WITH HIS FATHER'S SWORD

BOOK ONE OF THE EMPIRE OF THE BEAST

TM CARRUTHERS

Praise for With His Father's Sword

'The Count of Monte Cristo meets Kingdom of Heaven by way of Gladiator...I kept saying "Just one more chapter" about a dozen times when reading this book, and had a very hard time putting it down.'

Andy Peloquin, Author of Darkblade

'If you like characters that simply do not get a break and suffer relentless consequences for their choices, seeing someone be broken down to nothing and build themselves back stronger... you are going to love this book.'

Goodreads Review

'The world building was fantastic, the characters felt real, and the plot was a relentless sprint spanning years and countless tragedies.'

Goodreads Review

'A truly epic read and an easy 5 stars.'

Goodreads Review

'If you like A Song of Ice and Fire for its gritty realism and gripping plot twists; El Cid and Uhtred for their fighting skill, complexity, high morals and endearing traumatized souls, you should enjoy With His Fathers Sword and Harald Fairhair immensely'

Goodreads Review

This paperback edition 2025 - 1

Rights held by Carruthers Corporation Publishing and Troy Carruthers

Cover art produced by Sarah Dann Designs

Promotional art produced by Nenasmint

To my family.

My parents, the Triven and Sarah.

You're the best. This book wouldn't exist without you.

Chapter One

The difficult part of pushing the wheelbarrow was not losing the head.

Each jolt sent the body rolling; the severed head flopped like a fish out of water.

Some village yokel walked beside me, all gangly limbs and gapped teeth. He clutched two shovels in his left hand and did his best to walk just a pace or two behind.

Not for the first time I asked myself: why me?

But I knew the answer sure as I knew my own name. It was because bastards get all the worst jobs.

"Me lord," he said, "haven't we gone far enough?"

I looked up. Around us were the barrows of my ancestors. Tall hills covered in marigolds. And in the distance, you could see the mountain, sticking up over the valley like a sword rammed into the earth.

It wasn't far enough. Down below, I could still see smoke rising from the village. And my father would have a fit if he learned I buried the criminal alongside our forefathers.A smile spread slowly across my face. "You're right." I stopped abruptly. "Time to dig."

I upended the man out of the cart, head and all, and raised one eyebrow to the yokel.

"Go on then."

He offered me a shovel. I simply looked at him, expression unchanging. It was bad enough my father making me push the body all this way. Now even this scrawny little villager wanted to tell me what to do.

The grave the man dug was narrow and small, but it was deep enough to kick the body into. I looked down at the crumpled figure and the sightless eyes.

The poor bastard had been tall in life. In death, he looked smaller than me.

His words came back to me then. Screamed out as my father's blade came down. "Curse you fucking all."

I wondered if my last words would be so eloquent.

"Come," I said. "Pile the dirt. I'll fetch some rocks to mark the spot."

When we were done, the grave didn't look too bad, all things considered. A few heavy stones over a dirt pile. "Better than most criminals get, eh?" I said.

The villager nodded enthusiastically.

I sighed. "I'm going to walk back to the castle. You wait ten minutes and then bring the wheelbarrow. Am I understood?"

The villager nodded again, just as enthusiastically. At least he's consistent, I thought.

The way back was much faster. It was downhill, for one, and no scraping wheelbarrow to push either this time. It was almost beautiful, if I didn't know that I was walking back into the lion's maw.

My family's little fort stood behind the village huts, atop a small rise. I passed under the gates. A guardsman saluted me. "Your father wants to see you, my Lord."

"Of course." I sighed.

I would find him where I always found him. In his study, deep in the bowels of the castle.

My half brothers were already there, jostling and teasing each other. "Alright Harald, decided to keep us waiting," said Thomas, the eldest.

"Someone in this family has to do something useful," I bit back.

Thomas opened his mouth to respond, but our father raised a hand. "No squabbling. Not here." He eyed us all. Cold eyes, grey eyes. "There'll be a feast tonight. A toast for the execution. And for the marriage pact."

"Marriage pact?" James, the youngest.

All eyes fell on Thomas.

My father cleared his throat. "You will be aware that Thomas is no longer a boy. Well, a man must have a wife. And it so happens that Thomas's wife is to be the Earl of Bolton's daughter, though not before her father gets a good look at him. He's to travel three days hence, with a few trusted guardsmen, to the capital. Once the girl is wooed, he'll return to us, and the arrangements will be made for the ceremony. With that we'll have access to the Bolton's green pastures and tasty little pigs. After that maybe we'll eat something a little better than stringy pheasant."

"He'll be gone for long?" James asked.

"As long as he needs to be. Not that it should matter to you." He eyed each of us in turn. "Now boys, away with you. Help where you can with the feast."

I turned to leave but my father called me back. "Not you. We need to have words."

Dread settled in my stomach. I waited for the others to leave; Thomas raised an eyebrow but otherwise offered no support.

My father cracked his knuckles and stretched his legs. Whatever charm he'd used on my mother, he'd since used up. "You're not one of us. You're old enough to know that now. The others are young still, but you've grown up fast. You've had to. I hope you'll understand, then, that you can't stay here any longer."

"What?"

"Your family has been deposed, either dead or on the run. Your mother's vanished. Luckily for you a kindly uncle has agreed to take you on as his page. Keep you close in case the bloodline looks like it's running low. It'll be a decent life for you. You might even enjoy it." He smiled, but it never touched his eyes. "I've begun preparations. Have you gone and on your way before the wedding."

I did all I could not to scream. Bit my lip so hard I could taste the iron. "This isn't fair."

"And? It wasn't fair that you got left on my doorstep." He sighed. "It's not that I don't love you. We all bloody do.

But you aren't one of us, and every second you're here is a reminder to the rest of the world, that not only did I fuck some princess, but I was too scared of her family that I only could meekly face the repercussions. That's not the image I want to show the world, especially not the good Earl of Bolton."

"I hate you."

"Yes, you say that now, but you'll calm down. Now, go prepare for the feast. And say a proper goodbye to Thomas. It'll be the last time you see him."

I screamed my way out onto the hallway, vowing bloody vengeance. I don't remember much of the rest of the walk from the castle. I just remember walking and walking, until I found myself far away from the castle and the town and my goddamn family.

You'd think the forest would've calmed me down. Instead I punched the bark off a tree and almost broke my hand.

Cradling it, I walked on, on familiar paths. It got cold quick. I found a rise and pulled my cloak tight. Hadn't worn enough clothes that night, but my rage was too great to let me return to the castle. Firelight smoked in the great hall, though the rest of the castle was dark. Even from the hillside voices carried, laughter on the wind.

I shivered and shook. I hated them. I'd always hated them. I cursed them and denounced them. I vowed bloody revenge.

I wondered if any of them would miss me. If Thomas would spare even a single thought and look out over the valley. If my father would fear that I was dead, or whether that would just be another weight off his mind.

A real rattler of a storm swept through the valley that night. It could have killed me. I made a small fire with dry tinder and huddled beneath the back of a tree. Shelter in the valley wasn't too difficult to find; the land rose and dipped with wild abandon. Thick trees shielded me from the worst of it.

At some point I slept.

Rosy dawn light peered over the ridge of the mountain. I opened my eyes and stretched. Every single joint cracked. Birds played in the treetops and a badger trampled through the undergrowth.

I rubbed some heat into my arms, and, craving the warmth of a feather bed, set off home.

I didn't have much time to toy over that concept. Home. I was tired and needed food in my belly first. Plodding along, eyes half-closed, trying to rub some feeling into my shivering limbs, I didn't notice it at first.

The valley was quiet.

I heard the birds, and the pigs in their pens, but no people. A part of me would have been amused, but that celebration had not been hosted for me. They could drink themselves to an early grave but I wouldn't be happy for them.

The castle walls soon loomed over me. The gate was raised. No guards manned the gateway.

I snapped to attention. There was no way my father would not man the gate, no matter how great the celebrations.

If I had a sword, I would have reached for it. Instead, I inched inside.

The main courtyard was still and silent. The only noise came from the stables, where horses shifted and whinnied.

I ran to the double doors, leading to the great hall.

I cannot describe the carnage. Not then, not in all the years since. It would haunt my every nightmare to come. To talk about it, about all of this, is to reopen a wound that never closed.

Many would look to this moment and see the man that I became, fashioned in the eyes of a frightened child. I did not become a monster because I found a hall full of dead men. The world doesn't work like that.

I threw up. Mainly from the stench. Picked my way through the bodies of people I'd known my entire life. I did not move fast. I was scared for what I'd find next.

I went first to the rooms of my half-brothers. Each of them dead the same way, collapsed on their beds, headless.

I retched and heaved and spewed little brown chunks until nothing else could come out of me.

My father died the grimmest death.

Gutted, his entrails slipping from his stomach. His head had rolled behind the door.

"No, no," I said. "No, no, no."

I backed away, before falling over a body in the hallway. A guard, severed in two. I scraped along the floor, like a panicked spider. The corridors twisted and turned. I would have closed my eyes, but there were too many corpses underfoot.

I pelted outside, into the town. The silence was no better. Such stillness. Calm, even with the carnage that lay behind.

I screamed until my lungs were raw.

The sound of my voice dying brought the silence back. With it came a hollow quiet that stole into my heart. I was absent. Absent of mind, of willpower, of thought.

I walked into the forest, sat on the wormy stump of a tree, and closed my eyes.

My family were dead.

I sobbed into the back of my arms. Try telling yourself you don't love someone – and then having that person ripped away from you. There's no comparative experience. You have something, then you don't. And its absence weighs on you like a stone so heavy you feel your ribs breaking.

There was silence again.

I'd stopped crying. I stared sightless into the woodland as the midday sun filtered through the trees.

Reality settled in as a cold weight on my chest. I was alone. No family. Nothing. And somebody or something had murdered them all.

That brought a sharp red line of anger. A pain in the side of my head. I knew who had done it. What had done it.

I returned to the scene of my family's slaughter. I looked at them and swore I'd remember them. Vicious bastards the lot, but they were still my flesh and blood. Part of me wished that it had've been me that tore them to pieces, and that was a lie I let myself believe for a while. I had no other choice.

My father's sword was famous. Not proper famous, but famous enough that I wanted it.

A ruby in the hilt, a thick cross guard wrapped in leather. A heavy blade, but a well-balanced one.

I fixed the sheath around my waist and set off, following cart tracks through the town. The silence still shocked me, but I'd begun to get used to it. There was a prettiness to the valley that there never had been with people cursing and swearing and cluttering up the place.

The track went on for a half hour. I imagined myself with sword in hand, striking left, right, banishing my foe. Visualisation was a huge part of fighting my master of arms said. I'd visualised fighting my brothers often enough, but the reality had been different.

Not this time, I told myself.

I followed the forest path until we reached the barrows. The shallow grave had not stopped the monster from escaping. It had clawed its way out, leaving smears of blood and bits of skin behind on the rocks.

A draugr.

He'd vowed vengeance against my father. And he'd achieved it. That was usually enough for draugr's, but this one hadn't returned to the grave. He was out there somewhere.

Free.

I didn't know his name, nor even the crimes he'd committed. But I'd hunt him. I swore it on God, and my family. I swore it on my father's sword.

Chapter Two

I would go to the capital and tell the King. I was Harald, bastard son of a dead land. I would gather men at arms and ride for vengeance against the draugr.

I was resolute. I was determined.

I was not in my right mind.

Even with maps and food for a horse, it would be a long ride. Closer hamlets could offer help, but not revenge. Only the King could help.

I could barely ride for the screaming pain inside of me. I did not know how to camp. I slept against fallen trees and prayed for no rain. That is when I could sleep at all, and I didn't lie there, burning up, knees tucked to my stomach, trying to convince myself that it was all some kind of fever dream.

I ran out of water and the streams I filled my skin from were polluted.

I threw up, but I kept riding.

At some point, I fell from the horse. My lips were cracked and dry, head spinning. I don't remember what came next. I lost a few days to fever. When I finally woke it was in a hut, on the edge of civilization.

An old woman crouched over me, wet cloth on my brow. I lay in the most damnably uncomfortable bed. It was straw. So prickly and sharp I wouldn't even give it to horses for fear it would choke them.

I drifted in and out of consciousness for a couple of hours more.

When I woke, two other faces floated above me. Both girls, both little more than teens, pale and waifish. The old woman shooed them away and poured water into my mouth.

I drank so much she brought the entire urn. I drank and coughed and drank some more.

"Slow down," the woman said. "Your stomach'll cramp if you drink too much at once."

I shot her a dark glance, drank more, and spent the next half hour curled up on my side in agonising pain.

When the cramps ended, I was aware enough to look around the small hut. It couldn't have been wider than two men laid flat, the roof smaller than my father. I gagged on those dark thoughts, but pushed them away. The bed was big, but blankets had been lain on the floor, taking up most of the rest of the space.

They'd given up their bed to me, I realised, the old woman and the two girls.

I blurted out my thanks as she came through the door, holding a bowl of wild strawberries.

I ate, but not so quick as to give myself cramps this time. "What happened?" I asked, in between mouthfuls.

"Was hoping you'd tell us, son. Found you with your skull near enough cracked open, baking in the sun. Fancy clothes but stinking worse than a cow's backside."

Riding. I'd been riding to the capital. It all came back to me then and I threw up on the floor.

The old woman worked quietly, cleaning, while I mumbled my thanks.

Whilst she did, the two girls returned home, dirty faces with eager eyes. I didn't see much of them before the old woman shooed them and set them to new tasks.

"You don't have to talk of your past," the old woman said. "But we have your pretty sword in case you're worried about it."

I nodded my thanks. "Who are you?"

"Just call me Granny," she said. "The girls are Tava and Lot. I'll let you figure out which one is which." She laughed, a small sound that stood out in the quiet world.

"Would you help me to my feet?" I asked.

Granny did, and I hobbled unsteadily to the doorway. The reason for the silence soon became apparent. We were in a hut bolted onto the side of a hill, overlooking miles and miles of grassland and forests. Nothing manmade for as far as the eye could see, not even a trader's path. The mountains like dun pebbles on the horizon. "My horse?"

"No horse," Granny said.

I cursed under my breath; my knees buckled. "Take me back inside," I said. "I don't have the energy to stand."

I slept, then, in the long and dark night. It was the first day of my lucidness and the first of the nightmares. The cut in my scalp let reality sink in. My dreams were populated by ghosts clamouring for attention. I sat in my father's hall, in his throne, as the draugr served my family's severed heads.

It bowed.

"I didn't ask for this," I said. "I didn't want them to die."

"But that's what you wished for," the draugr said and its voice was my own.

"No," I said. "No, no, no."

The dreams turned darker. I don't remember them all. I try not to.

I do remember waking in cold sweats. I couldn't breathe.

In those first days, one thing in particular comforted me. The sound of breathing. The heavy snores of Granny, the two girls shifting and mumbling. I listened to the rise and fall of their breaths. I listened for each and every exhalation.

Eventually, I slept.

The girls wore wide brimmed straw hats while they worked. They were both slight and freckled from head to toe. Whereas Lot was blonde with wide blue eyes, Tava trooped across the countryside with a wicked look and her hair tangled and dirty. By some rather hopeful estimations, it could be seen as dirty red. In real terms, it was brown.

I mostly ignored them for the first few days. They buzzed about me like sprites, despite Granny's best attempts at keeping them busy. The questions were too much. I sat and watched the sun rise and sink, without saying so much as a word.

For some reason, that only made them more determined.

Whilst Tava gallivanted in the forests, collecting berries, Lot plonked herself down beside me. "Let's play a game," she said.

I said nothing.

"I'll start." She smiled a smile that could have made the moon blush. "The aim of the game is to guess what your opponent is thinking about. I'm going to guess. And you seem to have no problem thinking."

She was willful, I'd give her that. "I'm not much of one for games."

"Everyone likes games."

"Games are for children."

"Just cause you stole a sword, don't make you a man."

Anger rose in my chest; for a second I felt like myself. "I didn't steal a sword. It was my father's."

"And are you him?"

I remembered my father's harsh words. *You're not one of us.*

I looked at Lot. She was pure and sweet. Such concern in her eyes. Such...hunger. Desire.

I closed my eyes. I had been like that, but I couldn't remember when. The anger that I'd felt dissipated like snow in the sun.

"Go away, Lot. I'm tired."

"We haven't finished playing our game."

"I have." I sighed and stood. Guilt made me hesitate. "We'll play it another time."

"I won't forget," she beamed as I made my way to the silence of the bed.

It was a few days until we did. Granny fed me and didn't ask questions, though I caught her watching with an eager eye when the girls pressed me, pretending to stir her cooking pot.

Eventually, Lot caught me. I'd been feeling slightly more hopeful that morning. The sun was bright and pretty, like a polished penny. The normality of this life had grown on me. Lot spent most of her time with the sheep, or milking the decrepit looking dairy cow. Tava was a wild thing, sweeping from scene to scene like a character in a book. I was too sedentary to occupy her attention for long.

But Lot hadn't given up.

She cornered me, back to an outcrop I'd been staring out over. "We're playing the game," she said, with no small amount of force.

I sighed. "Fine." I planted myself down, feet dangling.

She sat beside me, a lot of space between us, as if I was a rabbit about to bolt.

"You're thinking about me?" she said. "About how interesting I am."

"About how annoying you are."

She laughed and a part of my armour melted away.

"You're thinking about how to get wherever you were going?"

I started. In truth, I hadn't been thinking about getting to the capital. It seemed an impossible dream. I was a thousand miles away, without a horse. More importantly, the draugr and the dreams of my family seemed so far distant. What would I do? What would I say? Everyone had been murdered by a mythical creature?

So lost in my thoughts, I hadn't noticed that Lot had asked another question. I looked at her with sad eyes.

She edged closer and wrapped her arms around me.

Her warmth broke something inside of me. Something that had been holding the flood. I cried and blubbered to a girl I barely knew.

I told her everything. We sat into the dark of the night. The stars took my breath away. Made everything feel so small. Made us feel so small, but so important at the same time.

When we returned Granny admonished us. No good being out so late, not even in the middle of nowhere. Bad things prowled.

I watched Lot. She had such happy, carefree eyes. For the first time there was something else. A weight. Now she carried my burden.

Still, she smiled at me as I slept.

For a little while before the nightmares came, I was happy.

Days became weeks. I gave up the bed back to Granny and the girls. I started to help out around the hut. I didn't have a gentle touch or a way with animals, so I mostly left Lot to her business, though I went to sit with her when I was bored.

I didn't say much. Words didn't come easily to me anymore. Looking back to my childhood, I'm not sure they ever did.

I was better suited to Tava's work, if I could keep up.

Sometimes you don't realise how sheltered you are. Tava taught me humility. I could have died a dozen times from eating poisonous berries. She knew which mushrooms left you feeling happy and contented and which would have you bleeding from your ears. Tava provided for the rest of us.

She did that without ever really considering the importance of her role.

"See that tree," she said, as we walked. "That's a heart tree. Soul of the forest."

"Things like that don't really exist."

Tava landed a soft punch on my arm. "Magic exists where you want to see it. Lot told me your story. You know the supernatural is possible."

I looked at the heart tree, leaves as ruddy as Tava's hair. Tangled roots gave way to a trunk squat and wide. Small yellow flowers sprouted from the leaves.

It was a good-looking tree, for sure, but I could see no magic inside of it.

"Non-believer," Tava said. "The heart tree protects us. Nothing bad can happen to us under the shadow of its branches."

"Are these fairy stories you learnt from Granny?"

"They ain't fairy stories." She stuck out her tongue. "Why do you think you know more about the forest when you've been trapped inside a hoary old castle for your whole life?"

"Because I've read books."

"Books. Pah! There's more to life right here than in some musty pages."

"Have you even seen a book?"

"I've heard stories."

I shook my head. There was no reasoning with her. Proud as a fox. "Come," I said, attempting to distract her. "I'll race you somewhere."

"Up," she said.

"Excuse me?"

"Up the tree. I'll race you up the tree."

"Thought you said heart trees were sacred," I muttered, eyeing the impossibly tall tree.

"Not sacred in a look don't touch way. Sacred in a real way. An enjoy and appreciate way."

We took up our positions at the base of the tree. I was no weakling, or stranger to climbing. The forest had been my home as much as Tava's.

"Go," she shouted and began scrambling.

Climbing trees is harder than it looks. From a distance you look – a hand hold there, a place for your leg there, easy. The reality is different. I got stuck about three branches up, with no obvious way to proceed.

Tava meanwhile scurried to the top of the tree fast as a squirrel. It took me almost ten minutes of sweating before I reached a canopy of branches. The floor was dizzyingly far below, but I was used to castles and mountains and tall trees – heights did not scare me.

Tava lounged against the trunk of the tree on a branch wide enough to stretch width ways if she had wanted. On either side, a bed of branches and leaves and flowers reaching towards the sun. I barged my way through a tangle of branches and plopped myself onto another one of the tree's thick arms.

"Still don't believe this is a heart tree?" Tava asked.

I looked around. Light bounced across the forest, the mountains molehills against the blue sky. The most beautiful sight of all lounged against the tree – freckled and red haired and proud as a mountain lion.

"There's something feral about you," I said.

Tava scowled. "Mind your tongue."

"Don't mean it in a bad way. You're wild. Free."

I turned my head away as her gaze sought out mine. She was a girl and I'd been having those kinds of thoughts for a while. Worst still, I'd been having them about her sister. I'd watched Lot as she bent down on her hands and knees, small buds of breasts straining against her shift. Wondered what my brother would say about a girl like her, and vowed to say exactly the opposite.

I'd no doubt they would have been whooping and hollering, strolling up to her with one hand on their hip. Announcing themselves as future lords, as great soldiers and intelligent men.

The same desire was in me. I could feel it. Like a pump in my chest, filling me with different emotions. I wouldn't be like them.

I realised I'd been silent for a while and looked back up to see Tava's eyes on me.

"You think too much," she said.

"Lot seems to like it."

"Lot thinks your special."

"And you don't?"

Tava laughed. "Do you?"

I hesitated. It was not an easy question to answer. Not now, not then. "I must be special," I said, carefully. "Else why did they die and I survived?"

Tava's expression softened. I realised again that she was only a girl, not a beast, not a creature of burgeoning sexuality. A girl with a heart and soul as soft as her sister's, if better hidden.

We stayed in the trees for a while. On our way back Tava checked her snares and found a young rabbit caught in one. She strapped it to her waist and when Granny saw it she clapped her hands together as if all her birthday's had come at once.

Granny had a pack. It was woven from straw and half the size of me. When it came time for one of their irregular trips to the market, they filled it with glasses of milk and granny slaughtered a lamb and salted it. The meat stank but she wrapped it in leaves and covered it with herbs from Tava's gatherings.

Ordinarily, she would go with Tava or Lot, whilst one of the others minded the house. Instead, I was given the honour of becoming their packhorse and Lot was to guide me towards the village.

Granny had a quiet word with Lot not to sell for any less than usual, no matter what the villagers said, and I debated bringing my sword before deciding against it, tucking it away beneath some clothes. The pack was heavy enough as it was.

We left before midday and would be in the village by nightfall.

Lot whistled as she walked. She always whistled. Soft tunes, folk tunes, the kind of tune your mother might hum – at least the kind of tunes I imagined my mother might have hummed, had she raised me.

"How did it happen?" I asked. "You and Granny. All alone in the middle of nowhere."

Lot shrugged. Wiped the hair from her eyes. "Some things have just always been."

"But you must remember. Didn't you have a mother?"

Lot's lips thinned to an uncharacteristic line. "Well I weren't dropped into Granny's lap by a wandering bird if that's what you mean. I don't remember my mum. Don't know what happened to her. Same as you. Must be out there somewhere. Hope she's happy."

The injustice in my chest, coiled about me since childhood, released like steam from a kettle. I wasn't the only one. The world was littered with orphans and forgotten children. "What do you think she's like? Your mum?"

"Kind, hopefully. Brave. Strong."

"Beautiful?" I asked.

She glanced at me out of the corner of her eye. "Why would she be beautiful?"

"Well..." I trailed off.

She laughed and in that moment I saw her and Tava as total opposites; whereas Tava was a wild thing, full of mischief, Lot had an earthliness that grounded you and magic in the sound of her head thrown back and her sweet laughter in the air.

"You're not sisters, are you?" I said, sudden realisation hitting me.

"We're sisters in all the ways that matter."

I nodded. Our conversations turned towards lighter topics. We laughed most of the day away. When it came time for us to break, Lot brought out a bowl of fruit and nuts and I collapsed against a fallen tree. "Heavy bag."

"Well you can't possibly make a lady like myself carry it." She pranced in front of me, doing her best impression of a noblewoman. "My hands are simply too soft and my bosom simply too big."

"What bosom?"

She dived at me and landed a soft blow in my ribs. "You're not like the girls in the castle," I said, as we fought in the dirt.

"I'd hope not," she said. "I am alive, after all." She grimaced after she said it. "Sorry."

I waved a hand, ignored the sudden prickling behind my eyes. "Don't worry. I may have lived alongside them my whole life, but I like you more already from this past month."

"Sweet talking, boy," she said.

"I'm no boy."

"Granny says all men are boys."

"Granny's wrong."

"Tell me then, oh mighty Lord Harald, what makes a man."

"Well." I thought for a moment. "A man has hair."

She held up her blonde curls. "We all have hair."

"I meant hair on our legs and our chests."

"And you do, do you?"

I hiked up my trousers. "Hair. See."

Lot pursed her lips and looked at me prettily. "What else makes a man?"

I thought about my brothers. "A man is strong."

"Prove it."

"I've been carrying this bloody pack all day."

"Carry me."

"I'm a man not a horse."

"I thought you were a lord. Capable of sweeping a princess off her feet."

I grinned. I scooped her up, not how knights in storybooks carry princesses, but like a sack of spuds over my shoulder.

She beat her fists against my back. "Release me, beast!"

Instead, I spun, before falling onto the ground with Lot on top of me.

She was close. Very close. Such big lips so near to my face. Hair falling onto my chest. My heart sounded like a band of musicians.

"What else makes a man," she said softly.

I pressed her lips to mine, soft and sure. I didn't close my eyes though she did. In that moment I saw what the players used to talk about when they performed for my father. I saw what drove my brothers to such frenzy around women.

I saw a perfect woman, golden hair glowing in the afternoon sun like a circlet of gold. I was not the royalty here, not even close. She outmatched me in every way.

When we pulled apart every fibre of my body wanted to reach back out to her, to grab her and hold her. Instead, she stood, patted herself down and grinned a smile bright as a penny. "Granny told us to watch out for you. Boys only have one thing on your mind."

"Then why didn't you?"

"Because girls only have one thing on their mind too."

She skipped away and I hauled myself to my feet, as if waking from a dream. Who was I? How had someone so beautiful kissed me? I thought about my brothers and all their talk of grabbing and hunting, of the thrill of the chase. In another world they would have chased Lot; my heart hardened against them. They had been vultures. They deserved to die.

I picked myself up and we ate lunch in quiet conversation. The woodland didn't seem quite real. All kinds of animals ran from the bushes. A deer bounded through the trees. We walked on, and occasionally Lot found my fingers with her own.

The village arrived before sundown. A cluster of a dozen or so houses nestled on the banks of a river. A couple of fishermen lounged by the water, smoking pipes and laughing deep from round bellies. "We stay in the priest's house, the pastor William."

The priest's house was possibly the largest in town. It was still no more than a single room, but a fireplace bloomed in the corner of it and a great steel cookpot gave off delicious aromas.

He was a gentle man, tall as an oak and slender as a willow. His wife bid us inside with an armful of babies. We ate on the floor – he asked many questions and I answered few of them. I have never been the easiest man to open up, even when the food is good and the company is pleasant. Fortunately, Lot guided the conversation – she was the consummate gentlewoman, even if her accent was a little less refined than my brothers' had been.

She sold pastor William a few pounds of lamb and a jug of milk in exchange for some warm blankets and two loaves of bread.

"You can sleep top and tail with me tonight young master, Harald," the pastor said. "My wife and children can sleep on the other blankets, and you can sleep behind the curtain all by yourself, dear Lot."

Lot patted the pastor kindly on his hand. "As courteous as that is, pastor, I rely on Harald for protection. If you have a spare blanket I would prefer if he could sleep near to me, behind the curtain. I'm so used to Granny's company, see, to be by myself will be frightfully lonely."

The pastor considered her proposal with a frown, looking at me, and back to Lot. For what it was worth, I did my best to look as sweet as possible, not that it has ever been in my repertoire of expressions.

"Alright," the pastor grumbled. "Can't see it as any different than how all of you women must be living up there in your hut."

He laid us a blanket down, whilst Lot lay on her newly traded goods. He pulled the curtain shut, snuffed the light and left us in the dark.

I lay silent for a while. Uneasy as a person always is in a stranger's house. There's something not right about it – something that makes you feel vulnerable right down to the marrow of your bones.

At least until I felt a small hand on mine. "Come closer," she whispered through the dark.

I shuffled towards her, all thoughts about uncouth behaviour in the pastor's house lost the moment my skin touched hers.

Two hands pressed on my cheeks, then her lips pressed to my lips.

"I can't believe I'm kissing a lord."

I can't believe I'm kissing a girl, I thought, but didn't say it. Instead, I kissed her again, long and hard.

We did nothing more. Hands wandered and held. But nothing more.

In those days, I believed myself a good man.

Chapter Three

Morning rose bright and early. I was beginning to get accustomed to the early starts after a life of relative luxury in the castle.

Lot sold the rest of our wares around the village, calling on each person individually. A crotchety old man tried to buy the goods for half-price, but she stood firm, and he paid up in the end.

We walked back through the forest light of load and light of heart. Lot sang as she walked, her voice more beautiful than the birds watching from the trees. We kissed beneath an old oak. We were in no rush, but our feet brought us, almost unwilling, back to the hut on the mountainside.

We glimpsed it, framed between tall trees, on fire.

Lot cried out.

She ran as fast as her legs could carry her, and I followed as quickly as I could encumbered by our goods.

When I arrived, Lot was crouched over a body, spitted upon the ground by a broken lance. I dropped everything, but Granny had been dead for long enough that it didn't matter.

I couldn't look at her face, frozen in agonising death. I stood, the world seeming to shake around me, scanning the hillsides for a sign of armed men.

There was nothing but stillness from the trees, though the hut smoked filthy clouds into the sky.

Where was Tava?

I ran to Lot, tried to pull her away from Granny, but she wouldn't come. She cried and clutched to the dead woman. "We have to find Tava," I said, but whatever words I said didn't reach her ears. Instead, I drew her close. "Stay here. I'll be back."

I checked the house for any sign of a body, but the fire was in full strength. I found my father's sword where I'd left it under a pile of clothes near the door. Whoever had burnt the house hadn't bothered to loot it. There were no tracks nearby, the ground had been dry and I had no real hunting ability to be able to tell otherwise. If I had've been one of my brothers...but I was not one of my brothers.

The only thing of note in the area was a broken horn beside Granny's body, like the type a troupe would wear when performing at the Midwinter Festival, becoming demons and monsters.

I couldn't be sure Tava wasn't burning inside the hut, or taken away by the raiders, but I knew there was one place she went whenever there was danger.

I made my way towards the heart tree.

In the shadows of the trees I saw armed brigands waiting to kill me, but when I turned there was always nothing. I saw my brothers standing like stone statues in the wood, felt their judging gaze upon my back.

"You've failed again," they said.

They were right.

I found Tava by the heart tree.

I do not want to describe her death. She never deserved to die.

I have, however, promised to be honest. To reveal my weaknesses. My truth.

And so I found Tava slumped against the heart tree, missing one arm and her head. She had come to the tree to save her, but the tree had simply watched as they cut her into ribbons.

I did not retch as I had done with my family's death.

I sunk to my knees and prayed to God, if there was any God, that he might spare Tava's soul. I searched for the rest of her, never finding her arm, but finding her bloodied and sightless head nearby.

Her sister couldn't see her that way. Whatever monsters had killed her had done their best to strip away her dignity, and I did what little I could to restore it.

The ground was dry and the forest thick. I built a fire beneath the heart tree, far enough away from the tree itself so the fire would not catch. I assembled Tava as best as I could upon the pyre and said what prayers I could remember.

When the fire was blazing, I returned to Lot. She wanted to see her sister and so I brought her to the heart tree. She wailed and screamed and asked me the manner of her death – did she suffer?

I lied and said the death was painless. That I found Tava with her hands clasped as if in prayer.

Lot quieted and clutched tight to me, heavy, as Tava's death weighed upon me that first night, one of many we spent in the wild.

Lot cried most days. Most nights too.

I kept my doubts to myself, but in the long moments when we walked, I wondered if it was my doing. I had been cursed, kept alive in a punishment much worse than the decapitation my family suffered. Whoever allied with me were doomed; whoever shared my blood, or who were close enough to consider me family, were condemned as surely as any poor fool at the gallows.

I looked at Lot, her head bowed as she walked, straw hat obscuring much of her face, and wondered when the world would take her from me.

No. I couldn't believe that. I may as well take out my father's sword and end it now, if that were the case.

But I was not brave enough for that, so all that remained was to keep living, and when the draugr came I would fight it, and either die like the others or be free of my curse.

"Come," I said, "what do you know of this land?"

"Nothing," Lot said. "Tava was the one who wandered further." She lowered her head and continued her silent trudging.

We had gone first to the village after finding Granny and Tava dead, but fires in the night turned us around. The raiders were ahead of us.

It was left to me, then, piecing together half-remembered maps, to guide us to some kind of safety.

I made our campfires. We sheltered beneath tall trees, in the shadow of the mountains.

We huddled close for warmth, but there was no curiosity in Lot's grip, no hunger. The passion had gone out of her, left only a grim determination behind, a desire to wake up, morning after morning, and keep walking.

There were days when she returned to herself. Quick to laugh and smile, like a princess amongst a field of wildflowers.

The long days of summer began to give way to autumn rain.

It fell in slanting gusts and we sheltered amongst the trees while thunder rumbled over distant mountains. The leaves turned to a patchwork of red and gold. The forest floor crunched underfoot in the places where water hadn't gathered, pools ever-growing with the onslaught of rain.

We survived off overripe berries and the few animals stupid enough to fall for Lot's traps. It was meagre pickings and it showed. Weight fell off us; I could see Lot's collarbone poking against her skin, legs hard and muscled but thin as twigs.

I fared no better. I was a wraith with dirty hair, a scarecrow with wild eyes and a growling belly.

There were few signs of habitation. We threaded our way through barely worn tracks, more likely to be the result of animals than trappers in the woods. There must have been villages, but we did not cross them, did not even see smoke rising from down in the valleys.

Our conversations grew as threadbare as our clothes. I no longer knew where I led us. To civilization, I told myself, west, west, ever west until we came across the wide-open plains and the stone roads towards the capital.

I began to lose hope.

Rain poured through dark clouds. The paths turned to mush. And, in the semi-darkness of what hour I did not know, we came across our first signs of humans other than ourselves.

We followed a trail up the side of a hill. I did not notice the path becoming wider, the trees drawing back, until a beast stood before us.

I jumped back. Lot looked up with beaten eyes at the creature staring us down.

It didn't move. Didn't blink. I would have laughed, if I wasn't so tired.

It was a creature carved from stone. In the shadows, on the other side of the path, there stood a second. Lichen grew over it, but that did not diminish its wide-open maw, jagged tail, angry eyes. "What is it?" I asked.

Lot shook her head. "Never seen nothing like it, nor heard about it, even in stories."

"It means people though. Civilisation." I almost grinned, but something held me back. "Come, let's walk on."

The path rose. We passed another set of snarling creatures, and suddenly broke through the trees. We found ourselves on the rim of a tall hill. The trees had been cleared and there was a rudimentary garden built on flattened land.

At the end of the path was a building, more akin to a castle than a house. Black stone slicked with rain; narrow slits of windows beyond which burned candles of strange colours. The world was muted. Apart from the candles, everything seemed a shade of black, or grey, even the bark of the trees we'd left behind.

"People," Lot murmured. "Food."

She began to walk forward, but I hauled her back. "Wait. Something isn't right."

"Food," she repeated numbly.

"I know, but..." I squinted through the dark. "I've heard of these. Monastic schools. Places children disappear into."

"Better than starving to death."

"I'm not sure."

We stared at each other, at an impasse.

My head snapped back towards the building. The candles flickered, flared, leapt to the air.

"Run," I said. "Run."

Someone, *something*, screamed.

I took Lot's hand in my own. We half-ran, half-skidded back down the hillside, past the monsters with frightening faces.

I stole a glance behind. Something followed. A figure, tall as a tree. A dark silhouette carrying a swinging lantern.

I did not look back again. Did not hesitate. I slipped, brought both of us down together, fell into the trees and slid down the hill.

A tree broke our fall, knocked the air out of me.

There was a light, there was a light on the pathway.

It waited, watching.

I looked at Lot, breathing shallow. I couldn't move. Couldn't even reach for my sword.

The light remained, the wind whistled. The light swung, as if on the end of a chain.

Everything went dark.

The light had gone. I squeezed Lot's hand so hard I could have broken her fingers.

I could not move, eyes fixed on the space the light had been, watching for any movement, a dark shape coming for us down the hillside.

Nothing came.

We picked ourselves up, never taking our eyes from the pathway up above.

And then we ran, down the hillside, past looming trees, until the ground levelled and the moon cast sombre shadows through the forest.

We walked through much of the night. Sounds, both real and imagined, terrorised us. The dark gives life to our wildest imaginings. It makes the impossible seem entirely real.

Lot stumbled, fell. Exhaustion brought me down with her. We could not afford a fire, could not trust a fire.

I saw the shadow of a swinging light in my dreams that night.

I did not see the creature behind it.

Only the darkness, only the shape of something terrible.

When morning came, ice had formed over our sleeping bodies. It cracked and broke as we woke.

Autumn seemed to have passed us by.

All that remained was the biting winter wind.

We could have frozen to death. We didn't have enough clothes. We didn't have enough blankets.

Wolves followed us, howls in the distance getting closer. I walked with my hand wrapped around the hilt of my sword, but I didn't have the strength to pull it free.

"Smoke," Lot said. "I smell smoke."

I sniffed the air. "I can't smell anything."

"Trust me," she said, taking my arm and pulling me forward.

I made no resistance. We were dead soon enough anyway.

We found a river and upon the river a series of huts, warm fires blazing in a series of bonfires either side of the water. A narrow rope bridge crossed the river teeming with silver finned fish.

A young woman knelt by the water, bucket in hand. Her eyes met mine – I can't imagine what she thought. Monsters of pale flesh walking out of the forest. Her eyes darted to the bonfires and the bucket dropped into the water.

She frowned as we came closer, muttered a prayer to God, but stopped herself midway. "You ain't demons," she said. "You's are people."

I nodded, smiled, fell headfirst into the ground.

I woke with salted cod hanging over me and Lot perched beside the pile of straw I lay on.

"This is becoming a familiar sight," Lot said.

I smiled, though it turned into a grimace as my headache throbbed. "Where are we?"

"A village. The kind that doesn't even need a name, cause nobody comes here, or leaves."

I puffed out my cheeks. "Are you alright?"

She nodded, though she seemed to look past me as she did.

I propped myself up. "Come," I said. "Let's play the game of questions."

"I don't feel like it."

"Of course you do. It's simple you see," I said, earning a smile, "I ask you a question, and I try to guess what you're thinking."

She looked at me, eyes wide and full. "You don't want to know what I'm thinking."

"Is it about Tava?" I said softly. "About Granny?"

"No," she said. "I have thought about them so much that all that I feel is a hollow quiet in my heart. I have used up their memory, and all that is left is a hazy image of what they used to be. I can't hear their voices. Their faces are nothing but swirling colours. Why is this happening to me?"

Tears fell on her cheeks. Words deserted me, so I took her hand in mine and held her tight.

I could remember them still – and that realisation only made her pain more unjust. Who was I to remember, and her to forget? An image of Tava's crumpled body beneath the heart tree flashed into my mind and selfishly I wished I had forgot.

"We're safe for now," I said. "We have to live for them. They would want us to be strong."

She smiled sadly and wiped the tears from her eyes.

"We've survived this long," she said. "It feels like we could survive anything."

I grimaced. "I have something to admit."

She looked at me, eyes entreating.

"The draugr that killed my family, my entire town." I hesitated, bulled on. "It cursed my family, everything my father held dear. That curse is on me, will always be on me, and I don't think anybody I care about will ever be safe."

"It's not your fault," she said.

"No. It is." I scowled. "Is it nice here?"

She nodded, shocked at the change in tone. "Yes, it's a small village. The river's pretty."

"Then stay," I said. "Leave me while you have a chance. Remake your life before it's taken from you."

Her lips thinned to a line. She rose without a word.

"It's for the best," I said.

"You don't get to tell me what to do. I've lost everything. Are you telling me I have to lose you too?" She shook her head and strode out of the room.

I waited in bed, but Lot didn't return. I slept, and when I woke it was with the fisherwoman above me, burning herbs and mumbling prayers.

"I'm not a demon," I said. "And I'm not going to die."

She cut me off mid-sentence. "That ain't a chance I'm willing to take."

I waited in silence beneath the choking smell of smoked fish and thyme. I didn't recognize half the words the woman said; her accent was thick as mud. Her last words fell into silence and she scowled at me. "Seem you ain't a demon after all."

"Sorry for disappointing you."

She folded both arms across her chest. "What are you's then? Your girl has kept her mouth shut. Said I should ask you instead."

"I'm Harald. She's Lot. We were...driven out of her home by raiders."

"Hmm, don't surprise me. Lots of savage things in these parts."

"Like the building on the hill?" I said quietly.

Her eyes narrowed, then softened. "Aye son – what did you see there?"

"A monster. Something I can't explain. Screaming."

"That's why we burn our fires. Keep the night bright."

I shook my head. "There were candles in the windows of the house. And the thing that followed us carried a lantern. They're not afraid of flames."

"Aye, but there's not just one dark thing in these woods. The world is frayed in these parts. A bit closer to the other, and what's beyond." She sighed. "I'll bring you some food in. You're welcome here for as long as you need to be, young master." Her eyes flicked to my sword resting against the timber walls, worth more than the whole house.

"Thank you. I would reward you, but right now I have nothing."

"I don't want for nothing."

She went to leave but a thought popped into my head. "Your people, they know the land well?"

She nodded.

"Do they know the closest town? Anywhere nobility might be?"

"There's a manor about three days from 'ere. Someone will guide you when you're better."

The next few days washed over me in a fever dream. I was hunted, chased, skinned alive. I woke up thrashing, damp with sweat, only to find Lot by my side mopping my brow with water.

"How are you so strong?" I murmured.

She smiled, but did not respond. "Sleep, if you can. You need your strength."

"I'm sorry," I said, though I did not know if those words ever came out of my mouth, because I was back in the dream-world.

The draugr waited for me, back-turned. He did not seem to notice me approach; he was dressed in silk and red velvet. He did not look like the grubby villager he had been when my father laid his head on the block. There was a rough seam across his neck where his head had been sewn back on.

He hesitated, sniffed the air, snapped around.

Only I was not there. I fell through time and space. I sat at my father's table as a child, listening to him describe the different parts of his sword. He smiled as I told him I would be a great warrior, better than my brothers.

"You have your mother's passion," he said, the first and last time he spoke of her kindly.

I fell further, into the heart of a forest, where a tree died and spewed blood.

Tava looked up at me in disbelief, a hole in her chest where her heart should have been. "This wasn't my destiny," she said. "I wasn't born to die."

I reached for her but found myself upended, lying in a chamber, on my back, a light burning in the corner of the room. I heard breathing but could not see the monster. "Leave me alone," I cried, squeezing my eyes shut. "Have I not lost enough? Have I not lost everything?"

"Shhh," a voice said, and moisture trickled down my nose, strangely salty as it touched my lips. "You're safe here, I've got you."

I fell again, into dreamless sleep.

On the fourth day the fever broke.

I woke feeling the freshest I had for a month. I stretched, clicked my back, and smiled to see Lot sleeping on the ground beside me. The fisherwoman had given us her hut, her time, and her food, and for that I felt a debt so overwhelming I could have cried.

Instead, I rubbed Lot awake and smiled as she blinked wearily. "Rise and shine," I said gently.

She bolted towards me, stopping when she was a hairsbreadth from my nose, on hands and knees. She peered into my eyes. "You're better?" she said.

She didn't wait for my response before sweeping me into a crushing hug.

"I thought you were going to die," she said. "You were fine the first day, then it was almost like a demon had left you, because you had no strength."

"No demon," I said. "I just got too cold."

I coughed into my arm and Lot drew back. "Not completely better then?"

"Mostly better," I amended.

We wandered outside – Lot providing a supportive arm to mine – and sat on the riverbank. A few fisherfolk laughed and cackled as they drank cider pressed from the trees surrounding us, now fruitless for the winter.

The fisherwoman came to find us after a time, after long silences and sweet laughter. She came with a man, short and stout, with a pointed cap. "He'll lead you to the manor, if that's what you want?"

I nodded, thanked her. Lot swept her into a quick hug.

"Travel well," the woman said, and that was that.

She'd given Lot a worn cloak, though I still made do with the clothes I'd worn when I'd set out from the castle what felt like an age ago. They had been washed but bore the use of our travel in frayed ends and jagged edges.

I had similar edges. The stray hairs of a beard began to spread across my cheeks. My hair was almost to my shoulders and tangled with knots. I couldn't remember the last time I'd seen myself in a mirror.

The journey to the manor was much simpler than what had come before. We were provided for – smoked fish on the first night, then a rabbit stew on the second. On the third day the hills grew less, the forests grew thin, and we broke out onto a plain beneath a white sky.

The manor was unmissable, dominating the landscape like a square shouldered brute. It was carved of smooth limestone and its glass windows shone with a razor's edge.

We thanked our guide and set off towards it.

Chapter Four

I rehearsed what I'd say to the lord time and time again. I made Lot roleplay with me, but she wasn't any more convincing as a lord than I was as myself.

I couldn't rely on fortune. I had to prove myself. I tried to remember what lord he could be – where even in the world was I? Since leaving the castle, how many estates had I crossed? Since befriending Lot, how many forests had we trespassed through?

I sighed.

I had my sword and a quick mind under pressure. What else did I need?

It took another couple of hours to reach the estate. Lot's nervousness showed; she squeezed my hand but did not hold it.

Hedgerows ringed the manor and two guards talked in a break between the hedges, the long walk up to the house itself. They snapped to attention upon noticing me and the sword at my hip.

"Who are you?" they called as one, before the senior guard stepped forward, spear out.

I raised both hands and Lot did the same. "We came to visit the lord," I said. "I'm Lord Harald – recently made due to the death of my father and my brothers. We have urgent business."

The younger guard scoffed but the elder frowned. "You look slightly worse for wear my lord," he said, keeping his spearpoint high.

"That would be on account of the recently deceased family I told you about." I huffed exaggeratedly, like I imagined the rich eastern lords might. "I did tell you my business was urgent."

"Are we at risk?" the guard asked.

"Not so long as you let me see your lord."

He lowered his spear. "So long as *you* give me your weapons."

I unbuttoned my sword belt and threw it towards them. "Be careful with it. It was my father's sword. Proof of my identity too."

The elder guard scooped it up. "Watch the entrance," he said, "I'll send others to join you after I've brought these two to the lord."

He led us to the manor house, so huge when standing before it I could not see its full width. We entered through great wooden doors, opened by a servant in black. We passed many rooms, walls lined with paintings, but at the time I took very little of it in. My hands shook and I clenched them into fists.

The lord's study was up a winding staircase, overlooking the rear of the building. The limestone walls gave way to thick wood panelling, and many lanterns burnt on the walls, for there were no windows to the outside world.

Two guards stood outside – and the elderly guard who guided us bowed slightly. "These two are here to see the lord."

The guards squinted, approached. They patted us down roughly for any sign of weapons, then shrugged. "Go in."

I breathed deep, shared a worried glance with Lot, followed the guard into the study.

The lord sat in a leather armchair, beside a blazing fire. Books lined the walls, far more than were in my father's castle.

The lord did not set his book aside immediately. He read until the end of the page, then closed it with a huff. "Yes?" he demanded, and I saw his face clearly for the first time.

Black hair just beginning to be flecked with grey swept down his face in a fringe. He was not young, nor old, but somewhere in between. He wore rich clothes, satin and silk, dyed black.

"I found these two outside of the manor, my lord. The boy says he is a lord and said he had urgent business with you." The guard stepped aside allowing the lord to examine me.

"Do you know who I am?" the lord said.

"No, my lord," I said.

He sighed. "They're nothing but vagrants, I'm sure. Take them – "

"Excuse me, my lord," I said. "But I would hazard you do not know who I am either. And such a quick judgement would not be enough for me to send you away without audience."

The lord narrowed his eyes. "Do enlighten me then, *lord*, of who you are."

"My name is Harald, bastard son, now last of my line." I told him my father's name and my brothers', and gestured for the guard to show him the sword.

The lord's eyes sparkled as he stared at the sword. When he looked back up he smiled. "Harald Fairhair, I shall call you, because you have a greater name than your father's, though it is not yet my position to tell you it. Your arrival is unexpected Harald, though not at all unwanted. In fact, you were due to come to my manor already. You are my nephew."

The weight of the past few months hit me like a brick. I remembered my father's words. "*A kindly uncle has agreed to take you on as a page.*"

"You're my uncle?" I repeated incredulously. "You were the one my father was sending me to."

"The very same. I am the Lord Alexander Calforth – your mother's sister was my wife. Though we are not bound by blood, I consider you an extension of my family." He smiled kindly. "I see that you do not come alone."

"No," I said. Lot had stood just behind me as we talked but came to stand by my side. "This is my good friend, Lot. She has saved me more times than I can count on this journey."

Lord Calforth inclined his head. "Then I am grateful to you for bringing my dear nephew to me unscathed. You may both make yourself as comfortable here as you desire."

"Thank you, my lord," we said at once.

Lord Calforth nodded, but the lines upon his forehead wrinkled. "I don't like to bring up trauma, Harald, but I must ask – what happened to your family?"

And so I told him. I did not tell him about Lot, how we met, but I told him of the draugr and the death of my entire world.

"I had heard stories," he said softly. "Folktales from the hills. But what credence do you give to the rumours of fools? Your brother had not met the Lord Bolton in the capital, but many of a groom has got cold feet before they are to meet their prospective father-in-law. When I met the great king of Amber to ask for my poor wife's hand, I couldn't even get the words out. Luckily my deep pockets spoke for me." He steepled his hands together. "You are truly the lord of that place now. I will send riders to *our* king telling him of what has transpired, though I warn you that few will believe the supernatural element to your story. I have been in this wild country, however, and I know that there is a darkness hiding on the mountaintops. I do not doubt you, Harald, though I worry. Have you seen the draugr since?"

I shook my head. "Though we have seen monsters in the dark."

Lord Calforth nodded. "You will be safe here. My own nephew is captain of the guards and a glorious fighter. When he returns from his scouting, I will tell him of the danger. For now, be content with treating my guards as your own. This entire castle is at your disposal." He looked to the guard. "Tell the chamberlain to prepare them rooms. I'm sure they're tired after their journey."

"Thank you, my lord,' I said again.

He nodded and gestured to my sword. "Don't let me disinherit you of your father's blade. I am sure it will win you much renown."

The guard led us out. My body flooded with relief – I could have leapt into the air and bellowed. The same feelings reflected on Lot's face; excitement shivered through her like a spark of lightning.

We had made it. We were safe.

Light flooded through my open windows. Birds chattered on the tall tree whose leaves brushed the stone. I woke and stretched and strode over to the window. I looked out – miles and miles of farmland stretched out beyond the manor gardens, and in the distance the heavy blanket of forest through which we had journeyed.

I looked across and saw Lot leaning out of her window in the room beside me, hair like a mantle of gold. "Hey," I called and waved. I had no wise words. Just pure excitement.

She waved back and disappeared. Within a few moments I heard a knock on my door. Lot sprung inside before I'd even turned the handle. "I'm in a manor!" she said. "I'm living like a lady from a story."

"You're prettier than any princess I've ever seen."

She looked up at me with wide eyes. Though I had slept in much the same clothes I'd travelled in, too tired to change, Lot had found a thin white nightdress from somewhere.

She reached up and touched my cheek. Hair had grown in a fuzz over my jaw. "Is this what makes a man?" she said softly.

I kissed her without thinking. Long and deep. She smelt of sweetness; she smelt of campfires; she smelt of a home I'd never had.

When we pulled away, my whole body shook. I grabbed her and lifted her off her feet, swung her about in a circle. "We made it."

I lowered her and she laid her head on my chest. We stood there, my arms around her, for a second that stretched on forever.

I wish that it had.

Eventually, she pulled away and wiped tears from her cheeks. "I wish Tava was here," she said and sobbed.

I pulled her close as she cried.

And so we spent our first morning at the manor of Lord Calforth.

Lord Calforth was a reclusive patron. He enjoyed books and writing poetry. As such, he spent most hours in his study or wandering the gardens, talking with a team of servants about the flowers. Letters flew from the tall tower almost constantly, missives and philosophy, thoughts about the state of the world.

We were left to the care of his chamberlain who showed us around.

I cannot tell you of the wonders of that place. It would sound trite to your ears. Most great lords live in grandeur that eclipses Lord Calforth. And still. There was a majesty in that manor that I could not comprehend, something more beautiful than my father's castle. It was a beauty derived from geometry – of shapes and distances. I don't comprehend it now any more than I did then. It was awe-inspiring and gorgeous, at the same time.

We stood in the chapel, a room of stained glass depicting the Beast slain. The light filtered through its narrow windows in a rainbow.

I looked through the roof of the observatory, where the stones had been stripped and a sheet of glass inserted – and a telescope sat in the centre of the room, a mechanical marvel of turning cogs, cast in bronze and steel. Lot clapped her hands to see it, and peered up at a blue sky empty of life save the formation of geese flying towards a coastline. Every corridor contained murals and tapestries: the Fall of Saint

Thomas, the slaying of the dragon over Loch Mere, God's punishment of the thieves.

Colour, such beautiful man-made colour. Pinks and reds, blues so deep I could have sworn that I was staring into a well. Colours that remade the sunset in paint and ink.

The garden was no less majestic. Shaped and cut, a hedgerow pruned, a tree remade into animals of many kinds. A kennel of sleek hunting dogs made their bed beneath a gnarled oak, each one with its coat washed and combed.

Part of me knew that I could never return to our castle near the mountain. I was its lord now, by right, but there could always be another lord of such a harsh and barren land. We had cousins, after all, cousins who would debate the fact that my father had legitimised me as his son. There were always new soldiers, hungry for land, happy to rebuild on that relentless patch of nowhere.

I looked at the garden of Lord Calforth and knew that my journey had just begun.

The deaths haunted me, but I couldn't see them as a punishment. They were an opportunity, a release.

I could be the person that I wanted to be.

I smiled and grabbed hold of Lot tightly. "We're alive," I said, laughing. "And look where we are!"

We soon lost the chamberlain and explored the garden at our own pace. It was strange, being at her side. My body felt awkward and wrong every time I became conscious of her walking beside me. But then the conversation would flow, and she would tell me about the butterflies flitting from flower to flower, and I would simply listen and smile. I felt the most fulfilled I had in my entire life.

How could that happen? A few days ago I thought I would die and now, like a curtain pulled in a mummers play, a new act had begun.

When the Chamberlain caught up to us, he proceeded to lecture us about how to conduct ourselves around the manor, but I was not really listening, and knew he had no real power. I was a lord now, whether I wanted that title or not, and people had to obey me when I gave an order, as they had obeyed my father.

That thought struck a discordant note inside of me. I did not want to be my father. I did not want people to fear me like they had him.

I came back to the world as Lot clapped her hands together and turned to me. "I'm going to be tutored," she said. "There's a man here who'll teach me to read."

I smiled. "That's wonderful."

"Will you be requiring lessons, my Lord Harald?" the chamberlain asked.

I pursed my lips. "No, I will not. I've always been one to teach myself anyway."

"The Lord Calforth is just the same, my lord," the chamberlain said, bowing. "Now, if you would follow me, I will show you the rest of the manor."

"There's more?"

"Yes. Of special interest to you I imagine, Lord Harald."

The chambers were deep in the renovated cellars of the manor, a series of circular rooms dedicated to fighting. "They came from the desires of my lord's nephew, who moved here when he was only seventeen. He's now the captain of the guard, my lord's most trusted lieutenant. And," the chamberlain said slyly, "the most likely candidate to become the heir of my lordship's entire domain."

"What's he like?"

The chamberlain thought for a moment. "Strong, brave, all the things that young men are. Careful with his words, if a little over exuberant at times. A good man."

I nodded. "How often does this place get used?"

"Once a fortnight the Captain holds a tournament, full of gambling and wine." He pursed his lips. "A lot of cleaning the next day for my staff. Other than that, the guardsmen spend their time sparring and keeping in shape. Only a small amount of my lord's forces are stationed here – the majority, including all of his knights, are in the town of Calchester, a little over ten miles from here. This is my lord's winter residence, after all. There is stuff to be accomplished in the summer, but the winter is a time for relaxing, for seasons ending, and the eating of copious amounts of food." He smiled. "You will both enjoy it here, I assure you."

The chamberlain left us alone soon after, bustling after a servant with a brace of rabbits strung over his shoulders.

That left the two of us free to explore the manor as we chose.

We were children. But like all children, we believed ourselves adults.

And so we did as adults did – we walked around the gardens arm in arm. Lot would say: 'oh what a magnificent flower, my Lord, what possibly can it be?'

And then we would both burst out laughing and chase each other around.

But I was not entirely uneducated in the ways of women. I'd heard my brother's advice, often without wanting to. I could read a dozen poems from ancient Ordrove, when our island was little more than a cluster of warring tribes.

Lot sat beside me, on a bench near a shrine to the Lord Calforth's late wife, eyes wide. I'd just completed *the Fairy Queen*, and feeling quite smug about myself I extended an arm over her shoulders.

"How do you remember all of this?"

I shrugged. "I just read."

She pouted prettily. "I will learn to read, then write. And then I will read my own poems to you."

"And what would they say? These poems?"

"They'd be love poems."

"Naturally."

"About a tall, handsome, dark-haired knight who saved me from a wicked blonde prince."

"I'm not a prince."

"But you are wicked?"

She grinned at me. Despite everything, I couldn't help but grin back.

We kissed. For a moment, everything was perfect.

I looked away.

Lot said, "I wish Tava could hear your poems."

It had become our tradition to eat our dinners, not in the great hall, but in a cosy room not far from Lord Calforth's study. He didn't eat with us often, but when he did he was a quiet companion, more keen to talk about the stars than anything of importance.

"There are more stars than you can possibly count," he said to Lot. "Always moving, from one month to the next, even as we are still upon this vast plain."

Lot pursed her lips. Asked question after question.

I did not pay much attention. I stared into the fire, my soup already devoured.

Despite Lot's attention and the Lord Calforth's kindness, dark thoughts had clouded my mind; thoughts of loneliness and self-hatred. I couldn't stop wondering how I had survived and the others had died.

Why had I been chosen? Why were they dead?

And I saw, time and time again, Tava slumped against the heart tree. That vain, glorious hope that the tree would protect her.

Those thoughts clogged my mind. In every silence I wasn't distracted by Lot, they resurfaced like bodies in water. Why? How?

I tried praying, small words in the silence of my mind. But the thoughtfulness of prayer allowed my thoughts to linger and stray, and always they would find the clot of dead bodies.

The door swung open, breaking me from my thoughts, bringing cold air inside.

A man stood there, still in travelling clothes, hair stained with sweat.

"Bloody Ordrove in winter," the man cursed. "Who would choose such a place as his home?" He pulled his riding gloves from his fingers and slapped them into the hands of a servant by the door. "If only we were truly lords of Amber – at least we'd have it a little warmer."

He paused, for the first time noticing myself and Lot. The Lord Calforth smiled.

"Gabriel," he said, standing. "This is my nephew, Harald, and his companion, Lot. Gabriel is also my nephew, the son of my dear sister."

Gabriel approached the table; myself and Lot both stood awkwardly.

"You are a prince of Amber," Gabriel said.

"I've never been acknowledged."

"Well, then we both have a distant parent in common. My father ran away across the endless sea to be away from me."

"Gabriel," Lord Calforth warned. "Your father serves nobly in the defence of Antonia against the heathens."

"Yes, yes," Gabriel peered at Lot. "You're a sight for sore eyes. I've been on the road for weeks with nothing but stinking, old men so you'll have to excuse me."

"You're excused, my lord," Lot said quietly.

"Excellent!" Gabriel sunk into the chair opposite us. He grabbed a fork and poked it into the turkey on the table. "A bit dry to serve for guests, Uncle?"

Lord Calforth sighed, but a glimmer of a smile touched his lips. He was bored, I realised, and Gabriel was the only one in his household who even had a normal conversation with him, barring his pet scientist.

"I'm captain of the guards here at the manor," Gabriel explained as he carved the turkey. "My Lord honours me and sends me frequently into the cold, dark, miserable countryside with barely any wine and the company of coarse, old men."

"Those coarse, old men are my men-at-arms. Some are even my knights."

"Yes, as I said, it's a great honour." He grinned. "Is there wine, Uncle?"

"No. We were having a civilised conversation about the stars."

"The stars." Gabriel gave a small laugh. "You haven't been talking to him about the stars, have you, Harald? A shame I didn't arrive back sooner. I could have saved you."

"I've been talking about them, actually," Lot said. She kept her eyes down as she spoke.

Gabriel did his best to meet her gaze, but she stared fixedly at her empty plate.

Instead, he shrugged. "We've been waiting for you to turn up for weeks, Harald. My men all want a go at you."

"A go at me?"

Lord Calforth stood. "His little underground fighting ring. You don't have to join in with my nephew and his masculine pastimes. It's perfectly legitimate to spend time around a dinner table, discussing stars instead. Isn't that right, my dear Lot."

Lot nodded.

"Now," Lord Calforth said. "If you'll excuse me, I'll be in my study. Gabriel, I will expect your report *before* you have a glass of wine. And think of your mother, will you? What will I tell her if she finds out you've become an alcoholic?"

"Tell her that it runs in the family."

With Lord Calforth gone, Gabriel leaned over to me. "Sorry to make such an entrance. My Uncle enjoys it, really. I was only meant to spend one winter here – instead I've spent most of my life. He'd be bored without it, so I have to play it up for him." He tore a rough piece of turkey between his teeth. "I wasn't lying though, my men do want a piece of you.

We'll be fighting tonight. I'll save you a space – I assume you've seen where we fight? Yes? Good. You don't have to fight. They've all been picturing you a bit older than you are, so I don't think any of the actual brawlers will challenge you – though from what I've heard about your family I think you're scrappy enough to take on most of my foul band anyway. What do you say?"

I nodded slowly.

"Excellent. Well met then, Harald. I'll introduce you to my men later on."

I left the room soon after, Lot by my side, unable to shake a nagging sense of dislike for the Captain Gabriel.

The guardsmen had families. They came from the countryside or they came from the big city. They were men, both big and small, sturdy, skinny, rich, poor. They were men just like any other.

Except, when you put them in the arena, they became animals.

I lounged beside Gabriel, on the only two chairs in the entire room. The other guards surrounded the competitors, a barrier preventing escape, marking out the limits of the arena.

Two men stood facing each other – one big, the other bigger, both topless. They didn't fight. Not in the sense you might imagine. This wasn't genteel boxing – the kind you might find at some gambling hall, frequented by nobles in silk coats.

This was anger, aggression, release. These men served in quiet times, warless times. They had trained for years to fight.

Gabriel knew the truth of such men. If you didn't direct their anger somewhere, one day you would have it directed back at you.

The competitors didn't smile or acknowledge each other. They'd served on duty with each other before, passed hours in companionable quiet. Now the quiet had a different tone to it.

A clerk from the house called out the odds, bets were placed, Gabriel stood.

"Begin."

A right hook, so fast I didn't even register it. The bigger man darted past it, moved in close for the grapple. Two hands locked together; a kick to the leg, release, knuckles cracking.

My heart was in my mouth.

The big man feinted, smiling. The smaller man patted his own bald head, daring a rash reaction.

Jeering from the guards around us.

Then, silence, as if a switch had been flicked.

A left hook from the smaller man crashed into his opponent's jaw. Head rocked back, feet went out from under him. The man's entire mammoth frame crumpled into a heap.

The victor wheeled away and was mobbed by the crowd, leaving the big man to be hauled away by arms and legs.

"Did you like it?" Gabriel's eyes glimmered. Torchlight reflected off the walls. Calls for the next fight had already begun.

"Yes," I said.

Here was something. A way to unleash. To take the anger inside of me and use it in a way that was permitted. I wouldn't be like my brothers – I'd find a use for my anger, a purpose for it than ran deeper than beating up unfortunate farmers, drinking in the wrong place at the wrong time.

"When can I start?"

"You're still a boy," Gabriel goaded, wine sloshing in his glass. "Do you think you can handle them?"

"They'll learn I'm a man soon enough, once I stick them on their arse."

"Fighting words." He sipped wine from his glass. "Perhaps you're ready now," he said.

My legs wavered and I was glad for the chair underneath me. I couldn't back down, couldn't be seen as a liar, a boy. I'd told Lot I was a man – and if this is what it took, then this is what it took. "I'll fight anyone," I said.

Gabriel rose and raised his glass. The room quieted without a word being spoken. "I hope you're all familiar with Lord Harald Fairhair staying with us. He's seen monsters, draugr, and lived to tell the tale." Gabriel's words bordered on the dramatic, but I couldn't tell if they were meant to belittle me. "Do any dare take on our esteemed guest?"

There was silence, but only for a moment. "He's a boy," said the winner of the last fight. "I got no business beating up boys."

"I ain't a boy," I said. "I'll fight any one of you. And I'll win."

The winner of the last fight shrugged. "You won't, my lord. You'll lose and you'll lose badly. But it's your business, not mine."

I scowled, but before I could respond, another man spoke up. "I'll fight him."

He was young. My eyes focused on him through the dark. Young, with shaven ginger hair, only a couple of years my senior.

"Two babes fighting," the winner said, "I'm older than both of you's together."

"Shut it, Margo." The young man pulled off his tunic and cast it on the floor. "You want a fight, lord. I'll give you one."

Gabriel turned to me. "Are you ready? Young Carrol here is a very capable fighter, even if he looks like a carrot."

Laughter from the men. Carrol bore the insult in silence, waiting.

I pulled off my shirt. I was still skinny from our travelling. Maybe even scrawny. The men laughed some more.

"You ready?" I said.

"Bets," screamed the clerk, not wanting to lose a profit.

Carrol moved in closer. "We don't wait until we're ready round here, lord."

And he struck.

A punch lightning fast. I caught it on my shoulder, rolled it off and stumbled backwards. Carrol advanced without hesitation.

Men jeered around me. I felt spit on my neck.

Only it wasn't spit, it was a smattering of rain. I wasn't in the arena any longer.

I was out in the yard, back home, practising with the master of arms. Rain and snow fell upon the parapets. Weeds sprouted in the courtyard. There wasn't a guardsman who could match me, not with a sword. Speed and power told more in hand to hand, but I was fast, and knew where to hit. Only my brothers could match me, only they had the same violence in their veins.

Carrol swung again. I ducked beneath his punch. It was wild, seeking to end the fight early.

I smiled, planted foot forward, let loose a combination. Left hand to face, right hand following it, left hand back and hooked into the body.

Carrol bent double; something cracked in his ribcage.

One more right hand – straight into the side of the head.

Carrol dropped like a stone.

I puffed a deep breath. Tasted blood inside of my mouth from biting my own tongue.

Something struck me from behind, then something else, and I was being hoisted aloft, on the shoulders of the guardsmen. "Harald. Harald. Harald."

I grinned, raised my hands above my head. Found Gabriel's eyes on me, still sitting, smiling slightly.

He raised his glass.

"Lot," I said. "Lot, Lot, Lot."

I was outside of her room, in the dark hours of the middle of the night, battered from my first real taste of alcohol, drunk on the feelings of my first victory.

Carrol had proved a good sport after he picked himself up, and we spent the evening drinking with each other, never losing pace. The other guards had cheered for us, set us both up nicely with a bottle of wine and a barrel of cheap cider.

Gabriel stayed for a time, but his humour was dark as the gallows, and when he talked it was about fighting and bloodshed, and we proved too tame for his tastes. Carrol, on the other hand, was a farmer's boy who'd spent his life toiling in fields and at least part of him wanted to go back. He told me the tricks of growing perfect potatoes – which I've sadly forgotten over the years – and how the wildflowers covered the hillside beside his village. He spoke about a girl he knew from back home that he'd half a mind to marry if he could.

All of this built – rose me up like a wave – until my ecstasy brought me to Lot's door.

It swung open. She stood in the doorway, a pale waif in a thin, white shift. She blinked bleary eyes, smoothed down golden hair.

"You're beautiful," I said.

She blinked again. "Have you been drinking?"

"Yes." I smiled. "I don't want to be alone."

She hesitated for a moment, opened the door. "We've lived the past few months with nothing but our clothes between us." She shook her head. "This manor house has brought so many rules, how it's not usual or right for man and woman to be in the same room together. But we slept in a hut on the mountainside, huddled together for warmth. Why do I need the loneliness of a locked door between us?"

I bounded after her, pounced onto the bed. I sat cross-legged and grinned. A hazy moon looked on through the gap in Lot's curtains.

She sat beside me. I spoke. No. I babbled. Like water from a brook. I talked about this and that, of the things I enjoyed, of the things I was looking forward to. No dark thoughts, nothing sobering.

Still, I brought tears to her eyes.

I took her face in my hands. "Why, why, why?" I said.

She bit her lip, squeezed her eyes shut. "You're beautiful," she said.

And then she was laughing.

The alcohol began to get to me. I rested my head in her lap and she rested her back against the headboard.

This time, she talked. She told me about the stars. About the way our planet shifted, how mountains sprung from movement deep underground. She told me of all the things she had learnt already and about how many more things she would learn in the future.

I smiled, and sometime in those beautiful hours I fell asleep.

The next few weeks settled into a familiar rhythm. We would eat our dinner with the lord, except when we didn't, and then we would eat by ourselves, always by the warmth of the fire. Lot would spend her days with the tutor – a half-blind eccentric who scared me half to death. If he cornered you, he would launch into rambling monologues about the state of society and so I did my best to stay clear.

He was supposedly present to look after the lord's younger relatives when they came to stay during the summer, but seemed to be tolerated or forgotten about for the rest of the year. And so he occupied a chamber not dissimilar to the lord's and they talked about the stars and things that never really changed, and Lot listened to them, and learnt, and before long she was reciting phrases from all the great writers of our civilization.

I was not, at that stage of my life, enamoured with the written word as I had been before in my life. The things that I'd seen had no answers in books. My only hope was to become stronger and hopefully I would be ready if the draugr returned.

I spent most of every day training.

I woke early to run through the fields and the farmlands, when the low morning mist still hung over the land. I startled farmers, stopped occasionally to talk to them while they sorted out their fields and their flocks. They were always grateful for comforting words from the manor house of their lord, always happy to hear no news of additional taxes or anything untoward occurring behind the hedgerows of the powerful.

I built a reputation for myself – from time to time I'd find a few young girls from the villages nearby gathered along my route, scattering as I ran past like a flight of doves. A few of the older farmers were daring enough to lodge a word of complaint or two about their affairs and I brought their words to Lord Calforth who proved himself fair in these matters, taking the time to look at the way the land was divided, which man harvested which grain, and what they were obliged to provide to their lord. To administer judgement he would journey to the farmsteads in long-legged boots and a long coat which dragged in the mud.

Part of me liked the man, though he had spoken few words of importance to me since revealing that he knew my mother's family. In truth, the thought of my other family might have occupied my brain when I was younger, but for now I had no desire. I had all that I wanted in Lot and the manor, and though I squashed my sadness deep down inside, for the most part I was happy.

That did not mean that I did not wake screaming some nights, or found sleep hard to come by. It did not mean that I didn't depend on Lot overly much, who has always been stronger than me. But it meant that I had found an outlet for my guilt, a way to deal with my anger. I had found a way to live, which is the only real goal people can set ourselves.

I trained for several hours a day with sword and shield, led by the guard captain. I ate magnificent feasts for lunch so ravenous had I become. The servants laughed at it and said that it was because I was a boy and I was growing – and they were right, but I was not simply growing up, but growing out. My arms transformed to lean muscle and my legs became thick as tree trunks. I kept my fair hair, shaggy as a mane by now, and earnt a reputation in the fighting arena. "The lion," Carrol called me, after I won my third fight on the bounce.

"The cub," Gabriel answered to a roar of laughter.

And so a new name was fashioned, used for familiarity by some, to mock by others, but mostly because in the firelight underground, with my teeth barred, I didn't seem much like a Harald any more.

"Cub," they saluted, when on duty. "Cub," they called when deep in their cups. "Cub," they yelled, when I floored another opponent.

Lot laughed when I told her, clapped her hands like the excited girl that in hindsight I know her to be. "Not just a lord, but a famous one. Harald Lionheart," she said. "Is that who you will become? Lighting towns like a beacon in the dark, all in God's name."

It was the first time I'd heard her talk of God. It wasn't that I didn't believe, but I lived in a barren place, don't forget. God didn't touch us much on the roof of the world. We had no great priests, only simple men preaching about good harvests and clear skies.

"Would you want me to burn towns to the ground?" I asked softly, to which she frowned.

"No, I just...."

"Were they the tutor's words? Preaching darkness and vengeance against the innocent?"

She sighed. "He's just such a knowledgeable man. How can he be wrong about God, when he's right about everything else?"

I shook my head. "Ask yourself if Tava deserved to die. And then imagine killing a hundred other versions of her. That's what would happen if I went around killing others in God's name."

She bowed her head. "You're right. I forget you're just as smart as anyone."

"You'll be smarter than us both the way you're studying."

And so on the days went – each one different, but keeping the same general pattern. Gabriel was rarely about, always ranging with the elite few men he clasped around him, led by the bald soldier Margo I had first watched in the ring.

At least until a message arrived from the King.

The rider brought the letter directly to the lord, and I came to stand in his study as he read the contents. He handed the letter over, smile on his face.

"The King has granted you your homestead. You are officially the lord we all knew you were."

I read the letter twice, three times. The words didn't sink in. I, bastard born son to a father who hated me, had inherited all of that cursed land. It made me one of the great men of the kingdom, rich beyond belief, no matter how barren and inhospitable the place might seem at times.

And I realised how much I didn't want to go back there.

I looked up – Lord Calforth was still talking: "...and of course resettlement might be difficult, but there will be plenty of people in Calchester, and others across my lands who would come if offered the prospect of a home and a fresh start. It'll be difficult, but we will manage." He broke off from his speech. "I thought you might be happier."

"I am, my lord. It's just..."

"You're happy here." He nodded. "You're a young man. This is a heavy burden to fall on someone so young." He placed his palms together, as if in prayer. "If you would allow me, I will send out the word to gather villagers. I will send out my troops to clear out the town. And by the time all that has finished, it might be a year, two years down the line. This will not be a quick process. But I am happy to share my wealth and my experience – I will govern your land in the meantime and you can learn and grow, and I can help you shoulder this unexpected and sudden responsibility. You are the blood of my blood, after all."

His generosity almost brought me to tears. "This is too much, my lord," I said.

"We are both lords now. And we have to look out for one another. We shall be allies, always."

"Thank you, my lord. Thank you."

He nodded. "We'll celebrate. A feast. And you shall sit at my side during the celebration."

I nodded, bowed, and slipped out of the room to cry.

The feast happened a week from the day the letter arrived.

I waited for it with no small amount of anxiety. It had been a feast which had brought the draugr to me last time. Perhaps the riders that Lord Calforth had sent out, bidding all nearby commonfolk to join us, would invite more unwelcome guests.

I slept alongside Lot most nights, and as always she proved my saviour. When I woke screaming – as I inevitably did – she would coo and hush me to sleep.

In those days I was young, as was she. We never sought to define ourselves, we never needed to. I thought, as we walked in the gardens and marvelled at the flowers, and the wind caught her hair and sent it twirling around her like a crown of gold, that I loved her more dearly than I had ever loved anyone before. I never told her, but she knew, she must have known.

Love wasn't a thing that a great lord felt – my father had drilled that lesson into me at an early age. But Lot treated me like a storybook knight – like I was all the things that I wished I could be, but wasn't. But I also saw, as she watched me from the high window of her room, that she did not believe she could hold me. That I would slip through her fingers like a handful of grain. I would go on to greatness, she would tell me, I would go on to be a great lord. Even though she never again told me of burning towns or religious fervour, she began to pray over me at night, warding off any draugr or foul spirits that meant me ill will.

She couldn't comprehend the truth, even though I told her it time and time again. I did not go back to my home, because my home was with her. It wasn't in a valley of dead bastards. People who had only cared for me because of the blood that ran through my veins. It was with her.

And so we slept and we fucked and we told each other all the beautiful things that we could think of.

On the feast day the servants dressed me in satin and silk, purple and gold, like an Emperor from a foreign land. Lot would not let me see her; the servants dressed her likewise, and she had spent hours marvelling at herself in front of the mirror. "I look like a princess," she exclaimed through a locked door when I came knocking.

"You must let me see," I responded, to which her laughter rang sing-song and sweet.

"You must have patience, Lord Harald. You will see this lady when she deigns to grace you with her presence."

I smiled wide at her words and left her to it.

Gabriel had returned from his most recent ranging and was marshalling the guards to sort and shepherd the commonfolk into the manor grounds. A great many tables and chairs and benches had been set outside, and fires already burnt, unleashing smoke into the unsuspecting sky. No clouds on the horizon for as far as the eye could see, but a white frost clung to the bricks and the bark of the trees. Lanterns were hung from low branches and the kitchen staff worked tirelessly, huffing and panting, baking loaves of bread and piles of sweet treats. Huntsmen bustled through the kitchens with their catches, and the serving ladies swatted at them with flour stained hands when they got in the way.

It was shaping up to be a party of the like I had never seen.

Only I couldn't bear the waiting. I holed myself up in one of the many small rooms throughout the manor, with book in hand, and proceeded to waste the next few hours. I couldn't tell you what the book was really about – I didn't read it, not really. I lost myself in the text and worried and waited.

Eventually, a servant found me and brought me before the lord. "This evening is for you," he said. "But it's also for all of these citizens to see you sitting at my side, as the guest of honour. Go amongst them. Talk to them. Make them love you."

"Is that all?" I muttered.

Lord Calforth smiled. "Don't worry my young lord. This evening will be smooth. It will be easy. And afterwards we can both return to our normal lives."

I made my way to the main hall afterwards. A pair of servants drew the door back and I stepped into a room, sweaty with the number of bodies. There were thirty or so tables, each bedecked with candles and linen, each housing more people than I could count. Some tables were full of rowdy soldiers, clanking tankards; some seated families, wealthy merchants and local businessmen, clinking small glasses of wine and eating with napkins on their laps.

All of this noise died as I stepped into the room. Absolute silence, barring the muttering of children. Their questions I heard all too loudly: "Who is he?"

My composure faltered. A bead of sweat gathered on my brow and I resisted all temptation to wipe it away. I did not go amongst them, smiling and shaking hands, as was my earlier intention. Instead, I walked straight backed, eyes forward, the kind of pantomime prince you hear about in the worst kind of stories. Haughty lords and evil step-sons. It took all of my concentration to not break into a run towards the high table, occupied only by Gabriel and Margo.

Gabriel granted me a flash of a smile as I approached. My perspective of him shifted again – perhaps he wasn't the worst sort, if a little self-important.

He gestured for me to sit flanking Lord Calforth's chair on the opposite side to him, and stood, clanking his glass. "Give a good welcome to Lord Harald, the cub," he said, flashing me a smile. "He is a good man and will undoubtedly lead us all to a better future."

"Hear, hear," the soldiers bellowed in the back, and made most of the noise, followed by some polite applause from the rest of the hall.

"Do you normally introduce people as they enter," I whispered to him, when normal conversation had begun again.

"No," he said. "But this is hardly normal circumstances. A new lord and a great party. My uncle hasn't hosted anything this grandiose for as long as I've known him. I didn't get this kind of treatment when I arrived here."

"When did you arrive here?" I asked, grateful for any opportunity to forget about my burning cheeks and the rest of the hall.

"Seven, maybe eight, years ago. Just before my seventeenth birthday. I'd caused too much trouble for my mother in the capital and they thought I would find a taste for civic duty out here in the sticks."

"Have you?"

He took a deep draught of his wine. "I've learned an appreciation for the finer things in life. For good wine, beautiful women, and the ring of steel."

I nodded. I didn't want to show my naivety but I knew nothing about politics in the capital. My father had talked about the king only to curse him. "Are your parents proud to hear you're the captain of Lord Calforth's guard?"

He barked a laugh. "My mother is proud of few things, Harald, and my career choices are not one of them. My mother is an ambitious woman – she left my father when I was young, and is busy wooing the most powerful men she can. He, on the other hand, is a simpleton with a broadsword. Minor nobility – punching above his weight in courting my mother, sent overseas from what I've heard. To fight in God's name."

"I'm sorry," he said.

He inhaled the rest of his wine. "What do you have to be sorry for? We're both bastards, one way or another, and we've both lost our parents, one way or another. Not that our parents were ever there for us anyway, isn't that right?" He went to pour himself another glass of wine, only to find he'd drained the bottle. He gestured to the one near Margo at the end of the table. "Come along," he said.

"Captain," Margo began, but Gabriel cut him off with a wave of his hand.

"Not tonight. Tonight's to celebrate Harald's parents being dead." He poured himself a glass, overflowing, and raised it up to me. "Let's hope someone can do the same for my parents."

I was saved from thinking of a response by the arrival of a new group of people – namely the Chamberlain, the tutor, and behind them, magnificent in gold, Lot.

I stared open-mouthed as they approached. I had met Lot as a girl wearing a straw hat, working in the sun. Since then, her tan had faded, made the freckles on her nose more visible.

And she had grown into a noble woman as beautiful as any in the entire world.

No. She had always been beautiful. I remembered the first time I saw her; a girl with an impish smile and a beauty greater than I had ever seen.

Now, though. Now she wore a gown that trailed and cut off in a slight V beneath the line of her neck. Back straight, pleasant smile on her face, smart eyes dancing back and forth. I realised how much this place had changed her – she behaved as if her blood was royal enough to ascend a throne.

She came before us, only Gabriel was there first, leaping out of his seat. He swept into a low, elaborate bow, the effect lessened only by the wine spilling over his fine white cuffs. "My lady, I've never seen a sight greater in all of this kingdom."

"Thank you, my lord. You do me too much honour."

Gabriel retreated to his seat and Lot stood before me.

All semblance of nobility fell away from her. She scrunched the length of her skirt in one nervous hand, whilst the other played with the ringlet of hair that fell down her forehead.

"What do you think?"

All clever words left me. "You're beautiful," I said simply.

Her face brightened as if I had paid her a compliment as fine as Gabriel's.

"Do you really think so?"

I grinned; she grinned back.

That was all we needed to say. She sat in the chair beside me, and before long my hand found hers underneath the table.

Lord Calforth arrived after a while and gave a halting speech that was met with loud applause and the thumping of tables. The evening settled into a soothing procession of food and alcohol until both me and Lot were giggling away, deep in our cups.

All the thoughts and fears that had plagued me before the evening had begun had vanished at the sight of her smiling face.

With Lot by my side, nothing could scare me again.

Chapter Five

Snow fell across the fields and I was forced to abandon my early morning jogging. Gabriel was out ranging and had sent a message ahead that he holed up in a town a good fifty miles away, and would wait out the first winter snows until it was safe enough to come back.

There was a sombre mood in the manor. The chamberlain bemoaned the lack of food shipments, Lord Calforth sat awaiting birds that would never make it through the storms. Lot's tutor demanded more and more of her – until she was sat reading in her room until the early hours of the morning, candle burning, pouring over manuscripts older than anyone still living.

With the intrigue of the outside world cut off from him, Lord Calforth turned his attention back to the manor, and mainly towards me.

We spent most days planning the resettlement of my ancestral home. If he sensed my reticence, he didn't show it – writing letter upon letter, tying small ribbons about them and securing them in his study until they could be sent.

He would send a few of his best men to oversee the growth of my old home, alongside dealing with the remains of those who had been left behind. "Granting them a proper burial," he said, and it occurred to me that my family had become dead skeletons in an unwanted castle far away from civilization.

No doubt looters had robbed the castle of its legacy, of my newfound money, but looters did not tend to bury the dead.

The thought sent shivers up my spine.

Within a week we had completed the majority of our planning, but the snows showed no sign of abating. Lot's tutor bellowed that it was the worst storm in fifty years, debated hotly by Lord Calforth who pointed to his data on the mid-winter storms six years ago. In the face of overwhelming evidence, or the fact that he owed his continued residence at the manor to Lord Calforth, the tutor wisely bowed his head in favour of the lord.

There were few soldiers to fight and it wasn't safe to go running. My anger bubbled and boiled, begging for some kind of release. No man is meant to be kept cooped up in a place, no matter how beautiful such a place might be. There is no entertainment that is substitute for the crunch of grass beneath our feet and the energy we take in from the sun.

It was in the midst of this cataclysmic storm that Lord Calforth finally decided to tell me more about my family.

"Take a seat," he said. His study had been outfitted not with the lone reading chair as usual, but an exact replica set across from it.

I sat, hands on my knees, awkwardly trying to appear proper in a seat that encouraged lounging and little else. He offered me a small glass of rosé – I began to understand how Gabriel's drinking habits had come to light. In many ways Lord Calforth was an unassuming man, but in others he was a man of great appetites, a devourer of both alcohol and knowledge.

"I met my late wife in the capital," he said, without small talk or explanation. "She was visiting, you see, one of seven daughters of a royal line that contained only two sons. Your own mother mustn't have been more than a child at the time, ten or eleven, but she was there with so many of the royal daughters to the throne of Amberleigh. They were of the family Wyland, so in one way you could be thought of as being Harald Wyland, if you were your mother's son and nothing else. But by that point they were long since past styling themselves as anything so mundane as Wyland's – they were Amber's, Amber like their whole country had come to be called. There was ruthless ambition in their family – I believe they coveted Ordrove as much as they coveted the heathen lands across the sea." He frowned at me. "Are you okay?"

"It's just a bit much, my lord."

"Hmmm." He swirled the wine in his glass. "I'm trying to explain why I wanted you to come here in the first place. Why you first came to my attention."

"I am listening."

He sighed. "I know. I just don't know how to begin. There's an ugly truth at the heart of this, nestled against a kind gesture." He thought for a moment. I waited, as patiently as I could. Part of me itched to be away from this conversation, back to my life in the manor. The other desperately wanted the truth, clinging to long suppressed dreams of my mother in a dark cloak stealing me away from the pain of my childhood.

"Before she died my wife used to talk about going home, almost every day in fact. When the sickness came she wanted me to send her body home. To my shame, I didn't. She is buried near the oak tree at the rear of the manor – I am sure you've seen her plaque."

I nodded.

"I missed the way she was, the way she brightened a room. Her optimism, her extravagance. This place has been empty for a long time. And then, I heard about you. A bastard son a hundred miles away. The only link to a place that felt more my home than this place ever has – it was through her words, her poetry, that she told me of Amber. The waves, the sea, the city on the water. It was a jewel in my mind's eye. Through her that place became my home. Then, I heard of the revolution – an upheaval in God's name. All of my wife's blood scattered to the wind. Executed or on the run. I was selfish, but I couldn't let her family die out, so like a hoarded treasure I sent for you, wanted you by my side. A memory of what could have been, if I had have had a son, born from Amber."

I waited for a while, after his words died out, to see if he would speak again. "There is no dark truth there," I said.

"But there is. I did this, not only to have a son, but in a vain, hopeless expectation. I dreamed that one day your blood might be useful, and the last surviving heir, the rightful king, would return home and take his throne. And then, with me at your side, we would go home, to Amber, the place where we have always belonged but never set foot upon."

Lord Calforth set down his glass of wine, buried his head in his hands, and began to cry.

"My lord," I protested, but the sentence died in my mouth. There was no comfort I could provide. No sweet words would banish the memory of a dead wife and a dream of a land more beautiful in the mind's eye than it could ever be in reality.

"Leave me," he said after a while, still in tears.

And that was the last we ever spoke about my family.

Dark clouds crowded out the light for weeks to come, though no more snow fell. Teams of servants cleared the tracks to the manor and the guardsmen who remained set to clearing the roads to Calchester.

Instead of running outdoors, I began to make loops of the manor, until the sight of me bare-footed no longer scared the scullery maids. Lot still worked constantly and I was slowly becoming a burr underfoot, distracting – always in a pleasant way – from the work she needed to be doing to complete whatever arbitrary task her tutor had set her.

"Why do you do it?" I asked. "Just say no."

At that point she closed the pages of her book and looked into my eyes with the most serious expression I had ever seen on her face. "You're a great lord. The world will part before you like a field of wheat. I am an orphan girl – nobody tells stories about orphan girls, except as cautionary tales, as if we can help our gender or our parents' wellbeing. I will learn everything I can in the short time I have. And I will make something of myself that would make Granny proud."

I shook my head. "You'll achieve whatever you want to. I've no doubt about it."

Since then, I'd given her space. When a person has something to do, it's best to let them get on and do it.

With my free time I sparred and trained. I beat every guardsman remaining at least twice; I beat Carrol near enough every day, but with every day he improved, until he was the match of any other guardsman in the manor.

Gabriel's return at the head of a mounted column of his rangers brought me bounding to the entrance to welcome him home.

"Bloody freezing," he said. "And with nothing to do for weeks. Some tin-pot town with buckteeth daughters and potatoes, so many goddamn potatoes. I need a good fight to get the blood boiling. Spread the word."

The rest of the soldiers saluted me as they entered, thick beards woven with ice. I felt almost like I could be a leader, toyed with the idea of taking Lot and heading back to my castle, but knew that both of our hearts were securely rooted in the manor.

For the first time in a few weeks, Tava dominated my thoughts. Would she have been comfortable in a lord's manor, hemmed in by red stone? I doubted it, somehow. I tried to convince myself it was better that she had died, still true to herself, but those were idle justifications and I felt guilty for having thought them.

It was then the first ravens arrived, bearing black words.

Lord Calforth summoned both Gabriel and me to his chambers. "The men that I sent to secure Lord Harald's lands were fell upon by looters and killed. All the while carrying our sigil. This news can only be greeted one way."

"You want me to lead a wild goose chase for bandits in winter?" Gabriel shook his head, still in chainmail and leather. "It's a fool's errand."

"It's your errand," Lord Calforth said sternly. "We cannot let any man disrespect our house, large or small."

Dismissed, Gabriel stormed from the room. "The old man's crocked. Likely enough that our men will turn coat and join with these looters if he sends them out in this weather. All for what? Protecting a castle its lord doesn't even want." He rounded on me. Jabbed a finger into my chest. "I blame you."

Before I could respond he turned, hesitating only to call – "tonight!" – over one shoulder.

Smoke and blood clogged my nose.

I was late – a fight had already begun.

Margo fought with the same mocking intensity he always did; his opponent Big Pete wasted no time in trying to close the distance, but was kept at bay by a steady right hand.

I found my seat next to Gabriel, no longer angry at his words from earlier, but awkward that my secret was so openly mocked. He showed no sign of even remembering his outburst and grinned with wine-stained lips.

"This will be a good one. Pete was chirping at Margo the whole ranging – they almost came to blows twice in the town. Anger and pride can go a long way to closing the gap to skill."

The entire room stank of beer and sweat. Lantern light flickered with each indrawn breath, sending the dancing shadows of the fighters out into the audience.

Pete closed the gap between them in one long stride, allowing a straight arm to strike him in the jaw and roll off.

Grappling is not a pleasant sport.

Whereas punching allows an element of strategy and control, grappling is a blind panic, fought closer to any man than you have ever been close to before. You can smell their smell, their masculinity, their power.

Pete wrapped two thick arms around Margo, pinning them to his side. He grinned a toothless smile, drew back his head and planted it into the bridge of Margo's nose.

Margo writhed, but there was no release. Pete butted him again and again with his iron hard skull. Blood trickled down Margo's left eye; his nose looked broken though it was hard to tell in the low light. Gabriel didn't call for a halt. He drank, eyes never leaving the fighting.

Margo squirmed, trying to break free, until suddenly it seemed as if he was successful. Pete released him. Only to follow it up by wrapping one hand around Margo's throat and lifting him off his feet. With his free hand he pummelled Margo's face.

Gabriel still hadn't stopped it.

Margo was going to die.

"Stop!" I bellowed, snatching Gabriel's glass from him and tapping it with my nail. "Stop!"

Pete released him and Margo slumped to the floor in a heap. The soldiers – freed from whatever bloodlust the fight had lured them into – rushed to Margo's side and turned him to lie face up. His left eye was a bloody mass, swollen shut, his nose shining with bone. Only his right eye saw clearly, darting frantically at the faces above him.

"Get him to the infirmary," one of them commanded, and they hoisted him up on their shoulders and carried him away.

When I turned Gabriel stood over me. For the first time I was impressed by the sheer size of him. Without stubble on his cheeks, it was easy to dismiss him as of an age with me, but the truth was something dramatically different. Gabriel had been soldiering since I was nine years old. He held himself with the absolute certainty that dangerous men do. Total belief that should they desire it, they can snap your bones like a kindling stick.

"We have our next fight," he said softly.

It wasn't in me to refuse such a challenge, though my knees almost buckled from underneath me as I walked to my corner.

Gabriel was a slick talking son of the capital. In many ways he embodied the kind of men that my father had always looked on with scorn. But there was rural power in his bones too – his was not simply a life of pampered luxury, but of sought out dominion. I could scarcely imagine the feelings of power granted to him by his ranging – the onlooking townfolk watching him with his black cloak streaming, knowing that he was the reason for their continued safety.

He stripped down to his skin and I did the same. He was lean and tall, with powerful arms built to swing a sword.

I breathed deep, tried to find some place of inner calm, and failed. I tried to imagine myself training as a child but found myself losing the fights in my mind. And in Gabriel's place was my brothers, with each swing wearing a different one of their faces.

Carrol patted me on my back. "Stuck a few pennies on you – do me proud."

I gave him a weak smile.

Nobody called for us to start. Gabriel stared at me, snapped forward like a sword drawn from its sheath. His first strike landed into my chest, his second went sailing over my head.

I backpedalled. I hadn't lost a fight yet.

And I'd never seen Gabriel lose one either.

I threw a long jab to keep him at bay, followed by another. He followed with his head tucked into his chin, hands raised, eyes glinting dark fury.

He threw again, and again, and again. I was inside of his reach, tried to step out but he pursued with small steps. Lashed a kick into my knee which almost knocked me off balance.

The alcohol had not slowed him. He caught me hard across the jaw.

My ears went funny, as if I'd fallen from a great height. My vision blurred and as it did another punch followed, landing hard on my cheek. Legs swayed – I pushed back, trying to buy space.

I saw the face of my brother, like a mask laid over his own. Violence seeped through hulking shoulders.

I stood, awaiting oblivion.

Only no final strike came. Gabriel watched me. He reached out – slowly – put one hand on my chest, and pushed me off my feet.

I stared up at him from the flat of my back. His hand offered me a route back to my feet and I took it.

Gabriel placed one arm around my shoulders. "Tonight has been a night of unwarranted aggression. Of tempers flaring. This cub has shown himself a lion yet, the match of a better man than me. I brought the rabid violence of a wolf into this arena tonight, and it has injured Margo, and could have injured Harald if I hadn't remembered myself in time. We are animals, baying at the moon, but we needn't be monsters. We'll open a few casks this evening and we'll drink together as friends." He smiled faintly at me – I saw perhaps he was my brother, but a better one than those dead ones, despite his poor qualities.

The last few bouts were tame things, as if Gabriel's words had taken the fight out of the soldiers as plainly as a sail would deflate without wind.

We withdrew to the main hall and broke open beer and ciders and clanked glasses until the hour was late. For the first time Gabriel invited me into his inner circle, those elite soldiers who joined him in his ranging and his confidence. There was a toast for injured Margo who slept in the infirmary and many dark words about the cold and the looters they were sent out to hunt.

"I would come with you," I said, found myself meaning it. "My brothers always said I would never be a man until I killed someone."

Gabriel shook his head. "There are many great men in this world who haven't swung a sword. When we go a-ranging we're not men anymore – I said we needn't be monsters, and that is true when facing our own kind. But there is a seductive pleasure that comes when you answer to no king, no authority but naked steel."

Big Pete laughed deep and low. "What our well-educated Captain means is that we like fucking women and raiding farms."

Gabriel shot him a dark look. "That's part of it," he grumbled. "But you have no idea of the power. How good it feels to do anything you want. No-one can stop you."

A dark cloud settled over me, bursting the alcohol soaked stupor I was heading towards. "You raid farms?" I asked.

"Anything," Big Pete answered. "We cause a bit of trouble. Loot a little. Just enjoy ourselves on the lands of other lords."

"We wear masks," another one said, "so no-one knows it's us." He pulled something out from his cloak; a mask of a demon with black horns.

"Though you remember when Lord Farley almost caught us," Big Pete said. "And we boxed in his son's ears."

Some of the men laughed, though Gabriel's lips thinned to a narrow line. "We cause some trouble. Annoy the neighbouring lords. Make the land a little more unstable. Burn a few crops. Kill a few farmers. Do what we're supposed to. All the *fun* is secondary."

"If that's what you say, o Captain," Big Pete said nudging him in the ribs.

"Did you ever kill a girl beside a heart tree," I said, barely able to get the words out.

"What the fuck's a heart tree?" Big Pete said.

Gabriel shrugged. "We've killed a lot of people, Harald. I'm sorry if it was one of the serfs you knew. You have to realise though – most commonfolk know nothing and think less. They're barely human."

There were a few "ayes" around the table. I nodded slowly. "I think I've had enough alcohol for the evening."

Gabriel caught my eye. "We'll be leaving in a few hours. Before you wake. Look after the manor while I'm gone."

I nodded, bid them farewell, held my anger around me like a shroud. Each step leaden, each breath threatening to turn into a scream.

They'd killed Tava. They'd killed Granny.

They'd killed Tava.

I knew it with absolute certainty. I remembered the broken horn that had caught in the frame of the door. It had been from one of the masks. I walked to Lot's room with barely controlled fury. My entire body yelled at me to turn around, to kill Gabriel, to kill them all, but I knew that was a vain, hopeless desire. Gabriel would just as likely kill me – and then what would happen to Lot?

I opened the door. She was sleeping in bed with a book laid across her lap, candle still burning beside her.

Could I tell her the truth? She had been happy here. She was somewhere she felt safe.

Sharing the manor of the men who'd killed her sister.

I had to tell her, but I couldn't bear to see anguish on her peaceful face. Instead, I pinched out the candle and sat in the darkness beside her, stroking her hair while my mind burned through a thousand possibilities.

The only man with more sway than Gabriel was Lord Calforth. Would he believe me when I told him what his nephew did when ranging? He must. He was a good man. He had taken us in, let Lot stay as if she were noble-born. He didn't believe in Gabriel's bigotry.

A plan formed in that long night. I would go to Lord Calforth when Gabriel left. I would tell him of the rapes and the murders of innocent people. I would have the guards in the manor to attest to it if he was not convinced, especially Margo who surely had reason to detest Gabriel after he had failed to stop the fight. And when Gabriel returned, we would arrest and try him for his crimes.

That was the reason why Gabriel's anger had almost boiled over this evening anyway. He saw that Lord Calforth treated me almost like a son. He was worried about losing his place in the succession. That I would be the lord of both my home and his.

He was like my brothers, in all of the wrong ways. His alcoholism, his violence, his lust. The only difference was the silver tongue behind his wine-stained lips.

My blood boiled. I watched Gabriel and the others leave on their black horses, with black cloaks soaked through with sleet and hail.

I let Lot sleep, even as the first splinters of dawn's fingers reached through her windows. I marched to Lord Calforth's study – knowing he would be there, as he always was, except for the three hours or so an evening he retired to his bedroom.

No guards were on the doors – Gabriel had taken most of the men ranging, and only a skeleton staff remained in the manor.

I knocked; no answer. I pushed open the door to find Lord Calforth with a wine glass to his lips, reading a treatise on philosophy from some long dead emperor.

"Welcome Harald," he said, then paused upon seeing the thunder on my face. "Are you alright?"

My anger burnt through my carefully constructed sentences. "I want Gabriel tried and executed."

"What?" Lord Calforth almost laughed, but the severity on my face kept the smile off his. "Why?"

"Do you know what he does on his rangings? He kills people. He kills innocent people."

"Calm down," Lord Calforth said.

"I won't. He's a murderer and a monster. He hides behind your power in order to rape and kill. He defames your name. He killed my friend for no reason. He killed Lot's sister."

My outburst trailed into silence. Lord Calforth shook his head. "Your dear Lot is a common born slut, and I kept her here to see you happy. But to demand I execute my own blood for her sake is beyond madness. Gabriel is like a son to me."

"A son you're happy to see murdering the citizens you swore to protect?"

Lord Calforth rose from his chair, wine glass still in hand. "Nothing happens in my lands or beyond them, done by my men, without my authority or approval."

Gabriel's words hit me like a club. *'We do what we're supposed to.'*

"You," I said, "You."

"Yes, little cub." He squared on me. "I do what's best for my land. And if that means the deaths of a few peasants, the burning of some of our neighbours' grain, then so be it. It's a small price to pay for prosperity. The commonfolk need fear. It keeps them docile."

I felt the sword slide into my hand without even realising I'd drawn it. I brandished it, like a candle to ward off the dark.

Mocking laughter fell from his lips. He raised his wine glass to drink.

"Monster," I screamed.

The sword slashed through glass, leaving a bloody red gouge across his nose and cheeks. Lord Calforth bellowed, blind.

Something bestial erupted from my throat. I charged, sword out, and punched a hole through his stomach.

Lord Calforth fell, still screaming, back into his reading chair.

With one smooth motion, I sheathed the blade. The madness that engulfed me, the rage that drove me, did not leave in an instant. Some men talk about feeling clammy and cold the moment the deed is done but my rage was not a simple one.

It wasn't born from a flash of anger. It was something deep, buried inside my chest. It hadn't begun with the draugr but stretched like the roots of a tree back into my childhood. Lord Calforth became the first victim of it, but the thing that horrified me, was that in that moment I finally understood Gabriel's dark words and dark thoughts. There was something seductive in power, in vengeance. Lord Calforth wasn't the culmination of the anger. He was merely the first of the many men I would kill as I tried to right the world.

All these thoughts flashed through my mind in the seconds I stood looking over Lord Calforth's body. No guards came to arrest me, nor did any servants bustle inside carrying breakfast.

That meant that I had time, though not much of it. I rooted in his office, taking a coin purse from his desk and another from his pocket.

There was blood on my clothes, though not much of it, and I stripped from my shirt as I walked. The months that I had spent running topless through the manor served me well – now I ran like a madman and no-one looked twice.

I found Lot still sleeping.

I knew I should wake her and tell her the truth, but it was too much at once. Instead, I shook her awake. "Quickly," I said. "We have to leave."

"Why?" she grumbled with sleepy eyes.

I grabbed her by the shoulders and pulled her into sitting. "Do you trust me?"

She nodded.

"Dress warmly. Quickly."

I gathered my own clothes while she dressed. I could almost feel my sword throbbing at my side, still slick with Lord Calforth's blood. I *wanted* to use it. To scream and shout and kill those who tried to stop us leaving.

But that would do no good, so I waited until Lot was ready and led us in silence to the stables. She hung on my arm – didn't ask questions, but the thoughts playing on her mind were obvious. Tava and Granny and that shadow holding a lantern in the dark.

"Saddle us a horse," I said. "Quickly."

The stablehand gulped, didn't move.

"I am Lord Harald and I will have you flogged in the courtyard." I didn't need to feign the anger in my eyes or my voice. "Saddle me the horse."

The stablehand bowed and saddled a black stallion. "Will you be only wanting one, my lord?" he asked, but I was already boosting Lot into the saddle. I placed foot in stirrup and swung on in front of her. "Hold on," I said and dug my heels into the horse's flanks.

Now at this stage in my life I was no great rider. Didn't know much about how to get the best out of the poor animal. I beat the beast bloody in an effort to get us moving, and moving fast away from the manor. If it had been a wilder thing, it would have bucked us straight from the saddle. Instead the fury had been bred out of it over generations in Calforth stables and it weathered my assault, the only response the quickening of its pace.

Lot gripped me tightly with gloved hands. I did not look back, but rode head bowed through fields and farmland, in the direction of the capital.

Neither of us had spent much time in the saddle, let alone riding fast enough to break your neck.

I don't need to tell you the pain we were in when we stopped by an overturned tree. The skin had chafed from my legs and my muscles ached in a way that told me they'd be sore for days. Lot was worse. The months at Calforth's manor had made parts of her soft and she winced and rubbed blood back into her arms and her legs.

We couldn't stop for long. There would be men sent out for us. They would be few in number at first, but when messengers found Gabriel, he and his rangers would fall on us with all the fire of the end days. We were woefully ill prepared, but I had money in my pocket, a lot of it. We would find a town as soon as possible, buy supplies and waterskins, then...

I looked up to find Lot staring at me. "Why are we running," she said softly.

The sun was still high. It was the worst time of day for riding. An even worse one for telling the truth. "Because I found something out. Something that I can't put into words."

"Did you put it into action?" she said quietly.

I nodded, could not find the words for what I had done. Not in the face of Lot's gentleness.

"We'd best get moving," she said.

And we got back into the saddle.

Night fell. A broad beamed moon scattered light across the sky and the trees all around us. We'd bought some food from a farmer on the road, drank water from a stream. We ached as if beaten and slumped with our backs to a tree, one of the few evergreens in a forest of skeletal branches.

The horse was tied nearby. A meagre fire blazed at our feet. I had no energy left.

"What did you find out then?" We sat almost back to back, with the trunk separating us. "And what did you do?"

With the exhaustion hanging heavily on my eyelids, it became easier to speak my mind. I could not see her, though I could feel her, tense like I was but with a tiredness coiled and ready to spring.

"Remember the horn I found, in Granny's hut. It was lodged in the door frame. I thought nothing of it then. It didn't mean anything to me. But I found out that Gabriel and his soldiers wear masks when they're ranging."

"No," Lot said, but I could not stop now.

"They had been talking about what they did on their rangings. How they killed people." *How they did other things.* "They raided farms and killed civilians. They told me not to worry about peasants dying. That they didn't matter."

Lot sobbed.

"I couldn't believe it, but I knew it was true. I went to Lord Calforth. He didn't deny it. He didn't show any remorse. It was all part of his plan. Tava and Granny died as part of his plan." Tears fell down my cheeks and I stared up at the moon to keep myself grounded. "I killed him. I stabbed him through the belly. I will do the same to Gabriel if I meet him."

There was no response from the other side of me. No crying. Nothing.

I pushed myself onto my side to see Lot staring straight, into nothing. Her cheeks were wet with tears but she did not move or answer me as I prodded her, or as I spoke to her.

She was empty and desolate. Something had snapped inside of her and I fell asleep cradling her as she stared sightlessly into the dark.

I woke to the cracking of branches and the sound of voices in the forest.

I shook Lot awake and pressed my finger to her lips. "They're here."

We crept through the forest at night, to a vantage point where we could see the valley ahead.

Trees covered most of the valley, but beneath their shoulders torchlight flickered. On the barren mountainsides too, men clambered over rubble and stone, seeking high ground and our trail.

I looked towards Lot who had her bowed, mouth moving to a silent prayer. "That's not going to help us now," I said, taking her arm and pulling her back towards the horse.

You might wonder whether we would leap atop the horse and race through the trees. That kind of thing might work in fairy tales but it wouldn't work for us. Noise would draw them to us like a hound chases a stag and soon enough we would be spitted.

Instead, we walked quietly as we could through the forest. We held no torch. We spoke no words. If they wanted to find us then they would have had to quite literally walk into us.

That's not to say we didn't take precautions. I wended our way through the bracken, using my sword to clear it where I needed to and boosting Lot into the saddle when she couldn't struggle through. We made new tracks through the forest that night; our signs of passing would be readily apparent when the sun rose, but when the sun rose I aimed to be on open plain, galloping away.

The night is a strange time even when you're not on the run.

Phantom noises rumble out of the underbrush and sinister shapes move on the edge of your vision. In a deep forest, with limited moonlight to guide us, it was a blind business, where often as not I felt for our path against the mossy bark of trees as much as anything else.

I knew Lot prayed. I wish I could have.

I did think of those old stories though, of God hunting the traitors who'd stolen from his Garden. I wondered whether he had dispatched his servants through the forest like firelight, and how many of the plotters had he caught and strung up from the tall branches of trees to die. It gave me a sick kind of pleasure to think of myself as one of those wrongdoers, stealing from his Garden. Some had been clever enough to even escape God, bringing all the mysteries of life to the world and away from the Mountain.

Though my family had treated them with a kind of revulsion – a don't misbehave or Risi will come to take your soul – there were some people who treated them with far more respect. In Amber, apparently there were even churches named after them. Harald – my own name – was the name of the traitor who had stolen the first sapling.

Lost in thought, my heart almost caught in my throat when through the darkness came a flickering light. The horse felt it first, becoming so rigid that Lot almost fell off.

I pressed a finger to my lips. We waited in silence for what seemed like an age, while the light stood silently. In some ways it seemed like as we watched it, so did the light watch us. But that couldn't be true – if so the searcher would have called out, or come storming over. Instead the light waited silently, and we waited silently.

Eventually, the light began to approach. I began to see the outline of a figure.

I took a deep breath.

My sword scratched from its scabbard.

The flame took a step backwards. The flame fell. A hand went to a sword, but my blade caught him first, punching through mail with a sickening wet sound. We both hit the ground, my sword embedded in his chest.

My hand scrabbled through the darkness for the man's face as he began to moan. I felt his wet lips on the palm of my hand. As I did, I fumbled for the dagger at my belt, and stabbed, and stabbed, and stabbed, and stabbed –

– Lot pulled me off the man. I heaved deep breaths; everything that wasn't me sounded so quiet. Every rustle of fabric, my knees on the ground, my sword as I pulled it from the soldier's cooling flesh.

And then I finally saw the soldier: Carrol's ginger head frozen in pain, with my bloody fingers smeared over his face.

I retched into the grass; my stomach heaved up indistinct chunks; my heart felt so heavy and low I thought I was going to throw it up too.

"We can't wait," Lot said, and in her I saw that unbreakable spirit that had carried us this far.

For all the leading I had done, I would have been lost a dozen times without her.

I nodded – I did not cry – and wiped my sword on the grass before sheathing it.

We walked on, until the forest edge approached, and a large open plain lay beyond. There was a camp on the plain, but it was far away from us.

I joined Lot in the saddle, and we rode without looking back.

After almost two weeks of riding, the horse curled up to die.

Two days of hard walking later, and we had made it to the capital.

Chapter Six

Morhagen sat beside a wending river, dusky and bronze. Hovels and tenements spilled out either side of the riverbank, but the city's old stone walls remained strong in most places, a dividing line between the city within and the city without. Two keeps towered above the rest of the city – Moor's Gate, weathered and bleak like a single block of stone. The other was Father's Keep, the royal residence, a sandy building draped in flags and banners.

I shivered, partly from the cold and partly from the anticipation of a warm bed. Lot felt the same – grabbed my arm and pulled me close. Together we stood watching over the city for a little while. Our journey had been hard, but its resolution neared, one way or another. Though that brought a queasy anxiety in my chest, my relief was greater, and we headed towards the city.

The hovels that first greeted us smelt like shit. The peasants here were different from the peasants in my village. They were filthy and stinking and poorly fed. Even Lot wrinkled her nose to be in the stench of the city.

As we drew close to Moor's Gate, a merchant stopped us, coming from the opposite direction. "Bastards closed it already, my son. You're going to have to stay in this mess."

"Can you recommend anywhere good to sleep?"

"I might, if you can spare me a bright penny."

I pulled a coin from my purse and flipped it across to him. He inclined his head and plucked it from the air. "The White Swan should suit you just fine." He gave us directions then doffed an imaginary hat. "Tell them Old Hal sent you."

"Will they give us money off?"

"No, but they might make you settle my tab." The merchant cackled and urged his horses away.

We found the White Swan without too much difficulty. I had little experience in inn's and drinking houses, but it seemed pleasant enough. Slender candles burnt in the windowsill and baskets of flowers hung either side of the doorway. Inside, a musician performed, only her high voice for accompaniment. Patrons drank tankards of ale; the bartender uncorked a bottle and the room smelt of strawberry wine.

I paid for a night and dinner. We had been careful with money and still had much to spare. I kept it strapped to myself, away from thieving hands.

Settling into a table beside the fire, I felt my eyes drooping. Lot stared past me, transfixed by the singer. "Never heard music before?" I joked.

"Of course, but..."

It struck me that she had heard Granny humming wordless tunes and on the rare occasions that Lord Calforth made an occasion out of dinner, but that had been fewer than five times. Music of the type performed in that smoky tavern near the waterside was completely unknown to her, and the woman may well have conjured a flame upon her finger as sung with that high, haunting voice.

I held her hand across the table. Soon after we ordered a glass of strawberry wine and spent the next hour in silence, watching the music. It was a perfect evening. I wish it had never ended.

In the early hours of the morning I woke, and knew I had to leave.

I rocked Lot gently. She mumbled something, blinked through bleary eyes. "I'm going into the city. I want you to stay here. If I'm not back by tonight, I want you to take your money and leave. Don't wait. Go somewhere else as fast as you can."

She frowned. "Why would you not be back?"

"Word will have gotten here before us. The boy who killed the lord who took him in. I'll be called a monster in most places."

"You're not a monster," she said softly.

I smiled and nodded, cupped her cheek in one hand. "I don't know what will happen. But we still have a fair amount of money, and you've never done anyone any harm. Just get out of here to somewhere safe."

"Nothing will go wrong."

"Promise me," I said. "Promise me you'll listen. If I'm not back, you will go."

She pouted prettily. "I promise."

My desperate words had given her much to worry about. She prayed over me three times before I left. Eventually, I peeled her hands away from mine, pecked her lightly on the lips, and left.

Moor's gate bustled with merchants and peasants alike. Barefooted. Filthy. Carrying produce in heavy bags. The merchants rode in small wagons and the farmers trundled in from afar with wagons of potatoes and bucktoothed sons.

I thought it would be simple to find my way, but Morhagen's streets proved impenetrable. People hawked at you from their stalls, and carriages rolled up and down narrow streets, panting horses urged on by foul-mouthed drivers, as likely to strike a walker with a whip as the animal.

I got lost a dozen or so times, even with Father's Keep to guide me, poking its head above the tangle of roofs. It was midday when I found it.

I rested my hand upon the pommel of my father's sword. It was all I had that stood between myself and total anonymity. It was my only chance to prove to the King who I was. Guards stood at the entrance to the keep, wearing the white cloak of his majesty. The silver sickle and the golden sun of his house had been engraved upon their armour. They looked nothing short of knights from a storybook; broad-shouldered, intimidating, hemmed in behind the visor of a heavy helmet.

I approached them, resting my hand upon the pommel of my sword to keep my hand from shaking.

They saw me coming from a long way off, adjusted their posture to my approach. They gave no outward sign that their hands crept closer to their blades, or that they suddenly had sensed danger, but something inside of them changed. If I twitched so much as a finger to draw my blade, I had no doubt that they would draw theirs first, and I would be standing before two of the finest swordsmen in the entire kingdom.

Instead I smiled, spoke. "I am Lord Harald, and I would seek an audience with the King to discuss the treachery of Lord Calforth and why fate has necessitated I flee towards the capital."

The guards did not speak. They only gestured for my blade, which I undid and handed over, then beckoned for me to follow.

I was not taken to the King. I was taken first to the Minister of Justice, a port-bellied man wearing a fine jacket. He looked me over, did not say a word, or introduce himself. He stared at me behind glassy eyes and gestured for the guards to pat me down further. I was checked thoroughly, and once they were satisfied I had no other weapons on my person, the minister wetted his lips and spoke a single sentence: "I will take you to the King."

A snake curled inside of my stomach. I did not know the King. He was as mythical as dragons. The minster took the sword in his hand and examined the ruby set into its hilt. "I once saw your father use this blade," he said. "He terrified us all."

"You knew my father?" I asked, but the time for words was past.

I was brought into a room, deep and long, with banners hanging from the ceiling. I saw heraldry I recognised – the Lord of Bolton's flew close to the King's own, my own father's heraldry hung closer to the edges of the room. I saw many more banners that I did not know. My father had never taught me anything about the realm. I had taught myself the world through books, but of the modern world I understood very little.

At the end of the room, upon an iron throne, sat a man hollow cheeked and tired. His hair hung to his shoulder like fallow wheat. A circlet of silver sat atop his brow, dull and lacking. At his side perched a young boy in a rich doublet, rose cheeked and fat of face.

Before those two arrayed a variety of petitioners, from rich stock judging by the cuts of their jackets. Guards ringed the old man – the King, I realised.

"My liege," bellowed the minister at my side, causing silence in the room. "We have brought with you a special petitioner – the Lord Harald."

I stepped forward and bowed. "My Liege, I – "

"You dare to disturb my court," he said. "You." He jabbed a finger towards me. "A murderer."

From the front benches stood a man I had not noticed at first, in fine black satin. He wore no weapons but his eyes shone with murderous intent.

The King scowled. "The Lord Gabriel Calforth has already briefed me on your crimes."

"He's a liar, my liege."

"Says the boy who claims monsters killed his parents. Whom trouble follows around with swinging swords. Tell me, then, great Lord Harald, how are you innocent of the crimes you are accused? Did you kill Lord Calforth?"

"I did, my liege, but – "

"Did you then flee with stolen gold and a common born wench?"

"She's no wench," I said. "And I didn't flee. I came to you to prove my innocence."

"Your innocence for a crime you have already admitted."

"Lord Calforth was a murderer. So is his *heir*. They were murdering people. They were a threat to your own realm."

"The *late* Lord Calforth was an eccentric and a recluse, I've no doubt. But he was a timely payer of tax and never once in all of my days, did a great Lord come to tell of how they had been offended by him. There was no talk of assassins in the dark. And to say the same of his young Lord Gabriel, who has spent many moons in front of my eyes here in the capital, is beyond foolish. I know the character of a man better than you, *boy*."

"He was destabilising your realm," I shouted. "Killing innocent people. Farmers and shepherds who never did anyone wrong in their whole life. Gabriel was his instrument and he was the player. I heard it with my own ears. What else would have driven me to kill him? Why would I hurt the man who took me in without reason?"

Before the King could respond, Gabriel spoke up. "It was over the girl, my liege."

"The commoner?" The King pursed his lips. "Elaborate."

"Lord Calforth, who was like a father to me, had tolerated the girl's behaviour for long enough. But she insisted on dressing up as a noble lady, playing the part, even becoming quite insolent to Lord Calforth when he spoke to her. He decided it was time she moved on, but Harald took the news badly. It was this quarrel that led to him stabbing Lord Calforth in a fit of rage, and why he fled with the girl immediately. We even found the stablehand dead upon his escape, his insides cut out."

"And the girl?" the King said.

"I assumed she would have been with Lord Harald, my liege. But we have many witnesses at a recent feast who will attest to the lady's actions."

The King scowled. "Where is she? The whore?"

"Not here," I said. "And she is no whore."

"You expect me to believe your words, bastard?"

At this moment the King's son let out an almighty sob.

The King swung to face him. "And what are you crying about, boy?"

"Don't kill them, father. He did it for love."

The King shook his head. "Love does not even begin to come into it. He did it because he has a temper. His whole family had a temper. His father had a temper. Proud as a king that one." He turned back to face me. "Even if your story were true, you took the King's law – my law – into your own hands without trial or judgement. The only man in this realm above the law is me. With that power I pronounce you guilty of the murder of the late Lord Calforth."

"No." The word escaped me, as if I'd been punched.

"Find the common girl, Lord Gabriel, and I'll throw her onto the same execution block as him."

Gabriel bowed and the guards seized me by the arms. I struggled but they pressed me to the ground and clamped great chains around my wrists. I looked up to find Gabriel towering over me.

"I'll find her," he said. "Then I'll fuck her. Then I'll kill her. Just like I did to her little whore of a sister."

He spat on me. I howled, strained against my captors, but their arms held me.

A blow across the back of my head sent me falling into darkness.

I won't describe my jail cell in great detail.

I'm sure you can imagine that dirty old thing without any help.

Instead, let me tell you of this tired, beaten thing inside of it.

An aching bruise spread down one eye from where I had struck the floor. My body was finally feeling the effects of our mad dash towards the capital. On top of that, worry about Lot ate away at me as surely as any poison.

My nerves frayed from the squawking rats. I scratched at the walls. Begged with the guards to let me go. Played every dirty trick in the book; cried like a child, cursed like a devil.

None of my actions drew the slightest bit of emotion from their impassive faces. The only time they swore was when playing dice, the only time they showed any emotion was when discussing women. My jailors were otherwise dispassionate, some distilled version of villainous masculinity.

Some time during my captivity the worry faded. In its place came a fire – a desire to destroy the King, Gabriel and the draugr. A madness descended on me. I cackled at the guards, talked to them, told them stories of what I'd do if they ever crossed my paths again. Their card playing stopped. Their conversations quieted. They watched me with shaded eyes, the candle flame dancing before them like a puppet to the tune of my voice.

In that cell some part of me grew. The part that had been nurtured by vengeance, strengthened by bloodshed, and now at rock-bottom, pulled me down a path of defiance. Most people would say that they were not themselves. But those people lie to themselves. Adversity reveals the naked emotion, laid bare when the skin is pulled back. There was fire burning in the pit of my soul. I would burn the world down before I allowed it to destroy me.

Time did not drift from me in that jail. With every grim new day came a dark anger that only grew. I counted each and every dawn.

I spent five months and four days in that prison cell.

When finally the jailors came, opened the door, and clapped me in irons I could barely remember what the outside looked like.

No lord came to greet me as I was dragged out from my cell, biting. I thought they were taking me to the headsman's block. Up a row of damp stairs and into a grey light. I was fastened into a wagon with a row of convicts and criminals and sent trundling towards the docks. A length of chain was tied between us, all pulling at every angle, some beaten and half-dead, others snarling like me, cursing our jailors.

We were not taken to the headsman, but rather up the wide ramp of a ship. One of my fellow captives attempted to throw themselves off and into the deep but the others held strong, knowing that the chains would drag us all down.

Loaded onto the ship we were brought before the priest, a balding man with fear in his eyes, who stood too far away from us to properly hear his blessings.

We were led down into the depths and shackled, not to each other, but to a ring of steel embedded into the wooden walls, like an animal on a leash. I was as prescient as I had ever been – part delighted not to be dead, part terrified to be leaving Lot and all that I had ever known.

But I wasn't dead, I told myself, between deep breaths.

I wasn't dead and that was the important part.

A soldier came to speak to us wearing rusted steel. His voice was snarling – he prowled through the darkness out of our reach, tailed whip in hand.

"Animals," he whispered, "you have a chance for salvation. The King in his infinite wisdom has not ordered you executed, nor has he pressed you into slavery and sold you to some foreign lord. Instead, you have been blessed, blessed to have been given to the Lord God, to become his defenders from this day and for all the days to come." He paused. Didn't try to hide his contempt. "Most of you are not worthy of God. Most of you are murderers and vagrants, thieves and fools, with the goodness in your heart strangled by your wayward ways. But now you are given a chance. A chance to join God in His Garden. To join the Almighty and have your sins scrubbed clean. You shall go in service to God, to war with the infidel, and you will find your salvation in either death or glory. This is a better fate than most criminals. You will not thank me now. I do not expect your hearts to be washed clean by my words like a light rain. But in the middle of the sea, in God's turbulent glory, you will begin to see that your future lies ahead of you and not behind. In service to God, and not to villainy."

He struck out with the whip onto the ground in front of him. "I will let you think on my words. For now, you will be held like the chattel that you once were. But soon you will have the opportunity to prove yourself and earn your freedom. The priest will visit you in an hour. And an hour later we shall depart and join the rest of the fleet." His eyes flitted between us in the darkness. "For now, I will not tell you my name. The only names you shall consider are your own, and that of our Lord God. Think on Him now and come to terms with the prospect of your salvation."

The old soldier left. The doorway to our room closed. And the men began to make such terrible sounds.

I slept with my knees huddled up to my chest. At some point the priest brought me some water, concerned look on his face. He said no words and I didn't have the strength to strangle him with the chains.

Instead, I thought of Lot. Service to God. She had always said it was my destiny.

That destiny had been a noble thought, at the head of an avenging army, bringing goodness at the tip of a steel sword. But armies were not made of good men and that reality weighed on me greater than the collar around my neck. We had been recruited to war but how could a God so powerful even be threatened by sword and steel?

I slept fitfully. The men still made noises. They wept and screamed. I had used up my anger and lapsed into deep thoughts in between intermittent sleep.

God, duty, honour. I couldn't comprehend any such notions. I craved fire and blood. I had a mission. Kill the draugr who killed my family. Kill Gabriel. And...

Did I want my birthright? I didn't want to go back to that haunted place, howling with winds. I hadn't in Lord Calforth's castle and even then, huddled in the belly of a ship, I didn't crave that life.

There are few moments in my life where I prayed. But I found myself praying.

I whispered into the darkness and hoped that someone was listening.

It turns out there were ears in the shadows and one of them heard the words lord, castle and home...

The priest brought me into his chambers.

They were not much, but they were more than most of us had aboard that titling, slipping boat. A large water damaged copy of God's words lay on his desk alongside a few other books and mementos. He was a balding man with a growing paunch over a thin frame.

"Come, come," he said. "My name is Andrew. You are?"

We had each been summoned to his chambers one by one, to recount our crimes and our villainy and repent. Those that wouldn't repent had their throats cut and were slung over the side of the boat. Those that came after were a great deal more susceptible to talking about God and how He could help them.

"Harald," I said.

"How did you become to be condemned, Harald?"

I almost laughed. "For killing a man, I suppose."

"Do you regret your actions?"

"No. He was a far worse murderer than I. I killed to stop him. I did the right thing."

Andrew laid his hands upon the table. "Killing is unacceptable in the King's Lands, where it is God's desire for us to follow the King's justice."

"I sought the King's justice. And this is where I am now. A lord in chains."

"Who are you?" Andrew said quietly.

I looked into his eyes with burning rage. "I am Lord Harald, and I am a better man than any of you."

Andrew sat back into his chair. "So, it is true. I've heard the stories."

"What are they saying?" I asked, my curiosity getting the better of me.

"Different things. A boy who killed for love, a monster who murdered for greed. The truth?"

"Neither of those things."

The priest laughed softly to himself. "Thought as much. You can boil down most of these slaves in here to men being reduced to a single word. Murderer. Thief. The complexity of the tale is lost. The motives of the man is lost. Until eventually the soul is lost. Do you believe yourself a good man?"

I thought about it for a moment. "I don't know."

"Do you believe you could do God's work? Fight for your fellow brothers with sword and steel?"

I nodded.

'Then Harald, you will have no quarrel with us. You are condemned to serve, but penance shall no longer be a steel chain. It shall be a steel sword radiant with God's light. You will be invaluable to our taking of the lands of our enemy."

I nodded my thanks, and guards shepherded me back to our dank living quarters.

The next few days passed similarly – our bulky ships catching the wind and finding ourselves adrift in the deepest ocean. We were allowed to go up on deck from time to time and the soldiers we shared the vessel with began to see us less like monsters huddled in the dark, and more like men. A few jokes were exchanged, then a few more.

I shared no jokes. The rocking of the ship barely affected me, but the way the prow cut through fevered waters brought more pleasant emotion to my heart than anything for the past months. Besides, I did not need to talk. The priest spoke enough for both of us, and by the time we'd been at sea for a month, many inclined heads marked my passing, along with mumbled 'my lord's.'

I was too deep in my melancholy to notice or to care, but men were bored on such a journey, and soon my noble blood became a source of competition. It began simply enough – bare chested on deck in the blazing midday sun, when the wind settled in miserly drafts and the sails hung limp.

They challenged me, some sailors with hair like silver wire on their arms, some soldiers with jutting chins. None were successful, even in my malnourished and underfed state. I began to get better rations – less stale bread and the occasional piece of fruit.

"He is a gift from God," I heard the priest preaching one night, to a room full of ruddy faces, lit by a single lantern.

The soldiers didn't care in the sunshine. They fought me in pairs, with wooden weapons. Sometimes they won; I was not that good to take more than two men at a time, though I could feel my potential, my strength waiting for me, just out of reach.

I could be more.

To pass the time I started training. With the sailors I'd hoist bags of grain, hold myself like a plank upon the shifting deck, climb the rigging. When we nestled into the few islands on our journey – for restocking and trade – a few of the sailors taught us to swim, in shallow waters clearer than anything I had ever dreamed.

My back blistered and burnt a dozen times, and though my milky skin never tanned bronze like the other men, I gained more than a few freckles.

Still, I could not shake the sadness. It coiled about me in the silent hours before dawn. It ate away at me in the loneliness while other men played dice and talked about their wives.

I thought about Lot. I thought about her too much. She became an obsession. I couldn't keep the darker thoughts from my mind; Gabriel's hands around her throat.

I prayed, because I thought she'd want me to. The priest took my confessions and said that all prizes would be returned to the righteous – that I may become a hero and a free man.

But Lot was no prize. She lived and breathed, and all the months I spent upon the ship were months where she would age, grow thinner, grow tired, wearier with the world. She would be hunted, she would be alone. She would forget me, until day by day I became no more than a spectre of a barely remembered youth. Her smile would pinch from her lips; her innocence and passion stolen by a grim world. Even her faith would be strangled by the merciless power of men like Gabriel.

I missed her.

Sometimes the men would talk about their wives. Some tales would be lusty, some disparaging, but I heard those same men weeping at night for arms they would never feel around them again.

I swore I would find her. I added her to the list of my impossible tasks.

After pulling into port on the island of Mercenae, the last stop before the heathen land we were to go conquering, a sickness crept aboard the ship.

The first men who caught it were not lucky. They died in piss and shit. Amongst them was the old captain, head of our vessel. He had no natural replacement amongst the troop and so Andrew took command – leading sermons throughout the night to combat the plague.

Whether through prayer or anything else, the plague seemed to get weaker the further we crept out towards sea. The next ones who caught it survived, though I couldn't sleep through the night from the noise of men coughing and turning.

I began to get ill.

I did not allow myself to feel it at first. A nagging cough into the crook of my arm, a sore throat dismissed from drinking too much rum. But I could not outrun my own body, and the plague caught up with me and dragged me down with all the rest of the men. By the time I took to the sick room over half of the sailors and soldiers were either dead or dying, or some halfway point between.

Coughs without end racked my body; my limbs turned wet and shivering. But the worst part was not those nights of unrestricted vomiting, of shitting so hard blood mingled with faeces. The worst part came afterwards. The body would shut off, as if you were a corpse lying in a tomb. I would see nothing but the swaying beams above my head for hours on end, be able to move nothing except my eyelids to blink.

The priest would be in from time to time pouring water through my parched lips.

I was almost grateful for the dreams.

The draugr stood before me, his face a shadow and his voice echoing as if in a cave by the sea. Still, I knew it was him, with the cold certainty of my end come to meet me.

"Living has changed everything," he said.

I drew the sword at my side – my father's blade rose to meet him like a broken piece of stone, gleaming with the heat of the earth. He sidestepped my wild swing; laughter reverberated from the shadows. "God does not recognize your power. You're a mortal who's lived too long, nothing more."

I screamed and swung, and swung, and swung, until my arms hung leaden and tired. The draugr towered above me. He took the blade from my hand and I looked into the ceaseless face of the creature who would kill me. In the shadows of its maw I saw darkness; a deep hunger that spoke of dark things beneath the ground, of the echoing quiet of death, of the final rest that would come to me if his blade plunged into my heart.

He reached out a hand and spoke. "Come."

I followed the draugr. To not follow would be my death. He led me through the darkness, to a window beyond which a great vastness stretched. The vastness shifted and changed as we watched,

A thousand burning ships under a remorseless black sky. Soldiers screamed and leapt into the churning hollow of the water. A mast snapped and cracked through the boards of the boat beside it. There were soldiers in the livery of God, the same flags which we carried to Crusade.

The scene changed before my eyes. Instead, we were inside a great cathedral – a place of gothic lines and the shafts of God's light pouring through stained glass windows. Before the largest window, a woman knelt, on hands and knees, face turned down in supplication. In the shadows behind crumbling pillars emerged assassins, carrying wicked knives.

The woman turned, and I saw her face too clearly. "Lot," I screamed, but the world shifted again.

A man rode a black warhorse, lance held aloft to the sky. Behind him a dragon surged, half running half flying, bleeding from a dozen cuts across its golden scales. The beast blotted out the sun and the rider wheeled, coming to meet it head on. The dragon swiped with a vicious claw, tearing the helm from the rider's head.

The rider left his lance embedded into the dragon's heart. It fell to the floor in a cloud of dust.

Gabriel emerged from the dust, sweat stained but smiling.

"No," I said, and the scene shifted again.

Nothing but blackness showed beyond the window. The screams of monsters in the dark, punctuated by great gouts of flame as they devoured the innocent. Cracked and broken stone, a looming mountain in the distance that I knew too well.

The draugr spun me around. "Your destiny is death," it hissed.

"I won't let this happen." I found my father's sword in my hand and plunged it into the draugr's belly.

It smoked and twisted and crumpled like hot metal. The draugr looked at me and for a second the shadow cowl of its face parted to reveal the villager my father sent to death, hopelessly confused, before he blew away in a gust of wind.

I stood in the silence of the darkness before my dream crumbled around me. I kicked and screamed and bellowed and the priest restrained me, before the next batch of dreams stole me away.

I saw all manner of terrible things in my dreams. But then I have seen all manner of terrible things in my life, and what is the mind but a reflection of what we see?

After a while, I realised I wasn't going to die. My toes twitched in the long hours of the night and my fingers managed to ball into fists. After a time, I struggled to stand, though my feet were unsteady beneath me.

I staggered onto deck. The moon shone between clouds, but the sea was dark as tar. I hobbled over to the rail. In the distance something smouldered and pumped smoke into the sky, lighting up the hillside, as if damnation itself had opened up over the town on the coast.

Fingers on my shoulder spun me and pressed a long spear into my hand. I looked into the wide eyes of a soldier. "Get in the boats. We're landing."

"Where?"

"That's Antonia. We've arrived."

I staggered, sightlessly, along with the other soldiers into the boats. They plunged into cold sea and the surf splashed. Waves rocked us, and for the first time since taking to the sea I knew the fear that some men felt. I retched into the open water, the tall dark waves rising on either side, foaming like a devil, tossing our small boat like a pebble in a man's hand.

There were eight of us per boat; an oar was thrust into my hand by a tall man with a hollow face. "Row," he bellowed, and we rowed.

Oar in, oar out, waves rushing against the boats sides; its noise much louder than the grunting of men. We pulled and pulled, dragging wood over churning water, to the flaming city on the horizon. There were a hundred other boats in the water. A thousand other soldiers, hunchbacked and panting with each stroke.

Time did not pass quickly. I threw up onto my boots and I could no longer see Antonia burning, nor the waves testing us, nor the men at the oars. I sat in a darkness, each heft of the oar accompanied by puffed cheeks and furrowed brow.

The only other soul visible was the captain who stood at our prow and bellowed: row, row, row, and we rowed, and he watched us with cheeks as gaunt as death and sharp white teeth.

His eyes were the only sign that Antonia still burned, for they were the only colour in the world, and reflected the burning city.

Time chugged past, like water emptied from a bottle, until the boat beached and we ran aground a sandy shore.

The captain pulled me to my feet. I left my oar behind and stumbled onto the beachhead.

The soldiers ran up the hillside, so I followed, carrying a long spear in my hand. Above, the city flaked and crumbled; an ancient cathedral collapsed into the sea raining rocks upon the heads of the soldiers.

We knew nothing. We were given no direction.

We were creatures of damnation, unleashed on a burning night, drawn to the flames and the foul smell on the wind.

It was said that Antonia was once beautiful.

A jewel, a last bastion for good godly folk in heathen lands.

But smoke obscured the famous stonework that the heathens hadn't already pulled down.

I found myself with other men I recognised, others from the boat, advancing forward through the broken city walls onto a street filled with infidels slaughtering civilians.

I did not hesitate.

Bellowing, I hoisted my spear and launched it with the full force of my arm through the back of the nearest enemy. He crumpled; the other heathens turned; and I was amongst them wresting a short dagger from an enemy, punching through mail and tearing off helms.

Soon I was not alone. Like a wave from the sea we hit them and crushed them beneath dagger and spear. Within seconds it was done; I had another spear in hand and we advanced into the city.

I was not myself. I was driven on by a madness deep in my soul. My spear found soft flesh time and again, and the soldiers flanked me. When one fell another took their place, but I was untouchable. The enemies seemed without number; but they may as well have painted targets over their hearts. My spear did not miss but returned after each thrust, sticky and thick with the gore of war.

We battered the disparate groups who'd clearly thought the city taken, until eventually we reached a square filled with the closed ranks of the enemy. They wore battered steel and golden capes that billowed in the smoke and the misbegotten wind. Their weapon was not the spear, but the longsword, and there were no chinks in their mail – it was battle-tested plate.

We halted to face them. A great many of us had fallen, but with every passing second more of us arrived, until we filled the square with bodies. Still, they waited, unmoving, like ghosts amongst the debris and ruin.

I hefted my spear. It would clang off plate, but not all the men were so armoured. They had been joined by their own reserves, a rag-tag band of militia wearing leather and wielding farmers' instruments. It was these I sought, and my spear flew true.

We followed my spear with our bodies. We fell upon them like a wave upon rocks. They stood with grim resolution and deflected our clattering steel. But I was amongst them, and where spears failed, the weight of our numbers succeeded.

We bore them down with the sheer power of us. I stabbed through the joints of plate, in armpits, the groin, the narrow slit of a visor.

From one man to the next I flowed; I didn't recognise any of the others beside me now, but even as others fell to heavy steel I rushed onwards, death, death, death, I cried.

They broke ranks.

We gave chase like hounds through the burning streets.

I ran without thinking. I ran without knowing my left from right, my up from down.

I ran, and killed, and ran more, until my legs gave way beneath me and I collapsed into the burning rubble.

For the first time I faced the night sky. There were different stars in Antonia, Lot had told me once. I tried to remember their names, but blackness took me and Antonia fell into the dark.

Chapter Seven

I slept for another tortured week. This time I did not dream.

When I woke, it was to the face of a nurse looking over me. I lay in what had been a banquet hall but had been converted into a field hospital, beds filled with soldiers still recovering. She passed me a cup of water and it tasted sweeter than any drink before. After so long drinking from long stored barrels at sea, to drink water newly raised from a well is a treat.

She smiled at me sadly, with bright blue eyes.

"What brings a woman to war," I said, though my words were rasping and short.

"I didn't come to war," she said softly. "War came to us. I lost a husband and a father in the fighting."

The stench of blood and the reek of death caught up with me. I retched into a pan beside my makeshift bed. "I'm sorry," I said, spitting a mouthful of red saliva.

"Don't be. At least I helped saved one lover to go home to his wife."

She offered me a small smile and moved off to care for the others. Her words brought me back to Lot and the darkness I had dreamt on the ship. She had died a hundred times in my dreams, but she was still out there, living, though we were separated by a thousand miles of sea.

I will find you.

Soon after, I was strong enough to stand. I ate some dry bread and admired the small silver scar across my forehead in a pane of glass. The larger wound was the puckered red skin on my stomach. I had been stitched closed – whatever blade had caught me hadn't cut too deeply, but the nurses warned me off any sharp movements. I was saved from their administrations by a young officer wearing God's mountain on his livery.

"The Lord Ashdown requests your presence," he said.

Lord Ashdown. One of the oldest families in our kingdom, ruling from the volcanic cliffs of the north coast, practically a king in his own right. He was also a man my father had spoken of fondly. *Hard as stone with a mind like a whip.*

I followed the junior officer out of the infirmary and into the city. Antonia was as devastated as it had seemed during our night attack. In the daytime the fallen buildings and ruined facades seemed as if they had always been that way, though just a week before it had been a vibrant city.

Lord Ashdown waited for us in what had been the magistrate's office, one of the few places to be relatively unaffected by the attack. His door was opened to us and at his side stood the priest who had been on the ship with me – Father Andrew.

"Harald," Father Andrew said. "So good to see you well."

Lord Ashdown grunted his agreement and beckoned for the junior officer to close the door as he left.

"Please sit," Father Andrew said, drawing out a chair from the opposite side of the table. "You must be exhausted after your exertions."

I sat. All the while Lord Ashdown didn't take his flinty eyes from me.

"You're a hero in the eyes of the men who saw you fight," he said, finally.

I shrugged. "I haven't asked for their adoration."

Father Andrew almost squealed his excitement. "But they saw God driving your spear arm! You glowed as if guided by His hand."

Lord Ashdown pursed his lips at this interruption. "Father Andrew, leave us."

The priest looked shocked for a moment, then bowed – to both of us – before retreating out of the door.

"You look nothing like your father," Lord Ashdown said.

"I'm glad I don't."

"You're not as pretty as your mother, either."

I eyed him. "What do you want from me?"

Lord Ashdown reached to his side and produced a sheathed sword, small in his thick hands. My father's sword. "The King gave me this weapon as a token of his generosity. Said you were unfit to wield it. The bastard son of a good man, a murderer."

"I'm not a murderer."

"There's dozens of heathens who would say differently."

"I thought murder was only the killing of the righteous."

Ashdown shrugged. "Save questions of theology for the priests. We're killers, you and I. You deserve your father's sword." I thought he would hand it over to me, but instead he placed it on the ground at his feet. "You may earn the weapon that is your birthright. But I will not cross my king to praise you for killing a few fishermen. You are a slave to God and glory." His gaze softened. "But you are the greatest of these slaves. I mean to make you their commander, leader of your own company."

"You want me to lead condemned men?"

Lord Ashdown nodded. "Lead them and I'll give you your father's sword and your freedom, when all this is done."

I shook my head. "Why are you doing this?"

For a second I thought he would not reply. He let out a long exhalation. "Because you're a weapon. Because the men are telling stories of you. And because I loved your father like a brother, once. The least I can do is keep his line alive. You're dismissed."

I rose. It was too much to process. So much had happened. I left Lord Ashdown's quarters and found a quiet corner to cry.

To explain what came next, I must first explain the things that in those days came to me as second nature. Things that you hear and know, but do not experience.

Antonia was the port city of the province of Dulac, the single territory owned in the name of our God. The region was governed by a Steward, a thin no-nonsense man by the name of Preston Miller, being the kind of common-born man who could rise to power in this land, if he were both religious and shrewd enough. He was backed by the Knights of the Mountain, a type of standing army formed of the devout who had kept the heathens from its borders.

Dulac had existed this way for the past three decades, since the last religious war won it for God.

The goal, however, had never been Dulac. It was a province dominated by sparse, rocky land, its only real trade the sale of fish and the production of richly dyed cloth to be shipped back home.

The goal was the Golden City and all the heretical magic that took place within it. The goal was the Beast, who slept below the city, speaking heresy.

And so our armies gathered, ships having been blown apart during our long sea voyage, and united under Lord Ashdown's banner in Antonia. There was Lord Pebbleworth, a champion swimmer who looked in his thirties despite nearing his sixties. Lord Cryston brought with him the claw of a dragon slain on one of his youthful journeys beyond the edge of the world. Lord Henderson brought with him over sixty of his kin, each one scowling their way through the city, ready to call out the unbelievers who sheltered behind Antonia's walls. Other minor heroes and rogues each skulked into Antonia until the city was stretched to bursting and the tents spread out from the city walls for miles.

"God, glory and riches," chanted the soldiers of God, as they drank Antonia's meagre supplies dry.

Priests led sermons between the tents. I had my own, set up by servants who I never saw or spoke to. I had been made a captain of the slaves, but I could not stand to be in the presence of their bowing and scraping. I bolted from their sight and sat huddled in my tent with my knees to my chest.

I could not lead the company. I felt like a serpent wearing a man's skin. I did not believe in God, nor in salvation. I did not love the men who looked to me as if I would be their saviour. I had failed too many people to have faith that I could save anyone.

Lord Ashdown, however, did not leave my leadership to chance. Edicts were issued around camp, in my name. Captains were appointed, from the few soldiers with a hint of knightly credentials. The man in charge of running my camp revealed himself to me one evening, while I sat alone around a campfire.

The other soldiers kept their distance. They skirted the edge of my fire, though I heard the whispers. Blessed by God, they said. Harald Lionheart. He's killed hundreds of men.

Each one I regarded with icy eyes. I did not respond to their questions. Did not even look at them. They sought a hero in a man who could promise nothing but pain.

A shadow appeared above me. "Mind if I sit here?" he said.

I fixed him with a steely glare. "This is my campfire."

"Aye, that's why I'm asking." He plonked himself down on the grass across from me. "Prickly sort, aren't you?"

"Who are you?" I grated.

"Sir Simon Slant, knight of Antonia, and the man who has been organising your camp for the past few days."

"I don't want to be disturbed, Sir Simon."

"I know, but that's why I'm here. Lord Ashdown is concerned. Your health is a priority for him."

I faced the ground, but stole a glance at Sir Slant through my eyelashes. He was a handsome man, older than most, but not yet grey haired. He rubbed a flask between two hands, before unstoppering it and drinking a bitter draught. He wore the mountain emblazoned upon his jerkin and kept a thin knife in a sleeve on his leg.

"I do not want to be disturbed," I repeated.

He shrugged. "Then I shan't disturb you. But I will be checking on you."

He rose. Hesitated. "Is it true you lived with Lord Calforth? Before you...came here."

"Yes," I said, hoping that would be enough for him.

"Did you know Gabriel?" Something like hope glimmered in his eyes. "He's my son."

My gaze snapped to him. I could see it in him now. There was the same handsome arrogance, the same love of drink, the same widow's peak. "Your son is a monster. Now get out of my sight."

"Wait," he said. "You can't just –"

I roared at him. There was no other way to explain the noise that tore from my throat. I charged towards him until we were nose to nose. "I will kill your son, one day. I swear it. He's a monster who tortures innocents."

"No," Sir Slant said. He stepped back. Tears crowded the corners of his eyes. "My son isn't a monster."

"Your son murders innocents. Rapes women. I will carve him like a turkey at a feast. *Do not return to my fire.*"

"I am sorry," Sir Slant said. "I must return. Lord Ashdown commands me. We will talk again."

He spun on his heel and strode away.

The routine repeated itself. Sir Slant would perch beside me, sometimes bringing meat to heat on the fire, sometimes bringing brandy that scorched your throat as it went down. He'd talk and meander, and eventually bring the conversation around to the son he'd lost.

I offered him little information. I had little to give. His son was a monster. The boy he'd cradled in his arms; taught to hunt in the King's own forests; who laughed when most children would cry; who used to dress in his mother's silks; who knew what dialectics meant at only five years old, a word his father did not know at fifty. That son – that proud and perfect son – had killed Tava and Granny.

Part of me wanted to exact my revenge on Sir Slant, but he had already suffered punishment enough. His clever eyes would dart left and right as he talked, even as he bemoaned the fact that he was not a learned man, just a devout soldier. He wheedled and sought those precious tidbits that would remind him of a home he'd long since lost.

He tortured himself. There was no other word for it. He loved the wife who had left him and the son she had taken.

"I've been campaigning in God's name for almost fifteen years," he said, between a swig of his flask. "People think that Crusades are a command. A moment where the high and mighty declare the virtue of God's will and seek to enact it. But those people are fools. Crusades are long in the making. They're border wars and political marriages. Constant fighting amongst peasants. They require the long hard work of men like me, so men like yourself can take the glory."

"I don't want your glory," I said.

"But you'll have it. The men may know the flags flying on the pennants of the great lords, but it is your name they'll chant into the dark of the night. Lord Ashdown saw it, and he had two choices. Either order your death, dump you quietly into a ditch, or reward you and let you become a beacon." He raised both eyebrows. "You should be glad he chose the second option."

"*Why* did he choose the second option?"

"Your father, I assume. They fought out here when they were just babes. Many in Antonia loved your father."

"They had poor taste."

"Don't hate your father, son. You don't know how much he sacrificed to protect you."

"You don't know how hard he tried to get rid of me." My eyes blazed. "What does a drunk fool know of my father?"

"I only know how much I sacrificed for Gabriel," he mumbled. "I meant no ill offence."

"You left him," I said. "What kind of sacrifice is that? You shirked your responsibility."

"I did nothing of the sort. You don't know what his mother is like."

"So you left him with her? So he can become a monster, just like she is."

"I left him with her, because the only other option was to bring him into exile with me. And no boy deserves to spend his life warring in the dirt of this place."

Soldiers had gathered at the edges of our campfire, bright eyes in the dark. I let their attention drift away before I started speaking again. "Why were you exiled?"

He pursed his lips together. In his mind he turned over all of the lies he'd told, sifting through them like a scholar looking for a quote, then sighed. "I'm not a good man. I've used the years to make up for the man I've been, but I don't expect to have ever been successful. I kept the company of whores. I smoked and drank and whiled away my good wife's dowry. And when it came time for me to answer my poor decisions, my wife gave me a simple choice. Either leave now and never return – volunteer in service to God – or she would use the power she had gained while I spent my time drinking, and she would ensure that my head would roll away. Our son would die soon afterwards. She would not put up with the child of a criminal as her legacy. But if I wore God's colours and promised to make something out of myself, then she would raise him true, and I wouldn't be stripped of knighthood nor my family's name." His eyes met mine. "So? Would you have done the same?"

I shook my head. "I would never have made those mistakes to begin with."

"And yet you did. A different set of mistakes, maybe, but the same outcome. We couldn't control our baser urges and now we're here. Fighting for God."

I seethed. "I only did what was right."

"Aye, I'm sure you did. And I was just a boy with a frigid wife and a fear of growing up. There's always an excuse."

"If nothing can ever be the right decision, what's the point of ever acting?"

"The right decision doesn't exist, from a moral perspective. The only *right* decision is the one that leaves you with all the power, and your enemies with nothing. I wish I had realised that at your age, but I was too entrenched in the system of knightly vows and the invincibility young rich boys feel. The *right* decision, Harald, is the one that leaves you able to do what you want. Nothing else, nothing more. Lives, honour, glory. It's all pish. Take your power. Rule with it."

"You want me to command this company?" I said. "This company of men who another year would have been left to dangle over tall walls until their bodies festered and the crows ate their innards? I'm better than them. I'm better than you. I'm not a criminal."

"So you say. But it wasn't me who cut a hole in Lord Calforth's stomach."

"That was the right thing," I said, but Sir Slant was already rising. "I did the right thing."

"You made a mistake. And now you're here. Start making the most of your position."

Sir Slant slunk away. My entire body screamed bloody vengeance, but the only outcome of that would be my head rolling. He was right in one way. I didn't have power. I didn't have anything. But if he thought that the way to achieve redemption was by climbing the ranks of men in this wartime army, then he knew nothing. We were tolerated because we were useful. The King had made it clear that I had no place back home and no-one would deny him that because I killed a few foreigners in a land most people at home pretended didn't exist.

It hadn't been much of a home anyway.

I would fight because I had to, but I would serve no man. I wouldn't bow before Lord Ashdown. I wouldn't scrape and beg for the return of my position and my titles, let alone my father's sword.

The beginning of a plan began to form. I didn't need to command the men in a formal sense. They didn't ever need to hear me speak. I would remove myself from them, become something so out of reach that I seemed almost a God to them.

And then I would show them why the world should fear Harald Lionheart.

Days of forced marching left the troops sweating and red from where armour rubbed against raw skin. There were towns on the way which offered either respite or were torched by soldiers in the night. I heard the scream of farm girls across the fields and did my best to shut both my eyes and ears to it. In this I was like most of the soldiers not already given to blood lust and slaughter. The army of us crusaders was as disparate as it could come. There were men of both Amber and Ordrove, of both my mother's birthplace and my father's, mingling freely. But our countries were as disparate as countries could be. Each fiefdom came with its own set of customs, each village with its host of perceived slights.

They fought each other as much as they fought the infidels. For once I was glad for my position as leader of the slaves. We were kept on a tight leash. Only a few lords were permitted to raid and only a few took the opportunity, Lord Ashdown amongst them. His personal encampment became a harem, as much as a war camp. The soldiers gossiped and talked, and I overhead bits and pieces, though I had no desire to see for myself.

Debauchery spoiled the nobles, freed from the rules of ordinary war. Still, there were few towns, and the ones that we came across were often as not settlements we had occupied in the recent past, before infidel incursions.

I realised that our enemy was not simply the rulers of the Golden City, but an entire continent of allied forces, each combined in the strength of their heresy and each opposed to any incursion from us.

I did not blame them. In fact, I began to see reflected in the faces staring at us from the roadside, the same dead eyed stare that I had worn since being pressed into service. We were all victims of power, enemies of peace.

I thought a lot, in those quiet hours, marching with the sun on your back.

I thought about why Lord Calforth had ordered his men to behave the way they had, why my father never cared for me. It was all politics, all game playing. They each sought power. They each grasped as best they could at the power that was granted them. They stabbed each other in the back. They didn't care who they hurt.

Sir Slant was right, in many ways. *They* had learned the truth. The only right outcome was the one in which you were victorious – morality, ideology, was simply the cherry on top.

How could I solve it? Smash the nobility? Give the power to the people? But would I not run into the same problems? Hungry, grasping individuals, each fighting for more, always more. You can apply no control on individuals who are free – you cannot force them to behave amicably, and so you always sow the seeds of your own destruction.

Could I wield absolute power? The power of a God? Morally righteous, impervious to criticism, impossible to reproach. Could I be a true leader uniting a people, or would the temptation corrupt from within? Does power make us evil, or is there the possibility that one person would be better at ruling than any others?

It was a dark path. The road trodden by a dozen despots.

There was no right answer, no matter how long I thought. Each system of government equally as constrained as the last, existing on half-truths and justifications, unfair definitions in order to precipitate their own success.

I could not solve it.

That will not surprise you. I have read many philosophers in my time. Under candlelight in my father's library, in the quiet corners of Lord Calforth's study, my intellect bent to the studious minds who have gone before me. In those days there was an arrogance to me, a belief that it would be my mind that solved the problems that dead men wrote about in books. Sometimes the solution seemed all too clear, but realising theory in the real world, how possible is that, when a person cannot even realise a happy life for themselves?

The sun drove me mad. So did the silence.

When Lord Ashdown finally summoned me, it was with some relief that I left my lonely campfire. Even when lost to our own quiet, I do not believe humans ever really want to be alone.

The camp was a sullen place, far removed from the chanting that had rung out around Antonia's walls. Groups hunkered close together, speaking long and low, over fast dwindling supplies of alcohol. They shot worried glances as I walked by.

Not all the camps were the same; each lord kept himself holed up in his own little world, with his own sentries, and his own laws. We were moving nations, on a single road in the middle of nowhere.

That is not to say there was no laughter. There was boisterousness and singing, though not as much as you might expect. There was also the bowing and scraping when people recognised me that I mainly wished to avoid, but which I would bend to my purpose over the coming days.

The noise grew louder as I approached Lord Ashdown's camp. At first, I had viewed him as a vicious taskmaster, bent on God and glory, but I saw in the eyes of his men that the Crusade was not about religion but about escape. They had lived a life too poor upon Lord Ashdown's estates and so had come to foreign shores to leave behind the squalor and hard work with which they had thought they would be burdened with forever.

It was here that many local women danced around campfires, either as slaves with iron collars, or as free women paid an iron penny to become one of those camp followers who walked in drips and drags behind our column. It was not much of a life.

Lord Ashdown's pavilion was the size of a dozen or so lesser tents, embroidered in sea-green and grey trim. The guards at the closed tent flap recognised me on sight and waved me inside.

Lord Ashdown reclined on a mountain of pillows, bedecked in splendid silk. He looked like a merchant, not the hard lord of a hard coast.

He was not the only person in the room. Five women lounged before him, in various states of undress, each one with empty, vacant eyes.

He smiled to see me. "Welcome, Harald Fairhair. How are your men?"

"Well."

"And Sir Slant?"

"He talks too much."

Lord Ashdown laughed and beckoned for me to bring over the wooden stool from his writing desk. Eyes that had been hard when I'd met him already mellowed, with crinkles around his eyes from smiling. The tent smelt like smoke and bottles of strong wine sat upon the table.

"Do you have a wife, Lord Ashdown?" I asked.

His expression hardened. "Yes."

I nodded. I sat and waited for him to speak.

Lord Ashdown pursed his lips together. "The cult of your personality has only grown greater since we last spoke. Your spats with Sir Slant have reached listening ears. A righteous man, they call you. God's champion. What do you think of their words?"

"I'm nobody's champion."

"Not yet," he said. "But I would like you to be my army's champion. When we send out an offer of single combat to an enemy general, I would like it to be you who faces him."

"Why?"

"Because you're Harald Lionheart. That's what they call you, isn't it? The masses?"

"I try not to listen."

"Well, I listen. You're touched by God. The priests are all saying it, no matter how much I might disagree with them. And so you'll be our champion." He smiled slightly. "And if you die in single combat, know that we will avenge you."

I scowled. "Is that all, Lord Ashdown?"

"Wait a moment." He stretched his arm around one of the slaves. "There are five beautiful women here, Harald. You're a young man, aren't you? Sixteen? Have you lain with a woman before?" He slapped the arse of one of the girls. "They're willing enough. They'd take your cock as happily as they take my own. Live a little. Let down that guard. We could achieve great things together. Return home as champions."

I rose, though not without difficulty. It felt a long time since I'd been with Lot. But I still had my resolve. *A righteous man*, the soldiers called me. I wouldn't let Lord Ashdown drag me down into the gutter.

"Thank you," I said. "But I'm committed to another."

"To that common born whore?" He laughed. "I heard the stories but I didn't believe them. You truly are just a young boy in love."

"I'm not," I roared at him. "I'm Harald, son of a bastard father and a deposed mother. I know what's right and wrong. That's why I'm here." I felt the desire for power rise inside of me. How easy it would be to wrap my hands around Lord Ashdown's fat neck. Cold sweat broke out on my forehead.

Is this normal? Am I a monster?

The fight went out of me. I fled Lord Ashdown's tent and pelted out into the night, past the ring of guards, to where men with torches guarded the perimeter. I toyed with the idea of leaving. Of slipping away into the night. But I didn't know where I was. And Lord Ashdown would hunt me down with relish.

What would people say about me, then? A scared little boy? Dragged back to camp in chains, or spitted and left to die on some forgotten hillside.

I breathed deeply. Sir Slant was right. I needed power. And the company of slaves was the best way to achieve that.

I returned to my tent and began plotting my tournament.

It was a simple affair. Something to keep the men busy during an evening.

The best fighters signed up, eager for a scrap. The rules were as they had been in the room beneath Lord Calforth's manner. The crowd chanted and bayed for blood. I watched the fights, giving my verdict with a single word after each bout.

Men howled at the moon that night.

I fought. Of course, I fought.

Not only did my anger need release, but I needed to prove as I was the invincible warrior the soldiers believed to be.

I wasn't, of course. The soldiers – for the most part – were pickpockets from Morhagen who'd never eaten a good meal in their life.

I fought three of them at once, and won.

I knew how I looked as I hefted the last one over my shoulder and sent him crashing into the dark. My hair caught in the torchlight, brilliantly blonde. My arms rippled with muscle. My barred teeth, narrow eyes, like a lion at work.

I didn't drink with them afterwards, as Gabriel had. I shook hands. Nodded firmly. I kept myself aloft. Alone.

When I returned to my tent, Sir Slant was waiting for me.

"We all lose one day," he said.

"I've already lost too many times," I responded, and ducked between the tent flaps.

Chapter Eight

We marched onwards. A soldier's main job is to walk. Fighting is secondary. It was almost five months since we'd left Antonia, and all we'd achieved was torching a few small towns and the begrudging surrender of the small forts we'd come across on our way.

Some of the lords had begun to pit themselves against each other. Each night they would return with a number of scalps, and a trail of slaves, and the winning lord would have the finest wine and the finest women from amongst the spoils.

However, the Lords had slowly begun to grow tired of their games, and the morale amongst the ordinary soldiers dropped lower. There was no singing and the army coiled closely together as we approached wide open plains.

Riders in bright colours watched us.

Men were dispatched to kill the infidels, but they scrambled away before our outriders could reach them. The sight of the riders made clear a truth to even the dimmest of soldiers.

The enemy was coming.

We were dogged from that day on by a ring of horses. Occasionally they would fire a speculative arrow towards us. Two sentries died the first night, another three the day afterwards. By the end of the week we were ready for them and our own outriders patrolled far and wide, pushing well ahead of the main column of troops.

It was these outriders who found the girl.

I first caught sight of her as they brought her back to camp, sitting upon a horse with her arms around her captor's waist. To say she was the most beautiful woman I had ever seen would be an understatement. There was something about her thin face and bright eyes that called to me. I was not the only one. The men hollered and jeered and I resisted the urge to tell them to shut up.

She seemed more than human.

They brought her to Lord Ashdown, who feasted on her with hungry eyes. She climbed down from the horse with unsteady legs. And when she spoke, her voice carried like a horn across the camp.

"I am Lady Linial of the Golden City." Men muttered and cursed but her curious figure held us away; a circle formed around her like a congregation around a priest. Even Lord Ashdown was lost to this crowd. "My Father is the Heptarch, ruler of the Golden City and elected leader of the lands beyond. He has sent me to offer you a peace – a final peace – between your land and ours. You have your God. We have Him too, only to us he is one of many, a single deity amongst a constellation of worship. We do not mean you harm. We have never launched a *crusade* upon your fair isles. Let us meet in negotiation, in friendship, not in violence and war."

A silence held us still and motionless, but only for a moment. Lord Ashdown shouldered his way through the crowd. "Beneath your city the Beast dwells. And since he rose from the sea he has whispered *heresy*. This same heresy you whisper to me now. Heathen! Heathen! I will smash your armies and lay your Golden City to waste."

Lady Linial's chest rose and deflated like a bellows. She was a girl. The magic she had weaved over the crowd fell away and they joined Lord Ashdown's chant: "Heathen! Heathen! Heathen!"

I could not join in. I simply stared. Even as they bound her wrists in thick rope and forced her through the crowd, towards Lord Ashdown's tent.

The chanting lasted for a long time. A ring of guards kept anyone – even myself, from Lord Ashdown's tent. My mind whirled with outrage – both at the Heptarch for letting his daughter come into such obvious danger, and also at Lord Ashdown for not treating her with even the slightest respect. War here would never end if all we wanted was plunder. How many lives were we condemning to death? How many years would go by before *infidel* and *heathen* fell out of use?

Anger bubbled inside of me. I had killed Lord Calforth, but there were a million Lord Calforth's. They all deserved to die.

I returned to my tent, but I could not duck beneath the flaps. My feet compelled me onwards, towards Lord Ashdown's tent. I couldn't let him get away with it. There was something about the girl. Something different. She wasn't another dim eyed slave to add to his harem.

The guards at the tent flap eyed me – they'd had orders to keep the men away, but I carried my own aura around camp. Since my victories in the melee no-one met my gaze. They mumbled quiet salutations; treated me as if I was a God come walking.

"I am here to see Lord Ashdown," I said.

They only hesitated for a moment. They stood aside and let me pass.

I expected to find her screaming. For Lord Ashdown hot and naked above her. Instead, the room I entered was silent. There were none of his usual whores, nor Lady Linial. There was only one body, laid completely naked upon the pillows. Lord Ashdown's head was missing, but otherwise there was no blood.

"Guards," I screamed. "Guards."

They thundered through the flap; pulled up short with wide eyes. For a Lord to die on the watch of a guardsman meant death. They would be lucky to escape with their heads.

"Lord Harald," one said, pleading. "It weren't our fault."

I nodded. The part of me that had stormed in here wanting to kill Lord Ashdown was satisfied. But the greater part of me was horrified. He hadn't just been killed. He had been assassinated, and his head had been taken as a prize.

"The Lady Linial was an assassin," I said. "She could have only done this through witchcraft."

"Aye, my lord," added the other guardsman. "We didn't hear a thing."

I nodded. "One of you sound the alarm. And you – let's talk about what you heard."

I didn't have the power to assemble the senior command of the Crusaders. But they had to invite me – I had found Lord Ashdown, and without him there was no lord great enough to unify all of our disparate troops. They needed my popularity.

We met in the evening, in a great command tent set up specifically for this purpose. We were each served a glass of wine, from the personal stores of Lord Arrowhall who buzzed frantically around us, hoping to curry favour and support for an expansion of his seat. He had issue with his cousins, the Custards. Even in a time of crisis, a continent away, the nobles couldn't resist their petty squabbling.

The entire tent was filled with obnoxious nobility, both great and small. Lord Pebbleworth chaired it – his mouth a thin line and his eyes watching the others like a hawk.

Lord Cryston was at his side, looking almost smug; the death of Lord Ashdown marked an opportunity for him. He was well thought of, particularly amongst the young men who came to Crusade partly because of the stories told about Lord Cryston. Swashbuckling clashes on stormy seas;

treasure stolen from foreign lands. He was the archetypal crusader, and despite the small paunch that gathered beneath his silks, he still had the aura of a man who lived life properly.

Lord Shimpert and Lord Revent were both border men, ostensibly from Amber, but who spoke our tongue with as much fluency as natives. The Amber Lords were numerous, but less important than their counterparts. Their names I had not caught, but I felt their eyes on me, some with open disgust. My family had not been loved, and a royal bastard remains a royal bastard, no matter how far away from the line of succession I was. One in particular stood out to me – a silver haired brawler with scarred knuckles and the kind of look that makes even the bravest man tremble. He watched me too closely.

The rest of our lords – Henderson, Helmley, Witorth and others – were pious and quiet, and the knights were stinking and dirty, here more from curiosity than an ability to effect change. Still, amongst their number were a few brave men and a few cruel men of some notoriety.

"Order," shouted Lord Pebbleworth. "Order you damnable gossips."

The room quieted, though a few of the knights still snickered at the rear.

"Lord Ashdown has been killed by the enemy." The news which many of them already knew, once confirmed, prompted a bout of arguing that didn't die for several minutes. When Lord Pebbleworth finally shouted them into order his face was red and he seemed, for once, close to his actual age "He was killed by a witch on the road. The enemy – it seems – are everything we've heard stories of. Their black magic means that it is time our boys stopped treating this campaign like a fun bloody holiday, and more like a war."

Jeers of assent from all around the room. "Now," Lord Pebbleworth continued, "I move to strike a single motion. First, no more consorting with the whores of this cursed land, at least not if you want to keep your head. Secondly, no more mercy on these foreign villages. There is no telling how these witches might conceal themselves, and no telling how much damage they might cause. We must burn the villages."

More nods, though one of the lords of Amber spoke up.

"If you kill the villagers, what then of our knights who are captured by the enemy?"

"Then they are with God now," answered Lord Henderson.

Lord Pebbleworth nodded. "This is a Crusade, for righteousness and the glory of God. This is not a war, in the conventional sense. We should not expect the ordinary rules of it to apply here." He looked around the tent, daring others to disagree. "I bring these matters of importance to you, before the election of our new war leader, because I'm sure you all agree that these are absolute musts, and I will not risk our Crusade failing because of petty politics." He puffed out his cheeks. "Now, Lord Ashdown was a brilliant man and he shall be missed. His organisation and leadership skills have seen us safely this far. But now we are in foreign territory. We need a leader with experience and knowledge. Someone who can set the right standard. Someone who – "

"I say we make the boy our leader."

The room turned as one to the speaker, the grizzled Lord of Amber with silver hair.

"Young Lord Harald is a hero to the soldiers. He is the unity of our two peoples. Why not let him lead?"

Lord Cryston burst from his chair. "Preposterous. He's a boy!"

"He's also your champion, should you meet the enemy in single combat. It is not as if Lord Ashdown did not trust him. Who's to say what they spoke about in their meetings? Perhaps he was being groomed as a potential successor all along." He looked to me with a smile in his eyes. "What say you, Lord Harald? Did Lord Ashdown talk to you of your role?"

Before I could answer, Sir Slant stepped forward from the rear of the room. "It's quite the opposite, milords. I have the honour of being both on Lord Ashdown's staff, and to be the secretary of Lord Harald's camp. Lord Ashdown did not trust Lord Harald – the boy is a firebrand and a liar, speaking untruths of our homelands, and with no appetite for war."

It was my turn to surge to my feet. "Liar," I bellowed. "Have you all not seen me fight? I've an appetite for war. I simply think there are better ways to do it than this morally vacant crusade. You promise condemned men salvation. You promise poor men riches. All for what? I see the mountain of God on the flags flying above you, but I see no piety in the heart of the men beneath it."

Lord Henderson nodded. "Perhaps Lord Harald is right – we need more commitment to God, and less to the spirit of adventure that has overtaken this camp."

Arguing erupted from every corner of the room. My heart beat heavily and the corners of the tent closed around me. I had been mooted as a potential candidate. From nowhere, control of the entire Crusade had almost become mine. What would I do with it? Would I turn round and find Lot, or press on to take the Golden City and win a return home.

It took a long time for Lord Pebbleworth to quiet the lords, and I did my best to appear confident and strong despite my fast-beating heart.

"I'll ask you now, as one, for nominations for candidates of our new leader. I've heard the vote for Harald the Bastard, but let me hear any others."

"Lord Cryston," Sir Slant said immediately.

From that suggestion came a series of nods around the entire table, and Lord Cryston allowed himself to settle back into his chair with a smirk.

Other names were mooted, but none carried the weight of Lord Cryston.

Yet despite his popularity I could hear my name muttered between tables.

When eventually all the suggestions had been made, Lord Pebbleworth raised his hand. "Both Lord Cryston and Harald have shown themselves to be heroes of this Crusade, so I'll tell you all now I'll tolerate no dirty talking or dissent from any of you."

Lord Henderson spoke first: "I won't speak ill of anyone in this room – but outside of it! Have you seen the state of our camps? This is meant to be for the glory of God. There's men here who think they've come to a brothel not to a war. Lord Harald is right, we need to remember why we're here!"

Lord Shimpert stood. "And you think a pretty child is the right man to do that? He's a murderer, not a lord, don't you forget it!"

The debate continued. I tried my best to make myself heard. My voice sounded small compared to the deep rumbling of the Amber lords. Lord Cryston had not moved and instead sat back in his chair, sipping at his wine.

For hours, the debate raged. Two minor lords fought and both were dragged out. Lord Revent called one of the lords of Amber a jumped up toad, and the silver haired lord of Amber had spat on the boots of Lord Shimpert.

Eventually, it came time for the lords to vote. Hands were raised and Lord Pebbleworth took an age counting each individual hand. He went through every candidate one by one – with some candidates receiving nothing more than their own votes. In the end, hands were raised for me. It was more than any of the other candidates so far, but it was still significantly less than half of the room.

"Hands for Lord Cryston," Lord Pebbleworth said, and the entire room seemed to raise their hands.

For a moment, Lord Pebbleworth attempted to count their number, but after losing his count twice he shook his head. "Lord Cryson takes the vote," he said. "Two thirds of the vote, I'd say." He sighed, and the wrinkles on his brow bunched. "Lord Cryston is the new leader of our Crusade."

My stomach sunk. I had not expected to win, and yet...there was a part of me that had dared to hope.

Finally, Lord Cryston stood. His speech was short and simple. We needed to return to the roots of this Crusade, he said. We needed to give the soldiers a standard to set themselves too. We needed strong leadership from an experienced campaigner.

"I've stolen eggs from a dragon, killed a whale with mine own hands. Taking the Golden City is just the next logical step."

I left the tent with my heart beating more than if I had run for an hour without stopping. I had not won, and yet even amongst the lords I had found a newfound respect. I felt the support of others solidify around me like something tangible. From nowhere I had power – the condemned company of men cheered my return to our camp and for once I favoured them with a small smile.

The biggest acknowledgement of my power came from Lord Cryston himself.

His guardsman – each of them dressed in richly dyed colours like foreign privateers – appeared like thieves outside of my tent. A group of my soldiers had already surrounded them. The atmosphere swung between jubilation and violence.

I stood to meet them wearing trousers and nothing else, my hair swinging around my shoulders like a mane. I looked like a wild man. Unwashed, bestial, lean and muscled as a wildcat. The pretty youth I had been growing up began to give way to something darker – the man that I would become.

Lord Cryston's guardsmen turned, faced their centre, and dropped to one knee. From their midst Lord Cryston emerged, bedecked in regal finery, his moustache combed and twirled. In both hands he carried a blade, sheathed, but I didn't have to see the blade to know it as my own.

"Harald Fairhair," Lord Cryston said, and all the soldiers quieted to hear his words. "With the power vested in me by this company, and by my own strength as Lord of Greenhold, I release you from the sentence pronounced upon you. I make you a freed man." He smiled brightly. "When this Crusade is won, I will bring you home, and you will always have a space in my halls."

I said nothing, merely stood, bewildered. He was counteracting the King's own command, in public.

Lord Cryston continued, as if I had graciously thanked him, as I should have. "You are the champion of this company, single greatest warrior of the Crusade. I offer you the sword of your father as my thanks for your support." He proffered the blade forward and I had enough sense to drop to one knee as I took it.

"My Lord," I said, voice breaking.

"Not a word," Lord Cryston said. "We are now one camp," he said quietly, "one people. Rise and take my hand."

I stood and we raised our joined hands to the sky. Soldiers bellowed and thumped. A conniving priest broke out into a hymn and within moments all the men sung along.

Cryston turned to me. "This isn't an idle gesture. In another life we would have romped across the southern sea, with women and wine. Instead, we are here, on this now all too womanless Crusade. I have come to expect a certain type of life and a certain type of treatment. I am used to being a hero. But here you are, upstaging me. And long may it continue."

His lips quirked into a grin. "Now young Harald, I have more swords to give out, so I hope you'll excuse me."

Alcohol flowed freely that night, despite the now constant threat of attack. Twelve men died, picked off by bloody arrows in the dark. The heathens weren't chivalrous, but how could I blame them? We torched every village we came to and slaughtered every foreign camp follower who wouldn't leave.

I distracted myself by training. I would get stronger. I would be unstoppable. I worked as I had done on the ship and at Lord Calforth's manor. I ran through the camp in the early hours, before anyone else was awake. But my presence was enough of a draw, and before the end of the first week I found myself with dozens of men jogging after me, red faced and sweating.

And then they were upon us in earnest.

No more attacks in the night, but bands of riders seen throughout the day. They shepherded us like cattle across the plains. We drew tighter. Our camp like the carapace of a great beast, rings upon rings of guards roaming the night.

I walked among them. I peered out into the night, wondering where the next foray would come from. But I was never there – it would always be another side of the camp, and there would always be more soldiers dead with arrows sprouting from their necks by the time I arrived. The enemy would vanish, and the men began muttering about witchcraft and sorcery.

It was not witchcraft, but they were well drilled. Still, even I could not help but worry. I found the Lady Linial in my dreams, a figure wearing nothing but thin black cloth, calling to me through heavy fog. I followed, but the sight that greeted me was no mysterious temptress, but a gibbet, from which soldiers swung and birds plucked out their eyes.

I woke in cold sweats. I did not smile when the soldiers cracked jokes at my side. Sir Slant no longer visited me but hung resentful in the shadows outside my tent. He was the consummate soldier still, organising our supplies and drilling the men, but what passed as friendship between us was dead and buried.

I had power, but it wasn't of the right kind. It was a power that could change nothing; a power that was inherently powerless. It was the power of a ship's captain, unable to turn the wheel of a boat as it collided into the land.

The collision happened slowly. A great cloud of dust appeared on the horizon, a thousand banners turning in the wind. The shapes solidified into men – thousands and thousands, led by officers in streaming gold cloaks.

Our camp contracted like an indrawn breath. Soldiers scrambled into position. Orders were bellowed across the plain. Lord Cryston rode to me, with his guard flanking him, and a spare horse. "It's time, Harald. Are you ready?"

I nodded, pulled myself up alongside him, and cantered towards the head of our defences. All the great lords had gathered, jostling for position, but we ignored their struggles, riding on ahead to where Lord Pebbleworth stood alone, watching the gathering army.

"It's quite something," Lord Cryston said as we descended from our mounts.

Lord Pebbleworth grunted. "God is on our side."

We waited in silence as the heathens drew closer, then halted across the plain, like a still block of cloud on the horizon. From their army a single rider approached, leisurely picking their way across the plain. It was a woman, I realised, wearing black silk.

"Let Lord Cryston do the talking," Lord Pebbleworth said. "Be ready."

The rider came closer, her features revealed. She was as beautiful as the last time I'd seen her, wide-eyed and small. Lord Cryston's mouth thinned to a line as she dismounted. "Welcome, Lady Linial. Have you come to offer your surrender?"

She laughed, her voice almost sing-song. "Well met Lord Cryston. And if I were to surrender to you – what would you do? Take me to your bed like your predecessor."

He showed no expression. "If you were to surrender to me, I would spare your people. But I would lop off your head with a single swing of my sword."

"Such a frightening man." She stretched her arms above her head. "Do you know they tell stories about you, even in the Golden City? Your adventures travel well, but not as well you. Your paunch is heavy and your face is red. What hope do you have of winning?"

Lord Cryston still did not react. "You're a girl," he said. "Your people taunt us by using you as their ambassador. You will learn the error of your arrogance. God is with us."

She laughed again. "But all the other gods are with us. You say I am young, but to us your people are children playing in a brook. You are naïve. And you will all die today."

Lord Cryston shook his head. "There will be much death today. I'm not naïve enough to know that both of our armies will bleed."

"Then turn around. Go home." She jutted out her chin. "You are the aggressor."

"You tell us that we are children. That our religion is false. Prove it. Show that your Gods are with you. Defeat our champion in single combat and I will turn this army around."

She pursed her lips. "I cannot make the same promises. This is our home."

He fixed her with his expressionless gaze. "The best of yours against the best of ours. Our God, against all of yours."

She breathed deeply, then smiled. Her gaze flicked towards me. "Is he your champion? The boy?"

"I'm not a boy," I said.

"A boy who rises very easily to goading."

I scowled, felt the pommel of my father's sword between my fingertips.

Lady Linial watched me with eyes like a cat, before turning back to Lord Cryston. "You'll have your battle. Sundown today." She vaulted onto her horse. "Afterwards, I expect to see your army retreating back to Antonia."

She didn't look at me as she left, but my heart thudded in my chest. It wasn't the prospect of death that scared me, of mine being the first and last name lost in this battle, but her dark eyes on me. Her witchcraft, I told myself. She was trying to bewitch me.

Lord Pebbleworth scowled. "What do you hope to buy us? Time? Time for what?"

Lord Cryston smiled easily. "I hope to buy us a victory. Give the men hope. We'll need them to fight as if they believe God is beating the war-drum himself."

"And if Harald loses?"

Lord Cryston turned to me and rested a hand upon my shoulder. "He will not lose."

I will not lose.

A dozen servants buzzed around me, lacing up my armour. They dressed me in heavy plate mail, Lord Cryston's own from better days. It was black with strips of gold and a heavy helm with only a thin slit visible outside of it. I opened the visor and heaved a deep breath.

I had fought in mail before. But never against a foe wanting to kill me. I raised my arms; every movement tired me, wore me down. I felt as if I had been sapped of all energy, before the fight had even begun.

Lord Cryston came to see me. His smiling face anchored me. "You won't die here, boy. You're destined for great things. Great things. My name will be a mere footnote compared to your own. Now, be brave. Lord Pebbleworth will ride out as your second. You'll meet the enemy champion and you'll kill him. You're the best noble born fighter in this camp, though I'd still wager Black Pip would give you a run for your money." He slapped me on my mailed arm and grinned. "This is fun. Don't forget it. These are the moments we are born for."

A sea of well-wishers spoke to me as I dressed. I didn't register any of them. Eventually, I was ready – I swigged a skin of water and mounted up on a black warhorse with angry eyes.

Lord Pebbleworth led, walking his horse through the camp. Soldiers lined a pathway out, bellowing encouragement.

It was too much. All of the noise turned into the same echoing drone. The light seemed too harsh. I couldn't focus on faces; I tightened my grip on the reins. **It was too much.** *It was too much.*

We broke out of camp and I heaved a deep breath. Lord Pebbleworth glanced back and arched an eyebrow. "God is with you," he said.

I laughed, wild and loud. "And that's the crazy part, isn't it? I don't even believe in Him."

Lord Pebbleworth shook his head. "Well, you better hope he believes in you."

I looked back towards camp. Thousands of people watched us pick our way across the plain, to the point where two riders already waited. The sun split the horizon with fierce light, though the rest of the sky had already been claimed by maudlin grey clouds. I raised a hand to try and make out the figures waiting for us, but it was no good. They were just dark blots hiding in the horizon's light.

"Remember yourself," Lord Pebbleworth said. "Count your breathing. Be calm and trust your sword arm."

As a response, I urged my horse into a canter, until the spot of the duel appeared suddenly out of the sun.

I dismounted – not an easy task in full plate. My gaze was drawn to the heathen army. So many flags flew: a white apple, a golden tower, a broken sword. I knew nothing about any of them. Heathens and infidels, but with banners as bright as our own.

Closer, two figures stood. One of them petite – the Lady Linial. The other, hulking in polished plate. His helm was open, revealing lank brown hair and a cleft chin.

"Presenting," Lord Pebbleworth bellowed from beside me, "Harald Fairhair, often known as Harald Lionheart, champion of the Host of the Mountain."

Lady Linial smiled. "May I present my brother, Lord Axel, on behalf of the combined forces of the seven nations of Gora."

The warrior clapped his sword against his shield.

I did not fight with a shield; my father's sword was all I'd never needed, perfectly balanced, but with the reach to keep even the most persistent of opponents outside of my reach.

Lord Pebbleworth laid a hand on my shoulder. "Be brave, Harald."

I looked back towards their champion, the Lord Axel, to see him snap his visor shut. Lady Linial half-smiled at me.

It began, without preamble or formalities. I drew my sword and brandished it before me.

The plain beneath our feet was hard, dusty and brown. It was also uneven. I placed my feet carefully as we circled, knowing one turned ankle would mean my death. The sword was not my only weapon; a thin stiletto of a dagger hung at my waist, if I got him on the ground.

When I get him on the ground, I told myself.

I began to speak, to myself as much as to him. "You're a cunt," I told him. "I bet you that you're just like my brothers. You're callous, cruel –" I struck midway through the word, overhead. He blocked well and stepped backwards lightly.

"Light on your feet, little nonce," I said, and I had eyes only for Lord Axel and his polished armour, bright in the horizon's light.

He approached by way of his shield. I went left, right, sending a clanking blow off his left shoulder. I heard the smallest grumble of exertion and Lord Axel stepped back, waiting for my offensive.

The nervousness I felt had blown away with the first solid blow. Energy coursed through my veins like roiling thunder. "Come here you fucker." I approached him, eyes half on him, half on the ground beneath my feet.

He snapped into motion quicker than I expected, batting my sword away with his shield. His shortsword went for a killing blow, straight to my skull. I reeled just in time, backpedalling frantically, and the blow glanced off the top of my head.

The world spun. Down seemed like up, up seemed like down. I kept my feet, one hand on my blade to steady it, the other out wrapped tightly around the hilt. I gritted my teeth as Lord Axel approached, impassive behind his polished steel.

He was the perfect semblance of a knight, uncaring, unmoved, by the events in front of him.

I bellowed and thrust, overextending, my blade scratching across his armour. I came in too close, inside of his reach and his shield backhanded me in the face.

My feet went out from under me and I hit the ground, rolling.

He was on top of me, shield discarded, thin knife in hand. He sought the narrow slits in my armour where a blow would be fateful, but I held him, thankful for the near constant training I had done over the past year.

"Get off me," I cried, throwing him backwards. I did not press the offence, instead collecting my sword and heaving a deep breath.

He retrieved his shield and we faced one another.

Cold sweat trickled off me. The armour chafed.

The last of the sun dripped below the horizon, turning the horizon the colour of a bruise. Night settled, all too fast. Back in our camps, soldiers would be straining their eyes, barely able to make out who was who.

Lord Axel put one steady foot before the other, marching across the plain. I swept into a low guard and steadied my breathing. We exchanged a flurry of blows. Shield, right leg, across the breastplate.

He stood unmoving as I stepped back, panting. An implacable monster who did not tire.

I gritted my teeth. I had beaten every opponent I had faced.

All but one.

Gabriel's face flashed into my mind and I attacked. He parried, at first. Then he began to grunt and fall back.

I struck into his shield and cleaved it in two. He dropped both pieces and raised his blade.

I battered that aside too.

It went rolling out of his reach. My next strike caught him in the stomach, driving him to his knees.

My last, swung without precision, dented his helm and sent him rolling. He lay upon the ground, dazed, reeling, half-dead.

He was not Gabriel. Gabriel would not be beaten so easily.

Still, he had given me my best fight in years. Instead of pursuing I gently tapped my sword beneath his chin. "Do you yield?"

"Yield." He ripped off his helm, spitting blood. "Yield."

I turned to Lady Linial. "Take him away. He fought well."

She rushed to his side as I picked up his sword, handing it to Lord Pebbleworth. "Keep it," I said. "It might be worth something if we get home."

"What's wrong with you?" the old man hissed. "Why didn't you kill him?"

"Why should I? What will it have gained us?" I gestured towards the infidels' monstrous army. "Perhaps at the end of this battle they might remember this mercy and spare us our lives."

Lord Pebbleworth spat at my feet. "You ungodly bastard."

"Careful," I warned, sword still in hand. "You do not want to taunt me."

"So, you would rather kill your own kind than the heathens? The King was right to exile you."

To that I had no response, so I mounted up and cantered back towards camp.

The cheer that greeted me made all of Lord Pebbleworth's naysaying irrelevant. I was champion of the Host of the Mountain.

I had won.

Chapter Nine

Lord Cryston sat atop a menacing black strider, bedecked as if he were going to court, not to war. All of the troops were arrayed in formation ahead of him. Bonfires burnt across the plain and the soldiers had spent the time I'd won digging trenches and palisades.

"It was a glorious victory," he said, no hint of his usual cheer in his voice.

In the distance, the army of the infidel began to move, thousands upon thousands of bright flames in the night. They outnumbered us five to one and meant to press their advantage as quickly as possible.

"Sir Slant has control of your units," Lord Cryston said. "I would rather you stayed with me, and then I can use you where the fight is thickest. You are our sword this night. I will use you with expert precision."

Surrounding us was a small army of servants and junior officers. Lord Cryston's fearsome guard stood behind him with worried expressions. The night was alive with the noise of shuffling boots. A bone-chilling cold had settled on me. I was tired already from the earlier fight and Lord Cryston's armour weighed on me in all the wrong places.

Lord Pebbleworth had the right-hand side, stationed alongside some of the more inexperienced troops. My own company was with him. On the left were the lords of Amber

– part of me wished I had spoken to them more, asked them about my mother. It was too late for that now. Lord Revent took command of them, despite being a border reaver known for sowing more trouble than he solved.

The centre was led by the pious lords of the Mountain, great banners flying in the breeze. I wondered whether they had asked my father to join this Crusade, wondered what other secrets he had kept hidden right up until the end.

I looked out over the steadily encroaching sea of soldiers, of flags and banners lit by torchlight, and the reality of the situation hit me. I could die on this battlefield. I could be one of thousands of men crushed underfoot. I would never see Lot again. I would never find the draugr and avenge my family.

My grip on my father's sword turned my fingers numb.

"They're eager," Lord Cryston said. "They want blood."

In answer to his words a troop of horsemen bounded forward from the heathen. In a fluid motion they raised their bows and lit fire arrows, sent them hurtling towards our troops. There was a shuffling en-masse, and the front lines hunkered behind large shields, the deeper lines spreading out.

"Now wait for it," Lord Cryston muttered.

The riders galloped onwards, notching another arrow to their bow, until suddenly the flames crumpled into nothingness and the night was shook by screaming horses.

Lord Cryston nodded, satisfied. "We dug trenches. As many and as deep as we could. I only had a couple of hours and would have loved a couple more, but your victory shook them. I was expecting we would have had the whole night, but their eagerness will cost them. They won't even see the traps I've laid for them."

The horses left alive retreated back to the main column of the heathen host. I wondered whether Lord Axel was amongst them, on the front line, or whether his defeat had broken more than his pride. For that matter – where was the Lady Linial? The daughter of a Heptarch wouldn't be on the front lines of the battle, would she?

I remembered Lord Ashdown's head, left spiked on the road for us to find. His complexion had turned rotten and grey and his eyes were black from whatever cruel sorcery she had used.

She wasn't an innocent maiden. Far from it. She was a witch and I shouldn't forget just because of a pretty face. If I met her in battle, I would kill her.

The heathen forces advanced slowly, horse archers tucked in behind ranks of spearmen. They were a barely distinguishable horde, except where torchlight illuminated one of their faces all too clear. In some ways they looked much like us – grubby and unclean and scared shitless.

"For my next trick," Lord Cryston said.

Before he'd even finished his sentence there was a roar in the night. Before the heathen front line an eruption of dirt and the bellowing of soldiers. Our soldiers. The heathen front line crumbled immediately and our soldiers went amongst them dealing death. From further back rose more men covered in dirt, each one with a shortbow, each one firing death into the enemy ranks.

It was Lord Henderson, I realised, and half of his brood. "It's suicide," I said.

"Aye," Lord Cryston said. "But they want to serve the glory of God so I gave them the opportunity. Only volunteers, most wicked old knights with some misdeeds to correct. A few pious boys, but I did my best to dissuade most of them."

Hundreds of infidels fell to them. The entire enemy army reeled like a wave thrown back off rocks. We were winning. I looked into the eyes of Lord Cryston and saw no pleasure, only grim determination. He saw my gaze and shook his head. "There's no victory for us yet. They fight for their homes. We don't dissuade them so easily."

Not for the first time I looked down at that horde of soldiers coming towards us and breathed deeply.

The figures of Lord Henderson and his knightly children fought bitterly, but the heathens recovered, and one by one they fell and were trampled beneath the feet of that great host.

Our archers loosed as soon as they came in range. Silent shafts that rose and fell without me seeing – only the crumpling of soldiers. The enemy doubled their speed, but the network of trenches that Lord Cryston had built slowed them; a particularly overzealous heathen charged with battle cry only to fall into a trench in a clatter of broken armour and bones.

Our soldiers heckled them.

Their heavy horse pulled wide. Lord Cryston sent a message to our own knights – be prepared to intercept. The imminent threat of a clash dissuaded the enemy, and instead they hung waiting, in steel, with banners flying in the light breeze.

The last few paces between our army and theirs narrowed. They charged. The army swelled and the ground between the armies suddenly did not exist. Screaming, the clash of steel on steel, of steel wedging in bone.

Lord Cryston began to bellow orders. Outriders came and went, each one galloping off – one to Lord Revent, another to Lord Helmsley. I stood, in awe. Everything was noise – all of the world bellowed with the sound of men fighting and dying.

I looked to the sky. A dark sky. They said the heathens had a God for every element and I wondered whether any of them looked up from a mortal wound, beseeching their Lord.

I turned, slowly. I realised Lord Cryston was shouting for me. "Lord Pebbleworth needs you. Go! Go!"

Someone handed me a horse, and I followed the outrider from our position on the hilltop down towards the fighting. If anything, the noise got quieter. There was silence the space of an indrawn breath, but that silence stood out against the screams of men.

The rider was shouting something to me, but I wasn't really listening. I drew my father's sword. It was strangely beautiful in the darkness, a pale shadow except for the gemstone at its base, smouldering like a coal at night's end.

"Where?" I said to the outrider, and he pointed to a gap in the lines.

A great brute of the enemy smashed soldiers aside, roaring as he did so. From the gaps he made poured dozens of their men, each one snarling like a creature from damnation. I looked to our soldiers – it was mine own company, I realised – bloody and beaten and dying, and hefted my sword above my head.

"For God," I cried. "For God and our souls!"

The call reverberated down the line. I slipped from my horse, clanking down in my plate. The soldiers parted and I found myself before the big man.

He was big, but he was slow. One slip of my blade through his lightly armoured frame and he was on his knees, no taller than any man in our army.

The soldiers bellowed and surged. My enemies moved too slowly – what my blade didn't catch my heavy armour did. I was a one-man army. I felled two men in the same movement, barred the hole in the line and pushed forward into their ranks.

Enemies stood all around me, but I could smell their fear puddling between their legs. They tried to bring me down, but my armour weathered the fiercest blows and I cut indiscriminately, wide strokes that caved in chests and lacerated faces.

Our line surged and their attack buckled. We had the advantage. We had the power.

I almost plunged further but a strong arm on my shoulder hauled me back. I had to stop my own counter-blow when I realised it was one of our own. It took me a moment to see his face in the light, but I knew his voice well enough.

"Save yourself, boy. This will be a long night." Lord Pebbleworth was blood spattered and grim. "You did well though. You did well."

I let the outrider fetch me my horse and trotted back towards Lord Cryston. That was all the rest I would get. Lord Revent had lost his arm in the fighting and was being dragged away, though he protested.

They wanted me to inspire the troops. I walked amongst them – took off my helm and held it aloft. Shook free my too-long hair from where it had been tucked into my mail.

Lord Shimpert greeted me with a mailed fist clasping my forearm. There wasn't a breach as much as there had been on the left, but the fighting was fiercer. Their troops weren't the same scared boys I had cut down earlier either. Broad shouldered, they attacked in sustained bursts, heavily armoured. This was the side they were trying to collapse, I realised.

On our left the heavy horse clashed, knights riding past each one another with broken lances. "To the front," Lord Shimpert shouted over the din. "I'll be at your side. Let the men remember this – for the rest of the night, at least."

We took our place on the front line, two titans. I left my helm in the hands of my outrider, so the men could see me.

It was like brawling. All about discipline. One blow traded here, another there, always on your guard, always aware. There wasn't the same kind of joy as trading death freely. My armour began to feel heavy. More strikes slipped through my guard.

When I thrust, my father's sword buried deep into the guts of the attacker. I'd cut some kind of cord and his bowels released. I struggled to pull my blade free.

I didn't see the other attacker. Just felt the sweep of his sword, clattering off my breastplate, up. My face burnt with blood.

Lord Shimpert yelled, but I couldn't make it out. I turned to him, smiling, sword finally free.

He yanked me from the front line and another poor soul filled my place instead.

"God! Are you mad?"

I reached up to my own face; my entire gauntlet came away coated in slippery blood. "You need a doctor," he said.

"There's no time for that."

As I spoke, my knees weakened. The world dropped away and I was swallowed in darkness.

I woke immediately. Or at least that's what it felt like.

I was in a tent, an old man fussing over me. I could still hear the sounds of the battle, though dimmer. He'd stripped me out of my mail, leaving only my undershirts on, stained red by blood.

"Where's Lord Shimpert?" I said, sitting up.

The doctor eyed me. "Been here, back to the fighting, then back here again, then dead. The tide is going against us from what I hear. Good you're awake though. A good strong lad to buy us a few more moments with that nice sword of yours."

I struggled to my feet. The world swayed around me, but I wouldn't be felled. I was stronger than a little scratch.

"The wounds ugly," the doctor said. "I wouldn't move too much or your stitches will come undone. With any luck you'll live long enough for it to become a long silver line from your chin to your forehead. With less luck you'll die tonight with the rest of us."

"Where's my sword? My armour?"

"They took your armour. Put some other poor soul in it, pretending he's you. Your sword is over there."

I grabbed it. "Lord Cryston? Where is he?"

"Do I look like a battlefield commander to you? I'm a medic. A doctor."

"Fucking useless is what you are."

I stumbled through the tent flaps. Bloodier soldiers carried even bloodier soldiers to the field surgeons. An array of tents only partially hid the sounds of bones being sawn and men shitting themselves. I saw the hill on which Lord Cryston and I had stood, but it was empty now. Even he had been called into the fray.

I could barely make out which side was which in the melee. Our lines had crumpled inwards and the heathens swarmed around the edges. Even now a group of riders wheeled around our lines, making their way towards the field hospital.

Mustering my courage, I strode to meet them. They expected me to be just another target to carve down, but they'd all lost their lances, and their vicious short swords required them to come too close to my father's sword. I felled one on the first pass with a sword through his belly; the follow through almost carried me with him, but instead he tumbled from the saddle and I yanked the blade free.

The second pass saw them come in stages, eager to see me dead. I cut the legs away from the first horse, crushing the rider beneath it, while the second cut a bloody slash down my right arm.

The next two thundered towards me at once. Instead of fighting I leapt to one side, only lashing up at the last minute to bury my blade into the horse's rump. The rider went tumbling but rose to confront me.

I couldn't let him be distracting me when the riders came again so I ended it with power I no longer knew I still possessed. I screamed and crushed his skull, splattering brain and blood.

The last two riders advanced together, but never reached me. Two of our soldiers pulled them from the saddle and stabbed them in the belly.

I saluted them; they saluted back.

I turned to see the mayhem of the battle. The doctor was right. We were losing. The wing closest to me was Lord Pebbleworth's. Hundreds of soldiers lay unmoving on the ground, but the main body of the men fought on.

Even as I approached, the faith of men deserted them.

Some turned and ran, vanishing into the night. Others held their ground. Now, the heathen heavy cavalry was coming to bear, rumbling across the ground like thunder.

I saw Lord Pebbleworth alone, desperately trying to turn his men to the attack.

He was spitted like a pig on the lance of the first rider. I bellowed, but it would do no good. I wasn't close enough and the cavalry charge had obliterated the entire right wing.

I slowed my headlong charge. It was over. The banners of the mountain fell one by one, until I could see nothing but a sea of the heathen rolling over us in the night.

Some men held up their hands; others fled blindly into the dark.

From the heavy cavalry, I saw a rider approach, slowly walking his horse as if it were a tournament and not a battle.

I settled into the same stance as I had confronted the soldiers earlier. Breathe deep. Steady. If I could take his horse, perhaps I could flee back to Antonia.

Instead of setting his lance and charging he pulled open his helm. He spoke, at first in the strange tongue of the Golden City, then slower, in our own language.

"Dyaa Yeld?" he said.

I frowned, did not respond.

"Do." He spoke carefully. "You." I recognised him now by his square jaw and cleft chin. "Yield?"

I looked at the devastation of our host and the skill with which Lord Axel guided his horse towards me. I threw down my father's sword and nodded. "I yield."

Lord Axel smiled.

I was bound and trussed and taken to a tent where they left me for the night, guarded by men with halberds and evil smiles. I was not the only one. There were other lords – Helmsley and Bryant most notably, then smaller knights of a little renown.

When dawn broke, I alone was brought out, pushed through the enemy camp to the jeers of the heathens.

Another tent awaited me, grander than the last, and this one occupied by heathens. A grey bearded man sat atop a wooden chair, with the Lady Linial and the Lord Axel either side of him. Kneeling on the ground before him, head pressed into the dirt, was Lord Cryston.

The bearded man must be the Heptarch, I realised – the Lady Linial's father.

The guards forced me down into the same pose as Lord Cryston and I spat dirt from my lips. The cut down my face burnt.

The Heptarch spoke in the heathens rattling tongue and the Lady Linial translated, butter-sweet.

"You two are the symbols of your Crusade. Commander of your pathetic host and its champion. To see you both, stripped of your armour and your jewels, shows us that you are both nothing but dirty scoundrels chasing the Golden City's treasure."

From the corner of my eye, I spotted nods from courtiers and ambassadors. The speech wasn't for our benefit, but for the representatives of the alliance of kingdoms who had come together to stop us.

"Your Crusade wasn't built upon piety. I have seen enough of your lords begging for release, if only they would convert to our faith. But such sentiment shows how little you understand us, your supposed enemy. You think we are of one faith!" Some of the nobles laughed. "We are an alliance of nations led by men and women from a multitude of towns worshipping a hundred different gods. And the strength of our alliance over you will always be our tolerance and our understanding."

"And yet. It seems that your people do not understand this. Eight times you have declared a Crusade. And yet each time you have failed, failing further and further away from the Golden City since the First Crusade where you sullied our walls with your stinking bodies. We are becoming stronger each time, and you are becoming weaker."

The Heptarch paused for a second to drink water passed to him by an aide.

"I have toyed with the idea of executing you both. Sending your heads back as a warning. But that would be your style not ours. Your soldiers – those who have surrendered – will be spared. And those of you who can be ransomed, will be ransomed. Those of you who cannot – will be sold as slaves in the Golden City and beyond, as a warning to your people not to test us again. I have sent messengers already."

My heart sank. There would be no ransom for me.

"I want you to remember this moment," the Heptarch said. "Teach this lesson to your children and let them teach it to their children. *We* shall never be conquered by the likes of you. And if we are prodded – if you come against us one more time, then I will personally sweep your isles from the map and drown you all in pitch and fire. Do you understand?"

Lord Cryston managed a meek affirmative and I did my best to nod.

"Good. Take them away. I don't want to see them in my presence again."

They gave me my own tent, which I suppose I should be thankful for, but I wasn't. The Heptarch had told me that the path to freedom would be through ransom – and I would not be ransomed.

I paced the tent, cursing myself for not killing Lord Axel. I could have been halfway to Antonia by now.

A light wind entered the room and I looked up to find the Lady Linial watching me. "What do you want?" I grumbled. "Come to gloat about your superior culture?"

Her expression hardened. "I came to ask how you are."

"Bloody brilliant. Can't you see? I love being a hostage almost as much as I love being a slave."

She shook her head. "I thought you might be a little less barbaric than the rest of your kind, but I can see I was wrong. You'll be ransomed soon enough, Harald Fairhair."

She turned to leave but I caught her by the hem of her dress.

"You don't understand. I won't be ransomed."

"And why not?"

"Because I'm an exile." I was almost shouting. I released her arm and staggered to the corner of the tent. "Nobody wants me back in Ordrove. I will be here until the end of my days."

To her credit, the Lady Linial looked upset. She skipped closer and looked at me with bright eyes. "I'll talk to my father," she said. "He'll listen. We'll find a way."

Her generosity stung me. "Why do you care?"

"You saved my brother's life. He's a fool, but he's all I have." With that, she slipped away.

The Lady Linial did not return.

Instead, a grizzled old man entered, followed by another in hood and cloak. The hooded man spoke first, in a rattle of that foreign tongue.

The grizzled man translated. "My lord and master Heptarch Cracus graces you with his presence."

The Heptarch removed his hood. He seemed smaller than earlier with deep, heavy-set eyes. He spoke, and the older man translated. "You have made quite the impression on my daughter with your genteel act of mercy. Twice now, she has come to me, begging for clemency for you. Once to allow us to ransom you, and now to either set you free, or allow you to be adopted as a soldier into the Walled Garden."

The Heptarch shook his head. "Both ideas are the wishfulness of a foolish girl. I will neither be setting you free, nor allowing you into my household. If you were more of a man, you would have killed my son. Instead, you showed your weakness. You let your people down. And I don't think you did it because you were knightly. I think you did it because you were weak. You lacked the moral fortitude to kill a man in cold blood."

My blood boiled. Here was a man denying me freedom, simply because he could. Because he thought not killing his son demonstrated some kind of manly weakness in me. "I wish I had killed him," I said.

The Heptarch laughed; he understood enough of our language, even if he would not speak it. "You will not make the same mistake next time, then." He fixed his hood. "This is the last time we will speak. You will not see my daughter again. You will be auctioned to the highest bidder in the Golden City."

"Why did you come to gloat?"

"Because I won, and you lost. Do I need more of a reason?"

The Heptarch slipped off into the night and I waited in my tent, knees huddled to my chest, wishing I was with Lot.

Chapter Ten

They put me in a caravan with the other soon to be slaves.

Now, as then, my almost mythical perception amongst the troops of the Mountain kept the men from talking to me. Still, I sensed betrayal in their wounded eyes. I was meant to be their hero. Their salvation. Instead, I led them into the back of a bumpy caravan. Instead, they were coming to the city they had come to conquer in chains.

My mind was given over to darkness. I thought nothing good, ate little, and when the barren landscape began to shift into rolling green fields, and rich woodlands and streams, I did not even notice.

Only the excited babble of the others kept me informed of events outside of the bars of the caravan.

And then, the first man spied it. "The Golden City," he whispered, and the others rushed to the bars to see out, then scattered like a flight of birds as I approached.

The Golden City dipped in and out of view, behind a series of barrows lined with lavender. It glinted in the sunlight. A place of giant domes and tall walls. Some men wept to see it, but I did not. It was another prison we were going to – and there was no telling the darkness that lurked behind its tall red brick walls.

They brought us through the streets, in full view of the crowds who jeered and bellowed and shook the caravan. Drums beat and others sang, and the world buzzed with their foreign tongue. I saw none of it, reclined as I was in the corner of the caravan, away from the bars.

Soon, we were away from the celebratory masses, brought into a marketplace where they unloaded us like cattle. We were separated, divided, and I was led away from the marketplace with a few other noteworthy captives, Black Pip, Small Harren, each one noteworthy for their looks or their strength, whilst none of them were noble born.

We were taken to a mansion, a place of great luxury, where a water fountain stood outside grand double doors and stone fish spurted bubbles into the air. Separated, we were brought to our own rooms, with wide open windows and a veranda. Some were put in a room by themselves, others in groups – I entered a room alone, accompanied only by strong soldiers with short swords.

It wasn't long until servants bustled in, hairless boys and delicate fingered girls, each in flowing white shifts. They stripped from me my clothes, scrubbed me until I was almost red raw, flossed my teeth, shaved the nascent hair from my chest.

They brought out scissors for my hair, and all my protests earnt me was bound hands. To my relief they did not shear me, but simply neatened my hair. When they brought out a mirror, the face that stared back at me was not one that I recognised.

I was a man, with stubble on his cheeks and hair long but fashionable.

They gestured for me to sleep and I curled up on silken sheets. It was the first time I had slept in a real bed since Lord Calforth's manor. Those thoughts brought a flood of memories, but for the first time in a long time, I didn't dream.

A hand over my mouth woke me. Two guardsmen towered above me and jerked their heads towards the door. I staggered to my feet, wearing a white shift, but with no memory of putting it on.

They loaded me into a carriage where some of the other soldiers from the host sat waiting. The driver cracked the horse's whip, and we were off. I looked for a chance to escape, but any failure meant my death, strung up in front of the Heptarch. I would bide my time if I had to. I added him to the list of revenges – the draugr and Gabriel had prestigious company.

Small Harren began to cry in the seat opposite. An open-handed slap from our minder soon silenced him. Whereas Black Pip would be destined for some workhouse somewhere, where his physical brawn could be used to the best purpose, Small Harren was a pretty little twig of a man. It would be the pleasure houses for him.

If I were a better man, I would have reached out and whispered to him – it wasn't all bad. Some of the best pleasure houses looked after their whores good, and they would have far more freedom than a simple labourer, and a more probable route to freedom.

But I was consumed by dark thoughts of my own future and said nothing.

Our destination was a warehouse of some kind. They unloaded us and filed us into a queue. Many people from our Host already waited in line, though few had been scrubbed and cleaned like me.

The night was warm and alive with the sound of cicadas. Clinking glasses and the sounds of revelry came from inside of the warehouse. I strained my ears, but could only hear dim, indistinct voices.

Soon, we were divided into subsections, then I alone was separated and held at the rear.

By myself, surrounded by guards, I sat up against the wall of the spotless warehouse. One by one the other would-be slaves disappeared from my view, called away, not to return.

It was an auction, I realised, from the timing of the gavel against wood. I could hear nothing of the auctioneer's voice. Only hear the beginning and end of the lots by the shuffling of more of our former soldiers, like the fallen shuffling through damnations gates, and the gavel slamming down hard, with the sound of our old lives ending.

How many people were out there? What were we being bought for? Slavery in Ordrove existed on the edges of society. We were fodder for armies, as I had been, or sometimes labourers in the arse end of nowhere, where the eye of the law turned a blind eye.

But the society of these people was built upon slavery. It was one of the Crusaders' favourite stories, a myth of our righteousness and their failings, despite myself walking alongside them in chains.

I thought it could not get any worse. That I was merely swapping one kind of servitude with the Host of the Mountain, for another in Liriam. But the chains I would wear in the Golden City were of a far tighter variety than the chains I had been used to.

Finally, it was my turn.

I rose, only for the guards to separate my shift from my shoulders with their burly hands, leaving me naked.

"Walk," one of them growled, in my tongue.

I walked, seething. Not only was I to be bartered and sold, but my dignity stripped as well. I saw the reason for the servants' ministrations earlier – every piece of me would be weighed and measured and like an animal I would be carved, piece by piece, and sold to the highest bidder.

I resolved to meet my shame with pride.

Straight backed, I entered the auction chamber.

Hundreds of faces stared back at me. Tables had been set out, draped with cloth, with small candles burning sweet scents. People gasped as the auctioneer read my name: the bidding started immediately.

I could not follow the numbers, but the three main interested parties soon revealed themselves to me. A fat man, in military garb. A man with a misshapen face, glasses, and an entourage of fawners and well-wishers.

And...

A young woman, masked.

Her disguise did not fool me. I would know her anywhere. She was alone on a table, and an empty bottle of wine sat drunk in front of her. When she raised her hand to bid it was with grim-faced determination.

The Lady Linial had come to save me.

I drew myself taller, planted my legs, fixed the kind of expression upon my face that statues might wear.

The fat man failed first, resigning himself to defeat with a knowing shrug at his neighbours. Still, the Lady Linial and the other man bid, price rising and rising.

The Lady Linial set her jaw. When she bid, it was with the precision of a soldier thrusting his blade into the stomach of his enemy. Her small face was a mask of concentration and control. She drank, and bid, and I knew that same resolve had once been mirrored in my face. Her expression said: *I will not be beaten.*

Until, her hand did not raise again.

She collapsed in her chair, beaten.

"No," I said, out loud.

The gavel sounded and I looked to the man in glasses as he rose to applause from the room. He gave a small bow and clambered onto stage. The auctioneer shook his hand and the two exchanged smiles like old friends.

I looked back towards the Lady Linial, but she was not there.

"You are mine now, great hero," said the man in halting Ordrovian.

He gestured to his hangers-on and they rushed around me, covering me in a sable cloak and nothing else. The atmosphere within the auction house turned to one of revelry. The auctioneer moved amongst them, shaking hands, and nobles laughed and pointed, some displaying their prizes, others eager to be away.

The man in glasses led us out of the auction house immediately and packed me into a carriage. Half an hour we travelled, over bumpy cobblestone, until we reached a low, squat building, built into the shadow of the Golden City's walls.

The hangers-on led me inside, removed my cloak from me, and left me standing in the foyer, naked.

"Do you know this building?" the man in glasses said.

I shook my head.

"It is home." He jabbed a skeletal finger in my direction. "For all fighters."

I frowned at him. "What fighters?"

He frowned back, then turned to one of the men beside him, who spoke a babble of Ordrovian. "This is the house of Ines Hollith, great master of the Fighting Pits of Liriam." The man in glasses looked pleased with himself. "Here, all of the foremost Ines Hollith's prized possessions – his great fighting men and women – are kept well fed and well looked after. You are the lifeblood of Liriam – the great entertainers and warriors, who pit your lives for glory and renown, and furthering your master's name."

I sighed. "So, you want me to fight for you?"

"Yes," Ines Hollith said. "You will fight for me."

I nodded. "Why did you want to buy me so much?"

"Er," the translator said, looking towards Ines Hollith. The master spoke sharply.

"It's not your place to question your master. But as you are new, he will permit it this once. Ines Hollith is the richest man in the city, but he has never had a fighter greater than the Heptarchs' own fighting school – the Walled Garden. He hopes that you will change that."

Once more, I was to be a weapon in another power-hungry man's hands. I sighed and nodded. "Is there anything else?"

Ines Hollith barked a command and I was given rich clothes dyed blue and gold – the colours of Ines Hollith the translator explained, only to be worn when commanded.

From there, I was brought into the main chamber, a room of around thirty bunks. Outside waited a large courtyard filled with training equipment and wooden mannequins. Guardsmen walked the grounds with swinging lanterns.

I was given the bunk closest to the entrance – it had once belonged to the great Orbello Moon, the translator explained, second greatest fighter in Liriam. The other fighters were either asleep or doing their best to pretend to be.

Ines Hollith and his entourage left, leaving me in the near-darkness of the hall. I exhaled softly. Strange thoughts crowded my mind. I was a continent away from home, sleeping in the famous Golden City. I was so far away from everything I had known. So far away from revenge against the draugr and against Gabriel.

I added Ines Hollith to the list of men I had to kill, filed them away somewhere at the back of my mind. For now, I had to survive.

The night did not pass easily. Uncomfortable lumps stuck into my back; somehow it was worse than making my bed beneath the stars.

Eventually I fell asleep.

Cracks ran through the ceiling. Plaster crumbled from the walls. Ines Hollith's house – famous though it might be – was in disrepair. I understood the importance of my arrival. I wasn't just another fighter to add to a famous yard; I was his last hope at unsettling the Heptarch.

I woke to almost complete silence. Dawn began to break, splintering light into the courtyard over the shadow of the city wall. I leant over the edge of my bunk, the wood grunting under my weight. Nobody slept beneath me, but on the bunk next to me, I felt eyes watching.

She was tall, for a woman. Propped up on both elbows, a nasty scar ran down her cheek and her eyes had a fierce intensity I had never seen in anybody, outside of battle.

When she spoke, it was in the infidels' rattling tongue. Upon my lack of response, she switched to Ordrovian, as fluently as a courtier.

"You're the Ordrovian killer?" When I didn't respond, she continued. "They brought a player in a few evenings ago, when there was talk of the Heptarch buying up fighters to join the battle. He sang about you. Do you want to know what he sang?"

I nodded, wary.

"He said you like to fuck little girls. Well, do you, pretty boy?"

"Fuck off."

"Finally some spirit." She laughed and swung out of bed, wearing nothing. Her body was lean and hard and griddled with scars. As a young man, I found myself paying a little too much attention to it and her gaze caught mine. "So. There is a little fire in you. Well, you are not my type, eastlander. Why would I want a brutish thing like yourself when there are pretty women in this world?" She smiled and jabbed a long finger towards me. "The player sang that you were a murderer in your homeland. A bastard prince. An orphan. Blessed by God. Shining with radiance with each sword swing. But some say you're not possessed not by your God, but by the Beast. That you were his instrument come to break him out of his chains. How much truth is there in what I say?"

"Some," I admitted. "But not about the Beast."

"We have our folktales, same as you have yours." She gave a small mirthless laugh. "I say our, as if I am one of them, but I was no more born here than you were."

"Where are you from?"

"Leagues and miles away. A frigid, cold place. You wouldn't know it. I barely know it."

"And your name?"

"Frisia. Finest female female fighter in all of Liriam."

"I'm Harald."

"I know." Her expression softened. "It won't be easy. Being here. He'll push you more than he pushes the rest of us. His dreams are riding on you."

"Who is he?"

She checked over her shoulders and shook her head. "You'll learn who the Master Ines is soon enough."

A figure burst through the doors into the room. Shaven headed and scowling. As one the room rolled into motion, two dozen of the most scarred, muscled men and women I'd ever seen, standing to attention. Even Frisia turned to face him, straight backed.

His gaze swung between us, like a lighthouse roving through the night.

He barked something in Liriam's sharp tongue. I didn't need to be a native speaker to understand it; I fell into line with the rest of the fighters. Almost all of us were in the nude, barring the few who had woken early and even they wore little more than a loincloth.

He spoke a smattering of words; there were a few laughs amongst the fighters. I thought perhaps that meant he was our friend.

I was wrong.

We headed out into the yard. In the morning light it was almost pretty, but I had little time to admire the scenery. He shouted again, and again I couldn't follow.

I tried to catch Frisia's eye but she was already resting on her elbows, body taut as rope. I looked around at the other fighters. They had done the same.

The trainer came before me. "Me Jakis," he said, in my own language. "You cunt."

Despite his words, his touch was gentle as he eased me down to the ground.

I followed the routine as best as I could. Running, jumping, long static exercises. After half of it I couldn't breathe. The first time I fell, Jakis kicked me.

I didn't have the strength to fight back, but I had enough strength to try again.

It felt like years; the sun barely moved in the sky.

When finally, Jakis called a halt, I searched out Frisia. "What in God's name was that?"

"A warmup." She raised both eyebrows. "We haven't even started training yet."

I laughed, or tried to at least. It turned quickly into a cough.

"I'm not joking, eastlander," she said. "Get used to it. And fast."

True to her word, the session started soon afterwards. We started out with a series of competitive exercises, chasing a partner around, feinting, dodging. The loser would do more exercises – the winner would get to rest.

I threw up twice before the first game had even ended. In my defence, it took me until my third before I retched again, and by that time nothing else was coming out. The other fighters weren't just fitter than me; they were stronger than me too.

By the time we came to the sparring section of our training, I could barely even raise my hands to fight.

A tall, scarred fighter put me into a lock with my head trapped between their legs. I couldn't move. I couldn't breathe. Blind panic grabbed me as I tried to grab at them, to no avail.

I didn't even notice when they released me.

I couldn't breathe. Couldn't move.

Strong arms lifted me. Then I was back in my own bed. I heard discussion above me, but I didn't want to open my eyes again if it meant going back out there.

"It's not going to get easier," Frisia said. "Jakis is the king high bastard of working us hard, but he's also what keeps us alive when we make it into the arena. You can't back out of this. You have got to get through it."

It was with some effort I opened my eyes. Frisia stood beside the bed, her eyes concerned despite the large frame on which they were situated.

"Get up," she said.

"I can't survive this."

"If you don't survive this, you'll never survive the arena. So, you have a choice. Fight now and live another day. Or give up. And Ines Hollith will bury you in a ditch."

I took her hand and swung from the bed. My legs almost gave way, but she held me steady.

"It's good talking your language," Frisia said. "I've had a whole twenty minutes not training."

"I thought you said that we needed to train to survive."

"I said you needed to train to survive. I could kill you with one hand tied behind my back after eating a big dinner."

"That's not true."

"Spar with me next then. I'll prove it."

She proved it.

I spent almost two months following a similar regime. I always thought I had been strong before, but I'd been strong by the standards of normal men. What I was becoming in the House of Ines Hollith was nothing short of a monster.

Though Frisia was my only friend in those first few months, she was a hard taskmaster herself. Where Jakis would occasionally grant leeway, she would drive me harder, and not just when sparring.

"If you want to survive here, you must not just be muscles on legs." She tapped her thick skull. "You have to be a brain too. You must speak their language."

"I don't want to learn your heathen tongue."

"It's not mine any more than it is yours, boy." She slapped me around the head. For some reason I accepted it, and not just because she was stronger than me. It was a small pain for the kindness she showed me. "You have to learn, otherwise you will always be alone. Do you want to be alone?"

"Of course I bloody don't."

"Then learn."

It was easier said than done. Whereas I could feel my body growing stronger, the mind has a stiffness that few other muscles possess. Even after two months I could barely understand more than basic phrases.

It was at that point that Ines Hollith entered.

I hadn't seen him since my first night in the House. Dressed in expensive satin with a small army of attendants and hangers-on, he floated into the room. He beckoned to Jakis and pointed to me with a long-nailed hand.

Frisia slapped me on the shoulder. "Good luck eastlander."

Ines Hollith spoke rapidly as I approached. Much to my shame I couldn't even make out one word.

His translator spoke: "It's time, Harald Fairhair, for you to prove your worth. You will fight tomorrow."

A brief spark of fear ran through me like; the hairs on my hand stood to attention. I breathed deep. Despite my trouble acclimatising to Ines Hollith's training regime, I knew who I was, what I could do when not exhausted by ten hours of training.

There wasn't a fight I couldn't win.

"What do I need to do?" I said.

"Do not ask questions of the master!" The translator slapped me. Dumbfounded by the small man's attack, I let the blow land.

"Don't fucking touch me again," I growled.

The translator looked to Ines Hollith who shook his head and said four sharp words.

The translator spat them back at me: "Be ready or die."

The Liriam Fighting Pits are part of the folklore of a dozen different countries. Every story has an escaped gladiator looking for a home. In some the pure-blooded noble fights in the Pits behind a mask, sweat stained and snarling. In others, the Pits are an oddity, where beasts slather over the bones of men.

But every story has the same end: bloody men, dishevelled and reeking of death. Wild-men, brigands, fighting for their life to the jeering of a hungry crowd.

The reality of the Pits was very different.

On the day of the fight, I was brought not to an underground slum, but to a tailor. Manicured fingers measured me, took my size, my worth. They dressed me as if I were just another customer – not a monster of tough flesh and red scars. I was dressed in a golden jerkin and shorts, my cheekbones drawn on with thick makeup.

My lips were painted golden, my cheeks rouged. When they brought me the mirror, I did not look like myself, but some artist's impression. They had made me inhuman, but not monstrous. They had shaped me into a god, like I had walked straight from the Mountain, my power still radiant with the blessing of our Lord.

From there, I was bundled into a curtained carriage, surrounded on either side by big men with plain faces. I considered breaking out, but where could I go? I was alone in a city I did not know.

The world soon took on a different sound. Heavy and dark and quiet. Voices echoed outside of the carriage, but distant, as if hearing people from underwater.

I was underground, deep in the belly of the beast. My heart fluttered nervously.

The carriage ground to a halt. I was bundled out of the door, through an opening in the side of a building, down a flight of stairs, and into a room of exposed brick.

Even in the backwater of my own castle I had heard stories of Liriam's Fighting Pits.

I walked through a brick archway and into an endless underground amphitheatre surrounding a central arena half sand, half dirt. Peasants waved rough banners commemorating their favourite fighters.

It was the roof of the arena that caught my attention, however, not the scream of the crowds. On each side the walls rose as a dome, creating that claustrophobic atmosphere the Pits were famous for. Only upon the space directly above the arena itself did the ceiling flatten and the wall shift from rough brick to a painted mosaic.

Upon the mosaic was a night sky, with all the thousand stars looking down upon us.

I had arrived in the Pits, the place that would become my home for the many years to come.

I did not watch the fights before my own, but I heard them.

The crowd roared with each bloody fatality. I wondered how many of the dead were soldiers of the Mountain. Poor souls lured on this Crusade with the promises of riches and righteousness. Instead, fodder for heathen entertainment.

I was alone in the cell. Guards waited at the entrance, armed. I could hear other fighters in between fights, in the cells opposite. I was the only one who had been secluded, singled out. The others talked in that quick chatter of Liriam's tongue.

Even Frisia's lessons would have been an improvement over the silence.

In the minutes – or where they hours? – before my fight, my mind wandered.

I imagined my own death with the crowd cheering. What would Ines Hollith think if his great champion was killed in his first bout? But there was still too much to do: Gabriel and the King, the Heptarch and Ines Hollith. The draugr. They had all tried to break me.

I would break them.

In time, the guards opened the door. One of Ines Hollith's hangers-on led me out.

I shielded my eyes as I emerged from the tunnels into the arena.

The crowd booed me. What else did I expect? I couldn't make out faces, just this wall of sound that rose on every side of the arena's walls.

They provided me with a sword; it was not my father's sword but a heavy longsword in the same style. With that they pushed me into the arena.

My heart beat curiously slowly. I cocked my head to the ceiling and looked at the mosaic on the roof. Death would not come for me, not yet. There was no *real* battle I hadn't won. And what rode on this battle but my life?

A paltry stake.

My opponent was a small man, wiry and experienced judging by his scars. His sword was similar, but even his hold was wrong. He held it like he wanted to hurt me with it, which of course he did, but holding it like that would never win him the battle.

An announcer spoke and the crowd quieted. He repeated it in my language: "Victor is the man who disarms his opponent. This is not a battle to the death."

I smiled. Ines Hollith wasn't going to waste his money on the first bout. He wanted to see my ability first. Well, I would show him the quality of the man he had bought.

They banged a gong, and the bout began. The crowd roared. Hawkers took bets.

My opponent wasted no time. He pumped his blade towards me in a vicious thrust. The aim may have been to disarm one another, but he showed no evidence of that in either his demeanour, nor his attack. I sidestepped easily.

The crowd roared their enjoyment.

Once I might have played to them. Enjoyed it, despite my present situation. Instead, I stepped into range of my opponent lazily, sword trailing along the floor.

Without hesitation my opponent attacked, blade flicking towards my throat.

Only I was not there. I leaned to one side, grabbed his sword hand, and snapped his wrist between my fingers.

The sword dropped to the floor and the crowd quieted. Nobody moved. No sounds, but the screaming of my opponent.

The boos began.

I planted my sword into the dirt of the arena floor and raised my hands to the jeering crowd.

Chapter Eleven

"I am greatly pleased with your skill," the translator said. "The manner of victory, likewise, suggests a keen intelligence. You play the role of the villain. It is a similar role to that which I play, in being the underdog, and taking on the Heptarch's own fighting school, the Walled Garden."

The translator looked to Ines Hollith who regarded me with a shrewd smile.

"We're nothing alike," I said.

Ines Hollith smiled wider but did not respond. Together he and his entourage swept from the room.

"You shouldn't bait him," Frisia said. "Your words won't make you free."

"So, I should be meek? Accept everything he says."

Frisia nodded. "I have been in Ines Hollith's House for six years. I fought at first. And I was punished for it. He enjoys you now. You are funny to him. But he will tire. And then he will hurt you."

"Unless I keep winning."

"Unless you keep winning," Frisia admitted.

I scowled. "I want to be able to talk to him," I said. "Make him understand."

Frisia smiled. I pitied whatever woman she'd snared before joining Ines Hollith's House. "You're asking for language lessons?"

"Yes. You're a sadist. You enjoy this too much."

"Welcome to my cruel world, Harald Fairhair."

When I wasn't with Frisia, I was enduring the small cruelties of the other fighters. Not all were foreign born like Frisia. Some were from the Golden City itself, and for some reason they still professed loyalty to the city that had enslaved them.

I would always be a heathen.

Still, I could endure their silent scorn. It was Jakis who proved the real thorn in my side.

He drove all of the fighters like a madman. Some days I was so exhausted, I couldn't even climb the ladder into my top bunk. I collapsed on the floor and slept there instead.

Despite my tiredness, I followed his orders without complaint. I knew the truth of Frisia's words. If I couldn't beat the fighters of my own house, how would I defeat the famous enemies of the Walled Garden? If I wasn't the best, I would be killed.

And so, the days passed, sometimes slowly, sometimes in the blink of an eye. Each day I became stronger. I had the fighting ability – it was only a matter of honing my body in a way that would suit the Pits.

The next time they came to collect me was without warning.

Silently, they took me to the usual places. They dressed me, not in my usual fighting gear, but in silk, softer than anything I had worn since Lord Calforth's manor.

They brought me to an arena already full, the remnants of a fight to the death still visible in the pit. A torn arm and a lacerated corpse carried away by the pit boys. Ines Hollith was not sat in his usual spot, but near the front of the crowd, surrounded by his entourage. He wore a hood, heavy velvet and deep red with gold trim.

It wasn't hard to see how the people despised him, despite of his patronage of some of the city's favourite fighters.

"You asked for me?" I said, with one of the phrases Frisia had taught me.

He surprised me by responding in my own language. He spoke it as fluently as he was rich, and I hated him for it, after my clumsy attempts to master his own tongue.

"I brought you to see the price of failure."

He gestured to the seat beside him, so I sat.

"Your life has a price. A cost to be measured. Your cost varies according to your skill, the quality you possess to undertake tasks that I desire. I may measure you priceless for your skill in fighting, my cook may view you as entirely worthless for your skill in the kitchen." He sighed, unhappy with his use of his new tongue. "Your father was a lord. He became valuable in relation to the structure of your government – but he did not possess value individually greater than most men. His value was relative to his position in your society. If I had raided your isle and caught him, your King would have paid me according to his status. However, the value is relative, for if the King did not care for your father, and valued him *personally* as worthless, he may attach value to certain traits – heroism, sacrifice, appearing strong – that dwarfed your father's actual value to me. And so he would have paid nothing."

He nodded to confirm his own words, never looking at me. "In this city you have a value that is relative to your position as a fighter, and a value that is relative to your position as a captive lord. A use value, determined by myself, and anybody who may wish to purchase you off me. But the *personal* value that I attach to you trumps your use value. My wealth allows me to disregard your use value; therefore you become both priceless and worthless at the same time. Your value is dictated by my own personal enjoyment of you; and if I tire of you, remember that only death awaits. I will not sell you. I value victory over the Walled Garden above all else."

"I don't understand," I said, as Ines Hollith grew silent.

He continued, as if I had not spoken: "Becoming valueless, subject to my entertainment is not so bad. Yes, you cannot measure your worth in traditional ways. As you shall see in a moment, there are terrible outcomes to being subject to a rich man's entertainment. But there is also much potential reward. Without value, with only my favour, you may become anything. If you succeed in your task – if the

Heptarch witnesses the defeat of his own greatest fighters – then you shall be released. Freed. For now I free you from value; from here you shall be my obedient pet, to live and die on my whims." Ines Hollith smiled sadly. "Let us watch."

From the doors of the pit, they brought soldiers of the Mountain, unarmed, but garbed in the ragged uniforms they had worn when marching. I saw some I recognised, minor nobility and common men, not valuable enough to ransom. Amongst these stood a leader, bellowing commands, ordering his men into a defensive circle.

I did not recognise him at first. Someone had beaten him bloody. A long red gash festered on his cheek and his hair was misshapen and long. Still, Sir Simon Slant mustered all the courage he had left as he organised his troops.

Ines Hollith waited expectantly for my reaction. I did not give him one. I sat impassively, even as my heart erupted in my chest.

Ines Hollith clicked his tongue to the roof of his mouth and began to speak:

"I bought them quite cheaply. Off cuts. Unwanted remnants of your little army. Everyone here knows this. They know I bought them, and they know how this bout will end today. Do you? You see, the people hate you. They really hate you. And if they hate you, they hate me. And though I do not care for the opinions of others, I do not like the connotations that I am a sympathiser with your pathetic cause. So, this is my goodwill gesture to the people. These men will die, so you can live."

The men who entered the arena next were some of Ines Hollith's own fighters, though I did not see Frisia amongst them. They entered wearing traditional dress, like the heroes of the Golden City from folklore. They waved their hands above their heads and pumped their weapons to the sky.

Sir Slant looked on in horror.

His gaze travelled the arena, glaring at each spectator, until his eyes rested on my own.

Shock spread over his features, followed by a mocking smile.

I imagined how I looked to his eyes. A well-dressed spectator to the death of the army I was supposed to lead. He raised a middle finger and the crowd booed – chanting back 'Harald Fairhair, he's one of our own'.

From that day on, the perception of me in the Golden City shifted. I was no longer the head of a heathenous army.

I was a traitor to my people and my home.

Though I felt no love towards Sir Slant, I could not stop the shame from flushing my cheeks red. I would have vowed bloody murder; I would have cared, if I could, but my captivity had begun to weigh on me like a sunken stone.

Instead, I watched, as one by one Ines Hollith's men danced between them, slaughtering their unarmed adversaries. The crowd didn't care. Ines Hollith's men were showmen and for every bloody thrust, they twirled their spears and swords above them like dancers. They knocked men down and made them beg for death, renounce their religion and their homeland.

Sir Slant did not beg. He stole a spear from one and ran them through.

The others rounded on him quickly, before his ill-discipline spread.

Spear thrusts protruded from his back, through his groin, through his throat. No man could have stopped it. He was spitted like a pig.

He fell with a short gargle, but otherwise gave the crowd no satisfaction.

He was a soldier to the end.

I turned to Ines Hollith. "Please don't make me watch this. I've seen enough death. I'll kill for you, but this is cruelty, nothing more."

Ines Hollith nodded. His guards grabbed me roughly and pulled me away. The sound of dying men and the cheering of the crowd soon fell away, but in its place came a quiet that I do not believe has ever left me.

What had the world become to make Sir Slant a hero and me a tool of the heathen?

I asked that question of myself nightly. I cursed under my breath, beat the bedsheets until the other warriors began to cast dark glances my way. How had I become this? How had I failed?

All dreams of revenge, of Lot, fell away. I lay awake each night. I did not laugh with the other fighters. I did not sit up late and talk of what would happen when I was a free man.

I would never be a free man. I would never break from my incarceration. One day Ines Hollith would tire of me and either sell me or kill me.

Others had faced the same fate. A young fighter by the name of Dulf, here one day, the next beaten so hard by Ines Hollith's guards that he never got back up.

All because of one lost bout.

Favour could turn quickly and I was well aware of that. Survival was the only thing that kept me going. I had no appetite for it. No desire. But a small part of me forced my way to the arena each time, and each time I won. For just a second I remembered what I was made to be – a wielder of death, destruction, and violence, before they led me from the arena and the chanting of the crowd, and I realised that I was never meant to be a man like that at all. That had been my brothers.

I was meant to be a better man, but I was not.

I wondered whether God was punishing me for my failure to kill Lord Axel.

Was Sir Slant's death a sign of his displeasure, or a sign of his non-existence? I wanted to believe, but with each day that passed any caring almighty seemed further out of reach.

Most of the fighters had their own gods. They came from all over the world and collected in the Golden City like waste spills from a slaughterhouse. I realised the futility of the word God. A singular. There was nothing singular about the religions in the Golden City.

Some gods were golden crows. Others rootled through the ground like animals. All of them existed in uneasy parallel, their areas of worship crossing over, their place in each of their respective pantheons uncertain.

I killed men wearing tusks around their necks and men wearing pretty steel stars. I killed men of the Totteringham brotherhood and men of the Apsalarian creed. I killed men who prayed before each bout and I killed men who whispered between bloody teeth a last dying request.

No absolution was ever granted.

Still, I tried my hand at prayer. I stole the tusk from the neck of that dead man, and I prayed over it.

I joined in with some of the other fighters as they prayed, mouthing the same foreign words with them.

It was all for nothing.

Each month I was dragged to the arena. Each month I stood like a statue, arms spread wide, enjoying the bellows of the crowd, and each month I grew closer and closer to Ines Hollith's eventual goal of defeating the Walled Garden.

It was not, however, all that he demanded of me.

The silks he brought me were worth more than the other slaves. He would summon me to the gardens in his estate and sit beside me, long fingernails trailing over the fabric, describing the expensive dyes and the length to which he had gone to procure such jewels.

He would smile as if I were just another heathen noble. He would describe his gardens; the marble archways, the sculpted treelines, the delicious ever-ripe fruit. He would tell me of the ash trees felled to make the bench we sat on.

However, it was my appearance that concerned him the most. We would often be surrounded by other slaves, combing our hair and cutting our nails. He treated me as if I were special, and in some way I suppose I should be thankful for such privilege, but it never felt like much of a privilege to be marginally less oppressed than others.

When the guards dragged me from bed in the early hours of the morning, I expected it to be another sickening encounter. But Ines Hollith was nowhere to be seen. In his place was a small, wiry man with spectacles that kept slipping off his nose. He said nothing to me and ignored the few attempts I made in his tongue to talk to him.

He led us, via carriage, to a number of different establishments during the day. First, we came to a balding man in a large white villa. He bid me sit down and shaved me, starting first with my legs, and then moving his way up, only stopping his war on all the hair on my body in time to arrive at my hair. This he neatened before engaging in fierce conversation with the little man which I did not understand.

The next location we arrived at was a jeweller. It soon became apparent that the argument had been about the type of headpiece I should wear; it was settled eventually that I should wear a red ribbon and two white pins made out of a type of bone that stuck from my head like an antler.

It was not the only ornament they dressed me in. On each arm and each thigh, they fastened a golden circlet that dug slightly into my skin. The small man nodded appreciatively.

I went from place to place silently, not even thinking to take in the city. I remember those days as if through a great haze, an incomprehensible fog that clouded my every waking moment.

Each place we visited was like a dream house, in which I floated through walls and down stairs without my feet ever touching the ground. There was an underground boutique where they found me a simple white shift made out of the softest silk, a shoemaker who tailored a pair of leather moccasins, and then finally, a perfumer.

I had lost most of my pride in the Golden City, and yet there were a few battered pieces of my dignity that I aimed to preserve. This the perfumer quickly stripped away from me, not just forcing me nude, but rubbing scented oil into every fold of skin until the air was filled with jasmine and apple. Such ministrations did not sit well with me; though in Amber, society was said to be rich and decadent, it was not in my homeland. It was a place of furs and cold, and personal affection came in the form of a stiff nod.

After my entire outfit was complete, I expected to go to the arena. I had assumed that some great fight was about to take place. Instead, we headed towards Ines Hollith's house.

To say it is a house is to it a disservice, but in those days every building I visited in the Golden City seemed to be a mighty encampment. Ines Hollith's house was no less mighty than any other. It stood inside the walls of the Golden City, though you wouldn't know it, because for a half mile all around a ring of tall trees blotted out everything, even the city walls. Within the wall of trees was an estate of cultivated hedges, expensive flowers, and babbling streams that arrived and disappeared at no discernible point. The house itself was a hodge-podge of styles. It had the classical golden dome upon the main building, but every other building (of which there were many) was differing in size and structure, as if built over the span of many centuries by many different artisans. Most had been painted white, except for the main building, which was painted blue and gold.

It was that building we headed towards, and it soon became clear that we were not the only ones bound for Ines Hollith's house.

In fact, it seemed that most had already arrived. Carriages by the dozen blocked our way. Black shirted officials rushed about and horses stood politely as carriage drivers swore at one another.

It was a party.

The Heptarch wore white and smiled at me with hungry eyes. His wife hung on his arm like a trophy.

The Heptarch whispered a few quiet words to Ines Hollith and my master threw his hands in the air and clapped. Guards brought me gently forward until I stood before the three of them; around us a party played out, uproariously, clanking glasses, cackling and a bustling brass band.

"You think he's good enough?" the Heptarch said in their quick tongue.

Ines Hollith grinned and tried to hide it. "The Walled Garden are, of course, the greatest fighters in the city. But, in the right circumstances, I believe we stand a chance."

"You pin your hopes on a heathen." His eyes flickered darkly. "Kneel, boy."

I knelt.

"He's a better trained pup than when we first picked him up."

"He is kept under the tightest guard," Ines Hollith assured. "Not allowed to spread his heathenous words across the Golden City."

I glimpsed the Heptarch extend his arm over the shoulder of his wife, tried to see the woman better, Lady Linial's mother. She was hidden behind the bulk of the Heptarch, however, and the words that tumbled out of his mouth were too fast for me to follow.

I waited there, head bowed, unthinking. I'm not too ashamed to admit I was broken.

I *was* broken.

All the tender pieces of my heart had hardened into stone. The only thoughts that occupied me was that of survival. We are all put into situations where we realise the identity we prise above all else is nothing but a fleeting mask, easily cracked or set aside. In this case mine was pulled from me, leaving behind an empty shell that only came clamouring with life when required.

I was a dog that would bark on command, kill on command.

"It's better this way," Frisia had told me. "If you don't have the energy to fight him, you will survive."

It took me a little while to notice that the Heptarch had gone. Ines Hollith was in hurried conversation with the guardsman – I caught little of the conversation, but that I was late, that I was due two hours ago, and that my robes were cheap and must be stripped from me.

And so, I was pulled to my feet. The fabric – expensive silk – torn by rough fingers that pushed into the hard lines of my back.

Naked, I stood. In nothing but the jewellery clasped around my arms and thighs.

"You will wait on my guests," Ines Hollith said. "Serve them what they desire."

In the kitchens, a staff team worked on entrees while the serving staff uncorked bottles of wine. I was given a tray of wine glasses and sent back into the room.

I was self-conscious, but I was not the only one naked. The entire serving staff was made up of young men, fully in the nude, though few were as well decorated as me.

Nothing like this could have occurred in my homeland. Men had affairs. Snuck about in the dead of night doing what society might frown on. But to host a party like this? I couldn't believe my eyes. I stood dumbstruck in the centre of the room, only just remembering to hold my tray of drinks aloft.

Men and women gathered around me. Pointed. They spoke in Liriam's rattling tongue, but I could only understand Ines Hollith and Frisia with any regularity – from the chatter around me, I caught perhaps one word in five.

Despite my servitude, I had a sort of freedom around the party. Guards watched me, of course. But I could walk and go where I pleased, so long as I was carrying my tray of drinks with me. I looked for the Heptarch, but he had disappeared into some private chamber.

I turned, and found myself face to face with the Lady Linial.

She laid a hand on the small of my chest.

"Harald."

"Lady Linial."

She stepped back, taking in all of me. Her pale cheeks blushed red. "I am so sorry."

"Why would you be sorry?"

She blinked. I saw the truth in her eyes. She blamed herself for what had become of me.

"I thought you might save me," I said. "But I didn't *expect* you to save me. At this point, I'm not even sure I deserve saving." I shook my head. "I got myself into this mess. If I had been smarter, I would have killed your brother and escaped."

"But you didn't. You trusted us to repay your kindness."

"I didn't have a choice." I looked around the room. "Where is the Lord Axel?"

"My brother doesn't have a taste for these parties."

"And you do?"

"I." She hesitated. "I had hoped to find you."

Why? I wanted to ask, but two guards appeared at Linial's side. "Your father wants to speak to you, my lady. Now."

Lady Linial smiled. She looked around the room. "A beautiful prison," she said, and was gone.

I had walked into Ines Hollith's party undefeated in eight bouts in the Pits.

I had walked into Ines Hollith's party a broken thing, finally brought to heel after months of rebellion.

I had left Ines Hollith's party still broken, but no longer alone.

That night, I did not dream of the draugr, or my monstrous past.

I dreamt of the Lady Linial.

I cannot explain what happened to me. We have words that barely scratch the reality of my emotion. Love. Lust. And so on. They pale in comparison to the pain I felt – for it was pain, as difficult as any I have faced.

I had worn Lot's love like a warm blanket through my most difficult days. I had faced darker thoughts than any found in the murky waters of hell, with only the memory of her face to guide me. I had become fixated on her, a gleaming end to my suffering, my would be reward for escaping bondage.

In doing so, she had become both more and less than she was. She was an ideal, sacred and saintly. She was also stolen by time, distance and difficult circumstances. I no longer remembered her warmth. Her love was a hollow, aching thing in my chest. When I thought of her, I thought of my broken homeland, that bastard king, the sunken, empty eyes of my father's head.

Linial – Linial was different.

I thought maybe it was fear at first. That twisting clench of my heart.

But. When I played back our meeting, in the mansion of Ines Hollith, pouting prettily in a black dress I could think of nothing but my hand on hers, my lips on hers.

I would dream of her own eyes setting upon me, and the spark that travelled between us lighting us both into brilliant grins.

She was real. Tangible. An equal in this twisted court.

Linial – ah Linial!

And so I replayed the memory of that chance meeting – her soft hand on my chest – for all the weeks to come.

It was not, however, the last party I would attend on behalf of Ines Hollith. Serving his guests had not been enough. I had become the entertainment.

The cage that kept me from his guests was a thin sliver of glass. A box, big enough for me to lie down three times over but small enough that I felt trapped and claustrophobic. I was not alone inside the box; they had cast me as Euridities. That meant that I was both conqueror and object.

The three women who surrounded me were naked, but not entirely. They were dressed in costume, each one of them a member of Euridities' famous harem. There was Alloa, pale and red haired, wearing a circlet of gold around her mane, with painted red nails on her hands and feet. There was Deve, blonde and big boobed, with a golden chain leading from nipple to nipple. It was not her only ornament; golden earrings and necklace glinted in the lights of the manor.

Finally, there was Cerdyce, Euridities wife and the princess of his own land. She was dusky and slim and small, and upon her naked body where painted a hundred ornamental letters. It was she who could not be touched by anyone, for it would disturb the perfect script, and reveal her betrayal.

And there was me, Euridities, naked barring the golden bands around my calves and biceps. I wore a laurel crown. Within the box I was an Emperor; outside of it the Golden City's high society watched with disguised lust. The subtext was plain. Euridities had been defeated, brought back to the Golden City in chains, then executed.

But, I soon realised, it was also a little less sophisticated than that.

Fear rose in me as Alloa laid a hand on my shoulder. "We are to bed you, my lord," she said in halting speech, in my own tongue.

For many people this might seem a dream. A fantasy. But I was little more than a boy, and I stood before these powerful men and women, naked and cold and afraid. My penis hung limp and a little shrivelled; I resembled the statues leading up to Ines Hollith's house.

"I can't do this," I whispered back over my shoulder.

"We have to. Or we'll be killed." As she spoke, Alloa stood with one hand on my shoulder, face serene and lips barely moving. "We are not whores. Just women. Just women who have become a game to them."

Her words gave me little comfort. I could see Dere shaking, and the chain across her nipples rang like little bells with each convulsion.

It was Cerdyce who knelt first. She had not made eye contact with me before I felt her small hand caress my inner thigh.

A genteel clapping followed from the crowd beyond; I found Ines Hollith watching me with his hand on a young man's shoulder and a woman on the other side with her hand in his lap.

Alloa squeezed my shoulder, bringing me back to the present.

She knelt beside Cerdyce. Dere still stood with wide eyes watching the other two women.

Fingers ran through my pubic hair and rubbed the length of my cock.

For what seemed like an eternity my body would not respond. My manhood would get the girls killed.

And then I saw her.

She was sat by herself, as she had been when bidding on me, drinking a glass of wine. Her face was thunderous, brows knotted and tight, but she watched the scene before her with the same rapt fascination as the rest of the crowd.

I quickened at the sight of Linial. How could I not?

Alloa squeezed my buttocks in appreciation.

For the first time that evening I felt in control. Linial's face anchored me.

And yet. She claimed to be a prisoner, but the Heptarch did not compel her to sit watching. She, like all the others, had come for a show.

Well, I would give them a show.

I grabbed Dere by the chain and pulled her close, so her breasts were pressed up against my side. She gave a small yelp and looked at me with too wide eyes.

I looked like a king. A God. Like every fucking teenage fantasy.

Let them watch, unashamed.

They could use me. Abuse me. Rape me.

And one day I'll tear their fucking throats out.

We spent the next three hours like that, in one way or another.

After the initial excitement, the nobles soon went back to socialising, but the guards had orders not to let us stop. I couldn't be too angry at them. The guards had their own issues, as drunken noblewomen tried to join in but were warded away on the words of Ines Hollith.

By the time they released us, the party had turned to anarchy.

What we had been doing inside of that glass box seemed tame compared to what was happening outside of it. We weren't the only ones naked. Many danced, led by a lively violinist.

It was all too much for me. I was spent.

"I need some air."

One of the guards led us outside. The wind froze my bare skin. I wrapped my hands tightly around my sides and tried to focus on the natural world beyond the artificial madness of Ines Hollith's estate. Some reprieve from that den of sin. The thick backed trees, grassy lawns, lines of marble statues. The flower garden, so bright usually, rendered to a colourless mass by the clouded sky.

The door opened behind me. I sighed, expecting the guard, on orders to bring me back in.

Instead, I found a tired looking creature, with eyes dark both from makeup and sleepless nights.

"Lady Linal," I started

"I'm sorry." She laid a hand on my shoulder. "What you went through just then..."

"...Was just another ordeal. My life has been full of them." I shivered.

"Here." She unclasped her cloak, thick and black like a raven's wings.

"I'm covered in...stuff."

"I don't care, Harald."

I slipped the cloak on. Its weight was reassuring after so long naked, though it cut off just above my knees.

"You looked at me a lot," she said quietly.

I hesitated. "Did I?"

She nodded.

"I had to get through it somehow. I was…scared. And you." I sighed. "I imagined I was with you. Not them. It was the only way I could get through it."

I closed my eyes, waiting for her angry response. Instead, I felt her small hand in mine.

"You'll get through this, Harald," she said.

I almost believed her.

Chapter Twelve

A man stares into your eyes across a floor of sand. He is a simple thing, in that frozen moment. Bloodlust in the snarl of his teeth, death in his stance, all these basic urges egged on by a baying crowd demanding blood.

It simplified the man, and in that sense it was a blessing. I could not have killed real men so often, or so easily.

But I knew that each man who stood across from me in the arena, who crossed their blade against my own battered blade – a far cry from my father's sword – led as complex lives as my own. All of his existence is about winning the bout ahead; he has been a slave; he has been a king; he has loved and lost; he will die a hollow, battered thing upon the sand.

It was enough to keep me up some nights. Most nights, even.

But in the ring, with the crowd booing, I felt unbeatable.

I stood with my arms aloft at the start of each bout, sword above my head. I fell into a lion's crouch. I sprang across the ring.

If there was one criticism of me from the masses, it was that I was too relentless. They did not appreciate the ease in which I killed. Without showmanship, as quick as possible.

I had been born trying to kill my brothers after all. I grew up during the Crusade. I was a beast of war.

Every day had become the same routine to me. Wake, train, sleep. Only a visit to the Pits would break that routine and I soon grew to look forward to the real fights – they were all that kept me going. Yet Ines Hollith did not arrange too many fights for me. In my sparse appearances the crowds grew even more hungry to watch me. Soon, I was no longer a villain, but a favourite of the arena.

The fight that changed everything was my first against the Walled Garden.

I stood before Ines Hollith, naked as he often made all the fighters stand. It was for his own perverted pleasure I've no doubt; he liked stripping people bare in every sense of the phrase.

This time, however, his face was severe.

"We are not friends," he said in his own language. "But we hate the same man. The Heptarch's own fighters, the Walled Garden, are the greatest in the arena. Today, you fight the Walled Garden."

I nodded. "Who is he?"

"Caius Favre. He doesn't fight to the death often. He's the old man of the arena. Once great. Once a champion. Now, back to kill you. You must kill him."

"Of course."

"He's only lost twice, Harald. Both in the past three years. Both when fighting with a partner. Do you understand? He's never lost when fighting by himself."

"And? I've never lost."

Ines Hollith smiled grimly. "Do not start now, then."

With that he dismissed me and I had the rest of the afternoon to prepare. I learnt a little of Caius from the other fighters. He was well respected inside of the Pits. He was a free man, with an entire life outside.

In the long light of the evening, they brought me to the Fighting Pits. I was always one of the last fighters to enter. I was the crown jewel of the evening's entertainment.

Another fight was already taking place as I entered, though I felt the crowd's attention shift as soon as I walked down the narrow galley beside the arena to the holding pens. Booing began almost immediately, and I began to understand just how well-loved Caius Favre was.

I don't remember much of the time before the bout. I sat in near silence, with my knees to my chest in the cell. It was better that way, sitting there and thinking about something else. No time for nerves, until suddenly you are walking out to the arena floor and the crowd is screaming, and the nerves hit you in that wall of noise, and your heart sings, and you feel both very small and very big, like the world is all for you, like you are just one among a million.

I arrived before Caius. There was even enough time for the booing to subside and the crowd to start gambling again, before eventually Caius entered the arena.

It wasn't cheering that greeted him, but a standing ovation from the audience. Everyone on their feet, clapping.

For the first time since I'd entered the Pits, I felt overawed. This was genuine love for a person.

And I was about to kill the man.

He stood across the sand, three lengths of a man between us. His nutty brown hair had begun to give way to grey. Late forties, I would have guessed, but strong and sinewy like a ram. He held a shield and short sword as casually as some men hold flagons of beer.

I nodded to him across the arena. He did not respond.

His eyes promised a cold end and the announcer read our names.

'To the death,' he said.

There is a pain that flashes across a man's eyes when he dies, far deeper than a simple fear of death. It is a rage, an anguish, an expulsion of unspent possibilities.

In each individual there is an infinite amount of choices that spread out before us. Each of these choices lead to a new reality, a thousandfold in number. There are lovers and lies, each waiting for a specific choice, and each choice creating more realities. But as soon as the sword slips in between ribs and blood bubbles from cracked lips, those realities collapse in on each other, until all that remains is the man holding the sword in front of them.

And then the blade is withdrawn, the body collapses, and even the reality of the swordsman falls around them.

It would be easy to think of Caius as a life already spent. He was a hero of the arena who had won fame, fortune and renown a dozen times over.

Yet he was a free man, with wife and family. With a home in the city, built on the power of his performances.

He could have lived another forty years. He could have raised his grandchildren on his knee and peered over his hard-earned beer belly. He could have been happy for so much longer, and brought more to the world than the simple violence and blood that the Pits demanded.

As I slipped the blade between the links of his armour, into the soft tissue around his heart, I saw these possibilities flash before me. It was not simple, as all the other fights had been. I had killed myself, twenty years older. I had killed a father.

I sank to my knees as his body fell.

I cried.

In that moment, I was utterly alone despite the masses in the arena. I cried for Caius and my own sorry position. I cried that I had to kill other men just to survive.

I had defeated one of the Walled Garden, the Heptarch's own, and yet I had never felt such a hollowness.

Somebody began to clap. More followed. Before I knew it, the entire arena was on their feet clapping, even more loudly than they had on Caius' entry.

I do not know if they clapped for me, or for their fallen champion.

Either way, I rose, neatly saluted the four corners of the arena, then bowed one final time to Caius before making my exit.

Word spread to the other fighters. For the first time since my arrival, they regarded me with more than just sullen anger. A quiet appreciation, both of my ability and my character, began to form. No longer did I have to persevere through hard looks and small cruelties. I was not poked while we stood awaiting the instructor. The water to wash in was not emptied before I could clean myself. Backs were no longer turned on my arrival to the room.

All these things washed away after Caius' death.

In the Pits, it was no different.

I won my next three bouts, all against up-and-coming stars of the arena. I killed each one of them and the crowd chanted Harald. Some of the younger fans brought banners onto which their parents had sewn a lion, glorious with teeth bared.

I attended another of Ines Hollith's parties. I was asked to wrestle with other men; by the end of the evening, I had senators in the ring, naked and red faced, brawling like they had in their youth. In the gaps between fighting, I snuck outside and met the Lady Linial.

She wore the same as she always did. I sometimes wondered whether she owned anything that wasn't black.

"I watched one of your fights," she said. "I knew you were good, but now..."

"Now what?"

"I don't think there's a single fighter in all the world better than you. My father curses you. He says, foolish girl, I should have killed him when I had the chance."

"And what do you say?"

"I agree. I tell him that you're going to kill him. And he hits me."

She pointed towards her cheek. I could see the dark outline of a bruise, mostly covered by her makeup.

I inched closer towards her and extended an arm around her. "I'm sorry, Lin."

She rested her head on my shoulder.

I didn't know what it was we had between us. I wouldn't push further, for fear of startling her away, or worse causing her father to punish her further. She was my only salvation, and I was glad for what little we had.

We cuddled up to each other in the quiet of the balcony, as inside the party disintegrated into debauchery.

One by one I began to pick them off. I defeated the 10th fighter from the Walled Garden. Then I fought the 8th and 9th together. Ines Hollith told me that he could get odds of five to one against during that fight. He bought me a new silver and diamond necklace to commemorate that victory and made me stand naked outside of his estate, welcoming his guests, wearing nothing but the necklace.

I barely even registered that anger.

I was unstoppable. Nobody could defeat me. I was resolute in my heart and my spirit. I would kill every single one of the Walled Garden, and then when I was so powerful, so loved, I would kill Ines Hollith and the Heptarch too.

I wasn't in my right mind. I was drunk on Linial's affection – my body craved her. Every quiet moment between training I would find myself thinking of her. And the training – it burnt through me like fire. My body was like a lash, sharp and lean. Every muscle jutted against my skin; even while relaxed I could see the lines of my stomach.

At this point, I was the perfect animal. I will always hate Ines Hollith with a passion, but there could be no denying his methods. They were effective. I was chained enough to never falter in my training. And like a dog, I was given enough lead to think that I was free every once in a while.

Without my brief encounters with Lady Linial, I would have crumbled. Broke down into all the various fragments of myself that were just about holding on.

With her...

With her I wasn't human. I was a beast. A barely lucid thing of passion and anger.

With her I was enough of a person to keep my sense of self. To not lose myself entirely to the Pits.

These were not the actions of a few days, however. I had already spent four years in the Pits, fighting endlessly. Competitions were not so regular, fighters not so in demand that there were more than five or six per year. Any more frequent and we would have all killed one another and there wouldn't be enough fresh faces to replace us.

More common in the city was the use of the Pits for professional boxing, often between freed men or even nobles with too much to lose to fight in the Pits proper. It was something akin to the grappling that took place in Lord Calforth's house all those years ago.

Gabriel was never far from my thoughts in those days. Ultimately, despite the crimes of the Heptarch and Ines Hollith, it was Gabriel who had started me on this path. It was he who had killed Tava and Granny. It was he who had testified to the King.

It was in one quiet night in the training house that the news came to me.

It arrived in the form of a new fighter, a pale red headed man also by the name of Harald. The moment he spoke an uncertain hello to the other fighters, I rounded on him. His accent was unmistakeable. He was from my home.

"You're Ordrovian?" I said. The other fighters deferred to me, peeling away but staying in earshot. I had earnt that privilege.

He nodded.

"And you're a Harald? Well, I'm Harald Fairhair. You'll be Red Harald, while you're here. How does that sound?"

He nodded again. I scowled. Our introductions weren't going fast enough.

"What's happened in Ordrovia?" I demanded.

"Since when, my lord?" Red said meekly.

"Do I look like a lord?" I barked. "Since I came here. Since..." It took me a moment to count the time since I'd embarked on the Crusade. "The past four years."

Red went white as a sheet. "You're that Harald," he said. "The unbeliever."

"The unbeliever?"

"Who lost the Crusade. Who now works for the Golden City. They say you betrayed Ordrovia."

"If I'm a traitor," I hissed, "so are you." I placed both my hands on his shoulders. He tried to pull away, but I held him close. "I don't have a choice. I was never ransomed like all the other cunts on Crusade. I was sold into slavery, just like you have been. *I* was betrayed. Now, I want to know what has happened in my home. What's happened to Gabriel? What's happened to the King?"

"The King is dead, my lord. Overthrown. His son is in exile."

"How?" I released him. The revenge I'd dreamed of had melted away. But then it had never been the King, really. He'd been poisoned against me by Gabriel. "What about Gabriel?"

"Gabriel Calforth?"

The bastard had changed his name; Sir Slant would be turning in his grave.

I jerked a nod.

"He's Knight Commander of Ordrovia. His mother's Queen Regent, so it's only to be expected."

I punched him.

I shouldn't have. He hadn't done anything, but I wanted to shut him up.

"How?" I demanded. "How?"

The other fighters were on me before I could say anything else. They pushed me away, talked to me about other things.

Nothing could take my mind from the truth.

I had lost everything, while Gabriel had become Knight Commander of the entire realm.

"Lot," I bellowed. "What happened to Lot?"

Red looked up from where the others were trying to reassure him. "Who?"

I stormed away, punching the wall as I went.

Under the rapidly darkening sky, I sat next to Linial.

It had been so long since we first met – for most it would have been easy to fall out of the passion that gripped us, but for us both it was a kind of drug, made only more precious by the scarcity by which we could both meet.

We savoured each and every touch. We did not dare get too close, or try to do or say too much, for fear of frightening the dream of what we were away. She was my salvation, I knew, and I think that I was hers too.

But it was not always smooth sailing.

Another year had passed, and though I was now closer than ever to the Walled Garden, I seemed to be further away at the same time. Ines Hollith used me more for entertaining than fighting, as it proved particularly hard to persuade the Heptarch to commit his most valuable fighters.

Despite that, I had killed the 7th, though the fight had left a jagged scar down the side of my neck in the process.

"I'm so sorry you have to go through this, Harald." Her eyes were downcast. "If I had have been able to bid more…things would have been so different."

"It isn't so bad," I said. "I get to see you. I've heard about some of the other fighters in the city. Whipped. Assaulted. Never leaving their small patch of training yard." I dropped my voice lower. "I hate Ines Hollith. But he allows me this. So I survive."

Lady Linial shook her head. Her voice was soft on the wind. "Have you ever heard of the Golden House?"

I laughed. "Of course. A thing dreamt up by desperate pit fighters who don't understand reality."

"The Golden House is real. It is Tytos' House. He keeps his fighters well fed. He never forces them to fight in the ring, unless it's their wish. He frees them. They walk round the Golden City as free men and women."

"And they're good?" I asked. "This Golden House? Good fighters in the Pits. Just because I don't remember fighting them."

"Harald, there's more to life than the Pits."

"Not for a slave. And I won't make it out of the Pits by dreaming of the Golden House to come and save me, offer me a better life. I'll earn my way out. I'll kill every member of the Walled Garden. I'll be loved. Then Ines Hollith will release me. Only by being the best will I be free."

Linial shook her head. "Life is not just violence."

"Were you saying that when the Host of the Mountain was bearing down on your city? Would your Golden House have saved you? No. Strong men saved you. Better fighters. Better numbers. Power saved you. Violence saved you. Life is about more than violence until you're pushed up to the edge of nothing, and then what's left. You do whatever you have to in order to survive."

"Things will be better one day. You won't always be pushed up against nothingness."

"Then everyone will pay." I scowled. For once, I felt no desire for Linial's company. "Why do you talk to me? I don't understand. Why me? Has the Golden City truly got no better men than *this?*"

"It might have better men," she said softly. "But no men like you."

I went to respond; bit my tongue instead. "Tonight has been too much for me, Lin. I should go."

She nodded. "Things will get better, Harald. I promise."

"I don't think you can make that promise anymore." I shook my head and returned to the feast.

I spent another two years fighting. I defeated the 6th, 5th and 4th until it became clear that the Walled Garden wouldn't risk losing anyone else to me.

Ines Hollith proposed a bargain.

I would fight the third and second together.

It was the only invitation the Heptarch would accept. I had stopped even attending the parties of Ines Hollith; it was almost an entire year since I had last attended an event with him.

"It has become too dangerous," he said quietly, as we sat in the gardens of his estate. "The Heptarch cannot kill you in the ring, so he will resort to killing you outside of it, if he can. I can't provide him such unfiltered access to you anymore."

"But Linial?"

"Will wait for you until you are released. You are so close, Harald. My ambition is so close to being realised." He ran a hand through my hair and I struggled not to flinch, even after all this time.

"Why do you hate him?" I said. I'd asked the question a dozen times since Ines Hollith had bought me, but he had never answered.

This time, he hesitated. "We are so close," he said, even quieter still. For a moment it seemed like he would continue. He set his painted nails on his knees and looked out into the distance. "He cost me everything, and he never even realised what he'd done." Ines Hollith shook his head. "When you are free, you will vow your vengeance against me, I have no doubt. You will curse me in your sleep. But you will not touch me, for you are not a man like I am. I have seen you. You are the heat and passion of a tiger at rest; you are not a methodical killer biding days and years to take away what I have. You do not know what it's like to be a man like we are. Our joys are small things, all experiences witnessed. We are proud in our fighters. We have risen like stars in the sky, that we must compete on the only avenue left to us, the training of others. You are a simple thing, Harald, but you must be ready for this. Only the Third has ever lost, and it was one of his earliest fights. The Second has never been defeated, except by the First."

I nodded. I didn't have the energy to disagree with Ines Hollith, or even scowl. I would kill the two fighters ahead of me. Then I would kill the First. And then I would be free.

The thought filled me with such a delicious rush of adrenalin, that even my hatred of Ines Hollith faded away. If I was free, I would be unstoppable. I was already unstoppable. The greatest fighter in the world.

My only issue was in who my talents were directed against. I didn't want to fight the Second of the Walled Garden. I wanted to fight the Heptarch. I wanted to fight Gabriel. I wanted to fight the draugr.

Even as Ines Hollith ran his hands through my hair, something inside of him feared. He was tentative. He had described me as a tiger and treated me as such – even as we were now, with all my hopes of freedom pinned on him, he feared that I would turn around and rip him in two.

"I'll kill them," I said. "And then I want to fight the First. Soon."

"You'll fight him, Harald. And then you'll be free."

I spent the rest of the week resting, with only light training in between. The other fighters would take me two on one – and eight times out of ten I would beat them. But fighting two on one is a difficult proposition, especially against the best opponents.

Technically, they would not be far away from me.

But I would not lose in the Pits. It was mentality, more than it was anything else. At a certain level, skill stops mattering. At another level, so does physical fitness. It is mentality that separates the good fighters from the best.

Ines Hollith dressed me in finery; perfumed me; spoilt me. He was almost giddy the day before the fight, dancing around his estate, with his entourage in tow.

And then it was time.

A banner rippled in the crowd, a golden lion on a red field.

There wasn't an empty seat in the arena. It wasn't unusual for my fights, but the energy that ran through the crowd was different. Nobody was seated – even the nobles in their boxes stood and clapped, and the crowd roared my name.

I breathed deep. It was impossible not to grin and I raised my hands aloft to the crowd.

Louder they roared.

I shook my fist.

Louder.

And then quiet, almost at once, as the doors at the other end of the Pit opened.

The announcer spoke, but I did not hear him. Leo and Thraides – brothers, two and three of the Walled Gardens greatest fighters. They never fought in the arena anymore, but the Heptarch had lost too many men to me.

He'd decided to end me, once and for all. Two of his best versus the one of me.

It was an impossible battle.

But they'd been telling me that for years at this point. An invincible opponent. An unstoppable fighter. Well, I'd never been beaten. I never would be, either.

Leo and Thraides looked enough alike to be twins, though Leo was the elder by three years. They were both tall and blonde, as I was, born in a fishing village on the coast to a minor nobleman. Sold to the Heptarch, and eventually freed by the Heptarch.

These two were his guards. They stood watch outside his chamber. They were his most trusted lieutenants.

When they fought, it was a precession. Their days of fighting every month in the arena was gone – they acted as the Heptarch's sword arm now, out in the real world. They killed his political opponents and intimidated his allies.

But I had gotten under his skin, like Ines Hollith had wanted. He was sending his best against me. All I had to do was win two more bouts – and then freedom.

I licked my lips. The air was dry. There was a storm outside, but nothing could have overshadowed the noise from the Pits.

I looked to the ceiling of the Arena, all the stars drawn upon it and said a small prayer. I didn't believe in God. I didn't need to. But today, I was two against one, facing two of the greatest fighters in the world.

I almost missed the announcer calling for the fight to begin.

The words *to the death* filtered through my subconsciousness, and I came suddenly alert.

The brothers prowled towards me, like panthers with clever eyes. They looked to flank me from the off.

I couldn't let them.

I would win this fight on the move.

Without hesitation I shot forward, striking at Thraides. He blocked with a shallow grunt of exertion and his blade flicked out.

I felt the unnatural feeling of torn flesh and look down to find the underside of my left arm bleeding.

Grimacing, I trotted back, as Leo came to stand beside his brother.

I kept to the edge of the arena, so close to the crowd that they could have reached out and grabbed me.

Thraides followed. Leo darted to my right, but I didn't let him pass.

Two overhand strikes; Leo weathered it well, retreating into the shadow of his brother.

Silence fell over the crowd.

For them, the initial excitement of the battle had worn off. For years they had chanted our names. Thraides, Leo, Harald. These men – these famous fighters would be dead in just a few minutes, and only now did the crowd begin to realise it. Men you had idolised, watched fight for years, would soon be bleeding out in the dirt.

This was the moment.

Sweat trickled down my brow; blood dripped from my arm.

It hurt, but I couldn't let it distract me.

Leo attacked again.

This time I let him, faking a stumble.

He came in close – I could see his bloodshot eyes – and I turned my stumble to a lunge.

It caught him in the stomach, piercing skin. His mouth formed an O.

Thraides struck hard – pinned me against the wall of the arena. Over his shoulder I could see his brother gasping, but I didn't have time to stare. Thraides hit well; I ducked, blocked, shoved, until I broke through.

I gasped a deep breath and staggered away to the other side of the Pits.

Thraides exchanged a quiet word with his brother. Leo straightened. He was hurt but not badly.

The crowd screamed for us to come together – to fight! – but we held our ground. Faced one another across the length of the arena.

More whispering between the brothers.

"Fuck it," I muttered, and launched towards them.

They didn't expect it. I didn't expect it.

My first strike forced Thraides backwards, but he wasn't my target. I struck Leo again; he barely got his blade up in time, but the force of my strike brought his guard down.

My second ripped straight down his stomach, spraying blood.

Leo looked dumbly down and crumpled to the ground.

Thraides bellowed. I couldn't admire my work. We locked blades, as he punched me with his free hand.

I took a step backwards.

Only

My leg remained rooted to the spot. I looked down to find the tip of a sword pierced straight through the top of my thigh. Down the blade ripped, and I screamed, forced down onto one knee.

It was Leo, still alive, somehow.

I looked to see Thraides looming over me.

I swung with all my might; he didn't think I had the power left.

The blade ripped across his midriff and brought him to his knees.

My knee screamed. I screamed.

Blood spurted everywhere and my vision flashed in and out of focus.

With one last burst I struck again, severing Thraides' head from his shoulders.

He toppled, a headless corpse onto the sand.

I followed him down, head over heels.

Leo stared back at me, eyes glossing over.

I couldn't hear the crowd.

It was over.

PART TWO

Tell me of better days, I said.

When God watched over us wielding a bright sceptre, when the rain fell and the sun shone in balance, when mothers and fathers raised their own children.

I dreamt of those days. I dreamt of a King fairer than any man you've ever met, who invited myself and Lot to his halls, and we feasted all day long and we drank with his servants, and I wrestled with his guards and laughed as I beat them. When I wanted to stop, I stopped, and I returned to Lot and scooped her onto a dance floor, and we danced.

I dreamt of a long sunset. The kind that hides behind the hills but lingers for hours.

I dreamt of my father smiling and letting me play with his sword; I dreamt of being a child, without worry, without care, without the anxious thoughts that crowded my waking moments.

And with the memory of those thoughts, the dreams began to break.

The king cracked like ice before me and shattered onto the floor of his castle. Lot receded into the darkness and became a memory again.

My father's sword hung at my side and as my fingertips brushed the hilt, my stomach turned and fluttered, and I thought of all the dead faces I had caused.

I awoke screaming.

I do not remember the moment itself, not like the dreams which preceded it. In some ways they felt, and still do feel, more real than the reality which followed them. But there was no prophecy in these dreams, so do not look for it. They were fever dreams, anxieties, hopes. I wonder if those men who die, but do not die, who are fed sustenance by their daughters, who lie sleeping in comas, dream such pleasant dreams as mine before waking.

I do not know.

All that I know is that I screamed, and I woke, and I slept some more.

When I truly regained my senses, I found myself in a bed, covered in fresh white linen. I was naked, but for the bandages encasing my left knee and thigh, almost black with dried blood.

I tried to move, but every twitch of my body sent some tendon screaming in pain, and all I could do was lie still and mumble softly for help.

Eventually a nurse arrived, and I gulped down fresh water.

I slept again.

When I woke, it was to darkness. I was alone. There was no sound anywhere, nothing in the room to occupy my mind, and no nurse close by, no matter how much my disused voice croaked for help.

On the battlefield I had never known fear. During my young life I had acted with certainty and assurance. I had not doubted myself, except to question whether I was too competent, too successful, too much like my brothers.

In that long night, the longest of nights, I questioned my failings. I remembered the cutting blow, that blood smeared face knotted in determination as his sword ripped down my thigh and into my knee. Was this the end? I wondered. Would I fight again? Would I walk again? Was I crippled, waiting in the pleasure houses of Ines Hollith, ready to become a curiosity, an amusement for whoever dared to come see me.

The Champion of the Host of the Mountain. Failed challenger of a fallen God. A forgotten legend of the arena, defeated and cast down by the Walled Garden.

I imagined the Heptarch, wine overflowing from his glass. Boasts on his lips. Harald Fairhair, fallen.

Better dead than whatever life of pain awaits.

I saw my father's ghost in the shadows. I did not feel the draugr, only the thread of that quest slip away from me with each throb of pain from my bandaged knee.

I could not move. More than that, I felt swollen, as if the leg was not my leg at all but a thing that should move normally but resisted my thoughts and the small twitching movements of my hip.

Sleep did not find me. How could it? I fixated on the throbbing, the sensation once noticed that would not leave my thoughts. I felt it, I felt it, all my muscles hanging like weight from tendons that could no longer support them.

My screams, held in for so long, part of my resistance from the madness of the night, erupted from me like a storm.

With them came a nurse and a cup of honeyed wine, and once more sleep.

When I woke, I was not in bed, but lying on a hill of cushions, one propped under my knee, facing a cloudless blue sky.

At first, I thought I was dreaming again, but the fly that kept landing on my face was too frustrating to be part of a dream.

The voice that spoke, likewise, was not one conjured by my subconscious, but had that rare quality that only real sacks of flesh can conjure.

"The Golden City is beautiful in the summer," the voice said. "It glimmers with the grace of all of the Gods."

I strained my body to see the voice, but my leg prohibited any movement, so I was forced to lay looking at the sky.

"You are confused, I'm sure," the voice continued, "about your current state. You are, I'm glad to inform you, alive."

I tried to spit out a response, but my lips were cracked and parched, and only a whining sound emerged. Soon, a rough hand tilted my head forward and a brass cup filled with spring water pressed to my lips.

After I had gulped the entire contents down, I got my first look at the man.

To say that he was bronzed would be an understatement. His skin had been baked by the sun, so that he was a canvas of cracked flesh divided by wide, almost bulbous features. These features would have looked barbaric on a normal man, but the man who waited upon me possessed a mane of white hair that shone in the sunlight. Though he was not young and dressed simply in a toga and sandals, his arms were cut with muscle.

As he spoke, however, his face became something very different. His eyes, pale green, even against the blueness of the sky, narrowed to form a keen intelligence. I was forced to revaluate my perceptions: he was not a brawler, a strong man, but a smart man too, with a quick mind that watched and waited on my imaginings.

"Do you know me?" he asked.

"No."

"I am Tytos, of the Golden House."

I knew him only by the reputation of the almost mythical golden house.

"You bought me from Ines Hollith," I croaked.

"Yes."

I almost laughed, but the sound came up tangled and twisted. "I don't think you're getting much of a fighter anymore." I held myself up on my elbows to look at him, though all of my body ached as if unused for months.

Tytos eyed me, a twist of a smile on his lips. "Perhaps. Perhaps not. Besides, there are more ways to fight than with your sword."

"Tell that to someone with a sword in front of you."

He laughed. "But what happens if I am unarmed, but I have two men at my side with swords? What happens if I have thirty? I will fight the man who draws a sword on me, but I will not lift a single finger."

I muttered something about lacking honour, but his point was made.

Instead, I asked: "Why did you buy me? What do you want from me?"

He shrugged. "I want many things. As to why I bought you...I bought you to set you free."

I hesitated. "Is this supposed to be funny?"

"It is supposed to be a kind gesture. From this day forth you are a free man. That being said, you are not a very mobile man." He looked pointedly at my leg. "May I ask what you will do with your freedom?"

It hit me. Years of plotting. Years of waiting for vengeance: on the draugr, on Gabriel, on Ines Hollith and the Heptarch.

And now I was a cripple. I couldn't move, might never swing a sword again.

I was not free. No freer than I had been in the Pits with the crowd cheering my name.

I thought of Lot. She would not be the girl I left. She was probably swollen with some farmer's child, if she lived at all. All that remained of her could be a ledger entry in some town official's book, noting her name and the sight of a mass grave.

"You do not appear pleased with your freedom," Tytos said.

"I have *lost* everything."

"You have not lost your life." Tytos crouched beside me. "You have not lost your mind. You have not lost that fire in the pit of your stomach." He shook his head. "I watched you in the Pits. With a blade you were brilliant, but you were not invincible. I know of a dozen men could have killed you, broke you like kindling over the knees."

"You're full of crap."

"Yes, indeed." He smiled. "But I saw the way you believed. You dominated men with the sheer power of your will. You never believed you would lose. And so, you did not lose."

"But I did lose."

"Eventually, but you were set up to fail. You fight each of them by themselves, you beat them nine times out of ten, but on the tenth they kill you. Fight them both together? It was a toss-up whether you won or lost, and Ines Hollith got greedy because he wanted to fuck the Heptarch."

"It's the only reason I was happy to fight for him anyway."

"Well, if the future feels too difficult to comprehend, let me offer you a solution. A short-term employment you may learn to love."

I shook my head. I had to return home, even if the country had a different king, if Gabriel was the fancy of the courts, if Lot was gone and never to be found. I had to return and avenge my family.

Tytos laid a hand upon my hand. I withdrew it in shock; it was not the custom of my country to be so intimate with strangers, like it was in his. If he was perturbed by my reaction, he did not show it. Instead, he said:

"You are young. You burn with the fire of a difficult life. You want to prove yourself. But now you are in no position to act upon your goals. You are a broken man, at least in body if not in mind. You must recover. Grow stronger. And in time, you will still be a free man – your goals will still await you. There is no rush, until you are my age, and then you must act before time does. It is the only enemy you cannot defeat, but it does not always need to be your enemy. Heal, and learn. And when you are ready, I will help you with your ambitions personally."

Before I could answer, he beckoned servants from out of my field of vision. They dragged me into sitting, propping me on plush pillows, so I could look out from the rooftop. The entire Golden City lay before us, domes of gold, rambling alleys, and fountains gushing into the sky.

"You are in my home," Tytos said. "My servants will fetch anything you desire. I will return tomorrow to hear of your answer."

I did not ask anything of the servants. I sat in stony silence, and if they talked about me, which I knew they did, I did not listen. My actions might seem foolish to you. If they do then I know that you have never lost the thing that makes you who you are.

Some men have a mind sharper than the blade of a knife. When old age and senility sets in, so does a kind of madness – they cannot live with the loss. It is what kills them – it is why in my experience the oldest men I've met are the stupidest. The stupid can bear the loss of their faculties better, as they never had faculties to begin with.

It is the same for the beautiful. Man or woman, it matters not. If you trade your currency on your beauty, then when the first heavy-set signs of age begin to weigh on you, it is difficult not to descend into hysteria. There were stories that had found me, even in the bunkhouse of Ines Hollith, of nobles throwing themselves from balconies as their jowls drooped and their eyes grew dark rings.

For me, it was different. Mine was not a vain, stupid desire. I had a mission. Without the use of my leg, what use would those years of training come to? Sweating as I jogged around camp, the rough calluses I earnt in Lord Calforth's manor. Wasted. A life wasted.

And yet...

As I lay in Tytos' rooftop garden, the sky a blazing blue, I began to find hope rising in my chest. In a few moments I was laughing, roaring like a madman.

Orphaned, exiled, captured, enslaved, crippled.

Free.

I shook with uncontrollable laughter. The servants stood and watched, faces impassive. Was I mad? They thought I was mad.

Was I mad?

I had survived damnation. I would survive it again if I had to.

And now I was a free man.

If only I could rise. I cursed and spat. I used my elbows, anything to try and propel myself upwards, but each twitch of my legs sent shooting pain so awful it was as if a blade cut into me.

There is no sensation like it. A feeling of wrongness. Of sickness and revulsion that forces you to gag.

The servants wasted no time in supporting me. They took an arm in each of theirs and they hauled me to my feet more gracefully than I could have achieved even in normal days.

I was not untouchable, even under Tytos' protection. My life of freedom began with familiar constraints to my life in the arena. Guards followed me around and servants checked on me every ten minutes. I could barely move without a trail of concerned faces following me. And yet for the first time I began to get a sense of what the Golden City really was like.

If you didn't see it then, in the vibrancy of its history and the tolerance of its many religions, it is impossible to explain. Few things have overwhelmed me like the free markets of the Golden City.

However, the Golden City was not perfect, and I will do my best to explain the state in which I found it upon my release.

I woke one morning, in the stillness of Tytos' house. White curtains billowed in the wind and the stone floor was cool to the touch. I was not even close to well enough to put my foot to the floor, but with great effort I used my crutches to propel myself towards the windowsill. Drawing a deep breath I inhaled the richness of the air, spices carried from market stalls lining the street opposite, of types and fragrances I could not point out to you even now.

I could not walk well, but under Tytos' watch I received privileges I would have scarcely dreamed about before. I travelled around Golden City via palanquin, a box borne by four standard bearers who guided me through the busy streets. I was in no fit state to be moving and every bump and jolt hurt, but I *needed* to be out.

I had spent almost six years fighting for Ines Hollith. I could barely remember what it was like to be free – to be in control of each day.

As much as the crowds had cheered for me, I was not a part of the city. I knew nothing about it. And so I descended upon the Golden City for the first time, in control of myself and my time.

Tytos had given me freedom, though I was flanked by four guards, other freed fighters from the arena. I also wore a golden mask, under Tytos' orders. It was the fashion amongst certain members of the nobility, and it would keep my identity secret.

My first destination might surprise you.

I've made no secret that I am not a religious man. I have spent my life trying to do the *right* thing, not the godly thing. But I had the weight of the world on my conscience, and nobody to talk to about it.

And so, I asked to be brought to the House of the Mountain, one of the hundreds of Godly establishments throughout the Golden City.

It was not like the churches at home. No tall, dark towers. The House of the Mountain in the Golden City was quite literally a townhouse in the centre of a market district. Stalls were set down the street and foreign scents clogged my nose as I was assisted out of the palanquin. Streaming banners flew from the roof of the house, in God's colours, and the windows were painted with small murals of Godly scenes upon them, but otherwise the house was relatively circumspect compared to the more garish merchant stalls nearby.

I entered the building, leaning heavily on both crutches as I did so, with my guards holding the doors.

The building was no bigger on the inside than the outside. In fact, it was made of narrow corridors, filled with paintings of various pastoral scenes – God's Garden, the Mountain against a backdrop of silver stars.

Further on was the hallway of portraits, where a number of woodcuts had been commissioned of the Traitors who had stolen from God's Garden and brought his wrath upon the world of men. It was strange to see them commemorated. In Amber, they were also regarded fondly – as heralds of the good of God, who sacrificed themselves to bring the joys of the Garden to the people of our world.

In my home, the view had always been more orthodox. They had stolen from God. They had betrayed God. In doing so, they forced him to turn his back from our world and reside only in the Mountain, his influence and support diminishing.

Still, I had a namesake among the Traitors. Harald. I stopped and looked at the woodcut of him.

He had a square, bearded face. He was the Traitor who had stolen the First Sapling, a tree of rowan or ash, depending on which branch of the church you believed.

As always when I saw him, I wondered why my mother had chosen his name as my name. A pang of sadness ran through me. I had dreamed for my childhood that my family would come find me, but civil war had come to Amber and most of the royals had been executed by the Church.

I wondered if that included my own mother.

She'd never come to see me, not once in all the years since I was born. I received no letters. I told myself that it was because my father didn't want her to write to me. Because my father would not allow it. But she was a princess of Amber. If she had've wanted something – it would have happened.

She had come to him once, in virgin white. When she left, it was with a child in her belly. To him, she had been a conquest. And then I arrived on his doorstep, a messenger from Amber with clear instructions. I was his child, not hers. I was his mistake, not hers.

I had to face the fact that my mother did not care for me, and she had died having only seen me once, as she pushed me out of her body and away.

"Saying a prayer to Harald," a quiet voice said behind me.

I turned to see a figure, bald now, and bent by age, though he had been a relatively young man when last I'd seen him.

"Father Andrew," I said.

The priest nodded. "You know me. I apologise, I cannot see your face."

I looked at him properly through the narrow slits of the mask, before taking it off. He'd been blinded. His eyes were sightless, though there was the scarring of acid on his cheeks and nose. "What did they do to you?"

"This? A small price to pay to continue serving God."

"Surely you could have gone home. They must have paid a priest's ransom. Surely you were not abandoned."

"I did not repent. I did not accept the ransom. I came to represent God and God had spoken through me. The Golden Ones accepted my piety, punished me appropriately for my transgressions against their city, and gave me this empty house to oversee, as the last Priest of the Mountain had been killed by a mob." He furrowed his brow. "You speak to me as though you know me, though I do not recognise your voice."

"I was...a soldier in your company. We took Antonia together."

"Ah, Antonia. What a joyous day. I remember the city burning, the boys on the boats. I carried the spear that day and God blessed my blade. I thought I was the last of that company left. How did you survive?"

"With a lot of luck. And not without my own physical sacrifice."

"Ah, I see." Father Andrew walked closer – the guards moved to stop him – but I waved them away. He placed a hand on my shoulder. "They said that Harald Lionheart had become a legend of the Pits. I went to see him once. To hear him, I guess. To hear that he still lived. And he did, and God blessed his blade then as surely as it did in our fighting all those years before. It is your voice, isn't it? You're older, but it's still you."

"Yes, Father. It's me."

He could not close his blinded eyes, but his shoulders moved as if crying. "God is not finished with you yet. I knew it then and I know it now."

"I'm afraid I am crippled too, Father. I'm not sure if I will ever be able to fight again."

The priest was silent for a long moment. "Then pray with me, Harald. If you will? It will do us both good."

I followed him further down the corridor to a larger room with cushions and various paintings of the Mountain. Cobwebs hung between the higher up pictures and the entire room seemed covered in a film of dust. Marble sculptures of various famed priests cluttered the room at odd intervals.

Father Andrew sank to his knees. I stood beside him.

"Oh Father, please hear these two tired souls who come to you today. We have sinned. We have faltered. We have erred. Like the Heralds – those you deem traitors – we have only ever sought the best for our world and sought to work with your glory forever in our minds. Somewhere we have failed. I ask you show us the light. Show us the right path. We are your children. We swear it on the sun and stars. We swear it upon the Garden and the Mountain. We swear it on our own true names. Guide us, please."

"Guide us, please," I repeated.

His words faded into silence and he rose. "I am glad I am not the only one left. If you ever need a friend Harald Lionheart, both God and I will be here for you."

"You weren't meant to reveal your identity," one of the guards said, when we were outside.

"Blind men know more than they can see. He knew me."

"You could have denied him."

"I could have. But I didn't."

I returned to the palanquin and they took us deeper into the Golden City. The Golden City unfolded around me like the petals of a flower – heavy with exotic perfumes, and laden with the nectar of a thousand cities. I had always known that the Golden City was a cultural centre, the heart of those seven nations which had formed a rough coalition for the last thousand years. But they were far more than that – it was the collection of seven different empires and all the towns that filled them, and all the further lands that traded with them, across distant seas.

Incense smoked in the bazaars. Merchants sold shiny trinkets; whalebones; mammoth tusks; black ore; silk tassels. I gazed out behind the curtains of the palanquin in open mouthed wonder. It was impossible not to think of the effort that went to procuring each valuable item that sat on those stalls. It was something we had never had, cut off on our island, with only Amber and the smaller islands nearby to trade with. Of course, some foreign objects made it our way, shipped from Antonia, but they had never made it as far as my father's castle.

Our next destination was a bar in the city – upper class revellers sat outside drinking tall glasses of coloured alcohol. Tytos had booked out an entire balcony and it was there I was taken, carried unceremoniously upstairs by the guards.

Alcohol was brought to us by silent waitresses and the guards took their place around me. I was uncomfortable in the centre of them – but the views from the balcony were breath-taking, and I tried to admire the golden rooftops, tall spires, circular domes. Bells rang from a distant place of worship. A flight of birds clawed their way across a sky that seemed almost to shimmer gold in the haze of the reflected light.

"Would you be wanting the entertainment? My Lord Tytos was unsure."

I looked around to see a tall, cleanly shaven waiter standing beside me.

"Entertainment?" I asked.

He nodded purposefully to his right.

In the shadow of the awnings, a young woman waited.

Pale, from my own islands, she clasped her hands awkwardly behind her back. She wore a bejewelled top and a short leather skirt. Her bright eyes fluttered up at me and down again.

"What is she here for?"

The waiter coughed. "For sensitive matters. She will disrobe if you desire."

"She's a slave?" I asked. "Did you take her in the Crusade?"

"Her origin is unimportant – "

"Her origin is important to me. Answer my question."

"She was taken in the Crusade, yes."

"And is she a pleasure slave for the establishment?"

"Yes."

"And you thought that I, a crippled former slave, would want her?"

She stepped forward. "I'm sorry if I'm not suitable, master. We have others who you might find more pleasing."

It took me a while to stand, without the guards' help, and even longer to hobble over to her. "Look at me," I said. "My name is Harald. What's yours?"

"I have no name. I am just a vessel in your hands."

"What was your name, before you came to war?"

She looked scared, but a nod from the waiter strengthened her. "My name was Eleanor."

"And did you travel here with your father? Or brother?"

She nodded.

"Are they dead?"

She nodded again.

"Would you like to be free?"

She looked again at the waiter, but I moved my head to occupy the space. "Don't ask his permission."

"What else would I do?" she whispered quietly. "I'm all alone."

I pursed my lips. Turned to the waiter and the guards. "Will you release her? Find her a place in Tytos' house?"

The waiter shook his head. "There are thousands of slaves from your assault in this city. You can't free them all."

"No, but I can free this one. Go to Tytos, tell him that's the price of my loyalty."

The waiter clenched his lips. Barked something in their language which even after all this time in the city I didn't quite catch.

Eleanor bowed and disappeared back into the building. The waiter couldn't hide his disgust. "I will send word to her master and to Tytos. We will see if you are as important as you think you are."

He vanished back inside, and I spent the next few moments sipping my drink, trying to calm my nerves. Had I done the right thing? I'd been powerless for so long. I'd *needed* to try and save her.

"Where now?" one of the guard's said. "Shall we find a brothel for you to save?"

I clenched my teeth. "That's a good idea, but I want to see the real Golden City. Take me to the slave markets."

The guards looked between one another. "We're not sure if that's appropriate."

I shook my head. "I promise I won't try to free the entire slave population of the city. I just want to see it."

With a sigh, the guards rose and carried me back to my palanquin. There the waiting servants carried me through the city.

I wanted to stop at every corner. There was another town house that had been converted into a religious building with tiger statues on the corner of each windowsill. A large mosaic had been drawn in ink rising up the building, like the stripes of whatever God they worshipped.

Onwards we went.

Slavery in the city was ever present. I knew a little bit of it from my former pit fighters. Some had been sold into slavery in order to pay for their debts. Some had been sentenced to slavery through criminal conviction. Some had been refugees, taken by underworld gangs. Some were captured enemy fighters, from my kingdom or others bordering the Golden City.

There were a million reasons – and that meant that slavery had become one of the Golden City's key trades. It was not just present in the slave market itself. Occasionally I would spy a street stall with collared slaves waiting behind their master, but these were smaller enterprises. They disgusted me, but I tried to save my energy for the famous slave market itself.

It bordered the richer districts. Slavery as a concept was not greeted with any contempt within the Golden City. It had become a legitimate way of commerce and business, unlike my homeland. That's not to say my people weren't indentured against their will, as I had been, but it tended to be a criminal punishment rather than a commercial enterprise.

The Golden City was trade ran amok – the colourful riches of a million different hungry minds.

Eventually, we arrived at the marketplace. A guard at a checkpoint stopped us, but let us through at the barest mention of Tytos' name.

Suddenly, I regretted my decision.

There were slaves of every different background. Most of them were women. Some were girls. Almost all were a in a state of undress.

I closed my eyes. Gripped hard the handle of my crutch.

The slaves wore collars, as if they were chattel. They were naked and dirty, sad and starving.

I had worn those bonds. I had stood naked before the crowds with my manhood on show.

I had been one of them.

You can't save them all.

The injustice of it rose like putrid bile in the back of my throat. I swallowed a heavy lump.

"Take me away," I said. "I've seen enough."

I drew the curtains of the palanquin and sat in the darkness until we reached Tytos' estate.

I struggled to the rooftop terrace.

My teeth ground. My leg screamed. My mind boiled with dark emotion.

Eventually, I found sunlight, and a waiting woman.

"Eleanor," I said.

She waited with her head bowed and her hands behind her back, as she had done before. Only this time, she was completely naked. Her dark hair fell across her collarbone, but stopped before reaching the small pink mounds of her nipples. Her soft white skin was stripped of all hair.

"They freed me," she said. "But I own nothing. I am nothing."

"You are not nothing," I said moving towards her. I placed my own jacket around her shoulders, as Linial had done for me so many times. "You have always been something."

"But how will I live?"

I was facing the same question. Without the sword, how would I live? Freedom from the system is not enough, there has to be something after.

"You can work for Tytos," I said. "He will keep you."

"And how is that different to what I was before?"

"You won't have to give your bodies to others."

"It was lighter work than some jobs. Besides, what is the difference between a servant and a slave? I will still work. I will still suffer."

"You have agency."

"What agency? I'm stood naked in front of you."

"Things can get better."

"I have hope." She shrugged and made a small sound that could have been either laugh or cry. "I guess that is something. Things might get better. For some reason."

And now she did cry.

I stood helplessly by her side. She was right. I had freed her without thinking of the ramifications. She was now Tytos' servant, alone in a foreign land with no skills. It wasn't that she had been better in slavery, but I had put her into a situation that was a different kind of bondage.

"I feel the same way," I said. "I don't know what to do."

Her eyes flashed in the light. "Then maybe don't make your mistakes with me too."

She subsided into tears. I called another servant over. "Take her away. Clothe her. Feed her. Find her a job."

The servant nodded and I collapsed into a chair as quickly as my broken body would allow.

On the fourth night in Tytos' house I slept fitfully.

I woke in the dead of night, no light but for the full moon casting its silvery gaze wide. And, bathed in the light, stood a woman so beautiful and perfect she could be nothing but a dream. I stretched out a hand, but instead of the soft illusory fabric of my dreams, I found soft skin.

Her eyes, frightfully wide, fixed on my own. She reached out and laid her palm upon my cheek. "I thought you'd died in the Pits."

Memories flooded back; of parties where I was paraded naked in front of the Heptarch, of Linial being dragged toward Lord Ashdown's tent; of her bidding furiously for my freedom. "Lady Linial," I said.

"Lin," she said. "Please call me Lin."

We did not speak anymore. She curled up in bed beside me, conscious of my ruined leg. She was a small, almost fragile thing, but I remembered the ruin of Lord Ashdown's body – she was no maiden in need of my protection. Still, that did not stop me from extending an arm around her and pulling her close. Her hair smelt of berries and sweetness.

I smiled until I fell asleep.

In the morning she was gone, and I wondered whether I'd dreamt the whole thing until Tytos arrived smiling at breakfast. We sat at his table on the veranda and drank orange juice looking over the city.

"We are not alone in our endeavours," Tytos said suddenly, without taking his eyes from the city streets. "We have allies in every hierarchy in the city. Lady Linial is just one of our sympathisers. All of them want an end to the Heptarch and this corrupt, lip service democracy. A strong leader who will make the Golden City a fairer place.

"What place do you want me to have in this new order?"

Tytos turned and laid his piercing eyes on me. "People say you were magnificent on the battlefield. Always where the fighting was strongest."

"I can't fight anymore," I interrupted.

"You do not know that yet. Injuries heal."

"You are waiting for something that might never happen."

"I am not waiting. The opposite, in fact." He placed an envelope on the table. "This contains papers that will grant you entry into Erresea."

"Where is Erresea?"

Tytos smiled. "You came to conquer a land you do not understand. Erresea is the capital of Cithia, one of the nations of Gora that you sought to crush between your heel."

"I was a prisoner too."

"But you enjoyed it, yes? The squeals of my people as you killed. The way your men looked up to you."

"I did what I had to."

"One day that excuse will not be enough. You will do what you must, not simply what you had to." He downed his orange juice as if it was a shot of strong liquor. "You are not an instrument guided by fate. You are the hand that guides." He belched into a small white napkin. "Though on this occasion my hand will happily guide until you are strong enough to stand on two feet again."

"When will I leave?"

"Imminently, I'm afraid. This city is a dangerous place for you right now. You killed them both, you see, even as they did the blow that rendered you here. And the Heptarch has been looking for you – the Walled Garden may make their name in the Pits, but they are capable of far more covert operations. And killing you in your bed would be far easier."

"So I leave? And do what?"

"You recover. You heal. And when the time comes, I summon you back and you return and kill the Heptarch. How does that sound for a future?"

I nodded. It was hard to feel positive with the throbbing pain of my knee, but I forced a grin. "As good as any future."

"Excellent. In the morning my men will prepare a caravan for you."

Tytos rose and extended a hand towards me. "This is the last time we will meet for a while. When you return, it will be at the moment of our triumph."

I could not sleep that night. How little I knew of the world, how endless civilization seemed on the shores of the Golden City. Erresea. I had never even heard of it, not even in the books of my father. I wondered whether our knowledge of Gora was a wilful one. It was much easier to murder those who appeared only as abstract monsters, after all.

But it didn't seem to stem from decree from the king. It was more a collective ignorance. Like nobody had ever really thought to examine the culture of our greatest enemy.

It was in that questioning state the Lady Linial came to me.

She was dressed typically all in black. A tight dress and dark leggings. She wore a heavy cloak that dwarfed her body and made her legs look almost comically small.

"Come," she said, without further explanation. "There is something you need to see."

I almost laughed. "I can't move, my Lady. I'm afraid the time for dramatic statements might be over."

A flicker of concern appeared on her face. "You're no better?"

"Doesn't seem it. Tytos says the operation went well but I don't know how much to believe that."

"Can you walk?"

I shook my head.

"Shit," she said. "There is something I really need to show you."

I nodded. "There's two walking sticks in the corner. Pass them over."

She passed me one and wrapped her arm around my shoulder. "I can be the other stick."

The way was slow going – it took ten minutes to even get out of Tytos' building and into Lady Linial's carriage. "I'm sorry about the bumps," she said.

"It's fine," I said, through gritted teeth.

We sat in almost silence, though I could feel her gaze upon me.

Our destination was not one I recognised and Linial hesitated in the doorway. "There's a lot of stairs."

"I've come this far."

The staircase descended into absolute darkness. Linial guided me down each grimacing step, as if she had the eyes of a cat. I stopped and waited several times, my hard breathing the only sound in all the world.

We reached the bottom, though I felt little relief; I would have to return up the staircase at some point, and I was dragging my leg like a leaden stump behind me with each step.

Up would not be easier.

We proceeded through another doorway and into a large chamber filled with torchlight. There was an altar at one end and carvings of demons and other creatures on the ceiling. Lady Linial offered no explanation and I was too exhausted to ask.

There was another doorway at the rear of the chamber. We walked down a long passageway and into a chamber with running water. She hesitated at the next entrance; this one engraved with a spiral of black text I could not make out. "I haven't really explained myself, have I?"

"No. But I'm used to not understanding."

"I want you to understand."

I peered down at her, but her face was deadly serious.

"You need to understand, Harald. If you are to join us."

"I don't even know who *us* is. Just that I have Tytos to thank for my life. And you. Well, I don't really know who you are. I thought you were a prisoner like me."

She sighed. She glanced down at her hands; her small pale palms were white in the torchlight. "Your people call everything they do not understand witchcraft. There are a great many Gods whose followers are benevolent and grant them the powers of minor miracles. There are priestesses and priests who are forces for good in this world. They are menders, doctors, builders. They are the foundation on which the Golden City rests."

"I've seen a few of them," I said. "Tytos told me it was a priest who saved my life and my leg."

"Good," she said. "Good. I do not want you to think that they are all like me."

"And what are you?"

She sighed again. Spoke: "Generations ago a monster rose from the sea, glorious, bedecked in golden crowns. It was taller than our tallest spire. A God come walking, we all believed. It spoke in clever words and soon amassed a following of people from all corners of the world."

"The Free Cities of Gora treated it with kindness and listened to its counsel. It is why in your country we are regarded as heathens – not because we do not worship your God, there are some here who do, but because we listened to the Counsel of this Beast. Its counsel tore the Free Cities apart. It pitted brother against brother and the land was riven by war."

"We tell this story to children," I said. "What does it have to do with you?"

"The Beast was captured, as the stories said. Imprisoned beneath the Golden City. The Heptarchs have always treated it as their sacred duty to keep it hidden and isolated. So it has no effect upon the world beyond. But there is still strife and war. Still so much pain. So, some of us decided to study it, to try and learn its purpose and to understand why a God came walking amongst us."

"You're one of those people," I said. "The Crusaders were right. The daughter of the Heptarch is a witch of the Beast."

"A priestess," she said. "But yes. Look Harald I don't expect you –"

My laughter cut her sentence short. "You know Linial, the amount of shit I've seen, I honestly don't care. My leg is fucked, everyone I love is gone. I don't care. Do whatever you want with the Beast. It's nothing to do with me."

"But that's the issue Harald, it is to do with you. The Beast asked for you."

I shook my head. Everything that had happened since my arrival suddenly made sense. "Tytos is a Beast worshipper too, I guess. You're all bloody heathens. That's the only reason you tried to buy me. It's the only reason Tytos saved me. It's all some bullshit religious gambit. And you know what? I've had enough of it. I lost everything in this Crusade."

"Calm down. Please. I tried to save you before the Beast said anything."

"Bullshit."

She shook her head. "You don't have to believe me –"

" – I won't –"

" – But at least let me show you. Please, Harald. Just let me show you. It's important."

I weighed her up. In the torchlight she seemed just like a fragile young woman, but I knew what she was capable of. The power she held inside of her – because of the Beast – and the steps she was taking to supplant her father. Had all of her kindness been a lie?

"You want me to be a heathen too," I said.

"Everyone lies to us. This world is so unfair. There has to be an answer. You know that. You think that. There has to be a way to change the world for the better."

I hesitated. The pain in my leg throbbed to a fever pitch. I wanted to scream.

"Okay. Fine."

She nodded. Wrapped her arm around my shoulders. Opened the door.

Back home I never paid much attention to the priests. We weren't that kind of a family. They would prattle on to the masses, but my father didn't much like sitting for services. Real men didn't sit and pray to God; they forged themselves in action. Whether it was hunting or hawking or scaling the mountains, he believed in finding God through real means.

And yet the Beast was a special story. It wasn't a story of pious nonsense. It was a story of a creature rising from the sea to lay waste to all beyond. Of poisoned kings and traitor princes. When the players rolled through town it was often as not a tale from the time of the Beast that they performed.

We had all been obsessed by it. Me and my brothers. They cast me as the villains of course, the ones to be killed, and they were the brave heroes. Still. I don't think they would have ever dreamed that I would stand face to face with it.

The first thing I noticed was the sound; my ears popped and our footsteps at once sounded both loud and quiet. It was a chamber far bigger than any I had ever seen. Running water ringed the room, emerging from great pipes built into the walls and tumbling into a moat around a raised platform.

Tall pillars supported the distant roof. Around those pillars were attached chains as thick as a man was tall, each link bigger than my fist. And attached to each chain was the Beast.

There is not an easy way to describe the Beast. You have seen him on the stained glass of Cathedral windows. You have heard him described in every way imaginable – as a Goliath streaming with sea water, as a shadowy trickster whispering untruths.

The reality was neither, both.

The Beast was a gigantic shadow that barely fit within the chamber despite its enormous size. The chamber had been constructed around the Beast, I realised, for there was no possible way it would have squeezed through one of the openings. It was hard to focus on it; its body was a mass of darkness that seemed to be made of nothing tangible, but rather wisps of smoke and shadow. And yet, upon its seven heads were seven crowns so tangible and thick and golden that all beneath became suddenly real, and I took a step back to realise the truth of the monster before me. Beneath its crowns, seven pairs of eyes turned to look at me, thin and narrow like a trickster, but as clever and as human as that of any man I'd met.

The chains rattled as It regarded us and I felt weak before its gaze.

Make no false statements. Do not say that I stood bravely before the Beast.

No, my legs almost gave way, and I leaned on Lady Linial so hard that I almost brought us both crashing to the ground.

It began to talk, but the Beast does not talk like men talk. Or rather it talks exactly how men talk. It uses your own inner voice. It uses you, your mind, as its mouthpiece. And accompanying its words come a rush of memory and experience as old as time, like breaking down the door of an ancient tomb and feeling the wind stir to life objects and dust that have otherwise been unmoved for centuries.

It was even more than that; a corruption; a settling of its mind on your mind, a heavy weight on top of you and a smell not dissimilar to a drunkard's breath in your ear.

Following the unpleasantness, however, came my own voice in a most amicable tone (a tone which I have rarely used in life itself).

YOU ARE CHOSEN.

I had no response, to give itself a voice, it had rendered me voiceless.

YOU ARE THE VESSEL OF CHANGE. THE BREAKER OF CHAINS. YOU ARE OUR SALVATION.

As it spoke, glorious memories flashed into my mind. They were not my memories. In each the people dressed as they had hundreds of years ago, in sandals and white linen. And in each men smiled and clapped and raised glasses and bowed and acknowledged me as their liege, lord and ruler.

SEVEN CROWNS FOR SEVEN KINGS. SEVEN CROWNS FOR SEVEN KINGS. ALL THE WORLD UNITED.

In my mind I saw them as they should have been. Great men with strong brows and long beards, each sat around a circular table, each wearing golden crowns.

ALL OF YOUR DREAMS DELIVERED. ALL OF YOUR DESIRES FOUND.

A room full of women, naked and heads bowed, offering subservience with their hands raised.

The vision changed. Suddenly I looked down from the Beast at Lady Linial, the same posture, same pose, same nakedness.

My cheeks flushed red and burning; I struggled to remember where I was, who I was, as my mind fought against whatever hold the Beast had on me.

The Beast seemed to sense my disquiet. It spoke in my own voice, more frantic this time, and in a tone I would never use.

SEVEN CROWNS FOR SEVEN KINGS. IT IS YOU. YOU ARE THE CHOSEN. YOU WILL DELIVER US.

I snapped from its hold.

Staggered. My leg gave way. I screamed. Went tumbling onto the flat of my back, just in time to see the Beast extend its seven heads over me, as if ready to strike.

Instead, the crowns fell from its head, all seven of them.

They struck the ground with a clear resounding ping and fell still without bouncing, a perfect circle around myself and Linial.

"I didn't know it would do that. I don't even know what it did."

Since the crowns fell, we'd left the chamber, the Beast falling silent and still again, and I'd found myself echoing its mood. I leant upon Linial, but otherwise had not spoken, as we made the slow and trudging return to the surface.

We had not been alone in the chamber, though I hadn't realised it at the beginning. There were archers waiting in perpetual suspense and other black robed priestesses acting as their shadows. They'd charged forward as I fell, shouting and rushing to collect the crowns.

"You have no idea what this means. The Beast has worn those crowns since it emerged from the sea. It has promised so much to so many. And yet it has given nothing, nothing but empty words. But it has given you each of the crowns. You don't understand."

"It's a monster," I said.

"Yes. And? It's a God, all the same. Who's to say all the Gods aren't monsters? It values you."

"It has cursed me."

"How? This is a gift. You're chosen."

"By a monster." I would have flung her away if I didn't need her for each step. "I have my own ambitions. My own goals. And now this? I'm a cripple. A useless cripple who can't even make it up a flight of stairs – who can't even control their own life. And you're telling me I've been chosen by the enemy of all civilization. Well, it would be just my luck."

"Harald," she protested, but I shook my head.

"No more. I'll go to Erresea. And we'll forget about that. Keep your crowns. Mount them on your wall."

"You can't forget. People have seen. I control this priesthood, but secrets come out eventually."

Everything boiled up inside of me. I wanted to strike her. Instead, I clenched my jaw and kept my silence.

The carriage waited for us on the surface. Carried us home in silence. On the wall of the carriage, I found a small splintering of the wood and set my mind to counting its each individual shard.

Linial did not break the silence. Even she knew better.

When we reached Tytos's house, she helped me to my room. I told myself there was no shame in it; in each laboured breath as we climbed the stairs; in her hands under my arms as she guided me into the bed; in the silence between us as she stood at the end of my bed and waited.

"You can't hide from this, Harald."

"Did you hear it?"

"You can't hear what it says to others."

"It was desperate, Lin. It promised me everything. Anything. Like it was running out of time."

To that she had no response. I shook my head. "Leave. Please."

She nodded. "Enjoy Erresea. I hope you feel better soon."

Chapter Thirteen

The road to Erresea was bumpy and my knee throbbed.

This was the low point. There had been many low points over the past few years, but none where I had so firmly felt like the end was upon me as in the carriage to Erresea. I considered leaving almost every night when we stopped, walking into the forest and hanging myself off a branch. What stopped me? My capability. Nothing else. I couldn't move enough to put on my clothes, let alone kill myself.

I'm sure you're wishing I had. Well, this was the moment. The day destiny failed you. All it would have taken was a nudge, a small release from the pain, and it would have been done.

And yet, I continued. Absently, the countryside passed me by, endless greenery beyond the carriage door. A door I could not bring myself to open, until the very end of the journey.

When at last the carriage driver told me Erresea was close, I joined him atop his perch. I had been so long inside that fetid box of a room, I smiled just to feel clean air upon my skin.

We peaked the last rise before the city and cold, northerly wind buffeted me almost from my seat. It shook loose something inside of me. For a moment, my brow relaxed, and the pain in my skull eased.

In the Golden City, I had not been myself. I had not even been human. For the first time in years, I felt again what to the rest of the world seems so ordinary. I felt the movement of the world around me; of seasons; of farmers sowing harvests; of skirts blowing in the wind; of all the precious, pretty moments of day-to-day life which had been stolen from me.

My mind came back to the day I had almost died, before we arrived at Lord Calforth's manor. That cold winter forest and the kindness of the fisherwoman who saved me, and the small pleasures they took in that simple life.

Could that be me? Could I ever be the boy I had been before the draugr ruined my life?

I was going to Erresea. And Erresea was not Liriam. Not the Pits. Not Ordrove. It was a fresh beginning.

I grinned from ear to ear as the city approached.

And what a city it was.

Erresea. The clue is in the name. Here is the sea. The city was a gateway to that proud and terrible sea.

Even as we arrived, lights glinted from houses; banners strung between roads caught the sun; washing lines flapped in the wind. The world was alive with colour, even against the backdrop of Erresea's pale, grey buildings.

Many of Erresea's streets were cobbled, so we took the long way round to our destination. I did not mind. I looked for the sea, in the gaps between buildings. It roiled and raged, a tempest of grey water.

Fear grew in my chest. I had no idea what kind of a man Tytos was. Linial – I had thought I'd known Linial – but behind that tender woman was a worshipper of the Beast. So, I worried. Who was it I was coming to stay with in Erresea?

I knew his name and his title. Master Gerhardt, a professor of Ancient History at the University of Erresea.

His house was high on the cliff, and behind the manse I could catch glimpses of a long and sprawling garden. Beyond that rode the pale horses of the sea.

The building itself was in the style of much of the town, just larger. Flower baskets hung marking the doorway and trestles beneath each window. Even from below I could make out rows of bookcases through the windows.

I thanked the carriage driver absentmindedly as I clambered down onto the pavement, leaning heavily on my walking stick.

I didn't even have time to take a breath, before the doors to the house exploded open with such force they almost fell off their hinges.

I would stop for a minute.

I have rushed through this story, breathlessly. And though they didn't give me time to think as they descended the steps towards me, I would spend a moment longer to describe them.

To rush would do them a disservice. To those three I owe as much as I have ever owed anything to anyone.

Their leader, wiry headed Alfred Gerhardt, was himself a foreign export in Erresea. He looked every inch of the University professor. Even in his casual attire he wore a waistcoat and pocket watch; in one stuffed pocket was a folded magazine; in another a pocketbook of some sort, giving him the grotesque appearance of his body jutting out at odd angles, as if his insides were pressed up against his clothes. His fingers were ink stained, his eyes large and bulbous, but all of this was put into the back of my mind by the beaming smile that he wore at almost every opportunity.

On his left was Margaret, his daughter, a tall woman who had reached adulthood in an ungainly manner. She walked as if her head and legs were possessed of a different centre of gravity, and even as she came through the door, it was her head that emerged through first. Despite all of this, she possessed the same good-natured attitude that her father radiated.

On the right was Cat. I almost didn't notice her at first; she was thin and black haired and moved smoothly across the ground like good noble young ladies are meant to in storybooks. She was similar in many ways to Linial, but whereas Linial was wrapped up in her own struggles, Cat seemed to be completely unaffected by the world around her. In many ways she would appear no different to one of that faceless crowd you could see at any noble gathering.

And yet. There was a subtle glimmer in Cat's eye. Even as she floated down the steps beside the other two, some inner working puzzled me over in her mind.

And, I guess, a word should be spared for the misshapen, crippled figure they found on their doorstep.

My hair was long. Not like a lion and more like a mop.

Heavy bags hung under my eyes. I leant so heavily on my walking stick that a passer-by would think I was trying to stab it into the ground. I had aged more in the past few months than in all the years previously. On top of that I was wasting away from inaction.

Alfred said, "Well it if isn't the Lion of the East, Harald Fairhair himself', and he took my free hand in his own and shook it with such force I would have toppled were it not for Cat's quick reaction to hold me steady. "A real pleasure it is, my young sir, to come face to face with one of those living legends of our time." And he peered down the not insurmountable length of his nose. "Though I would say you appear more as an apparition than a Knight of History."

Margaret had taken up a position at her father's shoulder and was doing her own altogether too close inspection of my face. "I think he's diseased, father. His eyes are much too yellow." She took my hand from her father and subjected it to her own rough scrutiny. "His nails are spotted, too."

"Hmmm," her father said, and suddenly he had a magnifying glass out and I had my hand thrust into the air.

It would have continued that way where it not for the delicate clearing of Cat's throat.

Alfred looked at her with her puzzled expression, before tugging my hand even harder. "Of course, dear boy! It's been a long journey, and you're wishing to be off your feet."

I hobbled as best as I could alongside him, Margaret still matching me pace for pace, her inspecting eyes close to mine. Their house was four stories and decorated far more richly even than my father's castle. That being said – it wasn't exactly fashionable; the skulls of dead things on the walls; antique maps; reds and purples; leather chairs; and books, so many books that there was almost no wall space free.

They shepherded me into a dining room where cheeses and breads sat on small brown boards. I slumped down into one of the chairs with a heavy sigh.

Margaret perched on the table beside me, Alfred stood with his arms folded, and Cat sat in the chair opposite me and folded a little napkin upon her lap. "There is cheese, crackers and bread," she said. "I'm sure you're hungry."

"He's depressed," Margaret said suddenly. "And suffering from a whole host of vitamin deficiencies."

"I think you're right," Alfred said with a gentleness that brought my gaze towards the old professor. He took my hand in his own again, with less force than the first time. "In my house, Harald, you are safe. No harm shall befall you here."

I thanked him.

I ate what I could. My appetite came in spurts. Some hours I would feel sick at the sight of food. Other times I would eat everything and anything I could get my hands on.

Alfred watched me, Margaret looked bored, and Cat concerned herself with her own plate.

When I finished my crackers, Alfred nodded. "I have known Tytos for a great many years. We were students together, once. Whereas his path took him to bondage, then to money, mine has taken me the more boring route of academia. I am a professor here at the University of Erresea and it is with profound happiness that I can repay my old friend by taking you in and giving you what help I can in both yours and Tytos' noble goal."

"You want the end of the Heptarch?" I asked.

"A false democracy is worse than no democracy. Tytos is a good man – he would be a great leader."

I thought of the Heptarch, and of the King back home. "I don't believe there's any good leader. Why don't you support a true democracy?"

"Because I'm a realist. The Heptarch is meant to be democratically elected. He's been in post for twenty-two years. Before him, his father was in post for thirty-nine years. If the choice is between despot and despot, I choose the despot I know to be a better man.

I hesitated. "You said Tytos was in bondage."

"Indeed. And if he comes to power, I know he'll do his best to end Liriam's rampant slavery."

I nodded. I didn't know Tytos, but if he had ended my imprisonment, perhaps he could end the imprisonment of others as well.

Nevertheless, he would give me a chance to kill the Heptarch and that would be enough.

"And do you know why he sent me to you?" I asked.

The professor smiled and threw open his arms. "Because it is safe in Erresea. Because the sea air is good for you to heal. And because you can learn a lot here – information that will help you kill your draugr and take back your birthright."

A hunger awoke in my soul, like a living thing. "He would help me now, so I will help him later."

"You are a miraculous man, Harald Fairhair. Not many have lived the life that you have. He wants you by his side but knows that you have your own mission too."

"Now," he clapped his hands together, "the girls will show you to your room. You can take some time to relax. And remember, this house is now your home. You're safe here."

Cat rose soundlessly and beckoned me after her, Margaret loping after us both.

Even being in a house was unusual for me.

I had slept in bunks at Ines Hollith's house, in a tent, on a ship, in the wind, and in a prison cell. Not since I was an actual child in Lord Calforth's manor had there been a house that I thought of as my own.

"Your room is a mess," Cat said as we reached it. She glared at Margaret. "But I hope that you will find it comfortable at least."

The room *was* a mess. Instead of being cleaned, white blankets had been laid over unwanted objects. Behind the blankets were shelves of forgotten books, each one dusty and unused. A large bed dominated most of the room, and that at least had clean linen.

"You must rest," Cat said. "You may rejoin us in an hour for tea."

She nodded and swept from the room. Margaret leant against the wall, one leg bent. "Don't think less of Cat. She's a proper noble, especially with strangers. But she'll warm to you quick."

I shook my head. "I'm grateful for your hospitality." The words sounded strange out of my mouth. I wasn't used to being polite to strangers.

She smiled. "You look a lot wilder than I thought, but you still have manners that befit someone of your status."

I didn't have the effort to respond. Margaret sensed it and kicked off the wall. "See you at tea."

In that first week I moved through the professor's house like a ghost, the only signs of my passing their rapidly diminishing larder.

Unlike almost everyone else I'd ever met, they didn't really care about me. That's not to say they weren't kind to me, but since Lord Calforth, almost everyone I'd met had wanted something. I'd been a story or an object for so long.

In the professor's house, I was Harald. If I wanted to talk to anyone I could. If I didn't, they would leave me to my own devices.

It wasn't easy. I had lived my life always running down the path laid out for me by someone else. Now, I had a new life, but memories do not go away overnight.

Sometimes, my worries crept up on me at night, or when I sat in the conservatory and ate biscuits with Cat.

One place, far more tranquil than any others, kept the worries at bay. In the morning, I would sit in the garden with a blanket over my lap and a second one over my shoulders. My mobility hadn't improved much, but I could still read. When it rained, I would hide away in the conservatory. The pattering of the droplets on the glass put me to sleep.

Time passed, without me really noticing. Flowers unfurled into spring, as if my arrival had somehow heralded the bloom.

Cat would join me from time to time in the gardens. She had an encyclopaedic knowledge of the different wildlife. It reminded me of a different time, in Lord Calforth's gardens with Lot. Cat wouldn't say much but I could see in the small smile that would play across her lips that she was happy for company from someone who thought about more than academia.

It was on one of those quiet spring days, while I was sat in the conservatory eating buttered scones, that Margaret approached. She perched on the arm of the chair and raised a quizzical eyebrow.

"You've not seen the city yet." It was a statement, not a question. "This afternoon I'll show you the sights. We'll take a carriage."

When it turned noon, Margaret collected me from the conservatory.

The sights, it seemed, centred around one specific location in particular.

The university.

"This city," Margaret explained, "is three dimensional. There are the lower classes who spend most of their time on the docks, working in shipping. We're the largest port in all of Gora. Most of the fancy trinkets you see in Liriam come through Erresea at one point or another. There are the nobles, who live on The Hill, which is where all the most expensive manors are, and where the parliament building is. We have a Prince, but he's mostly just a functionary. The real decisions are made by the wealthy merchants and nobles elected to the House. And then, finally, the jewel of Erresea." The carriage pulled up and I hobbled out. "The University."

I'd never seen a university before, and though there are some within Ordrove, they pale in prestige to the University of Erresea.

If you do not know what the university was like to the city, then it is difficult to explain. The two were so closely linked that it was impossible to tell where one began and the other ended. Though you could mark the end of the library and how it towered like a grey brick fortress over the surrounding manor houses, the university spread throughout the entire city. Its teaching took place in bright rooms wherever they could find them; its students poured out in droves to drinking houses after their studying was done. There were, however, three central buildings to the university and it was to these that Margaret had brought me.

The library was the largest of the three. It didn't seem to end. Grey walls were punctured by wide windows cutting through its austere façade. Students sat on the steps to one entrance, but there were a number of potential entrances, doors both open and closed, and it was unclear where they led.

Morton House was the original housing block of the university and was ringed by green gardens. Though many other accommodation blocks both large and small had been built or co-opted from around the city, the original building was still in use. It was taller than the library, but not as all encompassing. The windows much smaller, and each of the small rooms filled with an assortment of keepsakes the noble-born students had brought from their significantly larger family homes.

The final building was the Chancellor's House. To say that it is a house is to do it a disservice. It was a complex of interlocking buildings, centred around a manor that wouldn't have looked out of place in the countryside surrounding the city. The centrepiece housed the Chancellor and was closed to the public, but the other buildings contained the offices and bunks of senior staff members who worked and lived at the University.

"What do you think of it?" Margaret asked with eager eyes.

"It's big."

"And?"

"And what?"

"It's the home of learning. Biggest centre of education in all Gora!"

"It's a lot of big buildings." I forced a laugh. "Is that whole building for books?"

"The library contains most of the accessible texts to the general students, but there are more, smaller libraries. Special collections presided over by the professors."

"More," I said. It seemed impossible. My father's library had felt impossibly big and it was no bigger than the length of a tall man across. A slow realisation came over me. "Are there answers to every question in those books?"

"Not every question, but a lot of them."

"Draugr. Is there anything about draugr?"

She squinted down the length of her nose and pushed back her glasses. "You are strange."

"Yes," I said. "Please answer my question."

"There's books about draugr."

"How do I get in?"

"You're not a member of the university."

I frowned at her. "But you are."

"And? I'm not allowed guests."

I shook my head. For the first time since arriving in Erresea my purpose from before my injury returned to me. I couldn't let it go. "How do I become a member of the university?"

"Aren't you a soldier?"

I puffed my chest. "I am Harald Fairhair, exiled lord, champion of the fighting Pits. I'm so much more than a soldier."

She nodded, taking a step back. I did the same, shocked by my own intensity. "I'm sorry," I said. "It's been a long time since I've been around friends."

She smiled weakly. "We're friends, are we?"

"I wouldn't really know. I've not had a huge amount."

She took my arm in hers. "We're friends." For a second she seemed almost graceful, before taking a long lunging step and pulling me with her. "Come. We've only just started exploring."

We walked until my leg threatened to give way under me. Margaret summoned a cart and we made our slow way back to the Professor's house. "I'm not much of a people person either," Margaret said, looking out towards the sea. "I didn't want you here at first, when the Professor said we were taking you in. But, you're an outcast too, whether you want to be or not. We might not be the same, but at least we're different in some of the same ways, and I think that's enough."

She smiled her big grin. "What do you think, *Lord Harald*?"

It was strange to me, talking to someone who wasn't the Lady Linial or Frisia. But I knew the hand of friendship that Margaret was extending was something I'd never really had, not since...I struggled to remember a time when I'd had a conversation like this.

"I think I'd like to just be a normal person," I said. "With normal friends."

"Well, I'm not a normal person, but I guess everything is more normal than waging a war to take away everything that I've ever loved, eh?" She raised her eyebrows. "We need to talk about that Crusade at some point, by the way. For research."

"Another time," I assured her.

And so ended the first of many days I spent with Margaret, rambling our way across the city.

Chapter Fourteen

Of course, there were bad days.

Days where I didn't leave my room. Where I sat in bed, pouring over the books Alfred had brought to me, skimming pages even though all joy of reading had gone. I told myself to stop. To get up. Walk around. Just get some fresh air.

But the Compulsion had hold of me.

It was impossible to ignore. The only thing that satiated me was the food the servants left at the foot of my bed; dates from far flung cities; chocolate from across the sea; crackers piled with the most foreign cheeses.

I knew it was bad for me. The reading and the food. I sat in bed and told myself that I had to do something differently, that this wasn't working.

But I didn't.

It was even worse in the night.

In the day, the professor's house reverberated with the noise of experiments and hard study. In the night, however, a very different atmosphere sat heavy over the house.

I found it difficult to sleep. My room was crowded with all sorts of alchemical instruments, covered with white blankets. Behind those stood bookshelves that seemed undusted since the beginning of time.

From all these old things came a weight of silence so tangible it seemed to weigh down on my chest. Those sleepless nights left me haggard and worn during the day; Margaret conducted her own experiments on what was wrong with me, and Cat watched me when she thought I wasn't looking. But there was no answer. No physical one, at least.

It wasn't the house, or the night. It was my own tired thoughts.

But as I lay awake, I began to notice something. A quiet sound, every night, between the hours of one and two. Soft footsteps in the hallway.

At first, I lay in bed in terror, convinced that the Heptarch's spies had come. But soon my worry turned into curiosity, and I lay with my covers pulled up to wide eyes, straining for any noise.

It was definitely footsteps, and they were certainly furtive, almost no noise but the barest touch of fabric on cold tiles.

I tried following the sound of footsteps, but each night I left my bed to wait at the foot of the staircase the footsteps did not come.

It was why, one morning over breakfast, I broached the subjects of ghosts with the professor.

He laughed at me. "Ghosts, my dear boy, are nothing but the invention of tormented writers."

"But I've seen things worse than ghosts. The draugr..."

"The draugr is a vengeful spirit, true, but a tangible one. Born again to torment you and any others he's been wronged by. He's not an intangible, walk through walls, make soft footsteps just to annoy you kind of ghost. I fancy that draugr and yourself are bound. As long as you live, so does it."

"Could this ghost not be the same? A real spirit. A draugr."

"My boy, I think you'll find that before you jump to the conclusion of draugr's and ghosts, you should consider the very real people around you."

"You're saying it's one of the girls?"

"I'm saying that you shouldn't jump to conclusions. As far as I'm aware draugr's are rarer than finding a gold piece lying on the floor. Our souls are claimed by the Gods, whether we want them to be taken or not. Of course, understanding of the afterlife is one of the key topics studied, and the scientists who do so come to understand more with each passing year. Why, in a hundred years' time I'm sure they'll look back at our viewpoint as horrendously flawed – perhaps they'll have done away with the Gods themselves then." He laughed to himself. "Who knows. The only thing I know, is that this house is not haunted. And I have two wonderful young women under my roof who I don't ask too many questions of – so long as they keep their heads fixed on the straight and narrow."

With the professor's suggestion in mind, I thought about talking to one of them. And yet...

They did not want to be disturbed. Else why would they sneak out at night. And what I was doing – it was wrong in a lot of ways. I shouldn't have been curious, but I couldn't shake the paranoia. What if one of them was an agent of the Heptarch? What if they snuck away to plan my imprisonment?

I had to find out.

It was almost a month until I heard the footsteps again. My sleeping had not improved, though my leg was making a slow recovery. I had begun to walk unaided, though my way was slow and lumbering. Cat quipped that I looked like a scarecrow that had just come alive. Though I didn't like the image, I couldn't help but think she was right. My belly was soft. My hair seemed to stick up uncontrollably at odd angles (I blamed the sea salt). And worst of all, my walk made me feel less than a man, as if I really was stuffed full of straw, with no better purpose than to chase away the crows.

My relationship with the professor had only improved. I had nothing bad to say about him, apart from the fact he was always busy. He'd promised me he would try and secure me access to the library as well, so I questioned him when I could find him, and he would assure me that he was working on it.

Margaret continued to try and pull me out of bed and into the city, but for her, her studies took precedence, and the Professor kept her with him most days to help with his experiments.

Cat, meanwhile, was a ghost as much as I was. I wouldn't say we had become friends in the same way that Margaret and I had. But we exchanged kindnesses, polite nods on the way to and fro the kitchen. She would sometimes make witty remarks that could have been directed at me, but where always directed instead at some opposite point of the room. She seemed to have no trouble expressing herself around the others, who she chastised for being slovenly or tardy. With myself, she remained stiff and cold, even in our quiet moments in the gardens.

Her jibe to me that morning about being a scarecrow had come as a minor success. She'd made it directly to me, and not at the cupboards, or the tablecloth.

The day drew on. My morning's good cheer left. I clambered back into bed.

On that night, I lay awake, facing the ceiling, trying to dream of Lot. Instead, my mind conjured dark images – death and destruction, the worst possible scenarios.

And then I heard it. A soft pattering on the staircase.

This time I was ready.

Like a rusty spring I unfurled and staggered to the doorway.

The footsteps had fallen silent by the time I reached the doorway, but I followed where I thought they were going, down the steps and into the pantry. I arrived in time to see a head of black hair disappearing down a hole in the floor. As suddenly as it was there, it was gone, closing softly behind whoever had opened it.

I wandered over to the spot in the pantry. It was where bags of potatoes and other sacks of vegetables were stored. The handle of the trap door in the floor was covered in flour.

Now, I was curious, but I wasn't a fool.

I turned and went back to bed. Why? Because I didn't back myself against whatever spy the Heptarch had sent. A quick flash of a blade in the dark and that would be it. Cold steel sliding between my flabby skin, hot blood spilling into the shadows of the underground.

The professor wouldn't find me for days, until the kitchen started smelling.

Though one thought held me. The professor had warned me off chasing the figure. Had hinted it could have been one of the girls. But what if it was him who was the spy, who was granting the Heptarch entry to his house? What if the Heptarch wasn't even involved and the spy was here to report on me, and carry my indolence back to Tytos, to inform him of the failure of his project. Then I would be kicked out onto the street. My purpose lost. Pathetic.

Pathetic.

This was the word I repeated over and over again as I tried to sleep.

My paranoia was a weakness. My body was a weakness. My restless mind was a weakness.

Pathetic. Pathetic Pathetic.

It was on one of those lonely nights where I finally fought off the existential dread and slept, then behold, in my dreams a face both familiar and forgotten.

She was much older than I last saw her. She was both more beautiful and less. The childish innocence and soft cheeks had been replaced by lean muscle and lines of worry.

Still, my heart ached to see her.

"Lot," I said, though no words came out of my mouth, and she did not hear me.

She slept on a pallet of hard wood, her hands folded across her chest like a saint. The world around her seemed to fade into nothingness. She slept on a pallet bed, and the only thing of note was a candle on a dresser at the end of it. Beyond, was an impenetrable nothing that twisted and turned like smoke – no walls, no door, it was as if she was suspended on the bed in absolute nothingness.

Even as I watched, she rolled over. Her foot caught on the candle, tipping it over. The flames caught life on the sheet.

I darted forward before the flames could spread. I had nothing else, so I beat the flames with my own hands.

When I looked up, I found Lot sitting up, still against the inky blackness. Her eyes were wide, as if she had seen a ghost.

She said something, but I could not hear it, and as I reached for her, I found myself reaching up at my distant ceiling instead.

Lot was gone.

I heard the footsteps again. I waited a little while before following.

I'd mustered my courage. I was Harald Lionheart. Working knee or not, I wouldn't behave like a frightened child any longer.

I pulled open the trap door and looked into the darkness below.

Leaning heavily on my arms, I lowered myself down. It wasn't much of a drop and I managed to brace myself on my stick.

I descended through the tunnels, one unsteady foot after another. The smooth walls of the house soon gave way to subterranean rock slick with water. Both grip and step became slippery. And in the distance, I could hear the rumble of the sea upon rocks.

After a while, I began to smell the sea too. The sharp salty odour of dried seaweed and coarse sand. The tunnel began to enlarge. At first, I was aware of it by the sudden echoing sound my footsteps made, but soon enough a pale light began to illuminate what lay beyond.

And, as I rounded a corner, I was suddenly staring at the night sky. The rock gave way, forming a picture frame of black crags, looking out onto the sky and the bottomless sea.

In the corner of that frame of sky, sat a small figure with their knees pressed up to their chest.

"You could hear that shuffling gait of yours miles away," Cat said, not turning to look.

Before I could reach her, I had to make my way through a wide chamber with deep, pale pools of water that occupied most of the room. Torches had been lit in the corners of the room, giving some light that scattered and flickered across the chamber.

I said nothing as I approached, but hesitated a few steps from her, my anxieties turning to shame. I had followed her into this hidden chamber thinking she was a spy. Instead, she was just Cat, the same Cat who wouldn't look at me across the dinner table.

"Are you offended by me?" she said. "I think most people are." She gave a sharp laugh. "Why did you follow me?"

I hesitated. "Do you want the real reason?"

"I wouldn't have asked otherwise."

"I thought you were a spy."

She laughed, but it quickly dried up. "How could I be a spy? I've lived here far longer than you."

"I didn't know it was you."

"And what would you have done if I was a spy? Thrown me down onto the cliffs below? Flexed your big manly muscles."

It was too much. The tears came without me even noticing, but once they came, they wouldn't stop.

Cat was by my side in a second and her eyes held mine, even as I sobbed. "I'm sorry," she said. "I'm sorry. I just push everyone away."

"It's not you," I managed to croak between breathless sobs. "I'm just useless."

The last lines dropped from her narrow face and she wrapped her arms around me. "Gods, we're a mess, aren't we?" And I realised she had her own streaks of tears on her cheeks.

Eventually my tears subsided and so did hers.

We sat on the edge of the outcrop and looked out over the sea.

"I come here because you can't see anything but the sea. No people. No city. Just the water and the remains of what was washed away."

"It's beautiful."

"The pools behind us are warm too. This used to be a smugglers path to the sea, before the steps over the edge crumbled. Then it became a meeting spot for lords and their lovers, then a band of thieves. Then someone decided to build piping from the houses above down here – the pools aren't natural anymore, they're filled by warm spring water, but no-one really uses them."

I nodded, but I couldn't take it in. I'd let myself grow out of control. With so many years hiding my feelings, or suppressing them in service to Ines Hollith, I had no ability to control myself any more without the fear of someone else punishing me.

I told Cat as much, and she took my hand in her own. "It's not easy to live," she said. "Especially not for yourself. But you don't always have to live in fear. Live for something good. Live for Margaret. Live for me."

She smiled at me and I almost lost control again. Instead, I asked why she had been crying.

"Because I'm a stupid girl trying to be something I'm not." She took a deep breath. "I pretend I'm this noble woman, but what's noble about me anymore?"

"What do you mean?"

"The reason I live with the professor is because my parents died when I was younger, and our estates were taken by debtors. My family's name is mud. My family's old friends refuse to even acknowledge my existence on The Hill."

"I'm sorry."

"A minor tragedy," she said, trying to brush away new tears.

"Does the professor feel like your father?"

She shrugged. "I don't know. What's a father meant to feel like? I assume he'd be a big bear of a man, funniest in the room. He'd be clever and he'd look after me. I guess the professor is like most of those things, but I don't know what it's meant to feel like. I love him. And Margaret. But sometimes I feel like a creature that's just crawled from the sea compared to them."

"He loves you," I said. "And you love him. That's what's matters."

"Then why do I feel like this?" She bit down on her lip.

I opened my mouth to speak, then closed it again. What could I say? With my family history?

"You're an orphan too," Cat said. "I'm sorry, I forgot."

"I'm better off an orphan."

A guarded expression came over Cat's face. "But imagine if you still had your family. None of this would ever have happened. You'd still be at home."

I thought for a long second. Remembered that my father was about to ship me to live with Lord Calforth anyway. What would have become of me? I would never have known Lot. Maybe Gabriel would have killed her alongside Granny and Tava. Maybe Gabriel and I would have been friends...

"I've walked this path," I said. "It's been so hard. And I've spent every night wishing I was somewhere else. But now you've asked me this – I wouldn't change it. I'd change some things. But I've come this goddamn far, seen the truth of people, of places and things, that all I can do is go forward." My words lifted me like the wind lifts a sail and I stood to look out over the sea.

Beyond lay that long harbour, and beyond that the ruins of the sunken land beyond. No-one knew its name or how it had been sunken, but the raised hands of giant statues could be seen poking through the surface of the water. Below, was an entire civilization; houses and bones eroded by the tide.

It put my struggles into perspective.

"I will get better," I said. "And one day I'll bring evil to trial. I will destroy this world order that leaves you crying – for what? You're smarter than me. You're prettier than almost anyone. You're witty and you *care.* And you're still sad and crying and that's just not *fair.* So, I'll make this better."

The wind puffed out of my sails. I looked at Cat, who looked back with a half-smirk on her face. "You'll do all that?"

I nodded.

She shook her head. "I think you're crazy. You can't change the world. But you can have a drink with me. How about it?"

I nodded. "A drink is a good way to start."

Over the next few weeks, the sadness started to go away. It didn't leave me at once, like an expelled breath. Rather, it was as if piece by piece it chipped away, leaving some purer form of myself.

A large part of that was due to Cat.

We started off by walking. We'd both felt like outsiders enough in our lives to be uncomfortable always talking. But long walks into the tall trees and farmland surrounding Erresea began to heal us both. My knee tired from doing it, but each time I went out with her I felt stronger, fitter. I wasn't the same as I had been before my injury – and I didn't know if I ever would be – but as I walked I told myself that every step would make me stronger, each inhalation of that warm air would make me happier, and each piece of quiet conversation would heal my loss.

And yet.

The dread returned, in the dark of the night and lingered into the morning. I woke sweating and screaming. I woke in absolute stillness, frozen with terror.

For every good week there was a bad one.

I spent days where the only thing that really woke me up was the sound of Cat's voice as she stood like a wraith in the corner of the room.

"This isn't you, Harald. Remember. You have never let anything beat you."

"Nothing's beaten me. Anyway, what does it matter? I've done my piece."

"Are you satisfied, Harald?" she said softly, and I found myself damning her, because she was right and I would never be satisfied. Not until I'd killed the draugr, found Lot, and got my revenge on Gabriel. Certainly not lying in bed.

This was a lesson she had to teach me every few days.

It wasn't that I didn't remember it; it was just that I couldn't stop it. I was powerless as the sand is to the waves.

Sometimes, I would shout at her.

"You're not my mother," I bellowed from beneath the blankets.

"No, I'm not. And you're not a child, Harald. You've led armies."

I barked a laugh. "I failed everyone. I was a child playing at war."

"You've been used, Harald. It's normal to feel like this. You've not been able to make your own choices. Now you have to, and it's hard to know what to do."

And it was hard. There is a fortitude to live an everyday life that is beyond me. It's easier to walk a predestined path, no matter the weight of the expectation on your shoulder. When there is external pressure keeping you going, you can keep going. When there is just yourself, it's so easy to flounder, to fail...

And so my life was caught between these two counterpoints. Sunny walks over green hills. The sea breeze brushing over the sand. Forest lakes hidden between tall rocks. The cold, dark quiet. The dusty bedroom. The tightness in my chest.

But I will not wallow in my darkest moments, as sure as I didn't wallow too long in them even in that bed. Days were lost, but not a lifetime.

On we go, to drinking, foolishness, and the making of lifelong friends.

Sailors and students are the antithesis of one another. One life given to the open expanse, to the hard labour of the every day. The other is given to book filled rooms, hemmed in by the pressure of knowledge. By the insular communities whereby self-worth is determined.

And yet, they are joined by one inseparable love.

Drinking.

Margaret once boasted that Erresea contained the most drinking establishments of all of Gora's great cities. By her reckoning – and she insisted she had counted them personally – there was one for every single day of the year.

So, ever so slowly, the three of us began to spend our evenings in these drinking houses.

It had started with us drinking on a small table in the kitchen, but we were conscious of our noise and the professor's important work.

We flitted from pub to pub, like fireflies in the night

Despite Cat's class snobbery, she seemed at home in the dockside bars in a way she wasn't in her own house. She'd drink us into the ground, better than any sailor could.

"Where'd you learn to drink like that?" I asked her one evening, the three of us sitting round a table while dusk spread across the sky.

"When I was twelve," Cat began.

"Twelve!" Margaret repeated incredulously.

"When I was twelve," Cat continued, as if she had never spoken. "I was brought to the Professor's house. Margaret," she said slyly, "was a gangly, unfortunate child who never looked up from her books. It was terribly lonely, and no-one paid much attention to me. So, what was a girl meant to do but drink?"

"Twelve," Margaret repeated. "You did always seem like you had something a little weird about you. Like you weren't always all there. I thought it was just what noble ladies were like."

"No, it was the whiskey. And the scotch. And the rum."

I smiled. "First time I drank, I couldn't have been older than six. My dad forced me to drink a whole tankard of beer. I threw up so hard I never touched the stuff again until I was..." It struck me suddenly that I hadn't drank another drop of alcohol in my family's castle. "Until I was a lot older," I finished weakly.

"Well," Margaret said. "I can see I'm in the company of scoundrels and rogues."

Cat's eyes flashed darkly. "You have no idea."

"Oh really?"

"Really."

I pushed Cat gently on the shoulder. "You can't tease us."

She bit her lip. "I can tease anyone." She relented with an evil smirk. "Fine. Have you ever stolen anything?"

Margaret's eyebrows rose so high they vanished into her hairline. "You're a thief!"

She looked at me. "Surely you're no paragon of virtue."

I shrugged. "I don't think I've ever stolen."

"Just murder then for you. Not the heavier crimes."

"I don't like having to carry my crimes."

"Only mentally," Cat quipped.

"Gods!" Margaret said. "This is too heavy for my first drink. Come. Tell us of how you're a master thief, Catelyn."

Cat scowled at the use of her full name. "When my parents first died, I was passed around from house to house. Some of the people I stayed with – they meant well, but they were only after my family's money. When it became apparent that there was no money, I started being passed around more frequently. Every day would be another house."

"I hated them. I couldn't understand what was happening. So, I started stealing. I'd take their things, but I wouldn't keep them. I'd bury them in the gardens or throw them in a pond. A family signet ring. Gone. A precious gemstone necklace. Gone. The original Tytbetian Histories. Gone."

Margaret gasped. "You monster."

Cat shrugged. "I was a child. And a mistreated child at that. Still, I didn't stop there. I stole from the professor at first. Then when I realised, he was actually looking out for me, I began to steal from some of the other noble families we'd have dinner with. I'd bring the professor books that I thought he would like. It took him a while to ask the question of where the books had come from – he's always been wonderfully blind to reality. When he did, he made me apologise and return every single one. And that was the end of my juvenile career as a thief."

"I never knew," Margaret said.

"You were always absorbed in the professor's work. You weren't exactly the most social of children. Age has done you good."

I shook my head. "Do you steal still?"

Cat smiled slyly. "Only men's hearts."

At that Margaret laughed, too loudly. "Sorry," she said.

Cat scowled. "I get the point."

"Sorry," Margaret said again.

I took that as the perfect moment to stand. "More drinks?"

"Of course," they responded in unison.

When the professor finally secured my access to the library, I made it my new home.

Like most students, I alternated between those nights of drinking with Margaret and Cat, and the hard work of reading and note taking. Unlike most students, I wasn't studying for any exam. I was studying for revenge.

It might amuse you to know that with the gargantuan library at my fingertips, I didn't reach straight for the answers. I tried to. But I got side-tracked, caught up in what some call 'commercial fiction'. The long, often derided novels, dedicated to romance and revenge. And, as much as anything, they soothed me.

This isn't a book recommendation. I won't waste time on telling you of my favourites, of drama on the high sea and lovers separated each night at dusk. I will only say that there were many books about revenge. Most were simplistic, overblown, with kind-hearted protagonists and simple decisions leading to their eventual glory. Still, I loved them truer than I had loved any piece of literature. I could see myself in them. Nothing can do that like books. Nowhere else are you so thoroughly inside of someone's head – no matter how reprehensible or lovable they may be, they are your companions, your friends.

More than that – they are your guides.

And – without trying to sound like an arse – those books taught me how to talk and even think like a normal person again. I wasn't, mind. I never could be normal after all the shit I'd gone through. But I could pretend for a while, and those books allowed me to live that pretence.

It wasn't long, however, before I moved onto the serious business of my own revenge.

I'd already found my emotional salvation in books – I thought my actual salvation might come soon afterwards.

But it wasn't so easy.

Draugr have been a topic of literary discussion for going on a thousand years. However, two issues plagued me.

One. The majority of literature on draugr was written by residents of Erresea and other far-flung provinces near the Golden City. This presented one significant issue. Most of them were writing on hearsay and the facts of other writers, because the only ever recorded draugr sightings from even semi-reputable sources had occurred on my home island, and therefore were treated with scepticism.

Two. The literature – what little literature there actually was, for authors evidently didn't find draugr as exciting as say 'the taxation of the Hemelin Empire' – was primarily based on the assumption draugr were not, in fact, real.

Most authors spent their time debunking as opposed to examining the truth of draugr. Draugr were described as homeless men in the wilderness, practical jokers, or enemy clans seeking to drive their competitors away from fertile land.

At first these accounts frustrated me. I threw a particular arsehole of an author across the room. I had seen the draugr myself. He dogged me in my dreams. He was real.

But the sheer weight of the literature began to get to me.

I realised I had never actually seen the draugr. Only the corpses of my family and his dug-up corpse.

Could he have been framed? Who would go to such a length? Who would do that kind of a thing?

And my dreams?

The authors dismissed dreams mostly as the riot of emotions you couldn't bear to face during the day. A way to cope, rather than reality.

I spent several nights with Cat, drinking, pondering this issue.

"He has to be real," I said, more than slightly tipsy. "If he's not real, I've been living a lie."

"You've seen him in your dreams," Cat said. "Dreams are powerful. The nobles say the Gods speak to us through our dreams."

"The professors say our dreams are just a bunch of phallic innuendos, or stress release, or both."

"My dreams contain their fair share of phallic innuendos, but that doesn't make them any less real. It's more about my future."

"Your future contains phallic innuendos?"

"Less innuendos."

"Ah. I see." I took a shot of strong liquor. "This was a serious conversation."

"Was being the prerogative word."

"You're an arsehole."

"I'm your favourite arsehole," Cat said and grinned. "Now, your glass appears to be empty."

As such my fears were allayed in much the same way fears usually are. By making light of them until you forget.

Eventually I started feeling normal again.

And so, I searched deeper in that library, until I began to find what I was looking for.

Chapter Fifteen

"Run, Harald," Margaret said.

I ran.

"Now, turn."

I turned.

"And run back."

I looked at her with hatred in my eyes. Then began to run.

"Good," Margaret said. "You're making progress."

"I'm not good enough," I said between breaths. "I used to be able to run for miles."

"You are running on sand," Margaret said matter of factly. "And you have been injured. It will take time."

My entire leg ached. I felt pain in places I didn't even realise had a muscle – down the back of my upper leg, across the length of my shin. I wanted to collapse into the sand and pretend that I was nothing.

I looked at Margaret out of the corner of my eye.

"Again?" she said.

I nodded. "Again."

What had started as quiet walks across the beach had slowly turned into something else. Margaret enjoyed it. She made notes in her writing pads and otherwise enjoyed the sun and the sand.

She pushed me, like good friends do.

In turn, I pushed her.

When I arrived at the Professor's house, she'd told me that she hadn't set foot in the water since she was a child. I soon remedied that and together we ran headfirst into the water, much to the amazement of the other beachgoers.

This had become our routine, after which we would both go to the university.

From what I understood, Margaret was something of a prodigy. The university was not always kind to women; they struggled to find themselves in the highest ranks and highest paid positions, and often as not those positions went to lesser men instead.

This I learned from Margaret. However, some of the students upon seeing me with Margaret began to educate me on her own particular talents.

"A genius," one said earnestly.

"I've heard she's never dropped a single mark in a test."

"I've heard they've already offered her a doctorate."

The rumours grew even more outlandish daily. Nobody really understood what she was researching, though the general consensus was that it was one of the sciences. Which one, however, was the cause of much debate.

I asked her one day, while we ate lunch on the grass outside of the library.

"I study the stars," she said simply. "I think they're related to the Gods. We've had tangential proof in the past, but if our telescopes become strong enough, I believe we'll be able to see into the worlds of the Gods themselves."

"There's a lot of stars," I said.

"There's a lot of Gods."

"That's more than I've ever seen, even in Churches of the Golden City."

She nodded. "That's because there were more Gods, once. All throughout history. But as those Gods retreat, newer ones take their place. The sons and daughters of those who came before. Take your God, for example. After the theft from His Garden, your priests teach that he retreated into the Mountain, and turned his back on all humanity. That's why you must cleanse the planet – so he can return. But what if he doesn't need to come back, because he already has a home? But not some remote mountain. Up there."

She pointed towards the clear sky.

"Does it matter?" I asked, which I knew was the wrong question as soon as it left my lips.

"Does it matter? Does it matter? It could change everything. Tangible heavens. Think what we could do! Communicate with them. Potentially even fly up to them!"

"What do priests do, if not communicate with their Gods?"

"Priests wave their hands about and pretend they know where their magic is coming from. They're blessed, yes, but only the lucky and most devout have ever spoken to a real

God. We could all speak to them. We could understand them. Ask them for help."

"We do all those things now. They just don't listen."

"Then we could compel them. Find old Gods. Better Gods. The possibilities are limitless."

I shook my head. I've always hated things I can't see. "What about the Beast? If you wanted to, you could speak to him right now?"

"The Beast isn't a God," she said. "The Beast is...well, it's not clear what he is. Some corrupted monster. Something escaped from the stars maybe, or from some hell in the depths of the sea. He's interesting, obviously, but not a God in the way other Gods are Gods."

"Your father believes in him."

"I know. We've debated this opinion often enough."

"Why does he believe, and you don't?"

"Because if the Beast is a God, he is the only God who has meddled directly in human affairs since recorded history began. Because he is monstrous, and the last time he was released, his wars almost destroyed the entire world. And because when it came time for him to be chained, it was an army of priests who stopped him, not armed with weapons but with prayer. Their words chained him, became tangible chains. They laid the groundwork for his prison beneath the Golden City. They prayed and the Gods answered and *bound* the Beast. What God would be the enemy of them all?"

"Then why does your father believe?"

"Ask him."

"He won't tell me. I've tried."

She was silent for a long moment. "Because priests tell you they have power. Because they tell you it was because you prayed that your broken bone set perfectly. But the followers of the Beast don't tell you they have power – they have power. Legitimate power derived from his touch. There's been studies on it. The Beast can bestow the power to walk unseen, to steal another's voice, to force an action. But are they not the powers of treachery?" She shook her head. "Still, my father believes that God has walked amongst us. The God. And we have chained Him and pretended these images and idols that we have created are more important and greater than He."

I shook my head. "I hate religion."

"Weren't you the champion of your entire faith?"

"And look where that got me."

Margaret looked around. "Eating a perfectly nice lunch on a lawn outside of the University."

I sighed. "The Beast has plans for me. I just tend not to trust things that look like giant serpents."

Margaret nodded. "Remember, there is a reason for that. Your entire culture and upbringing has been telling you that giant serpents are the very sign of evil. That the Beast is worthy of sacking an entire city if you could kill it."

"I know. But you should see it. I don't think it can help trying to manipulate people. It didn't seem the most morally pure of beings."

"Neither are humans. I can't imagine a human chained underground for thousands of years wouldn't be trying to manipulate its way out of there either."

"I thought you said you didn't believe in the Beast. You do make a lot of excuses for it."

"I do not believe in the Beast. But that doesn't mean I am entirely closed off to it as a concept. We're not all sword swinging barbarians who think the world can be solved by stabbing the Beast in the face. The world hasn't been perfect with the Beast being chained up. I don't see why killing it would change that."

"I'm sure the theologians have an answer."

"Probably. They always have answers. If there's one thing that I've learnt at this university is that for every answer there's a dozen more questions. And besides, the answer is probably wrong, and someone will find a better answer in fifty years."

I laughed. "You can disprove your father's theories then."

"I'd already disproved half of them by the time I was 12. Anyway." She stood. "You have distracted me from real questions with this hot-blooded discussion of religion. I'll see you at the pub later?"

"Always."

I was working late in the library one evening when Margaret came to me.

"I've found something," she said. "In Manuscripts."

I followed her down into Manuscripts. It was a cold, dark place, buried deep at the bottom of the library. Very few people worked in Manuscripts, but you could see the few who did with small lanterns like enclaves in the darkness.

It felt like being underwater. There was a muted quiet even to our footsteps and nobody spoke above a whisper.

Margaret already had the manuscript out on her desk, spread out on a specific page.

I rushed over to it, taking her chair. Illuminated in brilliant gold and grey ink was a picture of a draugr, mouth open wide, scrawny body shambling forward.

The text was written in an archaic version of my own language. Margaret put a hand on my shoulder and leant in close. "The writer is called Harald Tibius, born to a mother from your isle and a father from mine. He wrote around eight hundred years ago – mainly a military scholar focused the Second Crusade."

It was difficult to decipher each word. They looked the same, but different. I mouthed each one as I tried to turn the archaic letters into modern words.

The draugr is a strange phenomena, located mainly upon the Ordovian Isles. Records of draugr on the isles are kept predominantly by village chiefs who keep a handful of folk remedies for the affliction within their houses. What is apparent to me is that draugr do exist. I have not seen one myself, but I arrived at a village only two weeks after one had been apprehended and burnt – all the villagers told the same story. A man risen from a grave to wreak havoc and torment others, imbued with supernatural powers.

Why do these creatures exist? I can't give a categorical answer. They existed before the Beast came to these shores. I have no doubt they will exist long after we have slain it. Draugr seem to be the dead who will not go to God upon the Mountain. They do not make the journey to his garden, for whatever reason. They exist in a limbo, neither dead nor alive. Trapped between worlds, between time and space. I have heard records say they walk out from our world, in the space between stars. That is why they cannot always be found, and why they are so difficult to catch.

I do not know how much I believe those stories. I believe I have found evidence to suggest that draugr are more likely to occur in the area from Thistledown to Longhorn Peak.

I stopped abruptly. "Longhorn Peak is the old name for the mountain beside my father's castle."

"Keep reading," Margaret urged.

The draugr in this area appear to have caused the most damage. Marg the Red set two villages afire. A farmer called Drumond killed the son of a local merchant. A brigand known simply as Coin reportedly lived in the wilderness for almost twenty years – waiting for the return of his band of thieves, until Coin was set upon and executed by some of the King's own men.

For what reason this area is significant is uncertain. My own research is filled with folk tales and old stories. King's blood was spilt here. God himself blessed the land. Some of the thieves of his Garden were hunted and killed here. Whatever the reason, there are certain requirements that cause draugr and remedies which seemed to prevent their return.

Unfinished business is the most prominent of them. Revenge or bitterness is a common reason cited by the village chiefs. However, a surprising theme amongst reported draugr is that they are in fact more likely to be Godly people. They are more likely to be men than women. They always seemed to be tied temporally to a specific patch of land – in fact, land disputes were the most common form of reason noted in Jon Palm's Big Book (a village chief in Thistledown).

To prevent draugr, the village chiefs each have their own remedies. It is not clear whether any of them work. Confession is the most prominent. Those who are to be executed or on death's doorway are brought to priests to confess their sins. The second most prominent is the burial. Burials must be deep – between eight and sixteen feet depending on which part of the world you are in. Some contend that the buried must be buried with some sign of God, some contend that burial must occur with an ash or rowan branch, on account of those being some of the trees stolen from God's Garden. Others include the grotesque chopping up of potential draugr, the bizarre, stuffing flowers in the mouth of the dead, or the practical binding of the ankles and arms with rope.

Killing a draugr seems less difficult than preventing their return. Finding them presents the largest difficulty. They are tied to where they were executed and seem to be unable to stray far from that spot. However, they do not always appear to exist in this world. The earlier rumour about walking between worlds is one such explanation. Others suggest that they walk in men's dreams when they cannot walk in the world around them. Either way, once found, draugr's are blessed with dreadful powers. Supernatural speed and strength are one such boon. Some say they can see in the dark. Others can walk without making a noise. There are a number of powers listed to them – but only one other that is important. Foresight. Draugr are reported to have visions of the future. They have seen what is to come, though often not fully.

The Mystic Triga who worked out of the King's own city was only revealed to be a draugr twenty years into her business. She had told the future of a number of individuals, including the Crown Prince. She was only unveiled when a young man came to her – the son of her first-time killer, and she ate him alive. Triga was afterwards executed on the authority of the King.

To finally kill them, then, they must be bound, and their heart cut out. Only then will they rest. I asked Jon Palm why this wasn't done before death – his response was that it had been done in my own childhood, but that the dead who had their heart cut out before death seemed more likely to become draugr, returning and placing the heart of another in their chest instead. Such practice quickly fell out of fashion.

Draugr remain a deadly phenomenon which, thanks to the diligent work of local village chiefs, are starting to become rarer and rarer. Jon Palm estimates that based on the reports in his Big Book, draugr will be extinct within the next two hundred years.

I sat back in the chair. I faced the darkness above, beyond the circle of lantern light.

"Obviously it's just one account," Margaret began, but I cut her off.

"It's the truth," I said. "I must cut out his heart."

"If what Harald Tibius writes is true, then they are more than dangerous. You will need help."

I shook my head. "I don't need help. This is one fight I will not lose."

Margaret squeezed my shoulder. "We'll make sure you're ready."

I nodded and rose. The world seemed suddenly too bright; too dark. Margaret sensed it for she stepped close and wrapped an arm around my waist, so I did not fall.

"It's a lot," she said. "It's a lot to take in."

I nodded and let her guide me from Manuscripts and back towards the main chambers of the library. We sat down together on a bench near the entrance. She waited for me to speak.

"I've wondered whether I was crazy for a long time."

"There's no such thing as crazy. If you've spoken to the physicians at the...I just realised you're speaking figuratively, continue."

"I just thought I was wrong. That something was messed up inside of me. But what he wrote. My namesake. They're what I've felt. The draugr does walk between dreams. It was over land disputes. And he must have been supernaturally gifted – my family were brilliant swordsmen. And it makes sense – if draugr are stronger near my own castle then it would make sense that he was particularly dangerous. I just...I never thought I would finally have answers."

"You have answers," Margaret said. "And you have friends who will help you plan. You will have your revenge."

I nodded. "God, I need a drink."

Chapter Sixteen

I'm not naturally inclined to liking people.

Blame my brothers. Living with the worst of humanity can have a lasting effect.

I've found it easier with women. I'm sure there's probably lots of theories – some savoury and some less savoury – on why that's the case.

I only know that when I see men, I see my brother, or Gabriel.

When I see women – there's the dream of my mother, and the anger of my foster mother, but both of those interactions were far removed. And then from Lot through to Frisia, the women in my life have treated me well.

And so, it's with some trepidation that I come to *him*.

A good man. Guileless. Honest.

Still, I did try to stab him.

Dockside bars were our favourite to drink in on account of the music, the atmosphere, and the waves. I liked the Shield and Sword, Margaret the Jagged Tooth, but it was Cat's favourite bar that we had ended up in – the Royal Waves.

It had a fiddler, red haired and handsome as a devil. It had a crowded taproom of fishermen and sailors, each one salty and loud. It had a view of the waves by lamplight, illuminating the rainfall outside.

As had become habit, we huddled together on stools, already two pints in. Margaret laid her cards on the table. "Sweep."

We played cards with the small allowance that the professor gave us. Cat was the best, unsurprisingly. Margaret counted the cards but didn't have the same knack for reading people as Cat did. I was the worst.

I shook my head as Margaret cleaned another row. "I need another drink."

"I'll take my earnings now," Margaret said. "A nice pint of ale."

I grunted my agreement.

I was still using my walking stick, though I didn't need it. Having it beside me meant that I could tell people that I was still recovering, that I had been injured. I wasn't better yet, and I wasn't ready to admit that I might never reach the level of fitness I once held. It was an excuse, and one I wasn't ready to let go yet.

I gestured to the bartender; he knew my order already.

Leaning against the bar, I surveyed the taproom. It was a busier night than usual. Most tables full, and several sailors lounging against the bar.

And one other, staring at me.

He was a young man, flushed red from drink. He was round of face, but square of body, built much like the sailors he stood next to.

"What do you want?" I growled.

"Are you Harald Fairhair?" the man said.

I turned away. I'd honestly expected more admirers than I'd had, but that didn't mean I had any patience for them. "I'm not interested in talking about the Pits."

"I don't care about the Pits," the young man said. "I remember you, you see. I was just a child back then."

I turned back to look at the boy. "You're still a child." I measured him. He was dressed cheaply and wore a short dagger at his waist. I didn't recognise him.

"I was more of a child," he said. "I always thought it was very tragic, what happened. I spoke in your defence, if you remember. Do you remember?"

I looked at him harder. I had never laid eyes on the boy before in my life, I would have sworn.

His guileless blue eyes looked back at me.

"You're the bloody prince of Ordrove," I said. I had his knife in my hand before I'd even finished my sentence.

His eyes grew even wider, until they threatened to engulf his whole face. He punched me.

I fell backwards, knife clattering away onto the floor.

I looked back at the prince, just in time to see a sailor clatter him from behind and send him crashing down alongside me.

I scrabbled for the knife. The prince scrabbled for me, grabbing my good leg. I kicked him off and had the knife in hand.

Above, the sailors fought. Who? Each other, I guess.

"I don't want to hurt you," the prince shouted.

"As if you could bloody hurt me," I shouted back.

I had the knife, but the prince was on top of me. He was heavy and strong and pinned my hands above my head.

"I don't want to hurt you," he said.

I butted him in the face.

He was saved by Cat. She'd bobbed her way through the maelstrom and held my hand, which in turn held the knife. "Stop it, Harald," she said. "You can't kill a man in public."

The prince picked himself up from the floor, pausing only to shove away a sailor who staggered into him. "Can we talk? Please?"

Cat nodded, smiling graciously. "Of course. Join us at our table."

"Cat," I warned.

She took the knife from my hand. "Behave, Harald. As far as I can see, only one of you is trying to stab the other."

Margaret looked up as we returned. "I'm going to assume that you didn't bring my drink."

"Sorry," I muttered, while Cat fetched the prince a seat.

"Introductions," Cat said, once we were all seated again, Cat between me and the prince. "My name is Cat, I am descended from one of Erresea's great families, and find myself living in the house of Professor Gerhardt. Now, you go Margaret."

"Margaret," Margaret said. "Daughter of the professor. What's happening here?"

Cat ignored her. "Now you, Harald."

"Harald. He already knows me. I don't try to kill strangers that often."

"And you?"

The prince nodded, rocking back and forth on his stool. "My name is Edward, exiled prince of Ordrove."

"Shit," Cat said.

"Now do you see why I tried to kill him?"

Cat shook her head. "Your father is the one who forced Harald into the Crusade?"

Edward raised his hand. "My father did a lot of things wrong. Even on that day, Harald remembers me speaking on his behalf, don't you? Tell them you remember."

I bit my lip. "What did you say again? He did it for love? And then your father ignored you."

"I tried!"

"You should have tried harder."

Cat laid a hand on my knee. "How old was he, Harald?"

"Old enough."

"I was eleven."

The two women turned to face me. I couldn't meet their gaze. "You don't understand," I said. "If the King had listened, everything would have been different."

Edward's round face was smiling again. "The King didn't listen to anyone. Especially not me."

"He listened to Gabriel."

For a second, Edward's expression darkened. For a second, I saw how he had survived so long by himself. "Listening to Gabriel is what got him killed. And what got me exiled. I've sworn vengeance on that bastard."

I looked at Edward from below my eyebrows. "He's mine," I said. "I'll kill him."

"Kill him together?" Edward offered.

Cat tried not to laugh. I couldn't remove the lump in my chest; instead I forced myself to extend a hand. "Kill him together."

Edward shook.

"Now, wasn't that better than trying to murder one another?" Cat said.

"I didn't get to try murdering him," I growled. "So I wouldn't know." I shook my head. If there was one thing I craved more than anything, it was news from Ordrove. "Tell me what happened?" I said. "I need to know.

Edward nodded. "It all started when I was fifteen..."

"My father had been sick for years. His hair had fallen out. He barely left the Court, but he was committed to his civic duty. He spent all day hearing petitioners, then all evening retching into chamber pots. He was a mess of a man. Since my mother...since my mother died, the servants tiptoed around him in fear. His Lord Chancellor was an old friend, just as sickly and as feeble as he was. The kingdom wasn't in a good state. We could all see it."

"I had a plan. I was on good terms with a lot of the younger sons. I was building alliances, but not everyone saw it that way. They thought I was playing at being a knight. Going to tourneys. Making friends. Trying to give the realm some cheer! But tidings were dark. Amber had fallen to pieces. Royals were executed, even if you had the slightest drop of Amber in you then you found yourself in some dark gaol on the waterfront. The religious government promised good things, but all we could ever see was bloodshed and violence. With it, came the outpouring of refugees from Amber to Ordrove. This movement of people brought with it plagues. My father contained them well enough, but his measures were not popular. Whole villages were isolated. Some were put to the torch. I didn't agree – but the prevailing mood of the nation was that action needed to be taken."

"My father created a special taskforce, the Council of the Autumn, to deal with growing unrest. On it he put the most influential men and women of the Kingdom. He didn't have the strength to run it himself, but he called it a show of faith in his most trusted and loyal advisors. We had the Earl of Bolton, Lord Smithfield, Earl Craddock, Lord Custard, and others, but most importantly, we had Lady Calforth. The

Earl of Bolton was appointed nominal head of the Council, but I could see the Lady Calforth's influence as plain as day."

He hesitated. His bug eyes stared out of the window. "They took your seat, Harald. It became the Lady Calforth's seat. Gabriel's seat became the seat of the late Lord Calforth. They stopped styling themselves as Slant's at some point around this time – once the news of her husband's death came from the Golden City."

"This Council of the Autumn took special measures against Amber. They strengthened the border reavers on our side. Most of Amber's best border men had died during the Crusade anyway, and too many had links to the Ambers to be trusted by the religious leaders in charge. It seemed like a good idea. It stopped the flow of refugees. But it didn't stop the darker things. There was an outbreak from a monastic school on Lord Gabriel's lands. Monsters, the like of which I had never seen before, murdering civilians. On the order of the Council, Gabriel led the King's own men, myself included, to hunt these monsters."

"And they did. Gabriel himself brought back a dozen trophies from nightmarish creatures. I, to my shame, was not so brave as he."

"My father's condition worsened. Soon enough, he stopped seeing petitioners. I stepped in, saying that it was my time to assume the crown, in my father's ill health. The Council must be disbanded. They disagreed, saying that I was not yet a man, and the nation needed strong leadership."

"I made a mistake. I called on the lords who were loyal to me. I had them march on the capital, intending to secure it for myself. Instead, the Council branded it as treason against my father. They said I had come to steal from a healthy king. My allies were loyal, but we were few, compared to the might of the great houses. They destroyed us outside of the city, on the battle people now call the Battle of Brimham Hill. You may have heard of it? No?"

"Well, I fled. What else could I do? Gabriel hunted me, but I've always been a coward, and I was much better at running than he was. I stole away on one of the merchant vessels sailing out towards Antonia. And I left behind my kingdom and my birthright. Gabriel, soon afterwards, was appointed to Knight Commander of Ordrove. The Council of the Autumn still govern, but now I hear people call them The Long Council instead. My father passed away a little over a year after I left. Natural causes, they said. He wasn't well – it was true, but stepping away from public life had made him feel better. He *was* getting better."

"I know what the Lady Calforth wanted. What she has always wanted. She wanted my crown, and now she has it. And when Gabriel has amassed the loyalty of the entire realm with his heroics on the battlefield, I have no doubt she intends to make him king. They've got the blood for it, on the Lady's grandfather's side."

Edward shook his head, as if trying to dispel those words. "I worked the next few years guarding merchant caravans. I went to the Golden City to watch you fight. I tried to learn, as best as I could, how to soldier. But my fortune south soon dried up – we were on the losing end of some skirmish, and I found myself running again. I boarded the first boat that would take me. And it took me to you. Here. I think that's fate."

"What happened to Lot?" I asked. His last words hadn't even left his mouth before I blurted out my question. "The woman I was with?"

Edward shook his head. "I don't know. As far as I'm aware, Gabriel never found her. Or at least we never heard anything more about her."

I sat back in my chair, nodding. I thought back to the dream, of Lot lying in bed while I patted out the flame. She lived. I knew she lived.

"It sounds awfully hard for you, Sir," Cat said, placing one hand on Edward's arm.

"It has not been easy. I have been...lost."

Margaret shook her head. "It sounds like you need a drink. Or lots of drink."

Edward laughed; he laughed like a prince, all spritely and sing-song. "I would appreciate a drink."

Margaret stood up. "The rest of you will owe me. Prince Edward, this one is on me."

"I'm not a prince anymore," Edward said. "Just plain old Edward."

I grabbed his sleeve. "Do you still want to fight for your kingdom, plain old Edward?"

"Of course."

"Do you still want your crown?"

"Of course."

I nodded. "Good."

I met Edward on the beach.

Margaret had come to watch, on a little stool she'd brought from home. I had two wooden training blades made up, one in the style of my father's sword, the other in the style of Crow Eater, the blade of the Ordrovian royal line.

"You realise your family have sat the throne for over two hundred years," I said. "I can't believe the realm would so happily accept your removal."

Edward shrugged; tested out his new sword with a few experimental swings. "My father sired a daughter on my mother, before she died. Emma. It's actually how she died." Edward grimaced. "She'll be five now. She's in the care of the Lady Calforth. So, the line isn't completely broken. Besides, my great grandfather had eight children, and the Lady Calforth comes from that brood – there's more of us than the realm knows what to do with."

"I never thought I'd meet somebody who hates Gabriel as much as me."

He swung his sword again, in a clear arc over his head. It wasn't bad technique. "Do you truly believe you'll have your revenge on him?" Edward nodded towards my knee. "I don't mean to be disrespectful, but he has the backing of a nation on his side. And you're..."

"A cripple," I said softly.

"No. Well."

I attacked before he could finish his sentence. He blocked well, but his footwork was wrong. I pressed the attack and Edward fell into the sand.

And through it all, I hadn't even felt my knee. "I might be a cripple," I said. "But I was the best fighter this world had ever seen. You don't lose that overnight."

Edward nodded from the sand. I helped him to his feet.

"This won't be easy. Nothing is. But surely as I'll come back from this injury, you'll come back to your throne."

Edward inclined his head in agreement and took up a ready stance.

I was better than him, despite the mobility problems. I was inflexible. At one point, my knee buckled, even lunging in the soft sand, sending me face first onto the ground, spitting the beach from my lips .

But it felt good to fight. I could see the road back to recovery.

Edward moped the sweat from his brow. "I knew you were good," he said. "But..."

We spent another hour together; I taught him what I knew, without needing to exert myself. It was strange running through what for so many years I had taken as second nature, my God given right. But I'd had a good teacher in Ines Hollith's House, so even after that first day, I saw an improvement in Edward.

"How often can we do this?" he asked, grinning. He was a boy. Quite a big boy, but still a boy.

"Every three days," Margaret shouted from her stool. "I've looked at the textbooks. That's what they say. No more, or you'll increase the risk of reinjury."

I shrugged. "Every three days. Got to do what the boss says."

I wish those days had lasted forever.

Six months spent, in that happy state. Edward became a much better fighter, almost good enough to enter the Pits. With Margaret and Cat, we drank our bodyweight of alcohol twice over, only this time we had Edward to accompany us.

I was glad for the boy. He was younger than me, and though there was a hard edge to him, he had kept his good nature. Being deposed might have toughened him up, in all the right ways. God knows, it was hard to imagine the snivelling child I remembered turning into the young man who sat before me any other way.

Cat, in particular, took a shine to him.

He was genteel, in just the right way. And though nobody cursed like Cat after a few pints, I don't think either I or Margaret fully understood the incestuous language of true nobility. They'd talk about spoons, about their nanny's, about fashion. We'd look at each other and roll our eyes.

Still, I was happy to see Cat happy.

She took us all into the caves below the professor's house. We spent an evening in the pools splashing and laughing until dawn.

The Compulsion was never far away, especially on the days my knee bothered. Sometimes I couldn't spar more than half an hour with Edward, and like a bird on my shoulder I could hear it calling. But I kept it at bay. I felt more like myself than...well, ever.

At the back of my mind, I knew it couldn't last.

Tytos had freed me for a reason. And I had my own quest.

But how easy it would have been to keep drinking, to idle away those long summer days, or huddle around the fire on those crisp winter nights.

But I knew the end was coming. It had to come at some point.

The end began in an unexpected way.

Town criers woke us in the night. We staggered from our rooms, in white nightgowns. "What in all of the Gods' names is happening?" the Professor bellowed.

Outside, men carrying lanterns, wearing strange snout shaped masks walked. The cry on the street was clear. A plague had come.

The city locked down. The University closed its doors, though the Professor and some others continued to access whatever manuscripts they needed.

The House stopped meeting; the Prince stopped organising parties. Erresea became a ghost town.

I started doing what I'd done on those first few days in the city; I sat on the bench, overlooking the sea, and read books.

A plague was bad news for all, and we took to drinking in our kitchen as opposed to the city's pubs. Ships still sailed, but often as not it was with grim tidings. The plague had travelled over almost all of Gora to reach us. It was worse elsewhere.

We smuggled Edward in when we could. Cat supported him with her own money, though I wondered where she got it from.

"My inheritance," she said.

"Not some stolen goods you've held back?"

She grinned that wicked smile of hers. "What's the difference?"

And so, I spent my last days in Erresea in worried gossip with both Cat and Margaret.

When the professor finally called me to his room, I knew what it meant. The plague was an opportunity, if you were planning on striking up civil unrest.

I sat in the small office chair across from the Professor's desk. It was too small for me. My arse felt stuck and the arm rests dug into my flanks. The Professor seemed oblivious to my pain. He agonised over the small letter on his desk. Reading it, rereading it. Looking up at me. Sighing. Reading it again.

Eventually, I broke the silence. Asked a hopeful question. "Why did you want to see me?"

He sighed, his body deflating like a balloon. It was the smallest, most exhausted, I'd ever seen him.

"Tytos has written to me."

I knew it was coming, but it had not prepared me for the reality. *Not now,* I thought. *I'm happy.*

"He wants you to return to the Golden City. It's actually his second letter. In the last I explained you were not ready to return. He insists."

I closed my eyes.

The Compulsion spoke to me, suddenly all too loud.

No no no no no no no no no no no nononononononono

I managed to croak out small words. "If I go back, I'll die."

The professor reached across his desk and took his hands in my own. "You are not quite as frail as that, dear boy. You are strong. Much stronger than you give yourself credit for. It is too early for you to return to the Golden City, but you are not so weak as to die. You will not be pressed into bondage. You will not falter."

"Please don't make me go."

The pleading in my eyes gave the Professor a moment's pause, but still he shook his head. "Tytos has called for you. When Tytos calls, it is our obligation to answer."

"Then I am already a slave again."

"You are your own man. With goals loftier than any twenty something I have ever met in all my years at the university – and believe me I know many an unrealistic dreamer. Not to say you're unrealistic. Merely to say that you have ambitions. And you will achieve them."

My voice was barely above a whisper. "If I go to Tytos. If he judges me unworthy. What then?"

"Then you will be a free man, free to do whatever you want."

"Could I come back?" I said. "If I fail?"

He gripped my fingers tighter. "There will always be a home for you here, Harald. Always."

I stood, the chair rising with me and falling back to clatter on the floor. I looked at it dully. Turned to the Professor. "I should tell the others."

"Yes," he said. "They won't take it much better than you, I fear."

"No," I said dumbly, and left the room.

"He cannot summon you like a dog. Who does he think he is?" Cat prowled around the kitchen. "You should refuse him. You are a freed man. There is absolutely nothing he can do about it."

Margaret, for once, was very still. She sat at the table beside me with my hand in hers. "This is Tytcs," she said. "He might not have been born with noble blood, but I can think of few more powerful men than him. You do not rise to that kind of power by accepting the wills of others."

"Well fuck him," Cat said. "He has to start learning at some point. Right, Harald?" She glared at me, as if this was my doing. "Harald?"

"I have to go," I said.

"Fuck you," Cat said, hurling a glass from the side to shatter over the floor. "We're happy here. We're a family."

Her voice broke, just a little. I beckoned her closer. Took both of them in my arms. Inside, the Compulsion agreed with her, but I was stronger than that voice now. I had become something of the man I used to be.

"It's time," I said. "I have to do this." There was something else, as well, something destructive. A different side of the Compulsion. *If you leave, you'll be alone again. Like you deserve.* I tried to shake that thought free, but I couldn't.

I would be alone again. But this time I would be leaving before harm fell onto my friends. They would be safe, unlike my family, unlike Tava and Granny, unlike Lot, unlike the entire Crusade.

"The Heptarch and Ines Hollith will pay," I said. "This is what I've been waiting for."

Cat was crying, fighting it, but only making it worse. "I fucking hate this."

"I know."

Margaret forced a smile. "Does this mean you're going to be a prude again, when Harald's gone?"

Cat tried to smile. "No. This is the me you've got to put up with. The cursing, blubbering idiot that I've become."

Eventually, we broke apart. Cat looked at the mess she'd made and sighed. "I suppose I'd better clear that up."

I nudged her in the ribs. "You're good at clearing up broken things."

She smiled. "I'll miss you, you dumb bastard."

I spent the next day preparing my travelling gear. There wasn't much I needed to take. Tytos was sending another caravan to pick me up, replete with all the guards that it would entail. Most of the city was under lockdown still on account of the plague, but rules like that didn't seem to apply to Tytos.

I spent my last morning in the garden, trying to enjoy nature, when a hooded figure snuck up to the bench beside me.

"You have the stealth of a blind pig," I said.

"Well, Cat told me you were leaving." Edward looked tired; his big eyes had even bigger rings.

"When did you see Cat?"

He blushed an altogether unexpected red.

I raised my eyebrows. "Don't tell me you're a...*thing*."

"I don't know. Maybe. Almost."

"Don't get married before I'm back."

His redness was replaced just as quickly by a white sheen. "No marriage. No, thank you."

I punched him lightly in the shoulder. "You're too young for that anyway. How old are you? I forget."

"Nineteen."

I shook my head. "You were a child. Twelve? When I saw you back home."

"Eleven, actually." Gave a small laugh. "It's been a rough eight years."

"You only lost your crown. At least you were never a slave."

I was so used to Cat and Margaret's banter that his honesty still surprised me. He sagged under the weight of my teasing.

"I know how bad you've had it, Harald. That's why I came back here today. To let you know that I'll be here for you...in a way I wasn't back then."

"I will reiterate my earlier statement. You were a child. I know we...started on the wrong foot. But my sentence was not your responsibility."

"But you were young too. I thought about it a lot, after you said. I wondered why I didn't have your bravery."

"I was born in different fires to you. Those fires shaped me early. They came later for you, but you've survived them, turned into a good man."

He pursed his lips. "Do you think we'll make it back there one day?"

I stood, drawing him up to stand with me. He was getting taller by the day. "I have a draugr to kill. I have Gabriel to chop into a million little pieces. If I don't make it back home, then I will have failed. All you have to do is follow me home."

He shook his head. "You should have been Prince, not me. My father would have loved you. When he was well."

"Your father exiled me," I reminded him gently.

"But he didn't execute you."

"Is that what counts for love in your family?"

"Pretty much." He puffed his cheeks. Stood back. Saluted me. "Prince Harald."

I laughed and saluted back. "Prince Edward. I'll see you soon. Look after them."

"I think they'll look after me."

I nodded and headed away. He was a kid, but he was a good kid. Still, I didn't know what Cat saw in him.

When I returned to the estate the carriage was there waiting for me, along with half a dozen of Tytos' men. I said another round of teary goodbyes and then I was in the carriage, waving out of the window, Erresea behind me.

I had come to the city a broken man. I wasn't exactly healed. But I was better. Reforged.

I didn't know it then, but I was already well on my way to becoming the type of weapon that Tytos wanted.

Chapter Seventeen

I took a deep breath as I sat in the back of that wagon, rolling ever closer to the Golden City.

I wore no sword; I had no walking stick. Without either, I felt naked.

Little comfort was to be found in my escort. They were hard men. Men that Tytos could trust. The blue-eyed man who led their gang had once been a soldier out to the far north, fighting some border skirmish against a kingdom I'd never heard of. Another was a pit fighter. One was a former merchant, exiled for trading illegal substances, who'd instead found work in the ferrying of people for Tytos.

They were a rotten bunch. Ears, noses, fingers; all were missing some body part. Most had scars that shone dully in the firelight.

Around the campfire, I studied them. I sat, massaging my own scars and the bony cartilage of my knee. I looked into their eyes and wondered what had changed them into dull eyed veterans serving Tytos.

They barely spoke. Still, they seemed to know what each other wanted without needing to speak.

I asked the blue eyed man how long they'd been working together.

He shrugged. "Long enough to know this is serious business."

In the whispered dark I could occasionally make out their private conversation. "Traitors," I heard a number of times. They were sullen and silent creatures, but I realised that they were also nervous. They were veterans of Tytos' employ, but something was changing.

They were no longer the muscle of a powerful businessman.

They were *traitors*.

I almost laughed at their worry.

I had been a traitor to every government I had ever served.

Still, it was useless conjecture to wonder about Tytos' purpose for us all. Until I met the man himself again, I wouldn't know how he'd put me to use. Kill the Heptarch he'd said upon our last meeting – I hoped the plan had become more fleshed out in the time we'd been apart.

Instead, I tried to focus on my surroundings. So little of the journey to Erresea was in my memory that I was determined to remember more of the return to Liriam.

We rolled through steep forests, until the borders of Erresea fell behind and the long farmlands and plains of the Golden City approached.

The plague had come before us.

Where once sheep grazed, weeds and thistle overran. Farms were silent. We met no travellers on the road.

The world was still, apart from the chirping of a million birds which twittered from branch to branch, flew from roadside to roadside.

One village had stationed armed guards upon the entry and exit points to their town. In truth they were little more than farmers with billhooks, but they stuck to their task with grim resolution, scowling at us as we rolled by.

More than once, we caught the stench of burning flesh on the wind.

The plague – as it had been described to me by my escorts – seemed similar to that illness which affected me aboard the crusaders ship all those years ago.

It was on the fifth day of our journey when my suspicions were confirmed.

The plague came to our campsite.

One by one it took them. None of them wanted to believe it. They struggled on at first, coughing into the crook of their elbows.

Then, the blue-eyed man fainted.

We stopped our caravan in a forest glade, just off the path, to wait out the worst of it.

Five days it took. Five days where it spread through men's bodies like wildfire. Shivering cold but burning to the touch. Shouting in unnatural dreams. More than one of them screamed about the Beast, as if it was towering over them, roasting them alive.

By the end of it, every single one of them was dead.

I had survived, as always.

Barely a cough had racked my body. I had cared for them. Brought them water. Food.

In the end, I burnt them.

When I re-joined the road to the Golden City, I was alone.

The Golden City was not how I remembered it.

Truthfully, I had only seen it from the outside looking in twice. But even still, it had been a tall, imperious thing, with strong walls and inviting golden towers.

It had become a different city in the time I had been away.

Hovels and wooden shelters spread from the walls in a haphazard way, as if carried by a large wave and left like driftwood at random heights and intervals. The city outside of the city was bigger than the city inside of the walls. I could not believe my eyes. I stood upon the rise and gathered my breath.

It should not have surprised me. Nine days into my three week journey I had joined a mass of refugees walking the long way towards the Golden City. They had stretched onwards before me, like a never-ending tide, and behind me as constant as the ripples of the sea. There were children and the elderly, carrying dolls and walking sticks. There were farmers with broad shoulders and tanned arms. There were seamstresses with red eyes.

The plague had ripped through small towns whose livelihoods were dependent upon local bartering and trade. When their key industries had collapsed, the survivors were unable to pick up the pieces. And so, they followed the mighty crowd towards the Golden City, where the Heptarch had issued a command to take everyone who was affected by the plague and find a home for them amongst the shacks outside of Liriam.

A young farmer with straw in her hair told me this as we walked along. It seemed too good to be true, but others confirmed her story.

Doctors worked like a storm in the Golden City, mending and healing folks, or so the rumour went. And the Heptarch was putting the displaced to work, in grand building projects or as soldiers in the guard.

Still, there were just so many people.

I made my way to join them.

Guards stood at checkpoints, taking names and filtering people out. Drawing the Heptarch's attention wasn't high on my list; instead I ducked out of the line of refugees as quickly as I could and into the maze of shacks.

The buildings were a marvel of casual engineering, each one precariously stacked against their partner, leaning like a drunk. Somehow, they worked. Somehow, they formed small living areas, in which I could smell stew and all the familiar delicious aromas of the Golden City.

Somehow the Heptarch had done good.

I gritted my teeth and walked on. Washing lines were strung between buildings and some sections had wood nailed across the passageways, so all beneath was dark as the night.

I had no doubt that this second city was full of plague and robbers. No soldier could penetrate through its winding streets and make a difference. People would rule themselves in such a tangled web of houses. I could barely find my way through the streets, with only the occasional sight of the Golden City's walls confirming my direction.

Three hours later and I was at a tall gate, one of the many leading into the city. This one wasn't full of refugees seeking entry, as I had feared. Instead, it seemed home to merchants with a market visible beyond, and a squad of guards in painted gold occupying the gates.

I breathed deep and approached.

The guards muttered between each other. One of them scowled. "No refugees in the city without the right papers. You're at the wrong gate anyway."

I pulled out the papers I had taken from the blue-eyed man after he'd died. "Will this be enough?"

The guard snatched them away. His eyes widened at the sign of the seal. "Sorry, sir. I didn't realise."

"An honest mistake," I reassured him. "Can I enter?"

"Of course. Will you be needing an escort?"

I hesitated. I had no idea how to find Tytos' house. I slowly nodded. "That would be perfect."

The guard nodded, mumbling something about it being his honour, before beckoning one of his unhappy looking friends closer. It wasn't long until they'd found us a taxi service, and I was sitting in the back of a horse drawn cart with the two soldiers trying to appear at ease beside me.

Eventually we reached a familiar location. Tytos's house. I wondered if everyone knew where he lived. But then, I'd never seen Tytos actually live there, even if I had slept there for almost a week. It was a visible front I realised, a place he could be found, but only if he wanted to be found.

The guards saluted me, and I stepped out onto the stone.

Jasmine and lavender drifted on the breeze. I sucked in a deep breath and knocked on the door to Tytos' house.

A young woman opened it after almost thirty seconds of waiting.

"Harald," she said.

I frowned. Realisation followed. "Eleanor."

She was dressed in a simple white tunic and black trousers. A rough ponytail pulled her hair back.

I hesitated. She'd told me she hated me the last time we'd meet. No words came out. She seemed to take this as a response. She nodded once and beckoned me inside and up a flight of stairs to the rooftop terrace.

"I will send word to the master," she said.

I caught her by the wrist. "You're not a slave."

"He's still the master." And with that she was gone.

The long wait for Tytos wrought havoc on my nerves. I struggled to contain my breathing. I tried to use the breathing exercises taught to me in Ines Hollith's house – but they only served to remind me of those terrible days.

Why had I come back? I'd thrown myself back into damnation. I was an idiot.

The Compulsion spoke to me, that same pitiful sound as when the professor had told me Tytos had sent for me.

No, it said. *No no no* –

"Harald," a voice bellowed.

I rose to meet it. It was harder than rowing towards Antonia. Harder than burying my father's sword into Lord Calforth. *I do this knowingly, of my own free will*, I told myself.

"Tytos," I said and reached my hand forward to shake his.

Instead, he clutched me in a bear hug, as if we were old friends. "I knew you could make it, you tough bastard. Standing without a problem."

"I have had problems," I protested weakly, as he shepherded me back into my chair.

"But to make such progress in such a short space of time. It would have killed normal men. And look at you."

I felt a brief swelling of pride. I had recovered. I might not have been as strong as I once had been, but I was better than I could have been. Sometimes that's enough.

"You're behind schedule though," Tytos said. "What did you do? Walk here?"

"Yes, actually." I relayed the story of the death of my caravan.

Tytos scowled. "I sent some good men to get you." His face twisted. "This plague is a curse, but it's an opportunity too. The opportunity I've been waiting for, for so many years."

I nodded, waiting for Tytos to continue. Instead, he pursed his lips and looked out over the city. "Do you know anything about me?"

"A little. People don't like to talk about you that much. They fear you."

"Aye." He shrugged. "Maybe they're right to fear me. I've done what I have had to do, to give myself this opportunity. But it hasn't always been pleasant. The death of those men won't be the last stain on my conscience before it's done, but I'll remember. That's all we can do, Harald. I think you know that better than most. Keep that goal in your mind. Keep moving forward."

I nodded.

"Good. I know much about you. I've had reports sent to me about you and your little play friends in Erresea. Now, don't get me wrong – you are young. It's good for you to be out drinking, acting your age. But men like you don't have the luxury of acting your age all too often. In other words, Harald, you've had your fun, and now it's back to the hard business of being a man. Can you do this?"

I hesitated. Tytos smiled and clapped me on the shoulder – I realised he didn't just know a lot about me. He knew everything about me. He knew my every response and he knew how he'd respond in turn.

"You were born a prince, Harald," Tytos said. "You are not like other men. You never have been. You have played at being normal – but you have never been *normal*. You were an outsider in your own house growing up. You were an outsider, even as you led your men to the Golden City. And you were an outsider even as you sat in those dockside bars with friends. Why? Because you have a calling. I won't call it a God given right – but it is something close to it. You are compelled down a pathway the ordinary cannot understand. You must do what is right. You must destroy those wrongdoers who've tried to destroy you – who have ruined so many lives both before and after you."

"But not you, Harald. They never destroyed you. You are something far more than the Heptarch, your Gabriel or even that hell spawned draugr can handle."

"I know it's hard to ask this of you. To willingly set aside joy. To act *for the greater good.* But any man can wake in the morning, fill his day with meaningless idylls, drink at the pub until all of his life is washed away and nothing remains of him. Very few are given the chance to make their mark. To strike back at the evils of the world – to look beyond their small bubble of bliss or misery and say 'I will be heard. And I will not be denied.' Are you that man, Harald? Will you stand with me against the Heptarch, and the institutional evils of this city? Will you stand for the slaves and the weak, for a better world?"

What else could I say but "yes."

Tytos knew me in a way I barely even knew myself. I had struggled day to day, living because some nagging sense of wrong kept me from just giving up. And now I had a chance.

That's not to say I wasn't wary. I had known Lord Ashdown and Lord Calforth. Great men had given me power before, but always revealed themselves to be monsters on the inside.

Tytos might be the same. Indeed, Tytos probably *was* the same.

But Sir Slant's words came back to me from all those years ago. "You have to dominate," he said. "You have to win and trust in yourself."

Tytos grinned that wide feline smile of his and beckoned me after him.

In the room beyond lay seven crowns upon a white blanket.

"Seven crowns for seven kings," Tytos said. "Every child of the Golden City knows what the Beast offered when he rose from the sea. Seven crowns for seven kings. Power greater than even the Gods. They were the greatest of men, but even the greatest of men were corrupted by his touch. He bent them to his will. Every single one of them fell into madness, lust, gluttony, wrath. They brought famine, pestilence and war upon our ancestors. Even still, the people who served were almost euphoric, absolute in the certainty that they were doing right. In the end, the seven kings fell, the seven cities were united under new leaders, and the Beast was bound by the combined will of the Gods, acting through his priests."

"I'm sure you know the saying: history is written by the victors." His eyes looked covetously upon the crowns. "What power might they hold? What lies have we been told to scare us from the Beast below? He *is* a monster, I've no doubt. What he truly is – I do not know. A twisted God, is my best guess. One who plummeted from the stars above into the cold dark of the sea, driven mad by the black expanse, until finally he roared his way to land." He sighed, for the first time since I met him seeming weak, pressing one hand to the wall to steady himself. He was breathless; his mouth had barely stopped moving. "You, Harald, were given this power. Chosen as his dark champion. No longer confident in seven kings, he has chosen one bastard lord. Do you want to take up the crowns?"

I shook my head. "He takes you," I said. "If you crown yourself with them, he would take you as his instrument. You wouldn't be you anymore."

Tytos nodded. "My thoughts exactly." He swept the crowns together in the blanket, loosely knotting it so it formed a small sack under which only the outlines of the crowns could be seen. "We play a complicated game with the Beast. He has guided us into the position we are in – the power we are in. But to take that final step and become His servant? I am convinced it can never be so. But where to draw that last final line? I deliberated long and hard. You are His champion after all. Whatever plan he has will put you front and centre. So, he has told me that my ambitions will only come to fruition under your guidance. Only you, Harald, can deliver us the dream which for so long has only been a fantasy to us. If you were a lesser man, I would have had you killed. He is a God, but I cannot risk him being released and another desolation coming upon us. But I believe that you see the Beast as I do – as a necessary evil we will use but not fall prey to. A monster we can control."

"I wouldn't see the Beast ever again," I said, "if I could help it."

"We need him. And..." Tytos hesitated. "...I will not so quickly dismiss the closest thing we have ever seen to a God as nothing but a monster."

It was my turn to hesitate. "What does he show you? When you talk to him?"

"Glorious salvation." Tytos smiled. "The world without the Heptarch. Without slaves. A truly free seven cities."

I nodded. "Don't you think he lies?"

"I did. At first. But all that he has promised me has come to pass, so long as I act as he commands. I *will* follow him, until I can follow him no more. Do you see, Harald? It is a mad balancing act. The greatest con we've ever known. The Beast is the tool we can use to create paradise."

"I don't believe in paradise."

"What do you believe in, Harald?"

I thought for a second. "That things can get better. Not perfect, but better. If those who do wrong are held to account."

"Better is enough for me." He extended his hand. "You are my soldier, as you have been the soldier of so many before me. But this time I do not ask you to fight for God, or for profit. I ask you to fight for your own conscience. Can I trust you in that? Kill the Heptarch with me, and I will help you in your own quests."

I shook his hand. "So, how are you going to kill him?"

Chapter Eighteen

History has a way of forgetting the small details.

In a story like mine, I can only touch on them where they enter my own story. Tytos' rise could be the contents of a dozen books – but if you are only hearing my story you might wonder where this man of hearty smiles and cold conviction has been, how he arrives on the scene.

I cannot tell you of the small events that tumbled like a rockslide together to bring us to the cusp of revolution. I, like you, found myself in this with so little knowledge of the politics or the happenings of those around me.

I knew only one thing – the Heptarch was a bastard.

It takes one to know one, after all.

I'd lost six years of my life to him. What other motivation did I need?

Trusting Tytos was a different matter. He'd already given me so much – I think other men might have been grateful. Gone to him on bended knee and professed allegiance. But I wasn't that sort of man. I didn't trust him.

Who gives so much to one man, with no expectation in return?

Well, there was an expectation. The Beast had chosen me. For what task, none of Tytos' inner circle could particularly agree on. Would me standing around in those meetings be enough? Or did I actually have to do something?

Tytos had an answer, as he always seemed to have an answer to everything.

I would be his sword in the night.

In the arena, respect filters from fighter to fighter. For every battle without a death, a man goes home and tells the story of the fighter who has bested him. All too often, the opponent was a brute, intent on doing as much damage as he could before the fight could be stopped.

But I had never fought like that.

I did what I had to do. I could be brutal. I could be cold. I could break a man's hand without blinking. But I had my own code of conduct – a quiet efficiency that had won me much renown. I barely even fought sometimes – I just *won*.

The Golden House, Tytos' own army of free pit fighters, knew me by my reputation. I'd even fought two of them in a melee, before they'd joined the House. They bowed their head in my presence, the kind of reverence usually reserved for the great and powerful.

But The Golden House was not the power that surrounded Tytos.

His inner circle was seven strong. I found it amusing. The Heptarch had also been one of seven once, before he seized Liriam's power.

Lady Linial was his 'left hand' as she put it – wielding the power and words of the Beast. In her corner was Tytos' spymaster – Dara Vernon – another foreigner from reclaimed islands off Erresea. I guess I was also aligned with Linial, if not with the Beast.

I had not seen Linial in almost a year. As I sat beside her at the grand meeting table which Tytos ruled from, I tried not to meet her gaze. For so long, she had been all that I had wanted. But we had left each other with harsh words, and I was not the same feral thing as I had been when fighting in the Pits. I wanted to study her, to see if she recognised the man that I truly was. But I could not look at her, not now, with the fate of Liriam resting on her. There was a time and a place.

Instead, I made note of the others around the table.

Galen was a captain of the guard in the Golden City. His military uniform remained crisp and golden, even while sitting. His medals shone brightly like polished stones. How he had found his way to Tytos' side was unclear – but his thick lisp didn't stop him from voicing strong opinions. He was old nobility, I soon realised.

Everything he said was backed by Claudia, a priestess representing the Many Gods, a type of elected official for all the disparate religions in the Golden City. When she spoke, it was with a clear, rehearsed voice. I noted her immediately as someone who felt as though she did not belong. She wasn't upper class in the way Galen was. She didn't resent that fact; she *aspired.*

Finally, there was the merchant Mysterious Rupp.

"That's not a name," I said to him, the first time we met. "I've met so many slaves. None of them have been called Mysterious."

The rotund merchant had only laughed at me. "They told me I could choose a name when I was freed," he said. "I was only twelve when my father sold us to the debtors. I was almost thirty when I was released. By Gods was I desperate to finally make a mark. And I'd learned a thing or two on that side – the ridiculous is often as powerful as the sincere. You need to be talked about. And so I became Mysterious."

He laughed. I frowned.

"Come Harald. A sense of humour will do you well if you're to keep sane through what's to come."

"I've seen my fair share of shit."

"So say all young men, until they find the thing that breaks them. It broke me, see. And I came out the other side laughing. It was better than the alternatives, trust me boy."

He was an outlier to the others – he thought with his wallet, not with grand ideals.

"Why do you bring him close?" I asked Tytos one evening, when we were sharing wine.

"Because Rupp has money," Tytos said. "And because he's an old friend."

"And you trust him? Even though he doesn't care if the Heptarch lives or dies, so long as he can turn a profit?"

"The one thing you can trust about men like Rupp is that if they're making money, they won't speak out against you.

And if you can promise them a lot of money, why, the world begins to turn a lot easier."

"What've you promised him?"

Tytos scowled. "Too much. But that's not for you to worry about. You're my sword, after all. I don't need a sword to court a merchant. I need a sword to kill a king."

And so, each afternoon our group of seven would sit around the table and debate the next step in order to overthrow the Heptarch.

"Everything is in position," Tytos said. "I've spent almost twenty years waiting for this moment. We must make full advantage." He nodded to Dara Vernon. "Stage is yours."

Dara Vernon stood and eyed us. She was stooped and grey, but none of the intelligence had vanished from behind her fox-like eyes. "The city is at boiling point. The nobility are pressed into living like normal people – no more parties, no more extravagant feasts. The merchants are struggling to ship anything of value into the city, and the nobles are struggling to pay for any of it with the new taxes imposed. The working class are just about surviving, but they're not happy about the curfews and the restrictions on public gatherings. The closure of the Fighting Pits last week has brought mass protests and the city guard are reported to have taken a dozen casualties in the fighting. Most of the key industries are still going – but the plague is amassing a body count that's forcing a choice for people. Work and potentially die, or stay home and potentially starve. This is only exacerbated by the cheap labour force that has arrived outside of the city walls. The poor families from other regions are making pretty much everyone annoyed, and the Heptarch doesn't have the backing of the elected ministers who in turn are facing stiff pressure from the nobility. Of course, some nobles are sitting on enough reserves to believe that accommodating everyone is the right course of action – the majority, however, are feeling the pinch. Never before has almost every key element of the city been set against the Heptarch. The only thing stopping public mutiny is fear of the plague. The implementation of these unpopular policies are predominantly falling on the city guard." She creaked back into her seat and beckoned to Galen.

The Captain stood promptly, chest puffed. "It cannot go on," lisp heavy. "The slum outside the walls is a den of thievery and rape. The people there have fallen into barbarity, and the city guard cannot even make it halfway into that maze without being assaulted. It is in danger of becoming a city unto itself and everyone knows it." He gathered himself, licking his lips. "If the Heptarch had any sense, he would have reallocated people to other towns and villages. Instead, he's fucked everyone, which I believe was the Lady Linial's doing when she whispered kindness into his ear instead of sense."

"Do you want him gone?" Linial shot back. "This is how it happens."

"I have lost brothers," Galen said. He shook his head. "Anyway. The City Guard is paralysed. The Lord Commander is powerless – the others realise he is nothing but a lackey of the Heptarch, and they will not follow him. They will not back us either. They just will not act, until it ends. Then they will help clear up."

"You're confident they won't attempt a counter coup?" Tytos asked. "Once we've taken the city, we'll be at our most vulnerable."

"The Guard will help," Galen said. "I will hang any bastard who mutters treason. But...it would help the Guard if the slums is burnt. It cannot be governed. And if we do succeed in taking the city, then we will have a thousand desperate mouths to feed, without any of the infrastructure that is currently feeding them, albeit poorly."

"You want to kill innocents," I said. "I thought you wanted to save the city."

"The slums are not the city. And they will die of plague anyway."

"You don't deserve those medals," I said.

"I won these medals by doing what is necessary, as I am doing now, committing treason. You cannot save them all."

Tytos raised a hand to stop further arguing. "I'll think on this. Harald is right in that we can't murder the people we want to govern – otherwise how are we better than *him*? But there is a solution to this. I'll talk to you privately, Galen."

The Captain withdrew into his chair, avoiding my angry stare.

"Lady Linial," Tytos said. "Update us on the Heptarch."

She rose, as always looking so small amongst her black furs. "We all hate my father, though for very different reasons. But for once in his life, he's trying to do what's right. He's turned the majority of his staff to helping feed the city. This includes members of the Walled Garden who've taken up key administrative positions, including amongst the City Guard. He spends most of his time hearing petitioners – he's already survived the plague so believes himself immune to it, though as I'm sure Claudia can tell you he's accompanied by a dozen priests blessing him and swinging incense during working hours. In the evening he sleeps in his chamber, guarded by the palace guard, of which my brother, Lord Axel, leads. Supplanted amongst the remaining staff members are the last few members of the Walled Garden who are foiling every attempt of our people to enter his inner circle. For now, only I have access to his schedule and his movements."

"Lord Axel remains against us?" Tytos asked.

"My brother won't even hear a criticism of my father. Father doing the right thing has only furthered his resolve. He thinks he's finally getting through to him." She hesitated. "He will fight us, but if father is dead, then he will come around. I won't have him harmed in the fighting."

Tytos waved a hand. "We've discussed this. Your brother is Captain of the Palace Guard. We'll take him captive where possible. But accidents do happen, and you must be aware of that."

Lady Linial sank back into her chair.

"Rupp," Tytos called. The merchant started in his chair as if he'd been sleeping. "Any updates on keeping the city provisioned through our little mess?"

The elderly merchant clasped his hands together on his belly. "An impossible task, but one we are making headway with. My caravans are waiting in nearby towns – I've kept them held up with some administrative issues." He chuckled to himself. "We'll have an influx of produce when we've seized the city. If you can keep the peace, then I can sell every piece. It will buy you some goodwill."

"And you a lot of money," Linial shot in.

"Indeed. Like all great plans. Anything else, *my liege?*"

Tytos scowled but didn't rise to Rupp's baiting.

"Harald," Tytos said. I sat up straight. "You've had some time to familiarise yourself with the Golden House. Do you think they're up to the task?"

In truth I'd only spent an afternoon with the Golden House so far. Their last leader – a pit fighter called Dossena – had died of the plague a little over a month ago. They were looking for someone confident to lead them. I wasn't sure I was the right person to do that. Still, Tytos expected a certain type of answer, and I would give him it. "The Golden House is in good condition. Over a hundred warriors in fit and fighting shape. They're ready to act. They're impatient. They want to kill their old masters."

Tytos nodded. "We're ready," he said.

Sadly, that didn't mean the meetings ended. I spent another three hours in that meeting alone, with another four meetings in the following four days.

When I was finally free of Tytos and politics, I made my way to the Golden House.

They were quartered in the rooms of a minor pit boss Tytos had bought out. They did their best to spar in the covered courtyard, but there was just too many of them and too little room.

They bowed to me, as if I was their master.

It filled me with disgust; I left as quickly as I could.

I missed Margaret and Cat and the Professor and Edward and Erresea and a good, cold drink.

I sat alone on Tytos' rooftop terrace, drinking wine. I'd worked so hard to get back to fitness. I was ruining it, but I couldn't help myself.

Apart from Galen, that Council knew next to nothing about war. They talked and talked, but they didn't know the horror they were about to cause.

The Golden City would run red with the blood of both friend and enemy.

I felt powerless to stop it. Worse, I was complicit.

This is what vengeance is, I told myself. You're not just following orders. You're choosing to do this.

All the sitting around was making me antsy.

I spoke to the staff. What has happening in the city?

The plague, they said.

Other than the plague?

Those preachers from Amber.

Curiosity piqued, I began to ask around.

Preachers from Amber had begun to stir up trouble – preaching the word of the Mountain, of one God, and damning non-believers to die in fire and blood.

But the Heptarch was once again showing his lenience. He had not executed or even exiled these priests from Amber, but instead granted them cushy rooms in one of the city's ancient temples.

I decided I wanted to see these priests.

I was from Amber after all, on my mother's side.

I needed some spiritual guidance.

Father Andrew had not left his position during my absence.

Though the church was closed to the public, Tytos' servants paved the way and had me admitted.

Father Andrew was in the middle of berating one of those servants when I stepped into the house.

"Father," I said, the blind man turning so fast he almost fell.

"Speak," Andrew commanded.

"What do you want to know? That I'm no more pious than the last time we met and only slightly less crippled."

"In God's name, Harald, what possessed you to bring this army of plague-ridden servants upon my doorstep?"

"Should you not welcome them all?"

"I remember what a plague can do, as I'm sure you do as well."

"It's the same one," I said quietly. "I think because we've had it before, it doesn't affect us as much."

The priest paused. "Is that so? It moves ever further west then." He hesitated. "I wonder, did we bring this here? I remember you storming Antonia."

"I was bloody out of my mind. I couldn't see straight."

"God acted through you."

"If he blessed me on that day, he's cursed a lot of people since."

Andrew sighed. "It has been a thing I've heard preached. A pestilence visited on the non-believers."

"It's coming from those priests from Amber, I heard."

"Yes, yes," Andrew said. "We're meant to be preaching peace, not bloodshed. Did our failure teach them nothing?"

"Well. Would you like to teach them something?"

"What?"

"I've decided to confront our friends from Amber. I'd like a bit of spiritual backing."

Andrew clacked his tongue against the top of his mouth. "Well, if I have got the plague from all your servants, where's the harm in spreading it to those bloodthirsty gnats."

"And they say that priests preach love."

"We preach all sorts of things, Harald. You know that. It's only since I lost my eyes that I began to see clearly all the lies I was spreading." He hesitated. "Though, I have never seen anybody move like you. Of all the things I would swear was an action of our God, it would be his blessing on your sword arm."

I hesitated. "I think you're wrong, Father. Gabriel was always a better swordsman than me. I think it's him God has blessed – judging by how things have been going at home. Me? I think it was the Beast that brought me here."

"Don't say such things." He dotted the sign of the Mountain on his chest. "The Beast tries to turn the best of men. You must not let him."

I shrugged. "I've never been the best of men. I think Sir Slant was right about me all those years ago. I'm a killer who thinks he's right. Same as every other killer who thinks they're right." I shook my head. "Come. Before we get lost in maudlin rememberings."

"I'm permitted maudlin rememberings. I'm older than you."

"You're not as old as you look, priest. And you're certainly not as old as you act. So come and be young for a while, and let's pick a fight."

The temple did not yield as quickly to Tytos' servants as Andrew's had. But still, like all things in the city, they yielded to Tytos eventually.

I entered the giant domed building, marvelling at how little of the Golden City I knew even after all this time. I could trace every path around my home, every passageway in my father's castle, even so many years later. The Golden City, however, remained a mystery.

"Almost a thousand people could fit in here," I muttered to Andrew.

"Aye, I wish I had've seen them all. Nowhere in the world has more temples than the Golden City. Even if I don't believe in those religions, I shudder to think of people crowded in here in normal times, witnessing the pagans in utter rapture."

"I assume they were probably as bored in this big building as I used to be in church."

"Harald, you are an outlier, not the standard."

I frowned. "I never did ask why you were on that boat with the rest of us. Did you volunteer to teach condemned men?"

"No," Andrew said. "I sinned in my enthusiasm for the glory of God."

"What did you do?"

"What I did is of no concern, except for myself and God."

A figure appeared from the upper level of the temple, shaking their first angrily. They were flanked by two others, all wearing sharp white vestments onto which they'd sewn the Mountain.

"Who are you?" The first of them demanded, a young man barely into his thirties, arriving onto the lower level. The two flanking him where little more than teenagers, dwarfed in their uniforms.

"Did the Crusade kill off all the real priests?" I asked. "Aren't you a little young?"

The priest from Amber scowled. "You force us from our prayers and now you insult us? I say good day, stranger." The priest went to spin on his heels, but I caught his elbow before he could move.

"I'm Harald Fairhair. Who the fuck are you?"

The priest sagged in my arms. "You're dead," he said simply.

"Not really."

One of the younger priests stepped forward. "We heard they executed you, sir. That's what they say at home. When the Crusade failed."

"It did not fail," the first priest said, pulling himself from my grip. "It was only the first part of God's plan."

"It bloody did fail," I said. "And I may as well be dead, for how much I've suffered in the past few years."

"Have you come back to lead us?" the younger priest said.

"No. Not that you want my support. I did fail. We lost. I..."

Father Andrew placed a small hand on my shoulder. "God deemed us not worthy. The Host of the Mountain was not righteous. We did not act in his name. And so, we have been punished for our failures, both Harald and myself. It is why we've come to talk to you. You musn't preach war. Have you not learnt anything from our ruin?"

The priest looked down the length of his nose. "Only that you failed. You were not worthy. And is it any surprise – you all treated *him* like some legend from the storybooks. He's just a man. But even still – how can you possibly expect us not to raise arms. The Beast is beneath our feet!"

"And there he will remain," Father Andrew said. "What is he doing to you from down there? No-one here worships him. They barely even talk of him. *They* think they're doing the world a service, chaining him down there for all eternity."

"Anyone who comes into contact with the Beast is corrupted. And It has its own priests – the Heptarch's own daughter is a worshipper. Or did you forget she murdered one of our own, in cold blood, and vanished without a trace!" The first priest breathed deeply. "We all know Harald Fairhair, but who are you?"

"Father Andrew. Ordained by the old King's hand."

"Ah, I see. The abuser."

Priests tell the world they're peaceful men. Even as they preach damnation for non-believers and war upon all the world. Still, you never expect a priest to throw a punch – certainly not an old blind priest like Father Andrew.

Still, that's what he did, and the punch was true.

The Amber priest rocked backwards on his heels.

"You hit me," he said.

Father Andrew didn't speak, but he raised his chin and stared at the man with his sightless eyes.

"You're both tainted," the priest said. "Like a plague you spread. Come," he said to his younger priests. "Come! Leave these heathens behind."

I couldn't even think of a comeback. Instead, I turned to Father Andrew. "What the fuck was that?"

"I'm sorry, Harald. I should be better."

"I think you should have hit him harder actually, but that's not the point. Why'd you punch him?"

The Father stayed silent.

"An abuser, he said," I continued. "That's what you didn't want to tell me. Who did you abuse?"

"Take me home, Harald."

"Tell me."

"Take me home! Has an old, blind man not suffered enough? Have I not paid the price? Must I always pay it? Forever and ever, always." His back stooped with each step he took away from the chamber.

I guided him. I did not press him further and we did not talk on the way back to his church.

"What happened today, Harald, was weakness. I have always been weak, Harald. I hope that the light in you can see the light in me. I hope that you will still consider me a friend, one day."

With that he slipped away, leaving me to ride the wagon back to Tytos' house alone.

Chapter Nineteen

I stood alone on the pathway to Ines Hollith's mansion.

The ancient statues still curled their muscles. The tall walls still stood. The flowers still bloomed. There was no sign of life though, within the walls, or guards stationed on the front gate. Everything was as it had been, bar the complete lack of life.

I was disguised, of course. It wouldn't do for the Heptarch or Ines Hollith to catch sight of me. I wore a mask of Euridities; Ines Hollith would have laughed.

The noise of a distant carriage turned me. I stepped from the path as it approached, trying to peer through the curtains. Was Ines Hollith coming home?

The head that poked from the window was much prettier.

"Lady Linial," I said. "How did you know where to find me?"

She smiled sadly. "It's the only place I could ever find you. Will you join me?"

I nodded and stepped inside. For the first time since my return, we were alone.

The Lady Linial removed her gloves and placed them on the seat beside her.

"I'm sorry, Harald."

"About what?"

"Where should I start? For shouting at you before you left. For not seeing you since you returned. For being so self-absorbed."

"Lin," I said. "I only have one question."

"Ask it."

I hesitated. Out of the window, I could still see the balcony where we had sat and talked. Eventually, I breathed deeply, and spoke. "Did you always know the Beast wanted me? Is that why you kept my company in Ines Hollith's estate?"

A flicker of discomfort crossed her face, a slight quiver of her lips. "Do you know when I first heard your name, Harald? I was eight years old. I had thrown a tantrum, and the High Priestess at the time, being one of my mother's friends, had offered to show me a secret. She brought me down those countless steps, just as I did to you. She presented me to the Beast. It showed me the Golden City from so high up. It showed me myself, as I would come to be, dressed in furs and feathers. It said: find Harald, and your path will be clear."

"When I first heard of you, I thought I knew what it meant. I had to kill you. Repel the invading armies. But then you showed my brother kindness. I realised I had gotten it so wrong over the years. You were not my enemy. I felt lost. My path wasn't clear. I went back to the Beast, but it showed me nothing more. I thought about it more. It said to find you, so I found you again, and again. And upon talking to you, my path did become clear."

She reached up to dab the corner of her eyes. "My path is with you, Harald. That's what I believed."

My world felt as though it was coming apart at the seams. I reached out a hand to steady myself against the carriage door. "Do you still believe it? Because it did mention my name again. You said as much. The night you took me to meet it."

She nodded. Took a shallow breath. "I am...confused. I had held your name since I was a child. I thought perhaps you would be a prince, to rescue me from my father. I dreamt it more times than I can count. As we sat on Ines Hollith's balcony, I had no doubt about it. You *were* my prince. But I realise now that the Beast doesn't show me happy endings. It did not tell me your name because we would love each other. It told me your name because you were important to It. Does that make you less important to me? Does that make what we had any less real?" She reached out to take my hand in her own. "I'm sorry, Harald."

I nodded. All I wanted to do was take her in my arms, but I held back. "Are you still a girl who dreams of love? I watched you at the table with all of the rest of them – I see you plot to kill your own father. I wonder is your service to the Beast your real purpose? I don't want to mistrust you, Lin. I want you. But you are not that girl of eight, dreaming of her Prince Harald. What are you?"

The Lady Linial closed her eyes. She fitted her gloves. She banged on the roof of the carriage and opened the door, even while we were moving.

“Where are you going?” I asked.

“I don’t know. You’re right, Harald. I don’t know who I am. I don’t know what I want. I’m still the confused girl you found on that balcony, but now I’m also something else. Maybe I’ve always been something else.”

She staggered away into the street.

“What would you like me do, my lord?” the coachman called.

I looked after Linial, waiting to see if she would turn back. She did not.

“Take me back to Tytos’ house.”

I slept in the same bed as when I nursed my ruined knee.

I say slept, but I did not sleep. I tossed and turned. Tried to get comfortable. Failed.

At some point, I must have drifted off, for I woke to a figure in the room.

I bolted upright in my bed, but Lin pulled down her hood and pressed a finger to her lips. “I’m sorry, Harald.”

“You’ve said that already today.”

She smiled and reached to take my hand in hers. “Plotting is bad for the mind. Without you, I’ve been missing something. It’s been almost two years since we used to sit on Ines Hollith’s balcony. I don’t know if it feels like that long to you?”

I shook my head. Up until that moment, I would have sworn it was six months ago.

She edged closer, further up the bed.

"I'm not wearing any clothes," I said.

"Do you think a woman creeping into your room at night minds?"

I shuffled over to one side to let her in. She slipped between the covers as graceful as ever.

The Lady Linial looked at me with wide, jewel like eyes.

"I don't know who I am, Harald," she said. "I don't know if I am always under the Beast's spell, if I can ever be my own woman. I accepted Its touch. I accepted Its power. But I would like to be with you. If you would have me. I don't think it's the Beast who wants to sleep with you." Her nervous laughter rang like a bell.

I smiled, though I couldn't shake the image that the Beast had presented to me. Of the Lady Linial suppliant and naked on the floor.

But I could not turn her down. Not after all we had been through.

I brought her lips to my own.

"I've been wanting to do that for almost half a decade."

"Then stop talking and do it again."

We kissed long into the night. Through it, the Compulsion whispered its own truths to me. I pushed them to the back of my mind; focused on her soft skin; on her slow, blinking eyes; on the wholeness I felt as I squeezed her tight.

And when I woke, Linial was still there, lying right beside me.

I kissed her softly on the cheek. She took my face between her small hands.

"We're free people," she said. "And we choose each other."

For the following days, she would steal into my room like a demonic spirit, often in the deep hours of the night. I would wake with her nipping at my ear, running her hands over my chest.

They say men have appetites, but they were nothing compared to Linial's.

We loved each other like dying people. Like people clinging onto a piece of driftwood to stay afloat in the sea.

It was a strange thing. It was different than being with Lot, both beneath the bedsheets and above them. With Lot, we had talked and laughed and loved. With Linial...

With Linial she was Lady Linial in the day, a traitor to her father and her country. In the night, she was Lin, the same worried girl I'd met on Ines Hollith's balcony, the same person who dreamed that she'd meet her prince Harald.

When she brought that daytime Lady Linial into our night-time activities, I didn't like it.

We lay in the utter darkness, only disturbed by the faint breeze turning the edge of our curtains. We were both awake, minds worrying.

"I know you don't trust the Beast," Linial said eventually. "But I think you should see him again. Demand an explanation, if nothing else."

"I won't see the Beast."

I could feel Linial sigh in the darkness, rather than hear her. "It can't do anything to you. And whatever It says to you – you're a consenting adult. Once you're free of Its touch, you're free of Its influence. You can make your own mind up. You're not me. You haven't let It inside your mind permanently."

When I didn't respond, she sighed audibly.

"The other members of the Golden House are going to secure the Beast's blessing tomorrow. The archers on rotation will be ones I know are loyal to me. The priestesses are *all* loyal to me. You could come. You don't have to interact. Just watch and see what you feel like."

"Why would I do that, Lin? I'm not a religious man – but can't you feel how obviously *wrong* that thing is."

"You don't compromise, Harald. It's one of the best things about you. But it's also the worst. You can't change the world just by being right. By being this idealogue. You have to make concessions. You have to use the tools at your disposal. And the Beast is a tool. You feel like it's wrong because you've been trained to feel like the Beast is wrong. Your religion exists to tell you the Beast is wrong."

I was silent for a moment. She was right. But she was also wrong. "I don't want to see it, Lin."

"Have you never dreamed that God would come walking? I know even in whatever mud huts you were born in, you had preachers. Did you never dream that God would come and offer you salvation? That one day you might find something better. Paradise. Did you never dream that when you died, you'd walk in the Garden, and all would be well?"

"I was a kid. I didn't think I'd ever die."

"You're trying not to understand me, Harald. I know you. You've waited all your life for a chance to make the world a better place. You've been given the opportunity. Why won't you take it?"

"Because I don't believe taking the crowns would make the world a better place? Look what happened the last time the Beast walked free?" I rolled to face the ceiling. "What would you do? If he had offered you the crowns instead."

"If the Beast promised me even half of what It has given you, then I would have been on my knees thanking It."

"You'd do whatever it takes for power." I didn't want to admit it, but I saw in her the same arrogance that I had seen in Lord Calforth, in Lord Ashdown and Sir Slant. *But she's only young*, I told myself. *And much sweeter than all of them.*

"I don't understand why you wouldn't," she said. "You think that having to make the smallest concession is giving away who you are."

"I'm not that black and white."

"You are. It's why you're terrifying. A truly righteous man. You don't waver, so you're easy to believe in. I believe in you." She rolled over and traced a line over my chest. "I wish we'd met sooner. Everything would have been much easier. You would have helped me choose the right path."

I turned so that we faced each other, her face resting in the crook of my chest. I stroked the small of her back.

"Why did you choose to become the Beast's priestess?"

"I'm surprised it's taken you so long to ask."

"I know what it's like to have done things others disapprove of. I don't like talking about myself all that much either."

She exhaled softly. "I forget how much you know me. Outside, I'm always fighting. Some days my heart feels so tight it might just explode."

"And now?"

"Now I feel relaxed. I think it's the first time in years." Her laughter didn't sound real; she was sweeter than a bird. "I owe you an explanation, for being so patient with me. But I worry you'll think my story predictable, stupid, compared to your own. An abusive father, who abused my mother, and abused his children. It's simple enough stuff."

"I know what it's like to have an abusive father," I said.

"No, you don't. Not like him." She shivered. "I can't talk about it still. I'm sorry."

I kissed her on the head. "Lin. We should be sleeping. The time for talking was three hours ago."

"Thank you," she said, and I held her until she fell asleep.

After that night, preparations for our treason continued.

Linial couldn't often visit. She was in the war room, planning with Tytos, arguing over logistics until the early hours of the morning. I didn't have the patience or the energy for it.

I paced across my room. Back and forth, back and forth. I should have visited the Golden House, but I couldn't bring myself to see the men sparring. I wished I was back in Erresea with Cat and Margaret and Edward. I had been getting better, but when I wasn't with Linial the whole world seemed to spiral out of my control.

Lin only visited me once more before it was time.

She was a pale shadow of herself, like a crow that had been dragged through a row of brambles. I soothed her, nursed her, put her to bed with a warm cup of tea.

She looked up at me, only her eyes above the covers. "Promise me you won't kill him, Harald? Promise me."

"Who?"

"My brother."

"I've never tried to kill him before, have I?"

She reached out and took my hand in her own. "This is different."

I nodded. "I promise." Still, she seemed uneasy. I laid a hand across her brow. "Are you still close?"

"With Axel? Not as much as we once were. They used to call us twins when we were children. Axel used to wear my dresses. I used to wear his mail and helmet. We were all one another had. Now, things are different."

"How?"

"He's forgiven father."

"And that's enough to separate you two?"

"That's enough."

"I don't want to pry, Lin. But what did the Heptarch do?"

Linial opened her mouth to speak. Only a low whine came out. I stroked her hair and whispered soothing words.

After a while, she fell asleep.

I sat in Council the following day, because I didn't want Linial to feel alone.

I couldn't even begin to understand the million moving parts that made up our rebellion. There were men a thousand miles away who had roles to play; smugglers who had braved storms and plagues; soldiers who stole into the city under cover of darkness; maudlin singers paid to incite the working class.

It didn't seem possible that Tytos could hold all of those infinite pieces of information in his brain. It didn't seem possible he could connect them together, join the dots between a buccaneer off my home island and a seamstress in Liriam's hovels.

After a while of sitting and listening, I realised that he didn't.

Tytos was an incredible man. I don't think anyone else could have filled the role he did. Everything seemed so effortless; he never tired.

And yet he was just one man.

The pieces that were to overthrow the Heptarch had been moving together for over thirty years, each heading towards the climatic moment, the now. Tytos couldn't have managed it alone.

It was the Beast.

It was the whispered words, threads sent scuttling about in the dark. It was the quiet conferences between the Lady Linial and that creature. It was all the small accidents that the Beast had orchestrated by doing nothing more than whispering a name, as It had for me.

I was only here because of it.

I toiled with that truth, turning it in my mind.

I wasn't fighting for Tytos. Not really. I was a champion of the Beast.

Tytos talked about choosing the right moment for betrayal, but the more I came to understand how the rebellion had come together, the more I came to understand that the Beast already knew whether Tytos would betray it. If he did, it knew the exact moment that betrayal would come, and it had already planned an answer.

"Harald!" I looked up. Tytos grinned wide as a wolf. "Did you hear? The rest of the Guard are with us!"

"Some of the Guard are with us," Galen amended. "We had a vote last night between the captains. Three companies are ready to take the city. The other seven will act when the battle is over, to arrest us as traitors, or to help us secure what remains of the Golden City."

Tytos looked at each of us in turn. "That means it is time. Send word for the Golden House to prepare. Send word to the Guard to ready themselves. The plan that we have been working towards is finally complete. Tonight, we will strike at the Heptarch. Ready yourselves for war."

The others bowed and left. Tytos called me back.

"Are you ready for this, Harald? You know what you have to do?"

I nodded.

"Follow the plan and you will kill the Heptarch." He clapped me on the shoulder. "Now dress yourself. I've had armour taken to your bedchamber. Your team will be here soon."

I nodded and bowed again.

After so long waiting for this moment, it had finally arrived.

Six years in the Pits. Six years of my life lost.

It wasn't only the Heptarch who would suffer this night; I had not forgotten Ines Hollith's torments. I would have my revenge on both before the night was through.

I waited in the silence of my room.

The house below was a hive of activity. Servants bustled from room to room; members of Tytos' inner circle gestured frantically to their followers; the Golden House gathered, buckling on swords and mail.

In my room, there was nothing but the whisper of the wind through white curtains and the distant chime of bells in the city. Night approached beyond the window, unaware of the chaos that would soon ensue.

Was I strong enough to do what was asked of me? Was I ready?

A tap on the door broke me from my worry.

"Come in," I said.

Eleanor waited at the threshold, head bowed.

I stood. Though she was ostensibly my servant, I'd seen little of her since my first arrival at Tytos' house. "Come in," I said again.

She moved into the room delicately; I remembered the life that I had freed her from.

"I came to help."

I hesitated. The armour that Tytos had provided me lay in a pile on the floor. I wasn't dressed in anything more than a white tunic and trousers. It had been hours since Tytos had spoken to me and I'd wasted them worrying.

I nodded. I *did* need help.

She closed the door behind her. Appraised the room. "You're not dressed," she said.

I shook my head.

"What do you usually wear under your armour?"

For years I had worn nothing but silk in the Pits. It had been over five years since I'd worn heavy plate. Part of me had thought to reject Tytos' offer, but another part of me realised that the rules of the Pits were simple. One on one. Man against man. Factors I could control. But fighting in the streets; arrows in the dark. I had to be protected.

"I have a gambeson and my braies – my trousers."

"Go on, then," she said. "Take these off." When I hesitated, she gave a shallow laugh. "Remember where you rescued me from, oh great lord."

"Fine." I disrobed. Looked away.

She did not look away. "You're nervous."

"You expected otherwise?"

"You forget who I am." She laughed sharply. Not for the first time I thought she was a bitter, broken thing. Shattered in the fall of my army. Remade, like I had been in the Pits, as a terrible version of what we once had been.

"We followed you because the priests preached. Because they told us you were blessed by God. We weren't convinced. But then seeing you. You looked like a miracle. You fought like you couldn't lose. It just ain't right seeing you look like a man."

"I never asked for it. To be worshipped."

"Yeah you did. You know what you did. You walked like you believed the ground itself owed you servitude."

I shook my head. I stood in the nude, in the centre of a room that I barely knew. "Life has been...uncomfortable to me since. I don't think I have the same notions."

"I could help remind you." She came to stand within a hair's breadth of my face. "Treat you like a king. I've been worse than a servant since I've come here. Everything I do is so slow. I didn't like being a pleasure girl. But I was good at it. I'm not good at this."

"You can be something else," I said, barely breathing.

"No, I can't. I was a peasant before the Crusade. We can't just go upping lives. Changing who we are. I can't read, like the rest of you."

"You can teach yourself. I knew someone who learnt once."

"And what happened to her?" she said.

My lips thinned to a narrow line. I took a step back. "My trousers are on the bed and my gambeson is on the dresser. Fetch them."

She pursed her lips. "Yes, my lord."

We dressed without another word. Despite her claims of poor quality, she moved with a quiet efficiency around the room. She had been born a peasant in my own land – she knew how to care for herself and her family. How much harder was it to care for me?

I fitted in the mail. I had forgotten how hot and heavy it was inside. Still, it brought with it a kind of comfort that I savoured. It had been months since I'd fought Edward on the beach. My body ached for a fight. My soul seemed to stretch across the room, pulling me forward.

And yet the Compulsion whispered *you are not ready.*

And I was not ready. After an injury like mine, I'm not convinced you ever are.

Still, I tucked my helm under my arm. Stood tall like a soldier would. Like Harald Lionheart once stood.

"We will discuss your service when I return."

Eleanor nodded, head bowed.

I hesitated on the threshold and spared one last look towards Eleanor." "Do you believe I will return?"

"I believe you will be captured and the rest of us will die. You always survive."

"This time is different," I said, though I did not believe it.

Chapter Twenty

In the street, the fighting had already begun.

The plan was clear. Incite the poor into violence. Force the Heptarch into committing the Palace Guard, as the City Guard pretended to struggle. Strike directly at the Heptarch's palace.

Flames flickered from outside the city walls. I felt a pang of shame; they may not have set the blaze themselves, but Galen and the City Guard had found a way to burn down the hovels. Even on the street around Tytos' house, windows were smashed, houses egged.

It would only get worse.

The people rioted. In that period between Tytos' ascension and the Heptarch's fall – there would be bloodshed like Liriam had never seen.

I took a deep breath.

This was a conscious choice. I was the master of my own actions.

And I had decided to kill the Heptarch, whatever it took.

The Golden House fell in beside me, warriors of renown, twenty soldiers in plate and mail. But the Golden House had never been the greatest soldiers in the city; I had been the greatest soldier in the city, but could I do what they needed me to do?

If called upon, could I kill the First of the Walled Garden?

I breathed deep again.

I could master these thoughts. Focus on what was around me.

One of the Golden House laid a hand upon my shoulder. A visor snapped back and a familiar face looked out at me.

Frisia grinned. "Happy to see me?" She looked me up and down. "You look tired, eastlander."

I could have hugged her. I put a hand upon her mailed shoulder.

"How?" I asked, simply.

"Ines Hollith has lost a lot of money. I was always his most valuable asset."

I raised an eyebrow at her confidence. A laugh burst out from my lips. When eventually my laughter subsided, I spoke softly. "I'm glad you're here with me."

She slapped me heartily on the back and clamped her visor shut.

I closed my eyes and listened to the sounds of our rebellion. From a bedroom window, a young boy crying. From the heavy steps of the soldiers beside me, the rattle of mail.

We began to walk.

One of the city's golden towers already smoked. In the bell tower, flames licked at wood. Within a couple of hours, the entire structure would be charred and black.

There are few ways in which a band of twenty soldiers can be inconspicuous. But the fear that comes from seeing silver swords and polished plate causes people to look away more easily than if they saw a figure skulking in the night.

On our route, I looked for the signs of Tytos' messengers.

Gold flags had been raised in windows if all was proceeding as planned. It would be a red flag if we had to prepare for trouble.

Flag after flag we passed. Each one of them gold. Each time I left free a held breath.

The Golden House did not speak as they walked. The amount of money it had cost to outfit them alone would have bought half of Ordrove.

I whispered a quiet prayer: let their quality be as good as the armour they were housed in.

From a window, I saw the flash of a red flag. I held up my hand.

Like a barbed carapace we stood, swords out.

On the street ahead, I could hear marching soldiers.

Do you believe in luck?

My father believed in luck. He always said that even the most well-planned endeavour could be ruined by bad luck. A guard captain could oversleep. A brilliant horse could go lame. A stone could go sliding down a rooftop, alerting everyone.

I didn't believe the Beast was subject to bad luck. I believe it had planned everything that was to happen. It hadn't left anything to chance.

So, what happened next, I had to believe that it had orchestrated it for some dark reason.

If that sounds suspiciously like what you might say about a God, humour me.

It had a reason. I don't believe it was a good one.

We advanced, ever so slowly.

Each footstep brought us closer to the sound of boots upon the ground.

We reached an intersection; the street split three ways.

The Palace Guard marched directly towards us.

I drew my own sword; the Guard looked at us from the shadow of a golden tower. They were at least thirty strong, and I could see Lord Axel at their head, a shadow in black plate.

We waited for a moment. The Golden House did not speak. The Palace Guard looked towards Lord Axel.

The question: is this an enemy or a friend?

They were outfitted well. Five knights in silver plate. Lord Axel with a sword almost as long as he. The rest in thick tunics, iron conical helmets and iron gauntlets. There had been over three hundred of them to start the evening – how they had been reduced to just thirty was a testament to Tytos' plan.

"With me," Lord Axel bellowed.

I did not move to meet him. The Golden House flowed around me; time slowed almost to a stop. Metal boots against hard brick. The world was too loud. Every sound shook my helmet, vibrated my sword in my hand.

Frisia carved open the skull of a Palace Guard and I remembered myself.

I joined the battle. A two-handed stroke caught some bastard in the chest. I took a blow in the ribs, barely felt it. Lashed out with a mailed fist and sent a man staggering backwards.

There wasn't time to think. A silver knight appeared before me; I braced for impact, but the man fell before arriving, a knife through his calf.

I saw myself as he fell, on the floor of the Pits. I looked into the eyes of my the brothers of the Walled Garden, even as the light dimmed. I faltered; the world too loud.

Two silver knights were already done. Three of ours lost.

A building across the street collapsed in a bellow of sparks. Flames reached out of the hole in the roof, licking at stonework. In the armour of the silver knights the flames danced, but Lord Axel's armour sucked the colour away.

He approached, implacable.

Had he recognised me? I tore off my helm – spread my arms. "I don't want to hurt you."

Sword flashed, scraping over my breastplate. I stumbled backwards, blocking overhead. He was silent beneath the shadow of his helm, a colossus, only the thin slit of his visor showing the anger of his eyes.

He struck again. I stepped backwards. I was not as fast as I once was; my knee tugged at me, as if the tendons stretched in all the wrong directions. I collapsed beneath his next blow.

I was not ready!

Lord Axel came down with us. He was big, but on the ground my mobility mattered less. I had trained for so many years in the House of Ines Hollith, and I had already beaten Lord Axel before then.

My confidence surged as we grappled. He didn't draw his knife in time, I flipped him onto his back.

I knelt above him, ignoring the shooting pain in my knee.

Beneath the visor, I could see his fear. Desperate, like an animal's eyes as it is put to the slaughter. His hands scrabbled against my armour, but I pushed down, one hand pressing him into the ground. I tore off his helm, leant into him, elbow across his throat.

His eyes bulged.

"Do you yield?" I demanded, in my language.

He found purchase on my heavy gauntlets, releasing the pressure.

"Do you yield," I demanded, in his language.

His left hand scrabbled for the knife at his belt.

"Do you yield?" I screamed.

He had the knife loose, scratching at my plate, trying to bring it to my face.

I had no choice. I pulled my own knife free; his grappling became desperate; a knee caught me in my armoured groin; I pressed down with the knife blade across his throat.

He made no sound. No desperate plea for freedom.

The knife cut down, severing his windpipe and spraying arterial blood in an arc above.

Lord Axel's hands fell away from me.

I had no time to rest. I staggered to my feet, absorbing a blow that caught me in my midriff. I had my knife in one hand, and my sword in another.

The flames danced before my eyes; the blood burnt. I swung wildly. My blade caught from time to time on dark shapes I couldn't blink into focus. My eyes stung.

Until there was nothing left to attack.

The other members of the Palace Guard had broken and ran.

From somewhere, someone produced a cloth. I wiped it across my face. The blood seemed too bright.

I blinked rapidly. It was still night. It was *cold.*

The Golden House *had* fought well. We'd lost six in the fighting – they'd lost more.

Someone clapped me on the back, though I did not know their name.

"On," I said. "The Heptarch."

The Heptarch's palace had once been the seat of Liriam's ancient king. Unlike Ines Hollith's manor, it was not set away from the city. Rather its golden towers sat at the end of a small garden, which branched into the Parliament building, and the home of the Lord Commander of the City Guard. Both those buildings were silent; the Lord Commander of the Guard had boarded his windows; parliament was conveniently out of town.

We were met with minor resistance as we entered. Two guards on the gate. A servant shrieking, soon quieted. Up the stairs, following the plans Linial had given us.

My heart thudded in my chest. It was like Lord Calforth's manor all those years ago. The violence never left my system, only lay dormant like a disease. I wanted to stab, kill, destroy.

I breathed deep.

Up a final flight of winding stairs, into a corridor beneath a glass chandelier.

And there, before the Heptarch's ornate golden doors, one man.

He swung his flail as we approached and unclasped his golden cape. He did not wear a helm; he did not wear a helm so I could see him.

"Are you ready to finally fight me, boy?" he said.

He was the First of the Walled Garden. I had waited six years to face him. As we approached, the Golden House flanked me, spread out in a line seven strong, two rows deep. I held up my hand to stop. I watched the man who had once been my salvation.

He showed no emotion, but the snarl of anger. He was a good dog, until the very end.

"I don't need to fight you," I said. "I've already beaten you."

I gestured to the Golden House. They moved out in front of me, approach slow. No-one wanted to be the first to clash blades. He was the First of the Walled Garden, greatest fighter in all of Liriam.

But no man can beat fourteen, though he did his best to try.

Three of the Golden House lay dead or dying before Frisia's sword caught him. It punched through his face, scattering skull and brains over the handle of the doors to the Heptarch's room.

So died the First of the Walled Garden.

I stepped over his body and brought out the cloth with which I had used to wipe my eyes. I wiped down the doorhandles, settled my nerves.

Only when I was ready, did I throw open the doors to the Heptarch's bedroom.

He waited for us. His wife was somewhere else and at my gesture, two of the Golden House peeled away to search for her.

Part of me had expected him to have fled down some secret passageway. My surprise served me right for doubting Tytos. Lord Axel lay dead with the Palace Guard. The Walled Garden had been scattered.

Still, he stood proudly in the centre of his bedchamber, sword out. His eyes narrowed as I entered. "Tytos didn't come to kill me himself," the Heptarch said. "Where's his honour?"

"We've grievance enough," I said.

"You?" The Heptarch shook his head. "You're a child still, a tool in the hand. You don't have half the history that Tytos and I have."

"And I don't care." I looked closer – the sword in his hand was none other than my father's sword. "But you care enough to take my sword."

"This?" He looked down the length of the blade. With a shrug he tossed it across the length of the room. "It was a trophy I'd been keeping on the wall. Nothing more."

I nodded to one of the Golden House who fetched the blade for me. For the first time in half of a decade I took my father's sword in my hand. My whole body yearned for it – every sinew from my fingertips through to some air starved piece of my brain.

I swung it in front of me – the release was like years of pain sloughing off me like an old skin. I stood straighter. Smiled wider. "Your daughter hates you," I said. "And your son is dead. How does it feel to have lost everything?"

The Heptarch looked almost sad, but he was a man who had spent years leading his people. Barely a quiver touched his lips before he shook his head. "I was good for my people and my family. If this is the end, then so be it." He put his wrists together. "Chain me. Take me to Tytos."

"You're not being taken prisoner."

"No?"

"No." I advanced towards the Heptarch.

"No," he said again, eyes wide.

With my father's sword I ran him through.

I removed the blade. The Heptarch collapsed at my feet.

"You can never govern this land," the Heptarch spat between bloody gasps. "It won't accept foreigners like you and Tytos. Our blood runs deep. We were one of the families who chained the Beast."

"Quiet," I said.

I brought the blade down gently, two handed, and pierced his heart.

For a moment, I waited. Blade buried in his flesh. His death mask a grimace. As I looked up, I saw the Golden House looking at me with a new kind of reverence.

We had defeated the Walled Garden. We had killed the Heptarch.

"Let's get out of this place. We're not finished yet."

The city was ours.

Fire burnt through the golden sepulchres and the air was thick and acrid with smoke. The famous markets of the Golden City burnt and released dust that may as well have been gold for all the treasures that were lost.

The City Guard and the rest of the Golden House had been hard at work. The strength of the Walled Garden had been crushed, each and every member eradicated. Every district had been seized. But there was still strength in the city – the Houses of the Masters of the Fighting Pits chief amongst them. Other groups of the Golden House had been sent to warn the Masters not to rise – to distract them with promises of compensation and inform them of the Heptarch's untimely passing. For those that would not listen to reason, the Masters would be put to death and the slaves given the opportunity to join the quickly swelling ranks of the Golden House.

I would not give Ines Hollith the mercy of surrender.

We arrived at the estate through thick clouds of smoke. Only five of us remained, including Frisia. The others I dispatched to other business, not least of which the capture of Linial's mother.

Despite this, we met no resistance.

He had forsaken the training arena where I had spent my time, for the manor house where he had held his parties.

He had not fled without taking precautions, however. Many of the fighters I had known manned the balconies of the estate.

I removed my helm and shook loose my hair. It was damp and matted with sweat, but I have always been easy to recognise at a distance. Frisia stood my side and removed her helm, holding her arms aloft.

"It's Harald!" the cry soon sounded. "It's Harald and Frisia!"

I addressed them all at once. "The city has fallen. The Heptarch is dead. All who had been slaves under the Heptarch's regime will be freed. The masters, however, must be punished. And it will start with Ines Hollith. Bring him to me."

My soldiers were uneasy. Who wouldn't be, when faced with the might of Ines Hollith's House? Ines Hollith's men were great fighters, but I knew they were not loyal, and Frisia would let no harm fall on me.

They brought Ines Hollith kicking and screaming through the doors of the estate.

His eyes widened to see me, and the words that rattled through his painted red lips were too frantic for me to understand.

I addressed him, not in his own tongue, but in my home language. "Did you think I was dead? That you were selling Tytos a corpse? Well, I am your very own draugr, back from the dead to punish you."

"You can't fight," he said. "Nobody can recover from that injury and be the same."

I switched back to his language. "Strip him."

Frisia acted without hesitation. Within seconds Ines Hollith was crying naked on the path before his estate. "You're pathetic," I said. "Did you ever really think you were the master of me?"

All the years of pain and torment at his hands came rushing back to me.

I bellowed, kicking him once in the ribs and once in the head. He reeled, weeping harder. I spat on him. The bastard didn't deserve any better. He was a monster in life. He wasn't even human anymore. With the remains of his clothing, I bound his wrists behind his back and loosely tied his legs together so each step was a waddle.

"Walk," I hissed, hauling him to his feet and pushing him forward. "Walk."

Ines Hollith began to walk. Nothing but a cruel, old man.

I would kill him, I knew. But first I would humiliate him, like he had done to me.

Through the wide streets of the Golden City, I walked him. Crowds began to gather, just about held back by the City Guard. Here and there the City Guard doused flame with buckets of water. And the people stood, open mouthed, realising the reality of our actions.

"This *thing* was stealing your food," I roared. "He caused the plague."

The crowd cried their approval and their disgust, surging against the raised shields of the Guard.

I brought Ines Hollith to a place outside the Heptarch's palace. Here, the crowds gathered in full force, thousands strong, upon news of his death.

"This is why your city has suffered," I said. "This monster has been bleeding it dry."

I slapped Ines Hollith with an open hand. He fell onto the cobbles.

"You have been starving," I bellowed. "Your children have been starving. You have been dying while pigs like *him* have been feasting away in their manor houses. They have stolen from you. Now you must punish them."

I hauled Ines Hollith to his feet. He blubbered, teeth chattering, a silent *no* forming on his lips.

The Guard pulled backwards as I approached their line; the crowd hesitated, unsure of what was coming.

"Punish him," I said, and pushed Ines Hollith forward into the crowd.

The first ones to grab him merely held him. But to the others he was little more than a child's toy. He disappeared into the crowd, falling out of sight within a matter of seconds. I watched for him, dissatisfied, until I saw a ripped off arm held aloft.

It was done.

Ines Hollith was dead.

Chapter Twenty-One

After my actions, the mob ran rampant.

Cries of pain racked the night. Women sobbed on street corners. My lips thinned to a line.

Galen was supposed to have control of the city. The City Guard was meant to protect people from such monstrosities.

But who was I to judge? I had encouraged the mob. I had been gripped by the same blood lust. They were simply following my lead.

In a square not too far from Tytos' house, there were three stakes, on which three bodies had been pinned, near a grove of burning trees. As I approached, the dead became apparent.

The three priests from Amber, faces frozen in agony.

On either side of them a pile of corpses – their attendants and servants. Their death had been premeditated; an opportunity seized in the chaos of the night.

That meant only one thing.

"It was one of ours," I said.

Frisia shook her head. Clanked open her visor and spat.

We were meant to be better than this, weren't we?

But I had seen the Crusade on its march. Seen what had happened to even good men, once blood lust got a hold of them. It was inevitable, in its own way. Surely a good leader could stop it, but I had not once met a good enough leader. I was not convinced such a person even existed.

Was I different from them? The Compulsion threatened to overwhelm me. Think of how many fewer would be dead, if only I had stayed in Erresea.

"No," I said out loud.

I had done what I had to do. What I needed to do. I had followed orders. I had only killed bad men.

And if I faltered, if I was excessive, then who can be the judge of that? I had suffered six years in Ines Hollith's House. I had been nothing but an animal.

If anything, the punishment was light. A night of pain and agony was nothing compared to six years of suffering.

It was a mercy.

I breathed deep. Centred myself. "Come," I said to my soldiers. "Let's report to Tytos."

The street was a bustle of soldiers, but all parted as we approached. Some removed their helmets. Some bowed.

We found Tytos in the meeting room, in serious discussion. On seeing me, he grinned from ear to ear.

"Harald! He's dead? They're all telling me, he's dead. Is he dead?"

I nodded.

The big man rushed me, crushing me in a hug so fierce that I felt it even beneath my armour. "The Beast was right! You were the right man to lead us." He released me. His eyes immediately fell upon my father's sword. "You got your sword back."

"I killed the bastard with it."

"What a man!" Tytos said. "What a man! We have the city thanks to you. The Guard have officially sided with us and are clearing the mobs out district by district. Thousands of former slaves have already approached me to profess their loyalty and thanks for their freedom. I've already started collecting names for a proper military – an expanded version of the Golden House. A Golden Army" He hesitated, clever eyes darting within his big face. "They say Lord Axel fell in the fighting?"

The sudden shift in tone caught me unaware. I nodded.

"Don't tell Linial about this," he said. "I'll tell her one of the dead Golden House did it? Somebody who served well in your group."

"But men have seen me."

"Men have seen you riding a flying dragon over the city tonight, Harald. You have become the stuff of legend – one great act leads onto a million imagined others. Only one thing is sure – the Heptarch is dead. That's all we'll ever acknowledge. Everything else will be the stuff of myth. And Linial will still be yours."

I nodded. A part of me was guilty, but another part of me was all too ready to accept Tytos' explanation. It could have been another soldier who dealt the final blow to Lord Axel's skull. It was such a melee after all, rolling about on the ground. It could have been anyone.

"What now?" I said.

"The city is a regrettable mess. Between the fire in the slums and the looting on the streets, there has been a great loss to housing and history. Many are dead. The Masters who have been receptive to the new order of things are being offered terms – help us secure the city with their knowledge and influence, and we will allow them to keep their estates. Offer their former slaves a fair wage and they will barely even notice a change in how day to day life happens. Once we have continuity, then we can undertake more radical changes. Within a few weeks, I will be crowned as Emperor. And we will be back to business – this is only one city of Gora's old empire. The others will fall into line soon enough."

"More fighting?" I said.

"More fighting, I'm afraid, son." He hesitated. "I don't want to lose you. You're a living legend, Harald. But I'm well aware of the terms of our arrangement. Ines Hollith and the Heptarch are dead. You've satisfied your honour."

I nodded. People conversed in the hallways of Tytos' house, but the mayhem of the outside world seemed so far removed. I blinked heavily. Tytos guided me to a seat.

"It has not been easy for you, I know. But you have always been a symbol of something far greater than yourself. Tonight, you are a symbol of freedom. Tonight, everything fell into place. You met the Palace Guard depleted and confused on the streets. All of the Heptarch's own men drawn away from his manor, or paid to disappear. And yet, someone had to lead the Golden House. Someone had to be a symbol."

Tytos unlaced the knots of my gauntlets and pulled them off delicately. "I do not want you to think you have been used, Harald. That what you did is not important. So, I have been working on your reward. Tomorrow. Tomorrow I will sit with you and give you your heart's desire."

I laid a hand on Tytos' shoulder; I was surprised to see it was shaking.

"For now, you must rest. Your work tonight is done, but mine is only just beginning. Go to Linial. She waits in your room. We're stronger together, Harald. This is only the beginning."

I staggered away. I found Linial, sitting in silence with the curtains drawn.

"It is done," I said. The words seemed to be the only ones that would come out.

She did not respond immediately. "I have lost a brother tonight, Harald."

"Your brother was an idiot." Anger ran through me. "You said your father was a monster. Why cry over monsters? Your brother chose his path. He's better off dead. It is done."

She rose. Tears stained her face in silver lines. The room darkened. The air around her grew stiff and solid. She spoke, not in her voice, but in the voice of a monster. "Do not talk about my brother like that."

The darkness closed around me, suffocatingly tight. It filled every available space in the room. I could not see. It writhed like snakes, smothering.

I stepped forward. The darkness moved from me, reverent. One steady step after another until I stood before Linial.

"It should have killed you," she said.

I took her gently into my arms and we stood in the blackness of the world.

I woke to the chirping of birds and the soft early morning sunlight. Linial was gone, as was the darkness she had summoned. I walked onto the balcony and surveyed the havoc; fires no longer raged, but the golden towers were blackened, buildings collapsed, and the streets almost empty. Liriam was a ghost town.

A knock on the door turned me. Eleanor bowed. "Lord Tytos asked for you as soon as you woke."

I followed her through the corridors of Tytos' house. Messengers pushed past, clutching bundles of paper. Soldiers marched down the corridors, stopping to salute as I walked.

Tytos was in the war room, sat at the head of his great table. Around him buzzed servants and high ranking members of the Guard. Linial sat at his left shoulder, back towards me.

He saw me first. Those clever eyes missed nothing.

"Leave us," he said, and the others scattered like a flight of birds.

Linial turned towards me, but could not meet my eyes.

I took a seat at Tytos' right hand. The big man beamed his golden smile.

"I won't tell you what you've done – you know it well enough. But know that if you weren't already a legend, then the players have a dozen new songs to write after last night. And – more than anything – such hard work deserves the ample reward promised. Before I let the Lady Linial lead, I want you to know that this is not the end of our acquaintance, Harald. Once your task is done, consider your next steps. Return to me and the Golden City, and we can subdue all of this land under our banner. But we don't have to stop there. Amber and Ordrove are a constant threat – at my side you can finally face Gabriel. We can be great together. And I can help you achieve those lofty goals of yours. Talking of which..."

He gestured towards Linial, who finally met my eyes. She looked like shit. There was no need for the dark makeup she usually wore; she looked like a crow chased by dogs, dark ringed, exhausted.

"I found your draugr," she said.

I stood. My seat clattered onto the floor. I gripped the edge of the table. Wanted to reach over it and pull the words right out of Linial.

"He's near a small fishing hamlet on the coast, not far from Antonia. He lives in a small hut, away from the rest of civilisation."

"And it's him? Definitely him?"

"It's him. Verified by a few survivors from local villages near your home who'd had dealings with him. I've been looking for him for a long time." She sighed. "Besides, the Beast showed me him. There's no doubt about it. He's had his neck sewed back – you realise how few men have stitches ringing their whole head? Finding him has been extremely difficult."

I leaned against the table, head in my hands.

Tytos rose and wrapped an arm around my shoulder. "I've prepared an expedition for you. Servants, soldiers and supplies. They're ready to leave at your command."

I shook my head. "If he's in Gora, why has he not come for me?"

I felt Tytos' shrug. "All we know is that he is here, and that if you want, you can take your revenge."

I looked up and found Linial's eyes on me. I bit my lip to stave away the tears. "Will you come with me?"

Linial looked towards Tytos. The big man nodded.

"Of course," Linial said. "Are you ready for this?"

"I've been waiting my whole life for this, Lin. I'm ready."

You might think me stupid. Naive. I was all of those things. But somebody had offered me a dream – and more than that, two of the people I trusted most in the world had offered me that dream. On top of that, I was tired. Exhausted from fighting. And not just the fighting from the past weeks. My whole life had been one long war.

I wanted everything to end. I wanted it all to be over. I wanted to win, finally.

Excuses, you might say. You might say these words make no sense.

Well, you will see.

We left the city the following day with an army of servants around us.

Eleanor and Frisia were not among them, which I was quietly grateful for, though Linial and several of the Golden House accompanied me. Our road would take us to Antonia – freed from my people years ago – and then onwards, skirting the coast until we reached the mountain lake and the draugr.

I would be lying if I said I wasn't nervous. For years the draugr had appeared to me in my dreams, and though his appearances had lessened since I had come to the Golden City, I thought about him almost every day.

We travelled in luxury, a moving fortress. Linial did not anticipate trouble in Antonia – it was a city that knew how to serve different masters – but we were prepared for anything.

I started training each night, like I had done when I was younger.

It was hard. Harder than I remembered it being. Each sprint up a steep slope would leave me bent and wheezing. My knees ached, and not just the one I had injured. I sparred with the Golden House – Tane and Virg were the best of them, and they were willing to duel in the dark when no-one else was around.

To say they were better than me would be an understatement. They thumped me, often literally, with their training swords. I wasn't just slow and unsteady in a one-on-one fight. My technique had slipped. A simple overhead counter just wasn't simple anymore. I should never have beaten Lord Axel, I realised. It was nothing but dumb luck.

They suffered my annoyances with encouragement and sympathy. It was the fear of every fighter to lose what made them special.

I howled through the night as I failed, move after move, time after time. I could read their moves, and for brief, glorious moments I would knit together an incredible flurry of attacks. But consistency? I would move too slowly, despite knowing exactly what was coming. I would thrust into an attack that would have ended a normal fight, only to find myself being rebutted with ease.

They were good. Obviously they were good.

But I had been the best, and now I was nothing.

I told myself the draugr had not been a fighter. He would not be skilled like the fighters in front of me. But, I remembered the wreckage of my father's keep. Even death relinquished him. Whether through skill or something else, my entire world had died at his hand.

I had to be better.

For the first time, I considered the Beast. Linial possessed his power; that suffocating darkness which had enveloped me. If I accepted Its blessing, would it go some way to making me as strong as I once had been?

Hot and sweaty from another night of failed training, I fell into bed alongside Linial. She bolted awake, free from the nightmares plaguing her.

"Could the Beast give me power?" I asked. "What kind of power?"

She blinked sleep from her eyes, squinting into the moonlight that fell across the sheets. "Bad session?"

"One of the worst."

"The Beast won't be able to fix your swordplay. Only time and hard work will."

"I don't need him to fix that. Can he make me strong in ways to compensate?"

She sighed. "You saw what I tried to do to you?"

"Kill me?"

"Yes."

The silence between us stretched on. We hadn't talked about it. If I hadn't been chosen by the Beast, I would be dead. And still we shared the same bed, though my extra-curricular activities took me away from her most nights.

"When I use his power, it is like opening a gate to a long and dark sea. The power rushes in. I'm just a conduit. It's the Beast who acts through me."

"What else can you do? You vanished from Lord Ashdown's tent in the Crusade."

"I can walk in the same shadow that you felt around you, like I'm not even there. I can crush the life from people. I can cloud people's judgement, if I let him speak through me. I can make people obey me. But none of it is really me, Harald. It's the Beast. You have to be prepared to sacrifice some of your own free will. But for what we can achieve – it's a worthwhile sacrifice. He's never asked for anything in return. Only given us the tools to remove the Heptarch."

I thought for a moment. "You asked me to be blessed by the Beast. You think I should accept Its power?"

"Yes. You should have taken one of the crowns and put it on as soon as they fell from his head. Just think of what you could achieve."

"Tytos is scared of them."

"Tytos will wear them himself! If you give him enough time, he will succumb to the temptation."

"So, you think I should take them first? Because I'm purer than Tytos?"

"Because the Beast gave them to you. He *is* a God, Harald. He knows what he's doing."

"He lost, Lin. He's chained to the bottom of the Golden City. He's not all knowing."

"You can think what you want. You asked for my opinion and I gave it to you. I have faith in the Beast. Tytos does too – though he's scared. He thought he was being groomed for something special. So much support, so many years. And then the Beast chooses you. Bestows you with the power of seven ancient kings. So, yes. You should accept the Beast's power. And I've no doubt it will far dwarf my own. But you'd rather try to do things the *right* way. You're a good man, Harald. So you can decide whether you want to be a good man, or a powerful man."

I shook myself free from Linial. I'd heard that same message so many times over the years. Linial was a good person – she cared about making the world a better place. And yet, she was a pragmatist. For so long I had stood opposed to people like that. And she knew, same as I knew, that the power of the Beast wasn't right for me. However much she might encourage me, she knew that Its power was different from where I drew strength.

But then from where had I drawn strength? Had the Beast guided me the whole time?

How many times had someone remarked upon the strength of my arm, as if blessed by God? And how were we to know that the Beast was truly evil? A curse, Linial had told me one night. That's what the Beast said. Once it had been changeable and beautiful; its power fair and growing. But the chains under the Golden City sapped it of strength. Made it seem evil, when it wasn't truly.

I sighed and rolled over to my own side of the bed.

I had wrested control of my life back. I had to remember that. I may be weaker than I was, but I was free.

And I wasn't finished.

The Heptarch and Ines Hollith were dead.

The draugr would soon follow.

And then Gabriel...

I would need an army to defeat Gabriel. To take my homeland back. I would need Tytos.

But I didn't need the Beast.

I was my own man.

Antonia was just as magnificent as I remembered it.

The years had been difficult. Some buildings slumped into roadways, little more than a collection of rubble. Tall towers bore the signs of scorch marks. People watched from behind closed curtains. Some doors were painted with the mark of the plague.

Despite this, there was a quiet solidity to Antonia. Grey stone and thick brick. A place that reminded me of home, despite all the years and miles between us.

We took up residence in an estate by the sea. The servants chased supplies through the city and Linial busied herself in the city library. I was left mostly to my own devices, with even the Golden House taking an evening to explore the city.

Many of the fighters who joined the Golden House had been slaves in the Pits. Part of me worried for Tytos' nascent army. In going to Erresea I had drunk too much – but luckily Cat and Margaret kept me sane. The others didn't have the same luxury or the same friendships. They would want to see the world, but they would have to master their own appetites lest it destroy them.

I sighed as I walked across the battlements overlooking the sea. Calm water for as far as the eye could see. Only the bay below the city and the jagged edges of the rocks churned with white surf.

It was the closest I'd come to home in so long.

I'd never felt proudly Ordrovian, but time ages us in ways that we never quite expect. My memories were like sand, filtering through a heavy net. Some had made it intact, but others were disparate, fractions of the events that had happened.

My brothers were like wraiths, but I could see my father as clearly as if he stood before me. The people were gone, but I could still remember clear paths around the mountain and the forests. Lot was there, but I had accessed my memories of her so often, even she felt like some faded painting.

I missed her.

I had yearned for Linial for so long, but the reality was beginning not to measure up to our fantasies. We had become political creatures, and the quiet conversations on the balcony of Ines Hollith's estate already seemed like memories. We were not naïve children – the innocence and concern she'd had for me as a slave in Ines Hollith's estate had turned into annoyance at the man that I truly was.

Intransient. Difficult. A bastard.

I felt in the deep folds of my heart that Lot would feel the same – if she was even alive. She would have changed so much in the intervening years. I would just be a boy that she once knew, now a man, now a monster.

I forced myself to take a deep breath.

I needed Cat and Margaret. Not in some silly romantic way. I needed them like you need family. Because they ground you, remind you of who you really are.

The world did not feel like it was for me anymore. Tytos was right when he offered me the choice between a life of mediocrity, and one of power. I shouldn't have taken it – the deaths of Ines Hollith and the Heptarch left me empty and cold. I couldn't enjoy the quiet of the sea. I couldn't do anything.

Linial found me huddled against the battlements.

She wrapped me in her cloak and ran her hands through my hair. "You're strong," she said. "Hush now, don't worry."

She took me and walked me back to our room. She saved me that night, and I felt stupid for ever doubting her.

We left Antonia the next day. Our group thinned. Just a few servants, Linial and I walked the coastal path away from Antonia. A boat had been prepared for us, Linial explained.

Tomorrow, I would kill the draugr.

Epilogue

The boat lapped over still water.

I could see our target on the far bank. A small, thatched house with candles in the window, straining against the incoming twilight.

I gripped the rails of the boat; my hands turned white with the pressure.

"You don't have to do this alone." Linial rubbed my back. I did not turn to face her, though her small white face appeared at the edge of my vision.

"You know I do."

"It won't make you stronger to have killed him by yourself."

"This is the moment I've waited my whole life for. He started me on this path. I'll make him pay for it."

She rubbed some warmth into the back of my hand. "I understand." She smiled. "You look good in black by the way."

I gave a small laugh, never taking my eyes from the hut by the side of the water. Like Linial, I was dressed all in black. A thick black cloak. Light mail over which I wore a black shirt. Black shoes and trousers. The only point of colour on my whole outfit came in the form of my father's sword.

I fidgeted with the pommel.

What would my father think? Had I done enough in all the years to satisfy him?

Don't think about him, I told myself. *Not now.*

The boat was manned by a skeleton crew of Tytos' staff. They went about their work in quiet excellence. The boat fought its way across the lake, and I counted each second as it passed.

I tried to visualise what would happen when I forced open the door to that house.

I would face him. We would stare at each other. Draw our swords. We would not speak. I would not ask him any questions – he wouldn't get that kind of satisfaction. I would slaughter him like the animal he was.

A deep breath. Yes. I took a deep breath. Tried to steady myself. The boat found the rough sand of the far bank.

I released my hold on the rail as the staff pushed the boat onto dry land. I descended from the front of the boat like a wraith. I raised my hood to guard against the low fog.

Linial said something but I did not hear it. The blood beat in my ears.

It was time.

The house the draugr had made for himself was beautiful, in a kind of quiet remoteness. There was nothing and nobody for miles around. It was just inland from the coast, but obviously close enough to home that his power hadn't completely waned.

For a second I wondered why he hadn't come to find me. We had been on the same continent. I was famous, in a way. Even the commonfolk talked about me.

And then I pressed down on the door handle.

It opened without hesitation, revealing a well-lit room. A woman sat with her back to me, feeding a small child. The man who sat at the far side of the table was unrecognisable to me – his face bearded and coarse. His eyes happy. Still, there could be no doubting the jagged scar across his neck – a head sewed on by some black magic.

They looked at me, as one, eyes widening with shock.

He'd haunted me. And for what?

To start a family. To marry. To whelp a child.

Their shock at my entrance turned quickly to anger.

The woman stood first, taking the child in her arms and retreating.

The draugr stood before me. He bore no weapons, but his eyes shone with rage.

He opened his mouth, but only a guttural, inhuman sound escaped his lips.

I took my father's sword in my hand.

Fear alit across his expression.

He scrambled for something to defend himself.

"For my family," I said.

I found my way back to the boat almost half an hour later, covered in blood and gore.

“You did it?” Linial said. “You won?”

“They’re dead,” I said.

Her eyes regarded me carefully and the smile fell from her face. She knew, same as I did, what that meant.

“It’s done. I cut out his heart.” I shook my head. “My family’s debts are satisfied. Maybe I’ll get a good night’s sleep for a change.”

“Harald.” She tried to grab me, but her hand slipped off and came away sticky with blood.

“*It is done.* Now, Tytos needs us.”

I boarded the boat and entered my quarters. I stripped from my bloody clothes.

I sat on my haunches with my knees to my chest.

And in the darkness of my cabin, I began to cry.

THE END

If you enjoyed WITH HIS FATHER’S SWORD, it would make me very happy if you could leave a review on either Amazon or Goodreads. I might even do a little celebration. If you’d like more from Harald and the rest of the cast, sign up to my newsletter via my website, where you can receive a free story focusing on Frisia called MY BROTHERS MUST DIE. (I promise, I have the most lovely and supportive family in real life. Honestly.)

Printed in Great Britain
by Amazon

62600029R00262